'I enjoyed *Arrested Song* immensely ... Karafilly succeeds brilliantly where I had decided not even to try. A very accomplished novel.'

Louis de Bernières

'A gripping, powerfully evocative chronicle of Greek island life. Nothing is black and white here, least of all her feisty, iconoclastic heroine ... hard to put this book down.'

Sofka Zinovieff

'An epic, page-turning story of longing and bravery. *Arrested Song* is a must-read.'

Nadia Marks

'*Arrested Song* is a highly accomplished, thoroughly researched, and compelling read.'

Dean Kalimniou

'*Arrested Song* is a wonderful novel, fully realized and absorbing.'

Anna Porter

'Wow! Beautifully written and riveting.'

Carol P Christ

'One of the best novels I've read about modern Greece. Karafilly combines impeccable research with skilful characterisation and plot twists, showing us the pettiness and greatness of life in an island village during war and peace, intertwined with a love story that defies all expectations. A truly original work.'

Diana Farr Louis

'A beautifully written, superbly detailed and addictive historical novel mostly set on the island of Lesvos. I savoured every word.'

Peter Barber

Arrested Song

Irena Karafilly

Legend Press Ltd, 51 Gower Street, London, WC1E 6HJ
info@legendpress.co.uk | www.legendpress.co.uk

Contents © Irena Karafilly 2023
The right of the above author to be identified as the author of this work has
been asserted in accordance with the Copyright, Designs and Patents Act
1988. British Library Cataloguing in Publication Data available.

Print ISBN 978-1-915643-96-4
Ebook ISBN 978-1-915643-97-1
Set in Times.
Cover design by Rose Cooper | www.rosecooper.com

Irena Karafilly is an award-winning writer, poet, and author of several acclaimed books. Her short stories have been broadcast, anthologized, and published in both literary and mainstream magazines; her articles have appeared in numerous newspapers, including the *New York Times* and the *International Herald Tribune*.

Karafilly was born in Russia, educated in Canada, and currently divides her time between Montreal and Athens.

Find out more at
www. irenakarafilly.com

For Ranya, my daughter

AUTHOR'S NOTE

Molyvos is the ancient name of a coastal Greek village situated on the north-eastern Aegean Island of Lesbos. Although its official Greek name is now Mythimna, the former name is still in demotic use. The island is separated from Turkey by the narrow Mytilene Strait and was part of the Ottoman Empire until 1912. In Greece, Lesbos is pronounced Lesvos and is often referred to as Mytilene, after its capital. The spelling of all transliterated names varies from source to source. *Arrested Song* is set in the twentieth century, during the most turbulent era of modern Greek history. Although the characters and plot are fictitious, the historic events on which the story is based have all been thoroughly documented. The reader may find it helpful to consult the historical highlights and glossary at the back of the book.

PROLOGUE

There were cats everywhere: on faded cushions and fraying rugs, on chairs and shelves and chests and tabletops. Cats blinking and swishing their tails, cats curled up in sleep, cats energetically licking each other's fur. The moment she stepped into the hallway, the intense odour caught at Calliope's throat. Zenovia the fortune teller was getting old and increasingly eccentric, living alone with her ever-growing feline tribe. Her only son had died in the Balkan Wars; her philandering husband had long since fled to Salonika. Calliope had been a child when all this had happened, but the villagers had immortalised the scandal in an amusing ditty echoing the national anthem. Whenever Zenovia's name was mentioned, someone was bound to recall the disgraced notary, though by the end of 1940, Molyviates were more interested in Zenovia's clairvoyant gifts than in her marital past. Months earlier, she had publicly predicted an imminent war that would take village men away from home to battle a new enemy.

And this prophecy had come to pass. Calliope's husband, Kimon Alexiou, had been among those drafted back in October to fend off Mussolini's advancing army. Not long after, the distraught Zenovia came down with acute pneumonia and was still recovering around Christmas when Calliope was charged with delivering a plate of her mother's holiday cookies.

It was a chilly December afternoon, with rain pelting the creaky Turkish shutters. Zenovia's house was one of the oldest and grandest in the village, but her kitchen was shockingly chaotic, as cluttered as most kitchens might be only during a spring clean.

'Sit down, sit down, my child.' The old woman set about making coffee. She drew an ivory comb out of her dishevelled hair, then reinserted it with a heavy sigh. There was an exchange of pleasantries, followed by a long talk of potential German involvement. Eventually, the conversation turned to Johnny the Australian, a local man who had prospered in Melbourne and had just returned to marry off his two sisters, and perhaps find a bride.

Calliope sipped her coffee. When the rain stopped and she made to leave, Zenovia reached into her sleeve and pulled out a none-too-clean handkerchief.

'Would you like me to read your cup?' she asked, dabbing at her reddened nostrils. 'I'll do it for free.'

The offer was received with a smile, a quick shake of the head. Staring into her cup, Calliope heard herself voicing a question that had surfaced one day when the old woman's putative clairvoyance was being rehashed in the neighbourhood.

'I couldn't help wondering,' she said, 'what you tell people if you ever foresee some misfortune – an accident or death, or some serious illness. Do you tell them the truth?'

The old woman cackled. 'People are right about you,' she said, wagging her head. 'You and your questions! No one else has ever asked me this, my child. No one.' Her face screwed up in a strange little smile.

Calliope waited. 'So?'

'So!' There was a barely perceptible shrug but still no reply. Zenovia sat casting about the room with her rheumy eyes, seemingly lost in thought. After a moment, both she and Calliope began to speak, their words colliding.

'I'm sorry,' said Calliope. 'You—'

'No, no, my child. Please go ahead and say—' She coughed, her eyes watering. 'Whatever you were about to say.'

Calliope hesitated, then went on to amend her question.

'I was going to ask… do you think that some people are born lucky and others unlucky?' She looked straight into Zenovia's eyes, thinking both of her drafted husband and her late father, Philippas Adham, who had died prematurely after contracting measles from his pupils. 'And… how is it possible that the dregs in my cup would have anything to say about my destiny?'

At this, Zenovia began to pluck lint off her woollen sleeve. She sat plucking it for a long, silent moment.

'I don't know about luck,' she finally said. 'Sometimes I believe there is such a thing, other times, I'm not sure.' She shot Calliope an appraising glance, then smiled obliquely. 'I can tell you one thing,' she added. 'I don't need to look into your cup to know that yours is not an ordinary destiny, my child.'

'An ordinary destiny!' echoed Calliope. 'So, you do believe there is such a thing as fate!'

'I'll tell you what I believe,' Zenovia said. 'Only… well, it's not exactly an original idea. Who said it – character is destiny – do you know?'

'Heraclitus, I believe,' answered Calliope, who had been mostly educated at home, by her headmaster father. Zenovia had been raised in Constantinople; she, like Calliope's own father, had arrived on Lesbos back in 1914, along with countless other Anatolian refugees. She was closely related to the local doctor, a victim of other political upheavals.

'Well, whoever said it was probably right, don't you think?' Zenovia was saying.

'Oh, I don't know,' said Calliope, eyes sliding towards the window. 'My mother says I have a difficult character,' she added.

Zenovia chuckled. 'Strong-willed women are often thought to be difficult,' she said. 'You were always different from other girls. Even as a child.'

'Oh yes?' Calliope studied her face. 'You remember me?'

'Of course I remember you! You were an ugly duckling as a child, your nose always stuck in a book.'

Calliope shrugged. Whenever she recalled her own childhood, what she saw on her mental screen was a pack of jeering boys, hands snatching whatever she was reading and casting it in the air, ripped pages whirling down like feathers. *'Book-eater! Book-eater!'*

A sigh escaped Calliope's throat. 'My mother keeps trying to teach me how to sew and embroider, but I'm hopeless at it. Everyone says I'm a born dreamer.'

Calliope's father had been the only one who seemed to understand her. She had vivid recollections of herself clambering up trees and hiding for hours among leafy branches. She was Amelia Earhart, bold and free! She was a young stowaway headed for exotic shores! Her father had a brother who had settled in Paris, and who was in the habit of sending fine chocolates every Christmas. The pleasure of the annual treat was eclipsed only by the collectable photographs in the fancy chocolate box: the Eiffel Tower and the Pyramids; the Statue of Liberty and the Taj Mahal.

'I used to dream of marrying a sea captain so I could see the world.' Calliope smiled to herself, eyes hazy with recollection.

Zenovia sighed. 'We all have our foolish dreams,' she said.

'I suppose.' Calliope stared out of the darkening window, thinking of the tantalising stories she'd heard over the years. Zenovia's husband had reportedly been frequenting a Mytilene brothel. One night, arriving home late, he found the door barred and his personal possessions strewn around the garden. For years, villagers spoke of a chamber pot being emptied on the notary's balding head, of pyjamas and shirts draped over fruit trees, trousers hooked on oleander bushes, belts and socks and shoes scattered on the ground, amid rotting pears and ant-infested peaches.

Calliope imagined all this, though all she could see just now was Hektor, the village fool, who was living in Zenovia's garden shed in exchange for help with domestic chores. He was standing outside the shed now, chopping firewood, while the wind kept gusting around him, strumming through bare tree branches.

'He's such a good man,' said Zenovia, tracing Calliope's gaze.

'Yes,' said Calliope vaguely. Hektor might be hare-brained, but he saw to it that Zenovia never ran out of food or firewood, and that her cats were fed whenever she felt indisposed. The rest of the time, he worked as a messenger and rubbish collector, trudging through the village every morning with the municipal horse, ringing his bell. The villagers were indulgent towards Hektor, who, despite his difficulties, seemed to be in on everything going on in the village.

'He's sharper than you might think,' Zenovia put in, as if reading Calliope's thoughts.

Calliope averted her eyes. 'I wouldn't know,' she said. One day, walking her dog at night, she had come upon Hektor in the hilltop fortress, spreadeagled on the ground, trying to count the stars.

'I don't know what I'd do without him,' Zenovia said, more or less to herself. She brought her cup to her lips, watching Hektor gather the firewood.

Calliope pushed her chair back and reached for her satchel, ready to go.

'Anyway,' said Zenovia. 'Please thank your mother for me. And happy new year to you both. I hope Kimon comes back soon, safe and sound,' she added, stopping to blow her nose.

Calliope thanked the old woman, turning down an offer to have her fortune read another day. She could not for the life of her say why she was afraid to have her cup read when she didn't believe it was possible for anyone to predict the future. She smiled down at the old woman, vaguely apologetic.

'Time tells the end of a story, *Kyria* Zenovia,' she said, quoting the village doctor, who was a dear friend. She paused to pet one of the cats, who had jumped off the banister and was rubbing itself against her legs. 'Happy new year to you.'

1941 – 1942

'How glorious it is – and also how painful – to be an exception.'

Alfred de Musset

ONE

I

The year began on a melancholy note, with the sudden return of two gravely wounded men. The younger one, Molyvos's football champion, had had his leg amputated below the knee; the second, one of the blacksmith brothers, had come back from the front with his head swathed in bandages.

Although the Italians had failed to repel the Greeks, both Mussolini's and General Papagos's troops had been thwarted by Albanian weather. The *kapheneion*'s wireless, which had once blared out exultant reports of Greek victories, was now broadcasting bulletins listing the names of the dead and wounded. As Easter approached, many believed the Germans were preparing to send reinforcements.

'They're allies after all – they've got to help Mussolini, like it or not!'

'They are allies, but if they wanted to help the Italians, wouldn't they've done so by now? Why didn't they send their troops all this time?'

'Why? Because they know those Italians are bumbling fools, that's why! Their fathers must have been singing arias while they fucked their mothers!'

The men brayed with laughter. A joke was a joke, but there was only one fact offering a modicum of hope: Churchill had offered to send expeditionary forces to Greece, to buttress the country's defence against potential German invasion.

Calliope had overheard the old men argue outside the *kapheneion* as she walked her dog. She, too, was anxious about the country's future, though in the past two months, her inner turmoil had less to do with politics than with matters of the heart. She had fought with her husband the night preceding the general draft and they had not reconciled before his departure. There had been occasional quarrels over Kimon's drinking and poker games in recent months, but their last confrontation in late October had nothing to do with either.

Kimon had come home on that rainy autumn evening looking oddly breathless, as if he had run all the way uphill. He followed Calliope to the kitchen, where she was preparing to feed him, and made for the ouzo.

'There's something I'd like to discuss,' he said.

'Oh?' Calliope lowered herself onto the day divan, mechanically groping for her open book. 'What is it?'

He pulled up a chair and reached for his cigarettes. 'I want you to listen to me, Calliope. Are you listening?'

'Of course I'm listening!' She tossed the book aside. 'I'm all ears!'

Kimon lit a cigarette. He took a sip of ouzo. 'Ioanna's gone into labour,' he said. Ioanna was his older brother's wife. She'd been expecting her fourth child.

'Good. She was overdue,' Calliope said, then stopped. 'Is there a problem?'

'No. No, we were just wondering what… what you'd say to adopting the new baby.'

'Ioanna's baby?' Calliope stiffened. She had been married nearly four years and, in all that time, had failed to conceive. 'Are you serious?'

'Yes, I… we thought that—'

'Absolutely not!'

The mere idea, Calliope's response suggested, was too preposterous for words. In truth, the adoption of a sibling's child was not uncommon, either because a family had too many mouths to feed or, as sometimes happened, because God had not seen fit to bless a couple with children of their own.

Calliope sat struggling with her inner havoc. 'We're still young. I'm barely twenty-five,' she finally said. 'Anyway—'

'What?' said Kimon.

Calliope hugged herself, listening to the grandfather clock tick in the hallway, the crackling of the fire in the hearth.

'Anyway what?'

'I don't like Ioanna's brats!' she finally blurted, her mind flying back to a summer day on which she had caught two of Kimon's nephews preparing to set fire to a pregnant cat.

'Ioanna's brats? We're talking about a newborn, Calliope! Ioanna might be a little too easy on her kids – all right, she *is* too easy – but the child… he wouldn't have to be a brat if you brought him up?'

Calliope raised her gaze, filled with intense but not quite diagnosed feelings. 'I can't do it. I'm sorry – I just can't, Kimon.'

'But why, in God's name? Just give me one good reason and—'

'I don't want someone else's child!' Calliope erupted. 'I already have a dog I adore,' she added, trying for a smile. She had recently adopted a delightfully playful stray: a black half-grown mongrel she had named Sappho. Her previous dog, Socrates, had died under mysterious circumstances

'You're so stubborn!' Kimon said, reaching for an ashtray. 'Like a mule!'

'Fine, I'm stubborn.' Calliope picked up her book as she had seen her mother pick up a dish of peas to be shelled or a skirt to be hemmed, declaring the subject closed. A moment went by. 'I can't help it, Kimon!' she suddenly cried, hands flying out, pleading for understanding. 'I can't help the way I feel about something so final, can I?'

Kimon said nothing. In the hallway, the old clock struck nine times, then fell silent. Sappho stirred, whimpering in her sleep.

Calliope rose, heading for the bread bin. Across the garden, their neighbour turned on the evening broadcast. For months now, there had been outrage over Mussolini's aggression. The Italians had sabotaged Greek fishing boats in the Ionian Sea, sinking a warship on a sacred Orthodox holiday. In spring, Kimon had been called up for military exercises. A national draft seemed all but inevitable.

It was as the news wafted into their kitchen that a sudden thought struck Calliope: *Kimon is worried about a full-scale war. He's afraid he might not make it back from the front!*

The insight struck her with the force of dire revelation. All at once, she could feel her will starting to weaken. *But does he want a child to avoid being drafted*, she wondered, *or does he just want to ensure that he has an heir?*

Slowly, mechanically, she put the knife down and turned to face her husband.

'Look, Kimon… let me think about it, all right? I *will* think about it, but… please, I'm not making any promises. It's not easy, taking another woman's child.'

Kimon made an ambiguous gesture, then rose, pausing to down his ouzo. 'I told Vangelis I'd let him know tonight.'

'Tonight!' Calliope stared for a long moment. 'Then the answer's no,' she finally said, bitterness flooding her mouth. 'I don't like Vangelis and I don't like Ioanna, and I don't want their stupid child!'

She turned to feed the fire. Her brother-in-law was bad-tempered and his wife a greedy, quarrelsome woman. Kimon himself had said as much in the past, but on that particular evening, when Calliope brushed past him, Kimon's hand flew out and slapped her face. Hard. She had never before been physically struck, not even as a child. Her father had been passionately opposed to corporal punishment; her mother had not dared cross him.

For a long moment, Calliope stood paralysed at the whispering hearth, a spurt of blood trickling from the corner of her mouth. Gingerly, she touched it, inwardly recoiling.

What now?

The question kept repeating itself in Calliope's head after Kimon left, slamming the door behind him.

She found herself lifting kitchen utensils at random, clutching them for a moment as if trying to recall their precise purpose, then replacing them with a shaky hand – on the wall, the shelves, the scarred kitchen table. There was something maddening about the kitchen's irreproachable order: the hanging plaits of garlic, the gleaming copper pans, the bouquets of wild herbs. The room was silent now, except for the wind rattling the shutters.

Dazed by her own impotence, Calliope left the kitchen and, heavy-footed, began to mount the stairs. Her mouth had stopped bleeding, but something within her had begun to ebb away and could not be arrested.

When the call to arms came in the morning, she and Kimon barely managed to exchange a word. They stood side by side outside the town hall, waiting with the other draftees for military transport. There had been announcements and speeches and patriotic songs. The women and children were saying goodbye to their men, whom they might never see again.

'We'll beat the stuffing out of those cocky bastards!' the draftees promised their weeping wives and mothers. 'We'll show Mussolini what we Greeks are made of!'

Kimon had never been one to bluster. He appeared pale and drawn in his khaki uniform, his bloodshot eyes blinking against the morning light.

'Forgive me,' he finally said, hearing the rumble of wheels. 'Please forgive me.' He made no attempt to kiss Calliope, but clasped her hand and stroked her hair, waiting for absolution. They stood facing each other in the rising wind, surrounded by the overwrought crowd.

What was there to say? The hand caressing Calliope was the same hand that, only hours earlier, had viciously slapped her face. She could still feel both sting and insult, but, at the same time, a small surge of wifely solicitude.

Her feuding emotions had left Calliope too muddled to respond. Though her anger would take days to dissipate, awareness was already dawning that solicitude could at times be almost as disconcerting as rage.

But she was still young on that late-autumn day, still getting to know herself, still resisting inner contradiction. What she longed for, in those final moments, was emotional clarity. Unable to find it, she stood barely breathing, inwardly agitated, outwardly as impassive as the façade of the freshly painted town hall.

Everyone's farewells were necessarily brief. But, in the months to come, Calliope would always recall how, in that short, chaotic interval, she had stood dry-eyed amid the lamenting wives, trembling a little, failing to answer her repentant husband's plea. She had wished him well as he turned to go, had managed that much. But Kimon had marched away towards the waiting trucks with death in his eyes, unforgiven.

Calliope could not forgive herself either. She was still grappling with her inner anguish in February when a letter finally arrived from the front. She read it over and over throughout the day, but her husband's tender words did nothing to placate her heart. That night, an unsettling dream jerked her awake: Kimon had returned home brain-damaged and blind, with his manhood blown off by flying shrapnel.

Flinging back her blankets, Calliope scrambled out of bed, her thoughts wild. For a moment she paused, muddled, then swept straight across the room, towards a massive wardrobe she had shared with her husband. The house was at its coldest just before dawn, but she ignored the chill, propelled by a mysterious force. Perhaps she was still dreaming?

She became aware of her own laboured breath, an odd taste clinging to the back of her mouth. Standing before the wardrobe, she reached out and opened the creaky pine doors with their floral motifs, then stopped, suddenly hesitant, as if some malevolent spirit might come leaping at her from behind the suspended garments.

For a moment, she was about to retreat and dash back to bed but found herself instead leaning deep into the old wardrobe, pressing her face into her absent husband's abandoned clothes: his trousers, shirts, his favourite cardigan.

What was she doing? What was she searching for?

In the years to come, Calliope would say that she must have had the sort of premonition Zenovia the fortune teller claimed to have experienced the night before her only son perished in the Balkan trenches. She had always laughed at such premonitions. But there it was: a portentous night that defied explanation, followed within days by an official confirmation from the Ministry of War.

Missing on the field of honour.

II

The village doctor was pensively jiggling the brandy in his crystal glass. It was Easter Sunday. Elias Dhaniel was thirty-nine years old, a sandy-haired, rumpled-looking widower whose facial expression somehow suggested a man listening to a joke with one ear and to some melancholy narrative with the other. He had unexpectedly become Calliope's confidant after his wife had died tragically giving birth to her fourth child.

When Calliope and Kimon became the baby's godparents, Dhaniel began dropping in for coffee when passing through the neighbourhood. It was to him that Calliope had first spoken of her failure to conceive, her reluctance to adopt Ioanna's child. The one thing she could never bring herself to share was Kimon's shocking assault. More than three months had passed since that final quarrel, but she was still too ashamed to speak of it, even to this most trusted of friends.

With his thoughtful eyes and ascetic features, the doctor resembled a poet more than he did a physician. Not that Calliope had ever met a poet, but she'd read about them in foreign novels. Dhaniel's parents and siblings had been slaughtered in Smyrna, trapped by frenzied nationalists bent on ridding Turkey of its ethnic minorities. Calliope's own father and uncle had also been orphaned.

Calliope was doing her best to enjoy the holiday, with the four boisterous children gathered about, absorbed in their new games. She had recently travelled to Mytilene, returning with gifts for the children and a dress for herself, the colour of ripe cherries. The frock had puffed sleeves and a dainty scalloped collar, its mother-of-pearl buttons going all the way down to the belted waist. If only her mouth were daintier, she thought, her hands more feminine!

She had helped her mother prepare a sumptuous veal roast with walnuts and pomegranate seeds, but Mirto was tired and, after dinner, went to have a nap. Calliope served the doctor his brandy, slipping into a discussion of Bulgaria's alliance with the Axis powers, the growing likelihood of a German invasion. And then of the headmaster replacing her late father.

Calliope had been invited to take over the junior class at nineteen, when a schoolmaster engaged from the mainland had suddenly died of malaria. The current headmaster was better qualified and increasingly sceptical of her idiosyncratic approach to pedagogy. She was a popular teacher, but one given to neglecting official curriculum in favour of Aesop's fables or a Hans Christian Andersen tale.

The doctor's children went on playing on the threadbare Turkish rug. The doctor sipped his brandy, his eyes travelling from the copper brazier to Calliope's wedding portrait. She traced his gaze, her thoughts wandering back towards her missing husband. All winter, she had thought she would never forgive him, yet there was no arresting her straying imagination: Kimon hunkered down in a freezing Albanian trench; Kimon felled by an Italian bullet.

At that moment, as if to distract her from her melancholy musings, the doctor's cherubic son came toddling in from the kitchen, startled by a shrieking owl.

He had hazel eyes as round as marbles and pale, silky hair yet to be cut. Yawning, he clambered onto his godmother's lap, thrust his thumb into his mouth and promptly fell asleep. Not for the first time, the thought that the child had never known his mother sent a spasm of pain through Calliope's chest, though she could not imagine loving little Aristides any more deeply had he been her own.

'Another brandy, Doctor?'

'Please.'

They went on to talk about Calliope's uncle, the village mayor, who had suffered a heart attack the day after the general draft, then about an elderly neighbour, who nearly died after taking a relative's medication.

Ever since a Mytilene man opened a pharmacy in the village, people had been buying drugs as if they were Turkish delights. If a neighbour had been helped by some medication, another would be sure to hurry and buy it. Why waste time and money on a doctor, they reasoned, gulping down heart pills for gout, antispasmodics for blood in the urine. There was as yet no law requiring a prescription.

'You have no idea how discouraged I feel sometimes,' Dhaniel said, gazing thoughtfully at his sleeping son. 'We live with one foot in the Middle Ages, the other in the twentieth century.'

Mirto returned then, bearing a plate of Easter cookies baked by the doctor's mother-in-law. After his wife's death, Stella Gravari had come from Mytilene to raise the children, but she was spending the holiday in the capital, with her elder daughter's family.

Mirto served the cookies, then the doctor said it was time to go.

'Oh, but it's still early!' Calliope protested. The doctor was the only one with whom she could still have a serious discussion.

'All right, one more drink, then we really must go.'

'One more cookie!' Aristides lisped. He had slid off his godmother's lap to join his sisters on the floor. Calliope noted that he had a chocolate smudge on his sailor collar. For some reason, the small stain tugged at her heart. In the shadowy garden, a passing bird called, its odd querying cry ripping through the night.

III

The Germans arrived in the village on a ravishing spring morning, shortly after Easter. The local *kapheneion* owner and his daughter, Dora, were on their way to work when they spotted a jeep roaring towards the village: a German vehicle, raising dust and stones, almost running over a stray dog dozing on the gravel road.

The girl was helping her father run the coffee shop. She had been known as Dora the weeper ever since her fiancé, injured in Albania, had written to call off their engagement after getting an Athenian nursing aide in the family way.

Dora did not write back. In the years to come, she would often be observed weeping, not only for her own melancholy fate, but for the entire world's sorrows. Even after the war, she would continue to be known for two things: her remarkable ability to start bawling at the slightest provocation, and her refusal, after being jilted by the baker's brother, to eat baked products ever again.

But on that historic spring morning, she was carrying a basket of fresh bread and, as the foreign jeep flashed by, she dropped the basket, letting its contents roll on to the dusty road.

'They've come! The Germans have come!' she was soon announcing, darting from shop to shop, spilling the news to merchants, shoppers, hawkers. She was a seventeen-year-old girl, with mellow eyes and flaring nostrils that gave her the look of someone perpetually trying to sniff out some peculiar scent. 'We saw them with our own eyes, me and my father! They're here – right here in the village!'

There were no Germans to be seen as yet, but having alerted everyone in her path, Dora fled to her father's *kapheneion*, sobbing, her headscarf askew.

'Ach, Holy Mother, what's to become of us? Why would God free us from the Turks, only to drop us into the Germans' clutches? Why, *Panaghia mou*?'

It was a question neither the Virgin nor Dora's father seemed likely to answer. A man of few words, Yannis Rozakis was often sought in times of dispute or trouble. If there was a solution to a problem or quarrel, the *kapheneion* owner was sure to find it. The one problem he seemed helpless against was the sight of a weeping woman.

Rozakis was a middle-aged man with a prominent nose and, on his left temple, a kidney-shaped birthmark he was in the habit of rubbing in stressful moments. He rubbed it thoughtfully now, then fled to the balcony, as far as he could get from the sound of his daughter's sobs. And there he stood, leaning over the sea, puffing on a cigarette, while Dora pursued her impossible questions.

By noon, the shopkeepers had all abandoned the *agora*; housewives had stopped hanging laundry and shaking rugs, bolting indoors with their whiny children.

A telegram had arrived from Athens, but Tomas the telegraphist could not find anyone to deliver it. Surveying the empty street, he spotted Rozakis and Dora locking up the *kapheneion*. Would they do him a favour and take the telegram down to the harbour?

The Rozakis family lived only halfway down to the harbour, but Dora quickly offered to go.

Tomas thanked her, scratching through his hair. He was a tall, freckled young man – an epileptic – with a deeply alert air, like a dog hearing a distant whistle inaudible to others. He was engaged to marry one of Calliope's favourite former pupils. They were both keen readers.

Tomas was still at his post when classes ended and Calliope came sweeping uphill from school, accompanied by a cluster of jolly pupils. They had been singing as they approached the *agora*, but stopped abruptly, taking in the shuttered shops, the deserted streets. The afternoon was eerily quiet. They could hear the mulberry leaves stir in the breeze, a stray dog scraping through an abandoned crate.

Spotting Tomas, Calliope motioned to her straggling pupils to wait while she tried to find out what was happening. But in her marrow, she already knew. A week earlier, a taxi driver nicknamed 'the American' had reported seeing a German troopship dock in Mytilene, accompanied by destroyers flying Italian flags.

'I think I'll take the children home,' Calliope muttered. She hesitated, then turned away from the telephone-and-telegraph office with her arms spread, like a mother hen uselessly flapping her wings to protect her chicks.

IV

Rozakis forbade Dora to go to the harbour alone. He would grab a cheese pie, then walk down with her to deliver the telegram and see what was what. His wife stopped him to brush dandruff off his shoulder. His younger daughter, who was betrothed to the erstwhile football champion, was preparing liquorice root for his chronic cough. Dora waited, staring out the window. Much later, she would recall that, right after they left home, a black cat crossed their path, and she forced her father to turn around and take another route.

As they made their way down the acacia-lined street, Dora and her father ran into the village seamstress, who was taking a plate of freshly laid eggs to her elderly aunt. The carpenter's daughter – a young deaf-mute who never left the house without paper and crayons – was sketching in her drawing pad. The doctor's mother-in-law kept chasing her grandson, a bowl in one hand, a spoon in the other.

Yannis Rozakis offered greetings but said nothing about the invaders, shuffling on with Dora past sun-drenched courtyards and blossoming fruit trees until they reached the entrance to the harbour. And then, all at once, Rozakis froze, his arm flying out to stop his briefly distracted daughter.

On the wharf, directly across from Fotini's *kapheneion*, stood a German officer, his binoculars aimed at the distant mountains. In front of the harbour master's office, two soldiers squatted by a parked jeep, replacing a tyre; another soldier stood guard, a rifle slung across his chest.

'*Kalimera!*' The officer was striding towards Dora and her father, a look of resolute goodwill pasted on his face. He was tall and straight-backed and, as Dora would eventually tell her sister, so courteous! So dashing! His uniform, she would report breathlessly, perfectly matched his eyes!

Despite the confident greeting, it soon became apparent that the German possessed a Greek vocabulary of barely a dozen words. Extracting a folded note from his pocket, he went on to read a sentence which he thoroughly mispronounced but which they understood to be an enquiry about Mayor Metrophanis.

Rozakis and his daughter were silent.

'Where-is-Mayor-Metrophanis?' the officer repeated, his 'r's like the sputter of a motorcycle engine.

The German's Greek might sound atrocious, but when he aimed his clear, enquiring gaze at Dora, the young woman found herself placing her clasped hands under her tilted head: the mayor was ill, she mimed.

The officer nodded; he seemed to understand. 'Police,' he said then, still speaking Greek. 'Where-is-the-police?'

Rozakis kept his gaze on the German's polished boots, but Dora began to gesture, doing her best to answer the foreigner's question. The police station was high up in the village, near the cemetery.

The officer glanced up. It must have occurred to him that he might not readily find the station. 'Come with me,' he said to Dora in German. 'Please.'

The girl did not understand the request, but her father said something that left the German looking fleetingly at a loss. He summoned his adjutant, then motioned towards the hill, asking to be guided. He said 'please' again. He introduced himself: '*Leutnant* Lorenz Umbreit.'

Rozakis hesitated. He instructed Dora to deliver the telegram and stay with Fotini until he came for her. Then he began to shuffle uphill, with the air of a man being led to the gallows.

The lieutenant and his adjutant followed. The sea lay on their right, frothing with white caplets. On top of the sea wall, a cat lay basking in the sun, its tail twitching, eyes slitted with sleep. Rozakis walked with his hands clasped behind his back, pressing his worry beads all the way to the police station, where children were shrieking in play, chasing each other around a shady plane tree.

Inside, the police chief was seated at his desk, trimming his new moustache before a small mirror set against the black telephone. Becoming aware of the Germans, Christopoulos dropped the scissors, jumped to his feet, and sent the mirror flying. He then uttered the only foreign words he knew.

'*Nasıl yardımcı olabilirim?*'

'What, you expect them to understand Turkish?' Rozakis sputtered. 'Turkish, you blockhead?' He stood for a moment, his birthmark throbbing. 'And why would you offer to help the bastards anyway?' He shook his head, made a disgruntled gesture, then turned and tramped out of the office, into the spring sunlight, the lilac-scented morning.

V

The village was perched on a hill, its maze of stepped cobblestone streets overlooking sea and pastel mountains. The main street led steeply to the *agora*, then sloped down towards the fishing harbour. In the heart of the *agora*, between the barber's and the main kiosk, was a small *plateia* with a mulberry tree and a faded bench. The tree was ancient, its leafy canopy offering shelter on hot summer days.

The day the Germans arrived in the village, Hektor the fool was coming up the wisteria-laced street, weaving his way towards the kiosk. A thirty-year-old orphan from nearby Stipsi, he wore an old man's Turkish breeches, often a turban and a cummerbund as well. He liked to change his turban at least once a week, choosing one from a collection of colourful scraps donated by the seamstress.

There was no telling where Hektor might turn up, or when. He was given to roaming the village, singing, occasionally climbing a tree to free a stranded kitten or help himself to someone's ripening fruit. On that sunny spring afternoon, Calliope had just dropped off the last of her pupils when Hektor stopped her outside the butcher shop.

'*Ky-ky-kyria* Ca-cal-liope,' he spluttered, his hair standing on end like a cockscomb. He had stationed himself in the middle of the cobblestone street, and waited with his arms spread out, the smell of stale urine coming off his clothes. '*Kyria* Calliope, I—'

'Ach, let me pass, Hektor,' Calliope snapped. For reasons of his own, Hektor was stamping from side to side, his eyes swimming in their bloodshot sockets.

'*Kyria* Calliope, I... I wish to say something, *Ky-ky-ria* Calliope!'

'Well, say it, for heaven's sake, Hektor.'

'I wish, *Kyria* Calliope, that you... that you was cross-eyed...'

'Cross-eyed?'

'Y-yes,' stammered Hektor. 'I... I wish you was cross-eyed so... so your eyes could see how beautiful they are!'

31

Any other day, Calliope might have laughed out loud, but today, all she did was let out a vaguely exasperated sound, then her deepest sigh. 'Oh, Hektor, Hektor.' For once, the busybody seemed to be in the dark about the latest news.

'Cross-eyed!' he repeated emphatically. 'Bea-u-ti-ful, beautiful,' he muttered, then plodded on towards the *plateia* without another word.

Hektor was not the only one smitten with Calliope. She was an auburn-haired young woman with bold eyebrows and amber-hued eyes that gazed at the world with the avidity of a child hopeful of new adventure. She was generally considered the most beautiful woman in the village, but, even as a girl, she had never been kept under lock and key. Not even the most permissive father would have allowed an unmarried daughter to wander through the village the way Calliope had been prone to do day and night, accompanied only by her dog. There were those who still felt that the poor headmaster should have known better than to let his only daughter become a schoolmistress, cramming her head with useless knowledge: French, German, poetry!

But now the headmaster was dead and, what with her husband gone, the young widow was once more free to do as she pleased. There were rumours of a domestic quarrel taking place just before the call to arms, but Calliope had always been deaf to village gossip and today all that preoccupied her was the grim possibility that Hitler's troops had arrived to stay.

There were no Germans to be seen anywhere, but Calliope had gradually become aware of her heart as a discrete organ. It felt like some panic-stricken creature, a swallow or a mouse, trapped inside a chimney. The sensation grew stronger as she began to climb home, all but bumping into an itinerant gypsy who came from time to time to sell tablecloths or yo-yos. She was a good-looking, colourfully dressed woman but unlikely to sell much today. All around, the neighbourhood houses stood mute and shuttered, except for one derelict Turkish house that had long since lost all its doors and windows.

For years, whenever she thought about their erstwhile Turkish neighbours, Calliope would experience a spasm of guilt, recalling how she and her cousins would amuse themselves by hiding shoes left at the entrance to the village mosque. The Turks would come out, swearing away, while three pairs of childish eyes peered through gate cracks, hands clamped over gap-toothed mouths.

Despite such childish pranks, there had been no animosity between Greek and Turkish Molyviates. They had not worshipped together and had not intermarried, but the men had worked and played backgammon together, and the women exchanged household tips and helped each other through countless domestic crises.

Then, one day, they were all gone, forced into sudden exile. By the time Mussolini had started to flex his muscles, the Turkish house was so decrepit there was talk of building a cinema on the site. Kimon, who loved films, had been one of the men championing this proposal, but now he, too, was gone. Everybody knew that 'missing on the field of honour' was just a euphemism.

The Ministry of War's telegram had arrived in winter, but Calliope was still being assailed by visions of Kimon's body decomposing on alien soil, maggots swarming through his wounds, vultures pecking at his lifeless eyes. A peculiar odour would accompany these random visions: acrid and vaguely familiar, like the smell of freshly slaughtered lamb dangling from butchers' hooks.

The mysterious odour was rising in Calliope's nostrils now, making her stomach roil. The beautiful spring day suddenly seemed unbearably hot. She turned away from the Turkish house, thinking to catch her breath in the shade of a sprawling pine tree. She took a step toward the public bench, only to find her legs revolting against her own weight.

On top of the hill, a German flag was being hoisted from the crumbling medieval fortress – a bold black swastika fluttering in the sea breeze, over burgeoning fields and silvery olive orchards, and the innocent blue of the placid Aegean, glittering in the sunlight.

VI

At the town hall, German and Greek flags were flying side by side. Calliope had paused at the wrought-iron gate. There was the familiar scent of roses planted by a Turkish pasha's wife, the sound of an aggrieved child whining over some parental injunction. Two stray kittens were toying with a bird fallen out of a nest. Chickens squabbled in some nearby courtyard.

A morning like any other. A morning like no other.

It was the second day of the Occupation. A megaphone was blaring the German national anthem. *Deutschland, Deutschland, über alles.* The anthem was making Calliope's stomach churn. She realised she had forgotten to bring her dictionary, but she had always been incorrigibly absent-minded.

She had been summoned through the chief of police, after Rozakis and the two Germans had turned up at the station. Unable to make sense of what the foreigners wanted, the chief had sent Sergeant Floros to fetch Dr Dhaniel from his clinic. He was under the impression that the doctor knew German, but Dhaniel insisted it was French he spoke.

Lieutenant Umbreit, however, turned out to have a much better command of French than he did of Greek. They had been given an interpreter, he explained to the doctor, but the recruit knew only classical Greek and had proven virtually useless. They were waiting for a replacement but had been led to believe that the Molyvos mayor spoke German.

'A little,' Dhaniel said. 'But he has had a heart attack. He wouldn't be much use to you.'

'Anyone else?' the lieutenant asked. 'We need someone... someone to act as a liaison officer.'

'Liaison officer,' the doctor echoed.

'An intermediary between us and the villagers,' the lieutenant elaborated.

'Yes. Yes, I see.' Elias Dhaniel sighed, paused to reflect, then – as he would later tell Calliope – decided it might turn out to be useful to have her working for the Germans. He gave her married name to the lieutenant: Calliope Alexiou.

The German raised an eyebrow. 'A village woman?'

'A schoolmaster's daughter.' The doctor studied the floor. 'Her German's probably adequate, but... well, she's a schoolmistress now. She's busy with the children.'

'Do not worry, Doctor. I'm sure we can compromise.'

Dhaniel translated the ensuing exchange. The police chief must get the schoolmistress to present herself at the town hall in the morning, when Major von Herden was expected to meet with the village council.

It might have sounded like a request but, calling on Calliope that evening, Chief Christopoulos made it clear: this was an order.

'Not mine, you understand. It's those bloody Germans. They want you there at ten a.m.'

And so Calliope came. She opened the gate, feeling hot moisture spread in her armpits. The armed sentries watched her climb the mansion's stairs: a tall, black-clad young woman wearing a widow's head-kerchief, her golden eyes bright with anguish.

They must have been told to expect her. Hearing her name, one of the soldiers promptly escorted Calliope indoors, announcing her to his superior.

'*Guten Morgen!*' The officer introduced himself, as amiable as a host dealing with some last-minute party arrangements.

Calliope did not return the greeting. She merely nodded, eyes riveted to the eagle-and-swastika badge above Lieutenant Umbreit's breast pocket. Eventually, she looked up. She noted that the German's eyes were the colour of a wintry sea; he had a dented chin resembling her father's, though the officer's face was more angular, as high-coloured as a mountaineer's.

The German anthem ended, replaced by the Greek. The lieutenant ushered Calliope into the former pasha's reception room, where the village council was assembled around 'the American' sitting in for the ailing mayor. They were waiting for the major to arrive, as restive as schoolchildren during a tedious lesson.

Coffee was served. Dr Dhaniel did not touch his, but the clumsy olive-mill owner spilled some on his carefully knotted tie. The German lieutenant had stepped out and was conferring with his adjutant. Calliope stared at her own hands with sudden astonishment. They were trembling like the hands of an old woman. They didn't seem to belong to her, to respond to her inner commands.

She hid the hands in her lap. The Greek anthem came to an end. There was the sound of clicking heels, a flurry of *Heil Hitler*s at the entrance. And then the lieutenant threw open the conference room door.

Major von Herden had arrived.

VII

Calliope had never met anyone with such pale, pale eyes – eyes virtually colourless except for the thin grey rim encircling the iris. A wolf's eyes, she would later think, recalling a picture book she had recently bought for her godson.

Von Herden was doing his best to seem like a friendly wolf. He was years older than Lieutenant Umbreit, but his speech and manner somehow suggested prolonged rehearsal in front of a mirror. The Germans had not come to the island as enemies but as well-meaning friends; the occupation of the region was only temporary; the Wehrmacht's aim was to protect the island against British attacks.

Von Herden stated all this with stiff courtesy, spacing out his words as if to avoid potential misunderstanding. He waited for Calliope to render his statement into Greek before continuing.

'Naturally, we shall not interfere with your authorities, nor molest anyone – provided the Occupation is respected, of course.'

Of course. Calliope, translating, observed the doctor exchange looks with the acting mayor. Kyriakos Himonas's tie was askew, his hair in revolt, as if he had forgotten to comb it on getting out of bed. Calliope thought of her husband rising in the morning and, momentarily distracted, missed the major's next words. Something about a speech Hitler had given.

'And I can tell you the Führer singled out the Greek people for special praise,' he was saying. 'No other nation has fought with the valour of your soldiers!'

Von Herden went on in this vein, but eventually got down to rules and regulations. That firearms had to be surrendered was to be expected, but the order to stop night fishing left Calliope staring at the major in utter bewilderment.

'In a few days, permits will be issued for daytime fishing,' von Herden added.

Calliope translated all this, seeing amazement spread on the councillors' faces. This was a fishing village! Its inhabitants had lived off the sea from time immemorial, accountable to no one but God.

A long silence followed. The birthmark on Rozakis's forehead had visibly swelled; 'the American' kept running his hand over his face, as if trying to decide whether a shave was called for.

'I'm sorry to say that school attendance will have to be cut to two hours,' the major continued, looking like a parent forced to renege on a promise. 'Two hours, six days a week, and—'

'Two hours?'

Calliope swallowed hard, then slowly turned toward the village council. 'At least they're not demanding we conduct our classes in German,' she added drily.

The comment was aimed at the headmaster but, shifting back to the major, Calliope became aware of the young lieutenant's querying eyes. He appeared faintly amused, as if he'd guessed the nature of her aside. Did he understand more Greek than he let on? He had a deliberate, distracted way of raking his hand through his hair, like a man absorbed in solving an intricate problem. The hair was wheat-coloured, as fine as a boy's.

'Any questions?' If not for his uniform, the major might have been a stern professor scanning his students' faces. His listeners looked more restive than ever. 'Please feel free to voice anything on your mind,' von Herden said: polite, encouraging. 'Anything at all.'

The *kapheneion* owner was the first to speak, asking about personal travel. He didn't state the reason for his concern, but Calliope guessed it had to do with his son, who had also failed to return from the Albanian campaign. There had been reports of families travelling to Epirus to scour the battlefields for their missing relatives' remains.

The major said that trips around the island should present no problem, but sea travel would require an official permit. 'Rest assured, you'll have permits for everything, including trade with the mainland.'

At this point, von Herden consulted his watch, conferred briefly with his lieutenant, then went on to announce a brief intermission. He must have a quick tour of the village, then hurry back to headquarters. Lieutenant Umbreit would conduct the second part of the conference. He would also be responsible for carrying out all further directives.

VIII

Calliope's anxiety had not quite evaporated but, stepping outdoors with the doctor, she was conscious of a surge of relief: she had never expected foreign invaders to be so civilised.

They went to sit on a garden bench. Now that the megaphone was off, birds could be heard, twittering in the garden; a distant goat had begun to bleat. The council members strolled about the garden, smoking and arguing. They lingered by the fish pond, trying to decide how best to disseminate the Germans' demands.

The doctor was not taking part in the discussion. He could not, he said, think clearly, with all of them babbling together. He seemed, all at once, unusually testy. When Calliope spoke of German civility, he made a small, disgruntled gesture but did not bother to answer.

'Von Herden even thanked me for my services!' Calliope added.

Dhaniel heaved a sigh. 'You mustn't confuse fine manners with good intentions.'

'What do you mean? Would you rather have them flashing swords like the Turks?'

The doctor was silent, his eyes wandering around the garden. Suddenly, he reached out and plucked a rose from one of the pasha's bushes, as if searching for consolation in the floral beauty. He brought the coral-hued rose to his nose, held it there briefly, then passed it to Calliope.

'The garden is technically theirs now,' he said. 'But why should they mind? After all, they're only here to protect us from the British.'

Calliope studied his face for a moment. 'You don't believe them,' she said.

'Ach, Calliopitsa. They're here to protect their own interests! They think the Allies might try to land here from the Turkish coast.'

'But why should they ban night fishing? Do they think our fishermen might collaborate with the Allies?'

'Yes! Or try to escape to the other side.'

'But why?'

'To join the Brits,' he said, 'or maybe our own forces in Egypt.'

Calliope mulled it over, watching the major and his minions briskly stride away. Her uncle, the mayor, was still bedridden, but he had at some point aired the view that Kimon might be among those fighting in Egypt. It was widely known that some Albanian draftees had joined the Greek Armed Forces in the Middle East, but even Kimon's mother didn't think her son was likely to be among them. Kimon had detested army life. He would have sailed home the moment he got his discharge papers. Calliope had agreed with her mother-in-law, though who could say what changes might come over a man after a few battles?

In the town hall garden, the councillors had reached a decision. *Papa* Emanouil had undertaken to speak to *Papa* Iakovos. The two priests would announce the new rules after Sunday Mass; the acting mayor would see to it that notices went up all over the *agora*.

The discussion was still in progress when the German adjutant appeared in the doorway. Lieutenant Umbreit was ready to resume.

IX

The first thing to disappear from store shelves was bread. It was mid-June and, walking home from her new duties at the town hall, Calliope came upon a gaggle of women gathered outside the shuttered bakery, clucking like distraught hens. They stood huddled together in the midday glare, gesturing towards the sign Petros Morales had posted on his bakery door: *NO BREAD*.

There was no bread because there was no flour anywhere on the island. There was no flour because sea transports from the mainland had virtually stopped. Morales could have stayed to explain all this but hadn't.

'There's no bread,' Calliope told her mother. She went to the cistern for a glass of water. 'No one knows when – if – we'll have bread again.'

'No bread!' Mirto crossed herself. 'Mother of God, what next?' She was stirring a pot of lentils, which were not quite ready. Calliope was hungry and irritable, itchy all over in her mourning clothes.

'We can always eat cake, I suppose,' she said.

Mirto, who had never heard of Marie Antoinette, shot Calliope an exasperated look. 'How can we bake cake when there's no flour?' She stood shaking her head. 'May their bones rot in pitch, Hitler and his cohorts!'

Calliope sat down to prepare her lessons. She taught only two hours a day now, but spent at least six at the town hall – morning or evening – translating the Germans' communiques, the mayor's questions, the villagers' complaints about permits, house searches, shortage of boat fuel. Even Hektor the fool had a grievance: there was too much rubbish put out by the Germans; he was having to make extra trips to the village dump.

The dump was behind the fortress, not far from the watchtower the Germans had constructed to survey the sweep of sea between the Turkish coastline and Eftalou. A military seaplane was frequently seen hovering over the village; German boats kept patrolling the sea, on the lookout for British submarines, contraband, National Resistance fighters.

The Germans remained polite but did not hesitate to requisition anything they needed, including Fotini's *kapheneion* in the harbour. The shop was now a German canteen, though old Fotini was duly paid for serving the Wehrmacht soldiers.

Lieutenant Umbreit had settled into a spare room at the back of the town hall; his adjutant was billeted in the cellar, next to what used to be the servants' quarters but was now a German detention cell. Eight recruits were lodged in the abandoned Turkish house. They had slept in tents while the house was restored and cleaned, with a skill and efficiency that left the neighbours agog.

There had been little left of the Turks' possessions, but the Germans burned whatever they found. They disinfected every corner, they requisitioned mattresses. Within a week, a swastika was hanging above the entrance. The place seemed deserted during the day, but sometimes, sitting at her window late in the evening, Calliope would hear the German soldiers singing their melancholy songs.

The town hall had come to house both Greek and German administrative offices. Calliope spent much of her time running between floors, working at the desk she'd been assigned in the mayor's office, keeping at bay any thoughts of Kimon. In the *agora*, villagers who had once detained her to enquire about their children's progress were now posing questions she could seldom answer. Questions about produce or leather quotas, about confiscated fishing boats or relinquished gold. Gold was one of the commodities the Germans had demanded upon arrival; hoarders would be subject to the death penalty.

'But it's not right – surely you can see it's not right,' Calliope's own mother-in-law protested. 'Expecting me to give up a family heirloom as if it was a sack of potatoes!'

Martha Alexiou was a widow in her late forties, with creamy, sumptuous flesh and blue eyes perpetually lit by fires of indignation. Since her husband's death and Kimon's failure to return, much of her energy had been expended in search of someone to blame for her various vexations. She would have gone on about the gold had it not been for the timely arrival of her youngest son, Pericles.

Kimon's younger brother had been one of Calliope's brightest pupils, a shy bookworm obsessed with world capitals. He was going on seventeen now, suddenly focused on his unruly hair. Every day, he would comb and comb his black mane, resolutely flattening it, only to have it spring up again.

Pericles looked older than his years, but his attachment to his former teacher seemed undiminished. He often came to see Calliope after school, offering to chop wood, or prune a fruit tree, or get rid of a large spider. All he asked in return was that she read a new poem he had just written, often two or three of them. Sometime around puberty, Pericles's interest in world geography had given way to a new, lasting obsession with the power of words.

X

What the Occupation demanded above all, however, was reticence and cunning. Due to the recent requisitioning of livestock, a medical certificate was needed to purchase meat. Calliope's mother seemed healthy enough, but the doctor officially diagnosed anaemia, offering the false document with a little ironic flourish. Oddly, as soon as the certificate had been issued, Mirto began to complain of real weakness in her limbs, sometimes of a malaise she could neither describe nor pinpoint.

Calliope was more robust than Mirto, but her job as a go-between and document translator had proven far more exhausting than teaching.

The Germans often confused her. She pulsed with resentment

against their authority, yet could not help admiring their manners and competence. She bristled at the exclusion of Greek history from the curriculum, at being forced to facilitate the invaders' purpose, yet could not deny the pleasure derived from the linguistic challenge. She would not admit this even to the doctor, but there was huge satisfaction in improving her command of a language that her father had taught her, and that she'd seldom had occasion to practise, except with her godfather-uncle, when his mayor's duties had permitted it.

But now her uncle was bedridden and 'the American' continued as acting mayor. He had time on his hands. Too much time, he grumbled, now that his taxi stood virtually idle because of fuel shortages.

As an adventurous young man, Kyriakos Himonas had sailed away on a merchant ship. He worked in Chicago for several years, then returned to purchase a taxi and marry the well-dowered cousin of a Kaloni man with whom he had shared a cabin.

Suddenly, the stonemason's son was a man of status and means. His achievements were widely applauded, but a few drinks, and especially the company of some passing stranger, soon had him lapsing into a boastful mood.

'I'm not like you aristocrats,' he was given to saying to his social superiors. 'I've sweated buckets for everything I've got. Buckets, believe me!'

He liked to tell stories of his youthful exploits, mostly involving women in various ports of call. He was at the time in his mid-forties, a handsome, solidly built man blessed with what was generally regarded as American drive and vigour.

Sharing an office with Calliope, Kyriakos did his best to emulate Mayor Metrophanis. He never left home without donning a tie, never used a simple word if a longer one could be ferreted out of his meagre vocabulary. He had brought a miniature of his own patron saint to the office, setting it next to a cherished American souvenir: the Statue of Liberty. Calliope thought her colleague foolish and vain, but always good for a droll anecdote. These days, you had to be grateful for the smallest distractions and pleasures.

Petra's Church of the Sweet Kissing Virgin was where Molyviates traditionally went on the Holy Day of the Assumption. Before the Occupation, most villagers would take the bus, or hire Kyriakos's taxi. Some rode a farm cart or a mule, but virtually everybody went. It was one of the most sacred days on the Orthodox calendar.

In that first summer of the Occupation, most Molyviates made the pilgrimage on foot. Molyvos's sister village was five kilometres down an unpaved road but, what with the fuel shortage, the public bus was no longer running.

The acting mayor had been granted a small quantity of fuel for medical emergencies. On that mid-August day in 1941, he had just enough left for one round trip to Petra. He was taking his own family but, at the last moment, his father complained of back pain, so Calliope's lame mother was invited to take the old man's place.

Mirto went, leaving Calliope to her own devices. Around six o'clock, after a swim and a nap, she took Sappho for a long walk. At the entrance to the village, two German soldiers leaned against the sea wall, keeping an eye on things.

The harbour was deserted. There was the sound of breaking waves, of seagulls swooping above the rippling water. The sun was still beating down on her head, so Calliope removed her kerchief. Settling down on the bench outside the harbour master's office, she reached for her satchel and brought out a French novel. Sappho stopped to nuzzle Calliope's feet, then went tearing after a cat.

Half an hour had gone by when Lieutenant Umbreit came strolling into the harbour. He paused by the canteen, his eyes sweeping the deserted quay. Absorbed in her novel, Calliope was as yet unaware of his presence.

'*Guten Tag, Frau* Alexiou!'

The officer had finally crossed the wharf, his cap in his hand. Though both voice and face conveyed friendly intentions, the greeting sent a dart of anxiety through Calliope. Had she overlooked some official request? Had she forgotten to hand in something before going home?

'*Guten Tag.*' She swallowed. She crossed her legs, hand at rest on her open book. She took in the lieutenant's binoculars, the pistol in his holster.

'Beautiful day,' he said genially, eliciting an inner sneer: a beautiful day in mid-August was hardly worth commenting on.

She made a vague gesture. His scent intrigued her. It was a fresh, soapy smell reminiscent of her father's shaving cream. But what was he doing here? Absently, Calliope's fingers stirred of their own accord – opening, closing, opening, closing – on top of the printed page. The lieutenant glanced down at her hand and smiled.

'What are you reading?' He had a way of crinkling his eyes, a habit that lent him a warm, friendly look. Not the look of a conqueror.

'A French novel.' Calliope picked up the book and turned it over, letting him see the dust jacket. Polite but impassive. In four months, they had barely exchanged a single sentence beyond the absolute requirements of her job.

'*L'Assommoir*!' Surprise flickered across the German's face. 'And in French!' He stood looking at her with his clear, foreign eyes.

'Well, why not?' Calliope said, mastering her irritation. 'As a matter of fact, I've already read it. Long ago, but…' She shrugged, letting the statement dangle.

'But?'

'I have nothing else to read,' she stated drily. There had been no new books since the start of the Occupation, but she resisted the urge to express resentment. 'I'm rereading everything in our library.'

The lieutenant regarded her for a moment. 'Have you read the sequels?'

'No.' Calliope glanced up. He was probably somewhere in his late twenties – not much older than she. 'Not yet. Have you?'

He nodded. He smiled. A German soldier who had read Zola!

'I'd really like to read Flaubert,' she said, thinking out loud.

'Well. I hope you will some day.' He made a small, ambiguous gesture, hesitated, then turned to go.

'Have you read Balzac?' she blurted, succumbing to curiosity.

Umbreit paused and turned to face her with a wan smile. He had studied literature and philosophy, he said, a little hesitant; had read all the French authors. 'At Heidelberg University.'

'I see,' she said, feeling herself flush. *Heidelberg University!*

Umbreit stood gazing at a soaring seagull. 'I miss my student days,' he said suddenly. He sounded sad, yet unusually relaxed. Calliope was accustomed to seeing him bustle about, issuing orders, talking on the phone. He was unfailingly courteous but also preoccupied, officious. He turned back to her. 'Have you read any German books?'

'A couple.' Calliope had finally risen, smoothing her black skirt. Her godfather had once been an ardent Germanophile. When Princess Frederika married the Greek Crown Prince, he had given Calliope two Herman Hesse novels on her name day. Reading them had been something of a struggle, but she had persevered. 'My vocabulary's still very small,' she told Lieutenant Umbreit.

'Not that small.' He smiled. One of his front teeth slightly overlapped the other. 'Your German's surprisingly good,' he said. 'Really.'

She managed a vaguely grateful smile. '*Danke.*'

She did not see him again until the next afternoon, when she went upstairs to submit an official record of olive oil production. She knew why the Germans needed the olive mill's records. It was the only way to determine how much oil they could reasonably expect. Umbreit took a cursory look at the sheaf of onionskins obtained from the mill. He tossed the file aside, reaching into a drawer.

'I have something for you.' He brought out a heavy black book embossed with gold letters. 'You may borrow it if you like. Nietzsche,' he added, the hint of a smile hovering around his mouth.

'It's kind of you, but—'

'It's all I have,' he put in, vaguely apologetic.

'*Danke schön.*' Her gaze veered away, sweeping over Umbreit's wall map: a German map of her own island, with red pins marking Wehrmacht garrisons along the coast. 'Unfortunately, I don't have much time these days and – well, as I said, German's still a struggle.' She paused. 'It's kind of you to think of me, though.' She spoke politely, concealing her satisfaction. A Greek village girl being offered a philosophy book by a German officer!

The lieutenant was silent for a moment, regarding her with a slightly perplexed expression. 'Wouldn't you at least like to try?'

She shook her head. '*Danke sehr.*'

'Very well.' He tilted back in his chair, putting the book away. 'You're free to go, *Frau* Alexiou.'

She left his office and returned to the Greek quarters. Should she have accepted the book? Was it churlish of her not to?

All afternoon, she kept struggling with herself. She would have greatly liked to read the German book – at least to try, as he had suggested. He'd caught her off guard and she had reacted instinctively: he was the enemy after all.

She tried to find vindication in this inner reminder, kept trying to settle her ongoing confusion with the memory of the way he'd looked at her yesterday, standing in front of the harbour master's office – his widening eyes, his raised eyebrows – when he first realised she was reading Zola.

It was the surprise she could not forgive.

XII

One day, a dispute broke out between the acting mayor and Captain Yorgos, the former football champion's father and captain of a fishing boat he had named *Eleftheria*. The Lyras family's new caique was the finest in the village, so it came as no surprise that the Germans would commandeer it for the transport of island produce. The supplies were to go by sea to Salonika, then by cargo train to the German Reich.

'The fucking bastards!' the captain fumed, storming into the mayor's office without so much as a greeting. '*My* boat to fatten up Hitler!'

He was a thickset man with flashing eyes and a mouth agleam

with gold. Looming over the acting mayor, he went on to demand that the council intervene with the German authorities. Their Italian allies had already got his son's leg, he thundered. 'Mimis is crippled for life, and now the motherfuckers want my boat?'

Kyriakos listened, toying with his moustache, as attentive as a newly ordained priest at his first confession. He let the captain speak, then leaned back and tried to explain: the council had no leverage with the Germans. 'None, I regret to say.'

The statement was made in a grave and collected manner, as befitted the dignity of a mayor. But Kyriakos's restraint only inflamed Yorgos Lyras. Waving his hammer-like fists, he insisted that a meeting be called to resolve the issue.

Kyriakos regarded him from under his bushy eyebrows. 'Can't do that, Captain,' he said. 'Anyway, the council—'

'The council should at least try to squeeze them!'

'But that's just what I've been trying to tell you: we've got no authority over the Germans! They take—'

'They take whatever they want because you let them! The Germans spit in your face and you say it's raining!' roared the captain. He was an ardent communist and Germany had just invaded the Soviet Union, compounding his outrage. He turned and spat on the floor. 'What are you, a man or a jellyfish? Is that what they taught you in America, to be the Germans' puppet?'

'What did you say?' The mayor sprang up, sweat running from his eyebrows.

Calliope, who had a document to finish, glanced up from her desk. 'Gentlemen, please! I'm trying to work!'

The men ignored her, their voices running into each other like hawkers' cries at Mytilene's central market. Kyriakos was jabbing his finger at the captain's chest; Lyras's sunburned face was contorted with rage.

'Stop now, both of you!' Calliope snapped. 'You're acting like children!' She had failed to catch the mayor's last statement, but the words tumbling from Yorgos's lips made her bounce up from her chair, jumping back to dodge the captain's flying spit. Were they going to end up punching each other like brawling sailors? Kyriakos was accusing the captain of cheating Mytilene fishmongers; the captain was scoffing at everything connected with the mayor, from his politics to his late mother's honour. He was still waving his fists when Alfred Reis, Umbreit's adjutant, happened to come by. He glanced at the two feuding men, nodded stiffly, then hurried on towards the staircase, as if nothing untoward were going on.

Calliope sighed, irritation giving way to a surge of shame. The German had said nothing, but oh, the disdain in those frosty eyes, the barely suppressed contempt for two grown men ready to go at each other's throats in a public office – in a woman's presence!

'Go ahead!' she spat out as the red-faced men went on trying to outshout each other. 'Kill each other for all I care!'

She snatched the page she was translating and swept out of the office. She wished she could go home, but she'd promised to hand in the finished document for typing and duplication. Would Umbreit be able to hear the men's voices in his upstairs office? Oh, maybe not: his office was in the back, overlooking the courtyard.

She collapsed onto the garden bench, perspiration trickling down her face. Her widow's weeds made her feel smothered in the rising heat. The black dye seeped from her collar and into her brassiere. It left stains on her neck and breasts. It made her want to scratch in intimate places.

The men went on shouting. Kyriakos was in no position to accede to the captain's demands, but he could have handled the situation more tactfully. Calliope was sure *she* would have, had she been in his shoes. But then, who would ever consider electing a woman to serve as mayor? Or, for that matter, even a village councillor?

XIII

At the end of that first, torrid summer of the Occupation, Calliope woke from an afternoon nap and, succumbing to heat and impulse, decided to burn all her widow's weeds. Hearing her mother stir, she hastened to gather all her black garments: the cotton dresses, the blouses, the traditional widow's kerchiefs. She then hurried out into the garden, hugging the hateful tangle with the look an overworked maid might wear while disposing of a soiled nappy. Soon, Mirto came shuffling out and found Calliope standing at the firepit.

'Do you realise what you're doing, daughter?'

Calliope struck a match. 'Yes, Mama, perfectly.'

'Perfectly, eh?' Mirto wrung her arthritic hands. She let a silent moment go by. 'Did you stop to think what people will say?'

Calliope jerked back from the leaping flames.

'Let them talk! I don't give a button any more!' She stood watching the sizzling clothes, her face set in ferocious resolve. There was the smell of burning dye in the air, a foul odour that seemed somehow to vindicate her impulse.

Mirto, too, was gazing at the flames. 'Ach, my daughter, you still think you can go through life doing whatever you like, eh?'

Silence. The underlying argument was nothing if not familiar. Watching the fire devour her mourning clothes, Calliope found her thoughts drifting towards her wedding day: the musicians accompanying her to St Kyriaki, playing their violins and accordion, the children skipping alongside the bridal entourage, the old women waving kerchiefs through the open windows, calling out their blessings.

But Mirto was going on with her melancholy rant. 'You heap scorn on everything I say, then—'

'Not everything,' Calliope interjected. 'Only the superstitious nonsense you keep trying to foist on me.'

'Superstitious nonsense, eh?' There was a glint in Mirto's eye. 'That's what you said when I warned you… didn't I warn you when you broke the mirror?'

'The mirror? Oh, God, not that again!' Calliope's eyes turned heavenwards.

The mirror in question had been broken six years earlier, but Mirto seemed unshaken in her belief that all their woes had been brought on by her daughter's carelessness.

'Did the Germans invade all of Europe because I broke the mirror, or is it just Greece I'm responsible for?' Calliope's lips twitched.

'Yes, laugh! Laugh all you want!' Mirto picked up an old garden broom and set about sweeping the leaf-strewn path. 'Most widows shut themselves up and cry their eyes out, but you—'

'Well, I'd much rather laugh than pretend to weep for a husband I no longer loved!' Calliope retorted, surprising herself no less than her mother.

She had spoken the truth, but it was a truth she had repeatedly averted her mind from. She had married Kimon in a spirit of affection and hope, spurred on by her father's dying wish that she marry and settle down. She had caused something of a scandal after a passing farmer had spotted her on St Basil's Day, entering the pinewood with Johnny the Australian. She had run into him by chance, after walking her dog on the deserted beach. He had said he wanted to talk to her, and she had followed him into the resinous wood, surrendering to curiosity. Although she hardly knew Johnny, his younger sister had been her classmate. What could he possibly want from her?

He had wanted her to be his wife. To go to Australia with him.

'Australia!' The proposal had snatched Calliope's breath. She might have been tempted by Paris or Florence but had no desire to live in Australia, a land of ex-convicts and hopping kangaroos! She was, moreover, not at all sure she wanted to marry anyone. Ever. She ended up saying as much to Johnny, who seemed taken aback, but wasted no time going to ask for the cobbler's sister's hand.

A few days later, there was a shocking assault on Socrates, Calliope's first dog, but neither the police nor anyone else could say who might have done it, or why.

Calliope's sick father feared the brutalised dog was just the beginning.

'A woman… a woman like you, *koritsi mou*, will only make people want to hurt her.' He entreated her to make up her mind and accept one of her suitors so he could depart in peace.

Calliope had not believed her father was dying; she'd argued and argued with him and, for weeks after, could no more arrest her devouring guilt than she could the setting of the sun or the waning of the moon. Was it her contrariness that had exhausted her enfeebled father? Her reckless behaviour on St Basil's Day?

Her mother was becoming a tight-lipped, aloof woman, moving about the house like a sleepwalker, rejecting all offers of help or solace. Her sigh-filled conversation had gradually shrunk to household requests, the occasional muttered rebuke. She was only in her mid-forties but whiled away her evenings polishing brass and silver as if her very survival depended on it. Calliope's own survival, she eventually came to feel, largely depended on her ability to escape the pernicious domestic fog.

In midsummer, she began to frequent the beach again, reading or watching children splash in the sea. Only the sound and smell of the sea seemed to soothe her, the sea and the books that her godfather had brought back from a trip to Athens. Sometimes, on her way home, she would stop in the *agora*, even when there was nothing they especially needed.

The *pantopoleion* often had something new for sale: toiletries or ribbons, imported chocolates or bananas. Crammed with crates and boxes, and sacks bulging with legumes and spice, the store had a musty-sweetish smell Calliope had always liked, slyly evocative of distant lands: teeming ports, mysterious alleys.

She was desperately trying to find her way back to her old self, and Kimon Alexiou, the sugar merchant's son, who co-owned the general store with his brother, seemed determined to help her get there. The older brother was moody, but Kimon had always enjoyed teasing Calliope, and was now teaching her to laugh again, making her rage against the fates gradually dissipate. One day, watching her cross the *plateia*, he said that her walk made other women look as if they were treading grapes for home-made wine. Her eyes, he told her another day, resembled the eyes of a tiger lolling in the sun. How she had laughed at that!

When, eventually, he came to ask for her hand, Kimon promised to let her continue teaching, if she so wished. Few men would have allowed such a thing and, gradually, Calliope felt herself being towed towards the shores of love. One year after her father's death, she consented to marry Kimon, relieved to be able to stay in Molyvos, grateful to find herself cajoled across the stormy river of filial grief.

By the time the Germans arrived in the village, Mirto had grown resigned to her own widowhood but not to her daughter's wayward ways. Calliope seldom listened to her mother, but she never gave up striving for understanding.

'I can't help it, Mama!' she blurted out the day she decided to torch her mourning clothes. 'I did my best to love him, I did, but…'

'But?'

'But it's not going to do Kimon any good, my wearing black for the rest of my life, is it?' She met her mother's baleful gaze, then stood watching Sappho head off in pursuit of a mouse.

'I can tell you one thing,' Mirto said after a long silence. 'It isn't going to do *you* any good to shed your mourning so soon.' She set the broom back against the stone wall, then busied herself picking acacia threads out of her coiled hair. 'Just think what your mother-in-law's going to say when she sees you tomorrow.'

'I don't care – I don't care, I tell you!'

She had worn black whenever she visited her mother-in-law, had done everything right, yet it all seemed futile before the blue accusation in Martha's eyes. *If only you had not been barren, if you'd borne my son children as you were meant to, Kimon would not have been drafted. He'd be alive today!*

'She acts as if I was personally responsible for Kimon's death!' Calliope reached out, sullenly plucking a plum from a sagging branch. 'She hates me, Mama!'

At this, Mirto stood for a moment, scanning her daughter's face. Then she sighed again, more deeply than ever.

'We shouldn't have pushed you to marry. You were not born to be a wife and mother.'

These words stopped Calliope's breath. They made her long to hug her mother, to wrap her arms around Mirto's narrow shoulders and bawl like a child who, lost in a seemingly endless forest, has stumbled upon a small, unexpected shelter.

XIV

Molyviates had begun to avoid venturing out, but, on the first day of September, Calliope saw Kimon's older brother emerge from St Pandeleimon's Church with his family. It was his uncle's name day, and he was carrying his god-daughter, the new baby Calliope had declined to adopt. She might have been more amenable had she known the child would be an adorable little girl, but Vangelis had often boasted that the Alexious could only produce sons, and everyone had expected the fourth child to be another rambunctious boy.

Seeing the family in the distance, Calliope quickly ducked into Dr Dhaniel's clinic, hoping to avoid an encounter with Vangelis, who had never forgiven her. Distracted by their children, neither he nor Ioanna had spotted Calliope, but she had observed them long enough to see that Vangelis was going grey and looking more sour than ever.

Ioanna had meanwhile grown much fatter, but the beautiful baby had done nothing to improve her disposition. In recent months, she had quarrelled with Calliope, accusing her of having married Kimon only for his wealth. The Alexious *were* among the richest landowners in the village, but Calliope had never given much thought to such considerations. She had never understood her husband's obsession with amassing money, any more than she had his royalist sympathies. She might have understood the former if, like some Dickensian orphan, he had been raised in poverty, but Kimon had been born into privilege and, in his mid-twenties, had still had the sleek, tender look of a pampered pasha. Every mother with a marriageable daughter had entertained secret hopes, and one or two among them had at some point joined Ioanna in wondering whether Calliope was even fulfilling a wife's chief duty. Why else would a healthy young bride fail to conceive after all this time?

It had turned out not to be a duty. Calliope had remained grateful for the conjugal blessings even after the drinking and the quarrels started. She had no interest in Kimon's financial affairs but had heard from her aunt that he'd lost a small fortune, playing poker at a neighbour's house into the small hours. Thousands of drachmas!

The irony had proven harder to digest than the loss. That a man so hard-working, so enamoured of lucre, would allow himself to lose so much in a single night! A man who had reproached *her* when, during a rare trip to Mytilene, she had splurged on an imported jacket.

There were also rumours that both brothers were short-changing elderly customers, and Calliope had both wanted and not wanted to know the truth.

One evening, she had stopped at the *pantopoleion* on her way home from a pedagogical meeting. The *agora* was virtually shut for the night. Kimon sat hunched over his desk, counting the day's takings. He was flicking through the notes with mesmerising speed, occasionally bringing his index finger to his tongue for a spot of saliva. But not stopping, not offering so much as a smile.

There was something eerily private about this nocturnal scene: the hushed interior, the flickering candle flame, the *pantopoleion*'s cat chasing a mouse across the dusty floor. Kimon himself suddenly seemed like a furtive stranger muttering an incantation. A reluctant voyeur, Calliope was both repelled and spellbound. She suspected that Kimon's gradual withdrawal was somehow related to her barrenness. Four years into their marriage, he was playing cards more and more often, drinking more than ever.

And all of it was her fault. Her fault.

TWO

I

Winter came early that year, evicting a brief, blissfully sunny autumn. One morning in late November, Calliope came down to the kitchen and found a grey rat the size of a half-grown kitten. The dying creature must have crept up from the cellar, perhaps scouting for food, or just a warm hiding place.

Calliope had been on her way to the outhouse, had removed her slippers and was about to thrust a foot into a garden clog when her sleepy brain registered: the shoe was not empty! The chamber pot in her hands was half full. It belonged to her mother, who was in bed with the flu, and who, in subsequent days, would be made to swear on everything she held dear never to breathe a word to anyone about the chamber pot or expiring rodent.

Since the end of summer, there had been numerous sightings of domestic rodents, probably due to the shortage of rat poison or the gradual decline of the cat population. Were villagers beginning to eat cat meat? Had the cats starved to death? In Athens, there had been reports of cat meat being sold as rabbit.

Breakfast was out of the question now. Cleaning up as best she could, Calliope sent for Hektor to dispose of the dying creature. She sent another message to the headmaster: she would be late today. Would he please give her class an assignment and ask them to work on it until she arrived?

Driven by some stubborn vestige of professional pride, Calliope carried on as if these were normal times, though her pupils' attendance had become erratic. Some, she knew, came only because of the corn bread she occasionally offered, a piece the size of a seagull's egg, which they would swallow without chewing, blinking at her damply as they bolted it down. It was the first winter of the Occupation. The children's eyes were beginning to retreat into their sockets, their teeth huge in their shrinking faces.

The school was warmer than most private homes. A stove stood between the two classrooms and burned for one hour each morning. The children sat huddled in layers of clothing, their fingers swollen with chilblains, their faces grey as trough water. Some mornings, half of them would drift off with their heads on their desks, scratching at their inflamed skin, muttering in their dreams.

Calliope let them sleep so that they might find the strength to go and sift through the Germans' rubbish, scavenging for scraps of food in the endless rain, perhaps a bit of kindling. Most villagers had only mule droppings for fuel.

Just before the end of the year, Calliope's godson came down with whooping cough. All over the village, people were coughing, sniffling, spitting into gutters. There would be no holiday celebrations this year, no children singing Christmas carols. Every day, pregnant women swooned climbing up the hill. Their infants were born underweight, some with shortened limbs, without fingernails. When both Molyvos's and Petra's midwives fell ill, people said it was from grief at bringing such pitiful specimens into the world. Molyvos's midwife had suffered a mild stroke; Petra's had a serious kidney ailment. All at once, pregnant women had no choice but to call on the doctor when their labour started.

It was the worst winter in living memory. The country had become isolated from the world, yet somehow the dire news kept trickling in: Hitler's armies had overrun European Russia; Japanese troops were triumphing in Southeast Asia.

Calliope and Mirto began sleeping together, clinging to each other under a heap of blankets. The walls of their house were half a metre deep, but cold winds swept in all the way from the Siberian steppes, howling day and night at the shuttered windows.

On the first morning of the new year, snow began to fall. Calliope spent most of the day at the kitchen hearth, reading and sipping mountain tea, and blowing her nose as she burned the last of the kindling Hektor had managed to find somewhere.

The doctor and his family lived on the other side of the village, but Calliope swore she could hear Aristides cough. The thought of her godson's suffering pierced her more deeply than the bone-curdling cold. She recalled the last time Aristides had spent the night, the way his ribs stood out as she bathed and dressed him. The village children had never seen snow, but even the elderly couldn't remember snow that didn't melt soon after it hit the ground.

The snow that fell on that first dawn of 1942 began as a languid dance of feathery flakes, but in no time turned into a tempest. By mid-afternoon, the entire village was cowering under the white onslaught. No one went to church. No German aircraft appeared in the sky.

By suppertime, Calliope and Mirto's kindling was gone and Mirto, who seemed to have a perpetual cold, wept as she opened a can of Christmas ham sent by the Germans. Calliope hugged her mother, started to say something, then spun and strode upstairs, her hand cupping a flickering candle.

She opened the study door, muscles taut with purpose. This used to be her father's favourite room. It was so cold Calliope could see her own breath billow. There was the familiar smell of old printing ink, of dusty book jackets. She began to scan the book spines, hands buried within armpits, desperately seeking warmth.

There were numerous novels and poetry collections on the bookshelves but no, not those. She was considering some essay collections when her eyes fell on her father's old French encyclopaedia. So old, she reasoned, that much of the information would be out of date.

One of the first entries in the *A* volume was *Allemagne*: French for Germany. She dropped into a chair and began to skim the closely printed page.

Allemagne. A German Empire... its territories occupied by peoples of distinctively Teutonic race and language. Published in 1910, the encyclopaedia had no entries dealing with the First World War, let alone the one that had brought the Wehrmacht to Aegean shores. Not a single line hinting at German aggression!

Calliope returned to the kitchen hugging a wobbly tower of morocco-bound volumes. Quickly, before she could change her mind, she tossed the first volume into the hearth, then stood before the fiery choreography she had set in motion, batting at her stinging eyes. The pages had promptly caught fire, the singed edges curling like evening primroses surrendering to the sun.

'Don't say anything,' she cautioned her mother. 'Come... come and sit by the fire. Just don't say anything, Mama!'

They sat together then, huddled in private thought, while the sparks went flying, volume after volume devoured by the hissing flames.

Before long, Calliope's eyes began to water. She thought of the Mongols' destruction of Baghdad's House of Wisdom. She had read about it in the very encyclopaedia she had just sacrificed, remembered her astonishment on learning that the Tigris river had run black with ink for several months. *Months!*

Calliope trembled, as much with repugnance as with the chill clinging to her bones. Watching the books gradually turn to ash, she began to weep, begging her father's forgiveness. She thought of him seated at his old desk, leafing through the encyclopaedia, and then of his haggard face just before he died, gazing at her with his eloquent eyes. He had opened his mouth to speak, had seemed intent on conveying something of vital importance, but had finally given up, raising his hand in a vaguely benevolent gesture, like an old man waving goodbye, or a weary priest offering a benediction.

II

The following morning, Mirto limped downstairs and began to shriek. Shattered roof tiles littered the kitchen floor; chunks of rotting masonry lay strewn over the sink, table, counter. The ceiling had caved in under the weight of snow, leaving the kitchen awash in dust and fetid water.

'*Aman!*' The exclamation, which the villagers had picked up from their Turkish neighbours, was apt to slip out during domestic crises. '*Aman, aman!*' Mirto crossed herself, hobbling about with the air of an earthquake survivor emerging to survey the ruins. 'Calliope!' she yelled, clasping her head. 'Calliope, come down! Quick now – quick, my daughter! Oh… may the saints preserve us. Cal-li-o-pe!'

Calliope was just getting out of bed. Arriving in the kitchen, she found Mirto frantically pulling at the roots of her hair, the way professional mourners did, wailing at a graveside. For a moment, Calliope stood on the threshold, unable to move a muscle; then she spun about, bolting for the laundry tub.

Ordering her mother away, she set the zinc tub directly below the ragged aperture. It was roughly the size of a manhole. The ceiling went on dripping, the foul water pattering against the metal with a dreary throb. Mirto could not stop coughing.

'We'd better send for Seraphim,' Calliope said. Seraphim Lemos was the building contractor, though the Germans' arrival had brought a virtual end to his business deals. All over the village, houses stood abandoned in varying stages of construction, like rotting teeth in elderly villagers' mouths.

By noon, it began to rain. The temperature had risen several degrees, but the house was as frigid and damp as an outdoor privy. Mirto was napping when Seraphim arrived. He leaned back from the waist and threw his chin in the air.

'Ach, ach, ach!' he said, contemplating the gaping ceiling. 'Ach, ach, ach!'

'Well?' Calliope mistrusted Seraphim, who was prone to

exaggerate problems so as to justify his inflated rates. Above all, she resented his restless, suggestive eyes.

'I can't do it – not right now,' the contractor said.

'Why not? Don't tell me you're too busy because—'

'No! What d'you take me for?' Seraphim looked offended. 'I wish I could say I was busy, but this… this here roof,' he said with a flick of his chin, 'it can't be fixed in this weather, *Kyria* Calliope. I'll need three days – three dry days – before my men can get up there.'

'Three dry days!' Calliope echoed. The weather in January had always been unpredictable. This year, it seemed to be in cahoots with the Germans.

'At least three.' Seraphim lingered in the kitchen, eagerly elaborating on the job at hand. 'You never know, we might get lucky with the weather.'

They were not lucky. There was the occasional sunny day, but then the rain would return, bringing down showers of dust and crumbling masonry. Calliope and Mirto had begun having their meals with Aunt Elpida, but they slept at home. Uninhabited houses were often invaded by rodents; the tub had to be bailed out at regular intervals.

It was February before the sun re-emerged. Calliope sent a reminder to Seraphim, who had promised to return once the weather cleared.

When the contractor did not show up, she asked Umbreit for permission to leave early so she could nab Seraphim before he sat down to the midday meal. She would finish her translation later, she promised, explaining the problem. If she didn't get the roof repaired, they might run into another long spell of rain.

The builder lived on the village outskirts, next to his vegetable farm. Calliope found him working his field.

'Welcome, *Kyria* Calliope! How are we today?' Seraphim leaned on his pitchfork, watching Calliope pick her way through the neat rows of green cabbage. 'To what do I owe the honour?' He grinned extravagantly, like a frisky, jovial horse in search of a playmate.

'Have you forgotten? You promised to come when the weather—'

'Promised? Did I promise?' Seraphim clapped a cigarette into his mouth, his eyes travelling around the contours of Calliope's body, as if assessing how much weight she had recently lost.

'Well, you did say you needed three dry days, you said—'

'Three days would be right,' Seraphim cut in with a judicious nod. 'But I did not promise, *Kyria* Calliope. Please don't offend my soul!'

Calliope was silent.

'How could I promise such a thing?' Seraphim flared up, gesturing towards the cloudless sky. 'You can see for yourself, the sun's shining! There's work to be done in the fields now!'

'Are you saying you can't do it?'

Seraphim raised his eyebrows and clicked his tongue in a gesture that was commonly understood as *No*. 'On the other hand,' he said, 'I have no objections to discussing it further, at least not—'

'Discussing it? What's there to discuss?' With a spasm of disgust, Calliope had registered Seraphim's eyes ogling her breasts. 'Can you or can't you do it?'

'Ach, ach, ach, *Kyria* Calliope… be reasonable. I have to do everything myself these days – everything! The world's going to the dogs with those German bastards! You know that as well as I do.'

Calliope hesitated. She opened her mouth, closed it, then pivoted and stalked off across the field, her lips clamped together.

She did not cry often. Increasingly, she felt herself retreating into a grim, private realm. But that afternoon, when Umbreit enquired about the damaged roof, Calliope shocked herself by bursting into tears.

She had, for months, resisted complaining to the Germans about anything connected with the Occupation, held back by a delicate sense of pride. As if to complain would be tantamount to an admission of weakness – or worse, an appeal for pity. But on that day, Calliope told Umbreit the building contractor had refused to come. So had two stonemasons she had approached.

'They say they have no supplies. Only Lemos has them.' She paused, struggling against more tears. 'I don't suppose you have any construction materials?'

The lieutenant looked at her. 'I'll see what I can do.'

A restless night followed. Calliope went to school in the morning, then to the town hall, where Umbreit did not mention the roof. She was beginning to regret having appealed to him. Though their relations were more cordial than they'd been early on, the lieutenant seemed busy. She decided she would try to get a neighbour, Odysseus the beekeeper, to take her to Petra in his mule cart. She would look for a building contractor there.

When she arrived home in the afternoon, however, the ceiling was intact.

'Oh... so he came after all!' she squealed, clapping her hands. She glanced at her mother. 'What's the matter?'

Mirto was bustling about with averted eyes, as if she'd had to pay with her honour for the roof repair. 'The Germans did it.'

'The Germans?' Calliope's eyes flew to the ceiling. '*They* fixed the roof?' She stood with her hand over her mouth, trying to absorb this extraordinary news.

'They came early this morning, right after you left.'

'And fixed it... just like that?' No one in the village ever fixed anything without making a song and dance about it.

Mirto shrugged. 'They had a work order from Lieutenant Umbreit.'

Calliope dropped into a kitchen chair. 'I don't believe it!'

'Well, you won't be the only one,' Mirto said and sighed.

Within three days, the entire village knew about the roof repair. Naturally, Seraphim Lemos heard about it too, though days would go by before he happened to spot Calliope, who was hurrying past the public urinals, on her way up from school. The contractor hastened to button himself.

'I hear you got your roof fixed *tchick-tchack*,' he said, sounding both wounded and reproachful.

'Yes... yes, I did,' replied Calliope. She had, after the roof repair, found herself wavering between gratitude and what she recognised to be unreasonable resentment. It was not her vague sense of indebtedness that vexed her – she knew the Germans were squeezing her for all she was worth – but the speed and efficiency with which the repair had been completed. Neither Seraphim nor any other villager could have accomplished as much in one morning.

'You wouldn't come!' she flared up, stopping in mid-stride. 'I pleaded with you, and you said—'

But Seraphim wouldn't hear her out. '*Kyria* Calliope.' He drew himself up, eyeing her severely. 'I can't help it if you'd rather deal with the enemy, can I?'

III

Oh, she would have liked to tell Seraphim the truth! What she wouldn't have given to watch the bastard flail and flounder, trapped by his own insinuations! Yes, indeed, she would have been willing to offer quite a lot, but the one thing she could not disclose was the simple truth: she had recently joined the Resistance. She had kept the news even from her mother, partly because those were the rules, but also because Mirto's perpetual anxiety might have led *her* to lose heart.

She had always thought of herself as a coward – a coward and a wimp, howling at the sight of her own blood! The very idea of someone like her being asked to help the underground had made her laugh when the doctor had broached the subject.

'I can't believe you're asking me – me!' she said. 'I'm a spoiled, selfish woman. Ask Mirto.' She smiled a little. 'She'll tell you it's all my father's fault.'

'Maybe so, but I don't have to ask her,' said Dr Dhaniel. 'I've known you since you were eight years old.'

'Then you know—'

'I know we need you,' Dhaniel interjected.

'You mean you're so desperate you'll take anyone?' The doctor, Calliope thought, was probably remembering her younger self, playing with her male cousins, climbing trees, leaping from rocks and sea walls. And yet, deep in her heart, she already knew she would end up consenting. It was not the first time she'd observed herself weighing a situation, scrutinising it from every possible angle, when a decision had already been reached in some other, barely examined chamber.

But how shrewd Dhaniel's timing was! Just last week, she'd found her hair starting to fall out in clumps; yesterday, her youngest pupil had fainted in class, and they'd had to summon the doctor to revive him.

'We need someone like you,' he was saying now. 'Someone strong and decisive and quick-witted. Someone trustworthy.'

Calliope was silent for a few moments. She then asked the doctor what would be expected of her and that was when she finally understood.

Someone was needed to deliver a coded message to Mytilene, to a priest named *Papa* Ioannis. She would ostensibly be going to attend a pedagogical conference; the priest was responsible for the curriculum's religious content. As a schoolmistress, Calliope was the ideal person for this mission. She would go in Kyriakos's taxi, along with two villagers in need of medical treatment. The priest would sit next to her at the conference. She would slip the message into a Bible and casually pass it to him. And that would be all. Her mission would be accomplished.

'What if there's a roadblock along the way?'

'You will carry the message in your socks. Under your soles.' The plan had been carefully thought out. Of course, every mission entailed some risk, but it was unlikely they would bother to search her.

'Oh, I don't know.' Calliope sighed.

'Extremely unlikely,' said the doctor.

And, at last, she capitulated. It occurred to her that courage was, perhaps, nothing more than the willingness to slam the door on one's imagination.

IV

Every year, just before Easter, parent-teacher meetings were held at the village school. It was doubtful many parents would bother to attend this year, but the occasion could be exploited for the transfer of provisions to the guerrillas. On Thursday afternoon, the headmaster had waited in vain for parents of pupils qualifying for middle school; Friday was the day assigned for the juniors.

Tense and alert, Calliope settled at her desk, listening to the swallows flitter under the eaves. Without the children's presence, the old desks looked sad and reproachful. Calliope waited, her ears pricking up when a passing horse whinnied. But nothing happened. The wagon rumbled on. For some reason, she felt voraciously hungry, as if every gram of nutrition had been extracted from her body.

Finally, rummaging in her satchel for dry chickpeas, she heard the anticipated signal; the whistled opening of the national anthem. *We know you by the sharpness of your sword.* The whistler was a woman; the food she carried was ostensibly meant for elderly parents living on the village outskirts.

The school was situated amid olive orchards. There was the beach across the road, but no immediate neighbours. As clandestine activities went, this one seemed less risky than her first assignment. The coded message had been delivered to Mytilene without a hitch; no one had paid the slightest attention to the casual exchange between a schoolmistress and a pedagogical priest. But the possibility of being spotted by a stool pigeon had Calliope leaping out of her dreams in the nights that followed.

And now her dread was back. She had stepped out to retrieve the baskets and found them, as promised, behind a flowering honeysuckle bush. It was a radiant afternoon, fragrant with spring blossoms, but even the breeze rustling the poplar branches sounded like a portentous whisper. Calliope peered about in case a parent arrived early or children turned up to play in the schoolyard. Both possibilities seemed unlikely. The parents would be too apathetic to come early, if at all, the children too feeble to kick a ball or play hide-and-seek.

There were two wicker baskets, both covered in fresh linen. As she bent to lift them, Calliope's skirt became briefly snagged by a protruding branch. She stopped and released the cloth, glancing over her shoulder. What if Umbreit happened to stop by? What if he decided to send someone for the document she was expected to drop off on her way from school?

But no one came. Nothing stirred, except for birds, leaves, insects. Breathing shallowly, Calliope strode towards the shed, where garden tools and broken chairs were stored for repair. There was no one left to do it. When people could no longer afford new furniture, the village carpenter had taken his wife and deaf-mute daughter and hastened to leave for Athens. Since then, broken furniture had been piling up all over the village. The school shed itself seemed to be subsiding into the earth.

The provisions were to be placed in an old chest at the back of the shed and eventually retrieved by another activist. Calliope's instructions were to leave the shed door unlocked. A lizard scurried by, quickly disappearing over the roof; a wasp circled above, its aggressive buzz somehow compounding her anxiety. The distance between the shed and the schoolhouse was negligible but might have been as long as the climb to the hilltop fortress.

She dashed back to the classroom and fell into her chair, shaking all over. There had been warnings on shop windows and telegraph poles: aiding and abetting the guerrillas would lead to summary execution.

Gradually, Calliope willed herself into a semblance of professional composure. She checked her watch, waiting for some stalwart parent to appear. Casting about for something to do, she took out the document she had been translating. Might as well review it once more.

The original had been written by the verbose von Herden. The major visited the village only once a month, but Calliope's work was apparently satisfactory, much of it originating in von Herden's own office. She received formal thank you notes from Mytilene; was secretly flattered to find her efforts praised by Lieutenant Umbreit, whom she had done her best to dislike.

She had not succeeded, for the German commander had a rare gift for making people do his bidding. He was the sort of man who, in times of peace, might have been called upon to settle disputes rather than issue orders. Calliope admired his manners, his air of competence and quiet authority, but their budding friendship was contingent upon her own ability to maintain separate mental chambers for her endlessly clashing musings. In her wildest dreams, she would not have expected the Germans to repair her roof. And how ironic it was, how maddening, that they'd done so just days after she had agreed to join the Resistance!

Calliope's thoughts and feelings might be at odds, but the war was one subject she and Umbreit resolutely shied away from. To listen to them, the Occupation did not exist, hunger did not exist; there were no arrests, no interrogations. Had Umbreit studied science or economics or law, Calliope told herself, they might never have exchanged a single word beyond the requirements of her job. But after their encounter in the harbour, after her rejection of the Nietzsche book, there was remorse on her part, a barely acknowledged need to make it up to him.

In short, she had let her guard down.

They began to discuss literature, to talk about this and that. They continued to address each other formally: he called her '*Frau* Alexiou', she called him '*Leutnant*', but not without a gleam of irony. Ten months after the start of the Occupation – two weeks after the roof repair – Calliope knew Umbreit well enough not to be surprised when he came back to her with the Nietzsche.

'Your German's certainly good enough now!' He held out the book, smiling obliquely. It came to Calliope that he might be less interested in her reading the book than in testing his own belief that, this time, she would not reject it. He was a man of keen insight and steely resolve.

She began to read with the furtiveness of a villager hoarding gold or arms. The book was *Beyond Good and Evil*, and she pored over it with the help of a dictionary, disconcerted to find herself hiding it from her own mother.

Aware of Mirto's snoopy ways, Calliope had always carried her journal with her. Now her shoulder bag contained the Nietzsche as well.

But why? Why should she hide a German philosopher's book? Why shouldn't she enjoy a purely intellectual advantage? No one else hesitated to squeeze every possible benefit out of their grim circumstances. Mirto herself had been happy to profit from the phoney medical certificate; she'd raised no objections to accepting foodstuffs from the Germans. What reason was there to turn down a book?

This inner debate was still going on as the first year of the Occupation drew to a close. When Easter came around, Umbreit sent Calliope and Mirto a box of Swiss chocolates, an unheard-of luxury; she gave him her own copy of Hesse's *Steppenwolf*. She had nothing else that might interest him.

Umbreit accepted the book with an enigmatic smile, thanking her and promising to read it as soon as he found the time.

Some time would pass before Calliope learned that in Germany, Herman Hesse was considered an enemy of the Fatherland.

V

The coffin was the size of the wooden crates used for storing dry cod in the winter months. As it was lowered into the freshly dug grave, the blacksmith's teenage daughter began to utter odd little sounds, like the cries swallows made over a storm-devastated nest. Eleni's eyes, as round and shiny as black olives, were today looking opaque and droopy. Her loose hair, normally gathered into a long, neat plait, was blowing across her face.

It was late April, but the afternoon was as damp and blustery as a winter day. *Papa* Emanouil's cassock billowed and flapped, exposing his hirsute ankles. Calliope stood next to her young brother-in-law, her gaze fixed on the gravedigger. There had been reports of villagers digging up coins and gold teeth in the cemetery, but the gravedigger's features were more gaunt than ever; his fraying clothes hung as loosely as rags on a scarecrow.

Calliope dabbed at her eyes. Eleni Bastia had been one of her favourite pupils. She had longed to go on to middle school, but her father would slap her whenever he caught her absorbed in a book.

She had been forced to marry at fourteen; her mother, the local herbalist's daughter, had occasionally expressed the wish that God had seen fit to bestow brains on her twin sons rather than on her daughter. You didn't have to be lettered to know that God worked in mysterious ways, did you?

Glancing at the bereaved family, Calliope noted that Eleni's father and his bachelor brother had both come to resemble vultures, that her husband Tomas's dark head had begun to sprout grey hairs – a man in his twenties! Standing beside his wife, the grieving father cast a few clumps of earth onto the tiny coffin, then stood gazing into the gaping grave with his arm suspended, like a mendicant's.

The couple had already lost one child to miscarriage. But the second pregnancy had been normal; the baby had died only because his mother's depleted body had failed to provide adequate nourishment. Calliope had done her best to help – had traded her favourite frock for milk and flour – but the infant had died after ten days of incessant howling.

The wind went on swishing across the cemetery. It muffled the young mother's heart-rending cries. It blew away *Papa* Emanouil's prayers. It was time to leave. Calliope embraced Eleni. She shook Tomas's limp hand.

'Let's go,' she said to Pericles.

It was late afternoon. She and her young brother-in-law were the only non-relatives at the cemetery, for who had the strength to attend every burial? Almost a year had passed since the start of the Occupation and the number of deaths was beginning to exceed that of births. Calliope's godfather had suffered a second heart attack and died; her mother was bedridden with pleurisy.

Pleurisy had become rampant on the island. The little energy people could rally was spent scouring the countryside for edibles, though there was always the risk of stumbling on a German mine. Even so, islanders were much luckier than city dwellers, who were said to be dropping off like flies. No one in the village had been reduced to begging; no women were prostituting themselves as so many were reportedly doing in the capital.

Molyviates had gradually learned to focus on such paltry

consolations. There were virtually no medicines left, but at least they didn't have malaria on the island; the shops had stood shuttered all winter, but at least they had wild greens and sea urchins and snails and, occasionally, a bowl of yoghurt sweetened with figs. There was little dairy because of the shortage of animal fodder; meat had become non-existent. Although fishing was theoretically permitted in spring and autumn, the caiques stood idle because of the fuel shortage.

Calliope left the cemetery with Pericles, her chunky footwear making a mournful sound on the cobblestones. The shortage of leather was forcing women to put on heavy clogs fabricated from carved wood and bits of cloth. The handcrafted product was both unsightly and awkward. It was a well-known fact that Greek leather was being shipped to the Reich, along with most of the island's olive oil.

Approaching St Pandeleimon's, Calliope spotted one of her pupils, whose father had been executed for being pro-British. In recent months, the Resistance had become increasingly effective in disrupting German supply and communication lines. There had been several instances of Greek sabotage: weapons had vanished from the German cache; jeep and motorcycle tyres had been slashed in the night.

The tanner's orphaned son was running around barefoot, his hair shaved against the ubiquitous lice. As Calliope and Pericles approached, Leonidas stopped in front of a fig tree, his chin tipping up. He hadn't been to school since his father's demise; had reportedly been taken in by his Petra grandparents. Yet there he was now, his head tilted back, his eyes in their hungry sockets scanning the twisted tree's canopy, where a collared dove was cooing. Calliope was about to speak when the boy pulled out a catapult. He ran his sleeve across his nose, then aimed the catapult at the tree.

The bird was invisible to Calliope and Pericles. They had stopped, she and her suddenly mute brother-in-law, and watched the stone go zipping up towards the treetop. As it hit the branch, the hidden dove came fluttering out of the rain-soaked foliage. It circled the tree for one chaotic moment, then flapped away towards the nearby church. The boy burst into tears.

'Leo!' Calliope called out. 'Leo! Wait, *pedhi mou* – I want to talk to you!'

The child ignored her calls. He bolted down the alley, vanishing around the corner. Calliope remained rooted to the spot, hand clamped onto Pericles's arm: she had, lunging towards the boy, twisted her foot in its wooden clog.

'Are you all right?'

'Yes... I think so.'

'Good.' Pericles was still staring at the treetop. He was now in his last year of high school, had grown taller than Calliope. 'I must write something down before... I lose it,' he said. Then he rushed off to write a new poem, like a man chasing a departing train.

Calliope turned and headed for the town hall, to type a document she had been translating at home during her mother's illness. The Germans' typist had also fallen ill, so Calliope had to type, as well as translate, the Germans' communiques. It would be past curfew when she finished today, but she had a night pass. A close neighbour was looking after Mirto, in exchange for the bread and soap Calliope managed to obtain from the Germans. If she was lucky today, she might get not only bread but a couple of eggs, maybe even coffee.

Despite all the obvious benefits, Calliope's thoughts were today flowing in hostile directions. She had just heard that high schools would soon be required to teach German as a second language. Pericles, who had shared the rumour, was about to graduate, but the proposed language law made one thing clear: whatever they said, whatever they did, the Germans had no intention of leaving the Aegean.

VI

Because of the ever-present possibility of capture and torture, Resistance members were kept in the dark about colleagues' activities. Calliope didn't even know that the town hall cleaner was an underground member, though they saw each other virtually every day.

Ourania Nakou had been the village seamstress. Despite a somewhat dour nature, her sewing had been much in demand before the Occupation. When people could no longer afford new clothes, Calliope used her connections to secure work for the fisherman's wife. Ourania was hired to clean both Greek and German offices and did it impeccably. The day of Eleni's baby's funeral, she had just finished washing the lobby when Calliope entered, reprimanded like a careless child for leaving tracks across the wet floor.

Everyone had grown snappish over the winter months. Calliope took off her clogs and was carrying one in each hand when Lieutenant Umbreit looked up to see her standing on the threshold to his office. He smiled at the footwear, then leaned back and sat scanning her face.

'What's the matter?' he asked, gesturing towards a chair. *Was ist los?*

'Oh, nothing out of the ordinary.' Calliope met his probing eyes, speaking with a sullen sort of irony. 'I've just seen a friend bury her newborn baby and one of my pupils try to shoot down a mourning dove with a catapult.'

Umbreit sat clicking the lid on his fountain pen.

'Don't you understand? He was doing it because he's hungry!' Calliope blurted with sudden heat. 'The whole village is starving to death – starving – while you ransack our land so *your* people can enjoy the fruits of *our* labour! Is that what you promised us? When you first arrived – is that what von Herden told us?'

Umbreit lit a cigarette. He gazed at her from behind his desk: silent, inscrutable.

'You came here claiming to be our friends!' Calliope continued. 'Is that how friends behave in your country? Is that how your mother raised you?'

At this, the lieutenant's jaw tightened. He seemed on the verge of speaking, but Calliope was not yet done.

'Now you want our children to study German – German! – when they barely have the energy for their own language!'

She sat with her eyes fastened on Umbreit's face, perspiration spreading in her armpits. She was the only villager who could risk making such a speech, but there was little courage in it, for her friendship with the lieutenant seemed secure by now; she could afford the sour luxury of speaking her mind. Oddly, though, the knowledge of her privileged position only seemed to fan her suppressed anger.

One of the things chafing at her was the Germans' condescension towards her people. Von Herden might claim they had come as friends, but his men were forbidden to fraternise with the natives. They were not permitted to pay social visits, or enter the *kapheneion*, and certainly not to indulge in intimate relations. Calliope and Umbreit had never had the slightest physical contact, but the affinity between them was beginning to seem stronger than that between many husbands and wives.

Having listened to the rant against the German language, and perhaps hoping to divert her, Umbreit calmly pointed out the obvious advantage of being able to read German books in the original.

'Just think,' he said, 'if you'd been teaching German all along, your young brother-in-law would be able to read Rilke in the original.' He smiled, releasing a plume of smoke. 'Wouldn't that be a good thing?'

But Calliope was not in the mood for banter. She went on with her diatribe, speaking of the useless food coupons, the idle fishermen, the children's thwarted education. 'You take everything we've got,' she repeated, 'then, as if that's not enough, you demand that we pay your expenses – the expenses of *your* Occupation!'

Twilight was coming on, flooding the office with a warm golden light. There was a sea urchin shell resting on the lieutenant's desk. White and brittle and exquisitely patterned, it was the only extraneous item in the austere office. Calliope became aware that Umbreit was offering her something. A pristine, lemon-coloured handkerchief, laundered and pressed and carefully folded. She declined it, shaking her head, as if to disclaim her own tears.

He returned the handkerchief to his pocket, then stubbed out his cigarette, waiting for her to regain her composure.

'War... war is never pretty,' he brought out at last, searching Calliope's face with his calm Nordic eyes – eyes that were sometimes like the sea on an overcast day, other times the colour of olives. An evening breeze blew in through the window, stirring the papers on Umbreit's desk. Calliope's nostrils caught the familiar smell hovering about his person – the scent of leather and ink and shaving soap. Most villagers seemed to smell foul these days. 'You know enough about history to know that, surely?' Umbreit was saying. '*À la guerre comme à la guerre?*'

Calliope turned this over in her head. 'But—'

She was about to continue but stopped on hearing the sound of Sergeant Reis's approaching boots. The boots crossed the landing, then headed downstairs.

'But what?' Umbreit was asking. 'Did Greek generals stop to consider Turks' pain when they burned their way towards Ankara? Did Venizelos give a thought to the innocent victims while dreaming of a new Byzantine empire?'

Calliope sat up, her eyes flashing. 'What Venizelos dreamed of was land the Allies had promised us before... before we got embroiled in their Great War!'

'Well, there you are... your Allies. They, too, claimed to be your friends?'

'They're not *my* Allies!' Calliope snapped back, knowing herself to be on shaky ground. 'Anyway,' she went on, 'the point is those lands – the lands Venizelos wanted – were Greek even before Alexander the Great's time. Surely you know that?' she echoed ironically.

'True,' said Umbreit, a gleam of amusement lighting his eyes. 'But how did the Greeks get to occupy those lands in the first place – have you ever asked yourself that?' He paused. 'There were ancient peoples there, you know, long before the Aryans invaded Asia Minor.'

Silence. Calliope swallowed, stumped for words.

'As for your Alexander the Great,' Umbreit continued, with his calm, relentless logic, 'when he went about founding his famed *polis* all over the map, do you suppose he was waving an olive branch? Is that how he succeeded in building his empire?'

'Oh! You... you're talking about an altogether different time!' Calliope flashed out, unnerved by her own inadequacy. 'This is the twentieth century – shouldn't your Hitler have learned something from history? Even Napoleon—'

'Shouldn't you?' he cut in, his eyebrows arching. 'Take a good look at human history – it's all blood and gore in the name of this ideal or that… often in the name of some higher civilisation,' he added, a note of disgust creeping into his voice.

'Yes!' Calliope cried. 'Exactly! But don't you see? You people pride yourselves on being so civilised – certainly more civilised than us primitive Greeks,' she couldn't help interjecting. 'Yet you… you torture and kill innocent people! You arrest simple men and put them through hell, just… just so…'

Calliope turned away, tears constricting her throat. She sat with her hands tightly clasped in her lap, hearing Ourania leave the town hall on her way home. Umbreit was gazing at her with his sad, foreign eyes.

'My dear Calliope,' he said, sounding all at once weary, seemingly unaware of the personal salutation he had just used. 'And what did your heroic Metaxas do, I ask you. To his own people?'

'Metaxas!' she shot out. 'Metaxas was a dictator – I'll be the first to grant you that! But I didn't vote for him, whereas you – you are supporting a… a ruthless imperialist!' she snapped out, feeling a tiny thrill of fear. She was suddenly not sure how far he would let her go before he lost his temper. Was he angry now?

No, he seemed rather sad, fiddling with his black fountain pen, staring moodily towards the open window. 'I wish… I wish I could show you pictures of my people after the First World War,' he said quietly.

'But who was responsible for that war? Who—'

'Whoever was responsible – and scholars don't agree, mind you – families like mine did not sign the Treaty of Versailles. They did not accept your Allies' outrageous conditions—'

'They may have had nothing to do with signing the Treaty, but they'd chosen the leaders that signed it for them! Aren't people responsible for the leaders they elect?' Calliope shifted her weight, doing her best to subdue the voice echoing in her head. *When two bulls tussle, it's always the grasshoppers that suffer.*

It was something she had heard the doctor say to her father years ago. She stopped now and mulled his words over, feeling sudden doubt. She watched Umbreit lever himself to his feet and go to the window, gazing out at the darkening sky.

'My mother was a widow with four children,' he said, speaking in a low, dispassionate voice. 'My father shot himself after losing his job during the Depression. My baby sister died.' He turned to face her. He had never spoken to her of his family. She had never asked.

She sat gazing up at him, deserted by words. 'I'm sorry,' she managed to let out. 'I didn't know. I'm very sorry.'

'So you see…' He detached himself from the window, his trousers ballooning above his boots, his thumbs hooked on his leather belt. 'Your people, Calliope, don't have a monopoly on suffering – I'm sorry to say they don't. And… well, neither do mine on ruthlessness.'

A long moment passed. There was the sound of distant waves, of frogs trilling in the garden below.

'Sooner or later, we all suffer,' Umbreit said at last. He spoke with averted eyes, his gaze landing on the swastika. Then he turned to face Calliope, tall and straight and mournful, fingers raking through his hay-coloured hair. '*Whose* suffering touches us most is – well, it's not really a question of choice, is it? Just… an accident of birth, *nicht wahr*?'

VII

In May, a subversive rumour began to spread through the *agora*: two foolhardy fishermen were said to be planning an escape to the Turkish mainland. Alerted by a stool pigeon, Umbreit ordered additional patrols, concentrating their guard along the Eftalou coast, where the fishermen had reportedly hidden their getaway boat. Night after night, the Germans patrolled the shoreline, waiting for the clandestine boat to fall into their hands.

The fishing boat did not appear in Eftalou. It was in Skala

Sykaminias that the father and son had found shelter, waiting for a moonless night, for the German patrol to pass on its first evening round, before launching their escape.

The two men were Captain Yorgos and his elder son, Takis. They were to share the boat with an unknown Allied agent hoping to join the British forces across the water; the fishermen's destination was Egypt, where the Greek Armed Forces had their wartime base. That was as much as Elias Dhaniel would tell Calliope when they last talked, on Saturday afternoon.

It was now Sunday morning. Mirto was attending Mass, while Calliope prepared dandelion greens for the midday meal. Waiting for the pot to boil, she marvelled at the Lyras men's daring. She could not imagine herself undertaking such a bold mission, or even joining run-of-the-mill guerrillas: sleeping in forests and barns, going for weeks without a bath, bitten by fleas and lice.

What she couldn't work out was how the neighbourhood women had got wind of the details, how they knew that the captain had sold his gold teeth to subsidise the escape. She had heard women whisper at the fountain, speculating on where the fugitives had found the getaway boat.

Yorgos's own boat had been sabotaged just before its German departure, loaded with some of the finest oil in the country. The captain himself had set it ablaze, then fled to the hills, eventually to Turkey, bearing forged documents.

The doctor had shared the news of the escape with Calliope, but only after the Lyras men had safely reached the Turkish shore. Calliope knew nothing about the Resistance movement's communication network, but Dhaniel had it on good authority: Yorgos and Takis had succeeded in circumventing the German patrol; the insidious rumour planted by the Resistance had worked exactly as expected!

Calliope understood: Umbreit had been outwitted.

The dandelions were ready to be drained. Setting them aside to cool, Calliope sat down to read Nietzsche, waiting for her mother to return from church. She herself had long since stopped attending Mass. Her mother was by now resigned to this fact, though she had insisted that Calliope prepare Sunday's dinner from then on.

'It's the least you can do, staying home when you should be in church.'

Calliope had smiled to herself. She was happy to stay home Sundays, reading in bed, cooking a simple meal. Today, the menu included beans as well as the dandelion greens, which one of the neighbours had picked and bartered for sugar and German coffee. The coarse ersatz coffee most villagers drank was made of toasted barley and offered as much satisfaction as a Lenten salad.

Calliope tasted the beans, speculating about Dhaniel's role in the Lyras men's escape. It was almost noon now. Sighing, she went into the pantry. She was getting the olive oil when her eyes fell on a jar of sour cherry preserves. Her Mytilene aunt had brought the preserves just before the Occupation, but Mirto was saving them for an emergency.

As far as Calliope was concerned, they had been living in a state of emergency since spring 1941 and might continue to do so until they all starved to death. There were, indeed, those who believed this to be the Germans' ultimate goal: 'Hitler's secret weapon'.

Calliope picked up her book and went into the garden, not bothering to change out of her sleeveless house dress. Their neighbour, the *hamam* caretaker, had recently died, so only his wife and sixteen-year-old daughter could see into their garden.

It was a fine morning. Sappho was slumped in the shade, eyes drowsily following a white butterfly. The garden was full of them, its air scented by wisteria blossoms. Every now and then, a sea breeze would rise, stirring tree branches. Sappho kept snapping at bean pods whorling down from the shady acacia tree.

There was something both comforting and maddening about nature's stunning imperviousness to human anguish. Babies died from hunger, men were arrested and tortured, but the sun went on shining, the peaches and plums ripened as wantonly as ever, most of them destined for the German Reich.

As she strolled towards the grape arbour, Calliope brushed

past a tray of chickpeas her mother had set out in the sun for tomorrow's meal. Legumes had become the mainstay of their diet.

'Thank God we've got something to put in our mouths!' Mirto was wont to say, as if to placate her own grumbling stomach. She served chickpea soup all too often, but why would she leave tomorrow's batch out in the sun? Almonds and vegetables were often set out to dry, but the chickpeas were dry already; what they needed was thorough soaking. Even she knew that.

Suddenly, she noticed the weevils: pale commas of wriggling flesh creeping out of the dry chickpeas, frenziedly crawling over their round, sun-baked dwellings. Back in winter, she'd heard that an old farmer had made a weevil paste, which he ate on crusts of bread thrown out by the Germans.

The memory was choked off as Calliope sprinted towards the outhouse, feeling her stomach heave. A woman approaching twenty-seven, she was still given to bouts of nausea in stressful moments.

But there wasn't much to bring up just now; all she'd had was coffee and a stale crust of bread, followed by that tiny taste of dandelions. Nor did she feel the hoped-for relief after she'd stopped retching. The nausea had vanished, giving way to a hollow sensation in the pit of her stomach; an odd sort of hunger that made her think of the cravings pregnant women described, so urgent that foetal welfare seemed to depend on gratification.

Sappho rose, shook herself and padded over, sniffing the air. Calliope gave her a perfunctory pat, then returned indoors. The kitchen smelled of dill and boiled dandelions. Two flies were mating with intermittent enthusiasm, buzzing at the windows for a moment or two, then settling down again on the warm panes.

Cherry preserves!

The moment she identified the craving, a peculiar excitement possessed Calliope, an intense physical urge impelling her towards the pantry. She was drooling by the time she reached for the *gliko* jar!

The cherries were plump and thick with syrup. Calliope unscrewed the lid. She had one teaspoonful of *gliko*. And then she had another. And yet another, the delectable sweetness sliding down her throat like ambrosia, spreading voluptuous contentment through her empty belly.

Oddly, though, deep as it was, the satisfaction only generated a new wave of greed, conquering her body as ardently as sexual desire. She had, at first, laughed at her own folly, only to find herself sliding to the edge of tears. There was something at once euphoric and terrifying about the irrational power subjugating her body.

She ended up finishing the entire jar. It was not a large jar and she finished it, spoon after spoon after spoon. Out in the garden, Sappho lay with her head on her paws, her droopy, reproachful eyes fixed on the kitchen windows.

Oh God, what have I done?

No sooner was the jar empty than Calliope was swept by a wave of guilt. She knew her impulse must have had something to do with the time of month: she had always craved sweets just before her period. The hormonal tension must have been compounded by prolonged deprivation, but this fact did nothing to assuage her remorse. She might have wept with regret but for the heedless joy coursing through her veins. She was beginning to feel both giddy and exhausted, as if she'd spent all morning carrying jugs of water under the blazing sun.

Sighing, she lay down on the day divan. Not reading, not thinking – just trying to hold on to the sweetness suffusing her body. This, she told herself drowsily, was the first time in months that she felt thoroughly sated. It was, it seemed, possible to feel remorseful and yet, however briefly, almost divinely blissful.

VIII

Coming home from church and a visit to her sister, Mirto found Calliope curled up on the divan, plunged in heavy slumber. She was ready to leave the kitchen when her eyes landed on the cherry jar: an empty jar standing on the floor, flies buzzing around its rim.

'I don't believe it,' she let out hoarsely. 'I don't… believe… it!'

Calliope opened one eye, then sat up, struggling with her mental cobwebs. She watched her mother stoop to pick up the sticky preserves jar.

'I'm sorry, Mama,' she said. And she was: both sorry and deeply ashamed.

'But how could you? How could you be so selfish?' Mirto shrilled, shooing away the flies buzzing around her hand. 'An entire jar!'

'I got carried away, Mama, I'm—'

'Got carried away!' Mirto grabbed the fly swatter. 'What are you, a child? Can't you ever think of anyone besides yourself?'

Calliope hung her head. She had hoped her repentant tone would mollify her mother, but Mirto was not one for silence once she got good and going. 'An entire jar!' she kept repeating. She was swatting at the flies with the gusto of a weary but sorely provoked warrior. 'As if there was no tomorrow!'

'Well, who knows?' Calliope rose for a glass of water, feigning sangfroid. 'There might not be a tomorrow,' she said, turning the cistern on.

'Oh, you! You and your clever tongue!' Mirto had given up chasing the flies and began to set the table with quick, nervous gestures. 'Your tongue's sharp, but your head's full of cotton, if you ask me.'

'Well, I didn't ask, did I?'

'There you go again, trying to get around the truth with your witticisms.'

'And what's the truth, Mother?' Calliope said, her mind darting to Nietzsche's views on the relativity of all truth. 'I got greedy and ate a jar of preserves. I said I was sorry, didn't I?'

'Ach, it's not just the cherry preserves!' Mirto pulled out a drawer and snapped up two cotton napkins. 'It's your general conduct. People are dying – dying – and you sit discussing books with the enemy! Philosophy!'

The last word was accompanied by a scornful glance towards Nietzsche's book, lying face down on the divan. Calliope had forced herself to stop concealing the book after her quarrel with Umbreit following the burial of Eleni's baby. She still felt the lieutenant was essentially misguided. At the same time, a long meditation on world history had made it impossible to dismiss his views.

'Well,' she said now, mulling over her mother's last comment, 'isn't it better to discuss literature and philosophy than to kill each other, Mother? Maybe—'

But Mirto would not let Calliope complete the thought.

'You know what they say. If you keep company with a blind man, you end up squinting. Squinting, my daughter!'

Calliope disdained to reply to this patently absurd warning. She permitted herself only the tiniest of smiles, but it was enough to set Mirto off all over again. She pulled out a chair and lowered her meagre bottom into it, glaring at her daughter.

'Yes, smile... smile all you want!' She spoke with sudden vehemence. 'It's no wonder people are saying you're like Metaxas's daughter!' The former prime minister's daughter had the reputation of being so intractable she was said to have broken her father's spirit long before the Italian betrayal. 'Anyway, you know I'm right. You know you don't give a button about anyone but yourself!'

The smile on Calliope's face faded. 'No, I don't know that, Mother.'

'You don't, eh?' Mirto had put her feet up on the divan. She sat wriggling her toes in their black mourning stockings, scowling at a tiny hole on her right foot. 'The cherry preserves are just the latest example,' she said. 'All you care about is satisfying your whims, and to the devil with—'

'Mother, that's not true! It isn't true!'

'Not true, eh?' The look on Mirto's face – the expression of pity mixed with lofty disdain – reminded Calliope of her mother-in-law. She thought of Martha's son, Pericles, whom she still loved, of the doctor and his children, of dear Eleni. There was no shortage of people she cared about, most of all Aristides, her beloved godson.

'No!' she heard herself say, her voice swelling. 'It isn't true! It's—'

'You're shouting because you know it's true,' Mirto broke in. 'Nothing hurts like the truth, as they say.'

'No, Mother!' said Calliope. 'Nothing hurts like being misjudged, especially by your own mother.' This was possibly true, but she was not sure Mirto had misjudged her. She *was* selfish. She *was* self-indulgent.

Mirto studied her for a moment. 'I'm misjudging you?'

'Yes, Mother.'

'You didn't just gobble up a whole jar of cherries? You're not cosying up to the Germans, getting whatever you can—'

'Mother!' Calliope cut in. 'You—'

'Whatever you can get out of them,' Mirto concluded.

'Yes! Yes, Mother!' Calliope was suddenly beside herself. 'I also risk my life! I do whatever I can to thwart the enemy!' she heard herself blurt out. Resistance members were under strict orders not to discuss their activities, not even with close family members.

'Thwart the enemy?' Mirto echoed. 'What in God's name do you mean?'

'Oh!' Calliope closed her eyes. She should have kept her mouth shut, but it was too late now. She wanted to tell her mother. She didn't want to tell her. She went and stood by the window, groping for a way out. Mirto wasn't stupid. It was probably better to tell her, make sure she didn't start asking dangerous questions. 'Do you promise not to tell anyone?'

'Y-yes.' Mirto gazed at Calliope's face, flexing her arthritic fingers.

'Not even Aunt Elpida?'

'Ach, I promised, didn't I?'

Calliope paused, then said, 'I've joined the Resistance.' She stood perfectly still, like a wayward child steeling herself against parental censure. Mirto, too, had stopped, staring with mute amazement.

'Mother of God!'

'Not that this has anything to do with the cherry preserves,' Calliope added, vaguely aware of a sudden need to change the subject, go back to bickering over trivia. 'I had a moment of childish weakness. I'm sorry!'

For a moment she hesitated, then, before Mirto could rouse herself, she spun, seized by an intense need to get away. Away from her own inability to control her tongue, from having to listen, now, to whatever it was her mother might say.

Seething with self-reproach, she flung the door open and stormed out of the kitchen. The garden was a hot, hazy, pulsing blur, but she surged forward blindly, ignoring her mother's calls.

IX

That summer, the doctor came up with an ingenious proposal. An afternoon excursion to the Eftalou springs, he tried to convince Calliope, would be the perfect pretext for carrying out an urgent underground mission. She and her mother could start by collecting wild greens, then Mirto would stay at the bathhouse for a therapeutic soak while Calliope went on with her assignment. Everyone knew Mirto to be in poor health; no one would ever suspect Calliope in her timid mother's company. It was, Calliope conceded, an inspired idea, though she was reluctant to involve Mirto in any risky venture. She would have to think about it, she said.

Mirto herself had turned out to be surprisingly brave. To think that she would be willing to contribute to Resistance activities! More than willing: eager. As eager as she'd been to help Anatolian refugees back in the early 1920s. Calliope, it seemed, had misjudged her mother no less than her mother had misjudged her. Mirto might be a handwringer, but she apparently considered some things worth worrying about.

'No sheep...' she'd pronounced on the evening of the cherry preserves quarrel. 'No sheep has ever saved its neck by just bleating, has it?'

It was the friendship with Lieutenant Umbreit that left Mirto shaking her head. She didn't see how it was possible to be friends with a German officer and simultaneously participate in Resistance activities. It made no sense to her, no sense at all, she said over and over, as if sheer repetition might help her grasp some small but elusive logic. And yet, Calliope had detected a note of relief that she was not quite the frivolous creature her mother had always believed her to be.

'Your father would have been proud of you,' Mirto said once she'd recovered from the shock of hearing about the Resistance. 'Can I do anything to help?'

Calliope had muttered something noncommittal. She had no intention of putting her mother at risk. And anyway, what could poor Mirto do?

It was only in early July, when a request came up to transfer live ammunition to the guerrillas, that she was forced to consider the merit of exploiting her mother's exemplary respectability.

Just before bedtime, she took Sappho to the fortress to mull things over. It had been a long day of shrivelling heat, but the moonlit night was clear and breezy, flaunting its stars across a velvety sky. By the time Calliope stepped out with her dog, half the village was submerged in sleep; the other half would be getting ready for bed behind blackout blinds.

The night seemed at its most radiant at the fortress, where the moonlight danced among the brooding stones. She sat in her favourite spot, her feet up on the parapet, while Sappho went snuffling along the crumbling walls.

It was cooler on top of the hill, with the sea breeze sweeping across the fortress, murmuring in the trees. Sappho was chomping down on something but had swallowed it by the time Calliope came down to see what the dog had pounced on.

She returned to the balustrade. The silence was deep and blissful. Among the surrounding trees, underneath each stone, invisible creatures pursued their nocturnal activities. There was the intermittent piping of frogs, the call of a distant nightjar.

Suddenly, there was a small, crunching noise: the sound of feet treading over twigs or pebbles – something. Calliope held herself very still, feeling her skin tingle. Sappho let out a volley of barks, then paused uncertainly, head slightly cocked.

'Don't be alarmed… it's only me,' Lorenz Umbreit's voice said from within the shadows. He stepped forth through a crumbling wall, tall in the light of the silvery moon. '*Guten Abend, Frau*

Alexiou.' He had taken off his officer's cap, stopping in front of her with a little mock bow.

'*Kalispera*,' she answered. She had recently taken to greeting him in Greek.

'I thought you were one of the sleepwalkers,' he said, a smile in his voice.

For unknown reasons, several village women had recently taken to sleepwalking, but she was not one of them. She had merely come out to walk her dog and to think, she said conversationally. She turned to lean over the balustrade, facing the Eftalou coast. Umbreit stopped beside her.

'Think about what?' he asked.

'What, is there a shortage of things to think about?'

She supposed Umbreit had been at the watchtower, had probably stopped at the fortress on his way back to the stifling town hall. He stood fumbling for cigarettes.

'So,' he said, 'why *are* there so many sleepwalkers in this village?'

Calliope shrugged.

'And all of them women, it seems. I was wondering why, just the other day.'

'I don't know.' Calliope swatted a buzzing mosquito. 'There weren't any before. Not that I know of.'

'Before what?' Umbreit struck a match, cupping it between his hands. The flare of the match briefly illuminated his face.

'*Before what?* Before you took over!'

'I see,' he said, drawing on his cigarette. They were both silent then, gazing at the moonlit sea. A breeze stirred, trailing the scent of primroses across the fortress.

'A sublime evening,' he said and blew a puff of smoke into the balmy air. 'Sublime' seemed to be one of his favourite words. *Hervorragend.* In recent weeks, Calliope had caught herself using the Greek equivalent with growing frequency. She was like a parrot, she told herself. It probably explained the gift she had for foreign languages. But the evening was indeed sublime. Umbreit began to say something.

'Shhh.' Calliope raised her hand. 'Listen.'

He stopped. He listened. 'A nightingale,' he said, chuckling softly.

'We used to hear them all the time,' Calliope said. 'I don't know why they stopped.' She spoke very softly. 'Strange, it's not even their mating season.'

They listened together, standing side by side. It was impossible to explain why Umbreit's chuckle should move her so deeply, and not only when accompanied by a nightingale's song. His chuckle made her think of an infant essaying laughter for the first time. The nightingale went on singing. And then, abruptly, it stopped, and the silence was like a physical blow. It seemed, somehow, to unleash cosmic disappointment.

'Have you ever read Hans Christian Andersen?' Calliope asked.

Umbreit smiled. His teeth gleamed in the dark. 'You're thinking of the Chinese emperor?'

'Yes.' She stood brooding for a moment, recalling her own indignation on first reading about the foolish emperor, who had turned his back on the humble plumed nightingale in favour of a bejewelled toy. 'I remember crying when I read the story,' she said, speaking into the night. 'I wonder how old I was.'

He turned his head sideways and chuckled again. 'What a sentimental soul you are.' *Eine sentimentale Seele.*

'Am I?' She felt vaguely miffed. She became aware of Umbreit studying her profile, the glowing tip of his cigarette circling hypnotically as he moved his arm.

He was a superb listener. She hadn't met anyone who listened so keenly since her father died. Elias Dhaniel was a sympathetic listener, but she often felt that half his mind was on his ailing patients. Umbreit listened as if nothing else existed. As if they had been cast adrift by some storm and there was nothing to do but listen.

There was a long silence. A sudden breeze brought a whiff of his scent her way. 'I'd better be getting home,' she said, pushing away from the mottled wall.

Umbreit crushed his cigarette under his heel. He seemed about to speak but finally didn't. They said goodnight. Calliope turned to go, while Umbreit leaned back against the parapet, watching her stroll away under the floating moon.

X

Odysseus the beekeeper owned a small farm on the outskirts, as well as an old mule cart. It was agreed that, in exchange for soap, Odysseus would transport Mirto and Calliope to the hot springs late on Saturday afternoon. He had tried to talk them into going early, before the day grew hot, but Calliope had to teach in the morning. It seemed best, moreover, to avoid venturing out when Eftalou was sure to be swarming with hungry women scouring the countryside for edible greens.

It was past five o'clock when they climbed down from Odysseus's cart, but the sun still had teeth, the beekeeper grumbled. He had let them off in front of the Eftalou bathhouse, promising to return in two hours. He made a vague parting gesture, then swung the cart around and jolted on towards his farm, prodding his reluctant beast.

They were on their own. The bathhouse was long and narrow, with one shaft of light slanting in through a tiny window. It reeked of mould and sulphur. The walls around the shallow pool were yellow with creeping moisture. There were cracks in the walls, caused by some long-forgotten earthquake.

'There's no time to waste,' Calliope said, glancing about tensely. The room had an echo. One of the cracks in the wall had sprouted a pale green weed straining towards the light. 'Will you be all right?'

Mirto was yanking off her shoes. 'Of course I'll be all right!'

'Fine then. I'll be back as soon as I can.'

Calliope picked up the two empty baskets. She left Mirto soaking her feet, then hastened across the dirt road, her skirt brushing bushes of sage and thyme. The countryside had been stripped bare over the summer months. Some farmers had taken to staying up nights, on guard against thieving guerrillas. The partisans were said to be worse than martens. They pounced on the little produce farmers still had, then bolted to the hills.

Calliope trekked down the dusty road. Some of her fondest memories were linked to Eftalou, the long summer days she and her cousins had spent here as children, staying at their *yaya*'s cottage. On hot nights, they sometimes slept under the stars, surrounded by legions of rioting crickets. In the morning, they would stuff their mouths with sun-ripened blackberries, the juice trickling down their chins, staining their hands purple. That was their daily breakfast. They would gobble up the fruit, drink some fresh goat's milk, then run off, squealing, into the sea.

Musing on all this, it suddenly came to Calliope that her feelings for the village of her birth were like those one might have for a family member, someone whose shortcomings one is familiar with, is occasionally vexed by, but for whom one nonetheless feels a deep, abiding affection.

Eventually, she came to an abandoned field. Squatting, she picked young dandelion greens sprouting along the fence, then, walking a little further, finally found the wild mustard greens she'd been looking for. She dropped the crinkly leaves into her mother's basket, shooing away a red ladybird. The countryside hummed with insects. It was still hot. She sat up and arched her back, then got down on her haunches and resumed picking. A few feet away, a lizard lay sunning itself on a rock.

Finally, she was ready. She stood swabbing the back of her neck with her handkerchief. Her cheeks blazed, her collar and back were drenched in sweat, but she had what she needed.

Retracing her steps, Calliope plodded down the dirt road towards a distant beach she had always regarded as her private hideaway. She stopped for a moment, surveying land and sea. Gingerly – she was still wearing her home-made clogs – she made her way among the sun-bleached rocks strewn along the shore.

She had been charged with picking up a cache of bullets for the mountain guerrillas. She had recently been involved in the transfer of hand grenades in the village proper, but such ventures were now considered too risky.

Although the remote beach had been her suggestion, she had no idea who had hidden the bullets. It was impossible to know who could and could not be trusted. Anyone who had not visibly lost weight in the past fifteen months was assumed to be a collaborator or black marketeer. Calliope, however, knew better than to trust any rumours. She herself was probably suspected of being a collaborator.

The cache of bullets was waiting in a pit dug to the left of a tamarisk tree where she had often sat as a child, reading or daydreaming. The beach was distant enough to make the location safe, she'd assured the doctor. Yet they both knew the truth: there was always the chance of being spotted by children or a roving shepherd.

Calliope paused and looked about yet again, then bent to dislodge a rock, feeling her skin prickle. The cache was heavier than she'd expected: a small burlap bag stuffed with lethal iron. The image of an unsuspecting Lorenz Umbreit being felled by one of these bullets surfaced in the back of her brain and was instantly quelled. *Calm down, calm down, calm down.* Her hands trembling, Calliope transferred the clandestine bag to one of the baskets, then quickly spread bunches of fresh greens over the top.

She was almost done, was shifting the rock back into place, when she heard a noise – a small rustling sound – somewhere behind her back. It lasted only a moment, but in that short spell, her body stiffened as if pierced by an arrow. Still crouching among the rocks, she whipped her head around, eyes wildly scanning the overgrown roadside. There were rocks and weeds and thickets of dry bush among the tamarisk trees, but it took another minute to identify the culprit.

A feral ash-grey dog was staring straight at her, a dead seagull between its jaws. A dog! *Breathe in, breathe out.* Just a hungry dog, already scampering away. *Don't panic. Don't let yourself panic.*

Calliope scrambled to her feet. She peered up and down the beach.

Nothing. Nothing but sea and rocks, the rustle of birds, the dusty, whispering trees. The dirt road was still deserted, the beach as tranquil as ever. Yet she couldn't stop trembling. Three raucous seagulls kept gliding over the shimmering water, calling to each other. The smallest had landed on the crest of a wave and sat there, swaying plumply, contentedly. But the other two went on screaming, like two frenzied parents issuing unheeded warnings.

It was time to head back.

XI

The beekeeper had obtained his mule from a Mytilene merchant who had for years been procuring honey from Eftalou. Unable to feed the mule, the family had traded it in for thyme honey. Odysseus's own mule had long since expired of old age. He himself was much too old to be tramping back and forth on his spindly legs.

All this the beekeeper shared with Calliope and Mirto during the early-evening ride from the Eftalou bathhouse.

'What can you do?' He sighed. 'Once you get past sixty, every day's just a gift from God.'

'Pah, and why only sixty?' Mirto demanded from the back of the cart. 'Every day from the time we're born is a gift from God!'

Odysseus made a noncommittal gesture. He was a shrivelled old man, with the melancholy eyes of a bloodhound. He kept scratching himself all over. The cart creaked and bounced. He talked, and prodded the mule, and scratched. Now and then he muttered about his eczema, or tried to entertain his two passengers, lisping through missing teeth.

'What's the difference between a Nazi master and his dog?'

'What?' Calliope said vaguely, wondering whether Umbreit owned a dog.

'The master lifts his arm!' Odysseus guffawed, swivelling his head back to glance at the two women. Mirto was leaning against her daughter, her hands clasped around her knees. The hands were small and delicate, but raw from years of washing family laundry. Something stirred in Calliope's chest.

'Look,' she said, pointing to the house of a man they had once hired to pick their olives. A dejected-looking child was lolling against the door of the stone cottage. The boy, Odysseus said, had been sick with measles, had not been the same since then, though the family had summoned Sultana the herbalist, offering an egg-laying hen.

'Poor little sod. But at least we ain't got typhoid.' Odysseus sighed, stopping to greet two farmers who had just emerged from a roadside orchard, their shoe soles flapping up dust. The older man had once been a prosperous farmer; the younger was Lazaros, one of Eleni Bastia's brothers. Christos, his twin, had recently joined the guerrillas, without so much as a farewell to his own mother. Athena cried for days, Odysseus was soon saying. Women didn't understand men's need to take action in dire times.

'A woman's a woman – she can cook, she can have children – but a man's a man, not a jellyfish, eh? A man's got to defend his land!'

Calliope managed to hold her tongue. The older farmer was one of Johnny the Australian's brothers-in-law, a man prone to grumbling about the four daughters Mina had given him. Many years had passed since Johnny had come to marry off his sisters; exactly seven since he and Calliope had run into each other on this very road. The thought was followed by a tired sigh. Not for the first time, Calliope found herself wondering how her life would have turned out had she accepted the Australian's marriage proposal.

The mule cart was approaching Odysseus's farm. The beekeeper offered to take his passengers into the village, but Mirto demurred, saying they wanted to dig up some wild onions before heading home. She fished a spade out of her bag and placed it conspicuously on top of the mustard greens. If there was time, she said, they might stop at the forest to look for pine nuts.

'Good luck!' said Odysseus.

Calliope climbed down from the mule cart, doing her best to lift the heavy basket as lightly and nonchalantly as if it indeed contained nothing but wild greens. She did not succeed. It was a good thing Odysseus was not as sharp as he used to be.

Calliope paused, setting the basket down while she adjusted her headscarf. Mirto had offered to carry half the bullets, but Calliope refused. In the unlikely event that they got caught, she would insist that Mirto had known nothing about the bullets; Calliope had simply exploited her mother's need for a sulphur bath.

The women tramped on towards the wood, each immersed in her own anxious thoughts. The plan was for Calliope to go into the forest where her contact was waiting, while Mirto sat guard on the wood's edge, as if taking a rest before climbing home. If anyone chanced to come by, Mirto would say that she was waiting for Calliope, who had gone in search of pine nuts.

But things did not work out as planned. Plodding towards the forest, they suddenly heard the roar of an approaching motorcycle. It was as yet invisible, but Calliope slowed her pace, peering up the road. No one in the village rode a motorcycle any more. The police chief owned one but had no fuel to keep it running.

The distant motorcycle had to be German.

'Keep walking,' Calliope said, her mouth going dry. Instinctively, she moved closer to her mother, fingers tightening over the wicker handle. Soon, the motorcycle was rounding the bend, drowning out the clamouring cicadas. An involuntary gasp escaped Calliope's throat: Sergeant Alfred Reis was hunched over the handlebars; Lieutenant Lorenz Umbreit sat in the sidecar, staring straight ahead through his amber goggles. Was it possible she had been betrayed?

'Try to act normal. We were just gathering greens,' Calliope whispered.

The motorcycle engine was cut.

'*Guten Tag!*' The lieutenant yanked off his goggles, shifting in the narrow sidecar. He had spoken lightly, pleasantly, looking relaxed and fresh in his summer uniform. 'A walk in the countryside, I see?'

'Yes. We have to eat after all.' Calliope shrugged. She'd spoken in a consciously offhand tone, but instantly regretted her response. The reference to food must have sounded churlish, given that Umbreit made sure they never went hungry. It was also redundant, since he knew that she liked swimming in Eftalou. Somewhere she had read that the guilty tended to over-explain.

While all this was getting tossed in Calliope's head, Umbreit's keen gaze shifted away from her face, briefly landing on her wicker basket. He then raised his sea-hued eyes and regarded her in silence, the corners of his mouth turning up slightly. Was that a smile? He was saying something about the benefits of living so close to nature. Sergeant Reis sat waiting, his lips pressed together.

He did not like her. Calliope had sensed this from the start, though perhaps it was simply that she did not like him, feeling something cold and condescending behind his civilised facade. His eyes, she'd told Mirto, were such an icy blue they might have been made of glass.

'I wish you both good health,' Umbreit said, smiling at Mirto.

He waited for Calliope to translate the message, then the motorcycle engine came to life again. '*Auf Wiedersehen!*' The lieutenant raised his hand in parting, still smiling genially, like a man who had chanced to encounter a couple of old friends on his way to work.

But could a German officer really be a friend? Calliope asked herself. He had, two days after she'd told him about the cherry preserves, brought her a jar of Bulgarian jam, telling her she was not to have so much as a teaspoon; it was all for her poor mother.

Yes, he certainly behaved like a friend. And yet, there had been something strained in his parting smile. Or had she imagined it? She glanced back over her shoulder, looping her arm around Mirto's elbow.

'Don't worry. It's all right, Mama.'

She had spoken as quietly, as evenly, as she could, but her flesh felt clammy. A tiny pebble had become lodged inside her clog, ignored for the past few minutes. 'Wait, Mama... just a moment, please.'

She set the basket down, her muscles knotted with pain. The pebble was chafing at her little toe. Leaning against her mother, Calliope yanked her clog off and shook it.

Suddenly, an inexplicable impulse made her turn, her foot fumbling its way into the waiting shoe. The motorcycle was too far off by then, too shrouded in dust to be seen very clearly, but it looked as though Umbreit had twisted around in the sidecar and was gazing back across the hazy distance. Yes, that was definitely his face, though there seemed to be something – some dark object – cutting across his features. She didn't think that it was his goggles. Something black, splitting his face in half.

His binoculars!

Reaching down for the basket, Calliope felt the cicadas' cries issuing out of her own skull: a shrill, derisive chorus. She darted a glance at her mother.

'He should be there by now,' she said, desperate to break the tension. She was referring to the waiting guerrilla. 'Are you all right, Mama?'

'Yes,' said Mirto. 'Don't you worry about me!'

'Fine, Mama. I won't.' Calliope took her mother's arm and squeezed it. It was all she could do under the circumstances. Perhaps Odysseus was right; perhaps women were not meant to take part in such hair-raising ventures.

The thought circled over Calliope's consciousness like a greedy vulture. *He knows*, a voice in the back of her head was saying. *He knows*.

1942–1945

'The heart has its reasons which reason knows nothing of.'

Pascal

ONE

I

God did not seem to be on the Allies' side. By the autumn of 1942, Molyviates were starting to point this out to their priests, as if lodging a formal complaint against divine arbitrariness. In North Africa, the Axis forces had begun to sweep into Egypt; in Russia, they'd penetrated the Caucasus, preparing to launch a massive offensive against Stalingrad. In Guadalcanal, American troops were still holding out against the Japanese, but German submarines went on sinking Allied ships, and thousands of soldiers had lost their lives in the disastrous raid on Dieppe.

The Germans had confiscated all the wireless sets they could find in Molyvos. But, huddled inside a wardrobe, Stamatis the headmaster listened to a clandestine broadcast, passing on the news as he saw fit. Calliope learned of recent events from Dr Dhaniel, who was in the habit of dropping his son off for a weekly sleepover.

Her godson's company offered so much pleasure that, one day in early October, Calliope let him stay up well past his bedtime. On Sunday morning, Aristides awoke in a contrary mood. When Mirto insisted that he sit down to eat a bowl of gruel, Aristides threw such a spectacular tantrum that, two decades later, he would still be teased about this early hint of his anarchistic leanings.

Mirto went to get ready for church. Calliope had just promised to take her godson to the beach when *Papa* Iakovos's wife turned up, seeking an ointment for the pus-filled boils that had recently appeared on her husband's body. She must have been counting on Calliope's friendship with either the doctor or Lieutenant Umbreit, but Dhaniel had no medicines left and Umbreit was away from the village.

All this was patiently explained, but the *papadhia* would not be persuaded, not even when Mirto came down, jumping in with talk of her own afflictions. The doctor was their friend, she readily conceded, but he hadn't been able to help her either, not even with common female ailments.

'I've got cramps right now – *poh poh poh*, you'd think I was giving birth!' She winced, rubbing her abdomen. 'You think he'd leave me in pain if he had medicines?'

The priest's wife was silent. She was a hefty woman with voracious eyes set in a face as pale and plump as dough. The pharmacist had long since closed his shop and returned to Mytilene, but the *papadhia* was not yet ready to relinquish hope. Reaching between her breasts, she brought out a gold locket, glanced at it sadly, then held it out towards Calliope.

'Take it, *kale*,' she said, speaking in dulcet tones. 'Take it. I—'

'Ach, put it away!' Calliope cried. The insufferable woman was not merely offering an heirloom; she was proclaiming her willingness to put herself at Calliope's mercy. A few whispered words in Umbreit's ear and the entire family would be arrested for hoarding gold. It was, Calliope understood, meant to make her feel powerful.

'What do I have to do to convince you, Olympia? I can't get you the ointment – I'm sorry. I couldn't get it if I had boils on my own skin.'

'God forbid!' Mirto crossed herself.

The *papadhia* looked from mother to daughter. Aristides was tugging on Calliope's skirt, wanting to know when they could go to the beach.

'Soon, *pedhi mou*, soon,' Calliope murmured. She did not like St Kyriaki's priest, or his wife, but reproached herself for her antipathy. The poor man's boils were hideous; his wife's suffering was clearly genuine.

'Ach, ach, ach,' she was moaning now. 'What shall I do, what shall I do, *Panaghia mou*?' She sat clutching the locket for a moment, then held it out again, with the mute appeal of a whipped yet tenacious dog.

'I don't want your locket!' Calliope erupted, her eyes flicking towards her mother. *Help me*, she pleaded mutely.

'Ach, we're going to be late for church!' Mirto exclaimed, leaping from her chair as the grandfather clock chimed. She would be ready in a jiffy, she said, clutching her abdomen.

Despite the theatrics, Mirto's female troubles were real. She had recently turned fifty-two, but her periods were heavier than ever. Not only were there no medicines left, there was no cotton to be found, not even on the black market.

Like all village women, Mirto spent hours boiling her bloodstained rags, soaking them in lemon juice, to be bleached by the sun. All over the island, women were cutting up dishrags, dresses, curtains, washing and rewashing them because who could tell how long this war was going to last?

One day, the late *hamam* caretaker's daughter had come upon her father's old army uniform and cut the trousers into rags, to the snoopy neighbours' noisy astonishment. Melpo was a little soft in the head, but her mother should have known better than to let the girl hang a war hero's ruined uniform for all the world to see.

The poor man must be turning in his grave, they said. That's what you got when you went looking for a bride among the *Turkospori*!

The *Turkospori* were the Anatolian refugees who had settled in the village back in the 1920s. Many of them had a mercantile background and were said to be cunning enough to provide for their families even under the Germans, while native villagers could barely stave off starvation.

All the same, in their calmer moments, Molyviates conceded they were lucky, at least in comparison with people in the German-choked capital or, for that matter, even nearby, in Molyvos's sister village. A new officer named Franz Dwinger had recently been transferred to the island and was now in charge at Petra. He had seemed, from the start, like an exceptionally hard taskmaster, but even the most astute observer could not have suspected the depths of his depravity, let alone foreseen the widespread impact of his sadistic actions.

II

A few hours before Aristides threw his memorable tantrum, his father had been awakened by a farmer whose pregnant wife lay moaning in a mule cart, deep in the throes of labour. It was almost dawn. The expectant father was in an excited state. The reasons were not immediately apparent, but were soon revealed to be only partly due to obstetrical concerns. The doctor asked a question or two, his head averted from his patient, his hand probing under the tented sheet.

He had entered into conversation between contractions, hoping to distract the fretting husband, only to find himself the recipient of deeply unsettling news. With a midwife, the father would not have been allowed to stay in the labour room, but no man would leave his pregnant wife alone with a male doctor.

The Petran hovered nearby while his wife lay labouring. She howled. She panted. She cried out to the Virgin. Every now and then, her hands would fly up in frenzied appeal, then return to clutch at her mammoth girth. Suddenly, she turned on her husband.

'It's all your fault!' she spat out. 'I curse the day I married you, you bastard! You want me to die, don't you? Ach, *Panaghia mou*, help me... help me!'

The husband blinked at the doctor. 'What's she saying? Why is she talking to me like this?'

'Don't pay any attention,' the doctor said. 'They go crazy during labour.'

'They curse their own child's father?'

'Who else? You must admit you had something to do with it.' Dhaniel achieved a smile, then steered the conversation back to Petra news. Three men had been arrested there the previous day, one of them the young man's own great-uncle. The doctor wanted to know about the other two.

'The other two were Germans,' the Petran said.

'Germans!'

'Germans.'

The young man fumbled for a cigarette, his gaze helplessly sliding in his wife's direction. He went on to offer details, oblivious to the change in the doctor's mien. The labouring woman was still moaning, but more softly now. Dhaniel muttered something vaguely reassuring, then went to stand by the window, watching the morning mists drift across the mountains.

A few minutes passed. The Petran sat smoking. Somewhere in the distance, a rooster began to crow. Suddenly, the patient let out a scream and the doctor dashed back, reaching for his stethoscope.

'You're going to have twins,' he said, smiling.

'Twins?' The young man jumped out of his chair. 'Impossible!'

'Twins. I can clearly hear two heartbeats.'

The farmer continued to protest but, before long, the mother herself provided indisputable proof.

'A boy and a girl,' the doctor stated with palpable satisfaction. He flicked a rueful glance towards the young father, who was shifting his weight from foot to foot, like a man forced to stand barefoot on scorching sand. Scratching his head, the farmer watched, wide-eyed, as the doctor slapped one infant's bottom, and then the other. He pronounced both babies healthy and quickly prepared them for their mother's arms.

'You should thank God they haven't forbidden our making babies.' Dhaniel chuckled at his own little joke. He clapped the young father's shoulder, then reached for the bottle of home-made brandy. 'May they live a long life!'

The farmer thanked the doctor, then downed his brandy in silence, a small hiccup escaping his throat. All at once, he began to laugh, madly, uncontrollably.

'Twins!' he sputtered, tears streaming down his stubbly face. He darted towards the bed and leaned over his wife, both laughing and crying. 'We made twins, woman! Twins! Aren't you glad they haven't forbidden it?'

III

Calliope's godson was sprawled on the kitchen floor, playing with building blocks, when the doctor arrived to fetch him. Mirto was upstairs, resting after the midday meal. Sappho could be seen through the kitchen window, snapping at flies.

'*Baba!*'

The boy leapt up, throwing himself against his father's legs. Dhaniel sat down and drew him on to his lap, listening to the child prattle about the beach. He looked almost dashing in his Sunday suit, but the sunlight picked out the lines in his smooth-shaven face. His hair was still thick, but the threads of grey were numerous now, giving his sandy-hued head a silvery sheen. Calliope had finally started calling him Eli at his insistence, but in her thoughts, he remained *The Doctor*.

Dhaniel removed his jacket. He planted a kiss on his son's crown and sent him out to play with the dog. He had something to discuss with *Nona*, he said.

Calliope set two coffee cups on the table. 'What is it?'

'The Turks caught Yorgos and Takis,' Dhaniel said. 'The foreigner too.'

'The Turks!' Calliope fell into a chair, banging her knee against one of the table legs. The thought that the Lyras men had succeeded in outwitting the Germans, only to be captured by the Turks, was not easily digested.

'They've been in a Turkish jail all this time,' the doctor explained. 'I just heard this morning.'

Calliope regarded him for a moment. 'What happened?'

Dhaniel couldn't say. All he knew was that the fugitives had been captured within hours of reaching Turkish shores.

'*Thee mou!*' Calliope looked away, watching Aristides frolic with the panting dog. 'What do you suppose they'll do with them?'

'They've sent them back.'

'Back? Back to the island?'

Dhaniel almost smiled. 'They must have figured the Germans would deal with them and save them the bother.'

'Have the Germans caught them? Is that what you're trying to tell me?'

'Oh, no. No.' Dhaniel shook his head. 'I'm sorry, I'm not being very coherent, am I? They've gone into hiding. They're safe for now.'

The words repeated themselves in Calliope's head. There had been reports of villages being burned down for aiding and abetting guerrillas.

'Don't tell me they're in Molyvos.'

'No. The Englishman's hiding outside Petra. Yorgos and Takis – I don't know – some small inland village, I suppose.' There were many such villages on the island, too insignificant for the Germans to bother with, except for an occasional raid. 'They were very lucky,' said the doctor. He watched his son throw a stick for Sappho to fetch. The boy threw it again and again, but the dog slumped under the tree, panting, her pink tongue lolling.

'Lazy dog! Lazy dog!' Aristides chirped, waving his arms. 'Lazy!'

The child's father and godmother exchanged smiles. There was another silence. 'There's something you're not telling me,' Calliope said, holding Dhaniel's eyes. 'There is, isn't there?'

'Ach, you know me too well.' Dhaniel sighed. 'I'm afraid you're right.'

'Tell me. I want to know everything.'

Dhaniel averted his eyes, silent for a long moment. Eventually, he cleared his throat, deciding to speak. Two German soldiers had been arrested in Petra and taken to Mytilene to be court-martialled. They'd been caught trading hand grenades in exchange for a slaughtered lamb.

'Lamb!'

'It was someone's birthday,' said the doctor. 'It seems even Germans enjoy lamb on special occasions.'

Calliope began to chew on a hangnail. 'Traded with whom?'

Dhaniel didn't know the man. 'Some old farmer living on the outskirts,' he said, lowering his voice. Mirto had woken from her nap and could be heard stirring upstairs. 'They took him to Mytilene as well. Kouches, I think he's called.'

At this, Calliope became aware of heat creeping up the back of her neck.

'I'm very sorry,' Dhaniel said, shifting his gaze towards the doorway. Mirto was coming down in her flip-flops. Calliope's lips parted to speak, but the doctor was quicker. 'Let's hope he doesn't know too much,' he said with a sigh. 'What were you going to say?'

Calliope sat cradling her head. 'You stole the words out of my mouth,' she said.

IV

Umbreit returned in early October, accompanied by von Herden. The major visited Molyvos on a regular basis, but he usually came at the end of the month. Why was he here now, Calliope wondered. Did his visit have anything to do with Petra?

As soon as she arrived at the town hall from her morning classes, Calliope was asked to interpret for von Herden, who was about to interview the local olive-mill owner. Calliope guessed that someone must have hinted that the oil production record might be falsified, but Loukas Stephanides staunchly denied the charge.

Lorenz Umbreit – a captain now – was present during the interview, calmly taking notes, while Calliope translated the German–Greek exchange, feeling no less edgy than the man being questioned. She had been tense around Umbreit ever since their brief encounter in Eftalou. There had been days when she felt sure he knew about her clandestine activities; other days she thought she must be in the sway of her overwrought nerves: Umbreit's kindness had shown no sign of flagging.

But if human decency seemed surprising in a Wehrmacht officer, Calliope's own feelings were far more perplexing. She found, for example, that while she loathed the army whose uniform Umbreit wore, she did like the uniform itself – at least on Umbreit's elegant frame. She could not imagine him in civvies, but the feelings generated by the uniform thoroughly muddled her. That the bluish-grey tunic, boots and officer's cap somehow heightened Umbreit's air of vigour and authority was perhaps understandable. But there was also an undeniable whiff of something like risk or danger, and her awareness of this often left Calliope viciously biting at her frayed cuticles.

She was doing her best not to bite them now, though she thought that von Herden's suspicions might turn out to be justified. Both the olive-mill owner and his son were known to be cunning as foxes, though the son, Kimon's best man, had returned from Albania with a limp and a serious drinking problem. Dimitris had been separated from Kimon after being wounded in a major battle and didn't know what had become of his friend. His nerves were said to be shot; he seldom arrived at the mill before eleven a.m.

When the interview was over, von Herden claimed to be satisfied but, as soon as Loukas was gone, he asked Calliope to contact Mytilene's olive mill and arrange a meeting. Did he want to compare his production with that of the village, Calliope wondered, or was the Mytilinios under suspicion too?

Although no reference was made to recent events in Petra, something in the air exacerbated Calliope's anxiety. Von Herden had always been brisk but today wore a feverish sort of resolve, like a man preparing for a trip, determined to put his life in order before his departure. When Calliope finished making the arrangements in Mytilene, he dictated a letter to Athens, then asked her to accompany him and his men on a house search.

House searches were common enough, and Calliope was often present to interpret. What made this search exceptional was the suspect's position. Eleftheris Yannopoulos was the harbour master.

At five in the afternoon, when the search unit arrived, he and his wife had just woken from their siesta and looked dishevelled and dazed, finding themselves presented with a search warrant.

The harbour master's son had recently married the baker's daughter, so the ageing couple lived alone, in Calliope's own neighbourhood. Although she had explained that this was a random search, Yannopoulos and his wife trailed the soldiers from room to room, with the air of people who had guns and grenades stashed in their cellar.

But the cellar had already been searched, found to contain only broken furniture and crates of dry cod and root vegetables. Following von Herden's instructions, the soldiers began to strip mattresses, empty trunks, inspect chests and wardrobes. Yannopoulos was silent, absently rubbing his jaw; Soula kept wringing her hands, exhorting the soldiers to go easy on her possessions.

Calliope dutifully translated every word, noting the bitter glances both man and wife kept flicking in her direction. Did they think that she had anything to do with the search, for heaven's sake? She watched the proceedings in silence until the soldiers arrived at the storage room on the second floor. Soula, turning to Calliope, finally snapped.

'Couldn't you at least have let us know they were coming?'

'I didn't know!' Calliope protested. 'Do you think they'd be stupid enough to share their plans with me?'

Soula made an ambiguous sound. She was a middle-aged woman who spoke with the voice of a little girl, heaving with indignation.

'What is she saying?' von Herden wanted to know.

Calliope shrugged. 'She's upset to see her house turned upside down.' Yannopoulos, who had been transferred from Kavala, was renting the house from a family who had emigrated to Australia. The owners' belongings were being stored in one of the bedrooms. The door had been padlocked, but the soldiers broke the lock and were now going through the absent owners' possessions: their trunks and chiffonier, their brass braziers, their mahogany credenza. There was the smell of dust and mothballs as they unrolled an old carpet pushed against the wall.

'None of this is ours!' Soula wailed. 'They emigrated long before the war!'

Calliope translated, but von Herden offered no reply. He only smiled a little, his wolf's eyes shifting between the harbour master and his wife with a look that was somehow both indulgent and sceptical. It came to Calliope that this might not be a random search; von Herden would not be wasting his time without serious cause.

She was both surprised and relieved when the Germans came up empty-handed. Yannopoulos tried to comfort his wife, who was darting from room to room, clutching her head at the chaos left in the Germans' wake.

Von Herden apologised for the inconvenience. He hesitated, apologised again, then signalled his men to leave.

V

He did not tell her where he'd been or why, and she did not ask. She had wondered whether Umbreit's absence might be connected to the Germans' North African campaign; had even found herself worrying that he would be transferred to join Rommel's army.

It was by now evening. Von Herden was gone, and Calliope had come up to the German office to return the Nietzsche, which she had kept for nearly six months. She was hoping to learn something that would shed light on the Petra arrests, but Umbreit seemed in a surprisingly sociable mood. He had taken off his tie and was down to his shirtsleeves.

'So, what have you been up to while I was away?'

Calliope was reaching into her satchel for the Nietzsche. She raised her eyes and offered a partial truth: she had been taking advantage of the free time to finish his book and review her German grammar.

'Well, I'm glad to hear that. I wouldn't want you getting into mischief just because you were bored.' Umbreit smiled, fiddling with his ink bottle, while Calliope paused to ponder his words.

Es wäre mir nämlich unlieb, wenn du dir nur aus langer Weile Unangenehmlichkeiten einhandeln würdest.

'I'm never bored!' she replied loftily. She placed the book on his desk and thanked him, her gaze landing on a small collection of beautifully patterned pebbles. Umbreit had collected them on the beach and placed them in a water jar.

'Thank you? Is that all you're going to say?' He chuckled, studying her with affable curiosity. 'Don't tell me you didn't like our Nietzsche.' He leaned back with his hands clasped behind his neck, utterly at ease.

Calliope shifted her weight. 'To tell you the truth, I'm not sure I understand everything – my German's still poor, but...' Her expression wavered. He was watching her so intently she suddenly remembered that her hair hadn't been washed for a week; they had almost run out of soap in Umbreit's absence. Was it possible that she was beginning to stink, like so many of her fellow villagers?

'But?'

'But I do understand most of it, and I... I can't decide how I feel about him.'

Umbreit said nothing. He swivelled a little in his chair, waiting for her to elaborate.

She was having trouble focusing, partly because of the subject, but also because Umbreit's gaze was beginning to fluster her. He was not handsome, exactly, but his features seemed to exert an almost magnetic pull, all the more so after his month-long absence. She liked his soldierly bearing, his boyish hair and dented chin, but it was the expression in his eyes – steady, intelligent, wistful – that moved her in some deep, ineffable way.

'I mean, there's so much I found wonderful. So much I do agree with.'

'Like?' Umbreit brought down his hands, reaching for his pack of cigarettes. His hands were a working man's hands: large-knuckled, with strong, prominent veins.

'Well, his thoughts on religion, for one thing – on God and sin – I agree with all that.' She paused again, plucking her journal out of her satchel and quickly thumbing through it. Umbreit was fumbling with the cigarette package.

'I also liked what he had to say about the compromises between moral theory and social practice.' Calliope said this with a little deprecating shrug: who was she to be passing judgement on the great Nietzsche?

Umbreit struck a match, then paused briefly, letting it burn.

'I knew it would appeal to you.' He looked rather pleased with himself.

'Yes... well.' She bowed her head, returning to her notes. 'I also liked his thoughts on the relativity of truth. The truth is such a slippery thing, isn't it?' Umbreit smiled, then turned to light his oil lamp. It was getting dark outside.

'Now tell me what you didn't like.'

'Oh... well, quite a lot actually.' Calliope rubbed her ring finger, where her wedding band had been. It was one of several nervous habits acquired in recent months. 'I can't understand Nietzsche's approval, his... endorsement of cruelty, of tyranny. He speaks of these horrible traits as if... as if they were virtues!'

Umbreit went on smoking, regarding her through the swirling haze with that infuriating Nordic calmness of his.

'Oh!' Calliope flared up. 'I knew I shouldn't discuss this with you! I knew it!' She stared at him for a moment, feeling her cheeks flush. 'All that talk about the master morality and the slave morality!' She let out a small, ambiguous sound. 'As I said, I'm not even sure I understand it but...'

The corners of Umbreit's mouth twitched. 'You don't understand it, but you know that you don't approve?'

'Yes!'

'Well,' he said, 'maybe we can discuss this further some day. I could perhaps—'

'I don't think so,' she said, forestalling whatever he meant to propose. 'We'll just end up quarrelling over your Nietzsche,' she added. The oil lamp had begun to flicker, and she watched him move to adjust the wick. Several moths had come in through the windows and were vibrating around the glass shade. Umbreit's shadow jiggled on the wall. She said, 'I'd probably quarrel with Nietzsche himself if he came to sit in your chair right now!'

'Would you really?' He chuckled and, all at once, Calliope felt vexed.

'You bet I would! All that nonsense about women – his total rejection of women as… as thinking human beings.' She looked at him with a schoolmistressy frown. 'It's shameful, absolutely shameful, coming from such a brilliant man!'

Umbreit laughed.

'Why are you laughing?' She bristled. 'Do you really find it so amusing that—'

'Forgive me,' he interposed. 'I'm only amused by how right I was in… predicting your reactions.'

She chewed on this for a moment. 'Well,' she said then, 'it can't take much insight to guess how offensive such views must be to any thinking woman.'

'You're probably right,' he said. But the expression on his face remained amused, fuelling her resentment: he was not taking her seriously.

She hesitated, then picked up her journal and began to read one of the passages she had copied in German.

'"What does woman care for the truth? From the very first, nothing is more foreign, more repugnant, or more hostile to woman than truth – her greatest art is falsehood, her chief concern appearance and beauty."' Calliope repeated the last three words with surly emphasis. *Erscheinung und Schönheit!*

She glanced up from her notes to see Umbreit stub out his cigarette, looking wholly unperturbed – perhaps a little bored? This, she guessed, wasn't the kind of discussion he would be having with his German professors and colleagues. She was just a village woman and for some reason she seemed to amuse him.

The thought grated on her. All at once, she was determined to make him take her seriously.

'Here's another one: "When a woman has scholarly inclinations, there's generally something wrong with her sexual nature."' She looked up from her open journal. 'I'd like to know something about *his* sexual nature!' she tossed out. 'He might be a brilliant philosopher, but—'

She stopped abruptly.

'Why do you keep smiling like that?' she demanded. 'You look at me as if I was a child – a naive child spouting nonsense!' She began to stash her journal away, conscious that she was losing her temper, despite her resolve to emulate Umbreit's exemplary equanimity. 'I can't understand how you can agree with all that,' she continued. 'Why? Just because he's a famous philosopher? Even philosophers are only flesh and blood! They have their own problems, they make mistakes, just—'

'Calliope…' Umbreit cut into her tirade, amusement giving way to sudden gravitas. The room was dense with shadows, but the light from the lamp fell on his flaxen hair, his foreign face with its wintry eyes. He ran a hand over his jaw, then rose and came to stand beside her, leaning against his desk.

'I don't think you understand,' he said. He paused, sighed, then, for the second time that evening, words seemed to elude him. He stood regarding her mutely, his arms folded, his eyes dilated with feeling. Calliope stirred in the office chair. The silence between them was a menacing cave she had wandered into in a distracted moment.

'If you're hoping to change my mind, please don't!' she said, the words erupting out of her mouth. 'You're good with words – I know you've occasionally managed to convince me, but not this time!' She gestured towards the book on his desk. 'There really is no point in discussing this, since you're bent on agreeing with everything Nietzsche says – just because he's German!'

'Calliope.' He was beginning to sound simultaneously reproachful and hopeless. He stood with his legs apart, his hands tucked into his armpits. 'It so happens I don't agree with everything Nietzsche says – certainly not the passages you've quoted.' He paused. 'My mother's one of the most intelligent people I know. I might have told you this if you'd given me half a chance.'

Calliope regarded him. 'Why then… why did you keep smiling like that?'

Umbreit was silent for a long moment. Something was happening; some new emotion was flickering across his face. Suddenly, he blurted, 'Your eyes, Calliope... your eyes are like the golden sky in Byzantine paintings.' He smiled at her sadly. 'They're magnificent when... when you feel provoked. Did you know that?'

'Oh!' Calliope sprang to her feet. She had always been given to anger in moments of profound confusion. 'Here I am, trying to have a serious discussion, while you... you try to appeal to my vanity!' Her eyes flashed at him. 'After all, I'm just a woman... my chief concerns are appearance and beauty, right?'

'Calliope... Calliope, you're not being fair!' Umbreit protested. He lifted a hand and spread it through his boyish hair. 'You misjudge me,' he added, his eyes looking wounded. *Du schätzt mich falsch ein.*

'Do I?' She tossed this at him rather aggressively, then recalled that, only recently, she'd thrown the same accusation at her mother. 'How do I misjudge you?' she asked, relenting. She sat down again.

'I take you very seriously,' he said. He gave her a penetrating gaze, a look so intimate it made her body tingle. She wrenched her gaze away and let her eyes roam over the shadowy room. Umbreit's office had two windows facing the back courtyard and, beyond it, a long, narrow alley. There were dark blinds at the windows, blocking the room's dim light, but the windows themselves were open, letting in the pulsing sound of crickets and chirruping frogs. 'Look at me, Calliope,' he was saying. 'Please, look at me.'

Umbreit's shadow stirred on the whitewashed wall. He had unfolded his arms, detaching himself from his desk. He bent forward slightly, reached over, and gently laid his fingers on Calliope's hand, which was just then fidgeting with the pleats of her summer dress. He kept his fingers there for a moment. And although his touch was as light as a feather, it made her heart start flapping; a trapped bird blindly beating against an unyielding wall. She sat for a while, breathing shallowly. Some sort of insect had flown in and was buzzing around the lampshade.

And still she would not speak, would not look at him. Only when he went on to press her fingers did Calliope snap out of her mental haze. She snatched her hand away, as if accidentally scalded. He was still gazing at her with his mournful eyes, but the look she gave him was opaque with fear.

She averted her face, muttering something about having to go home… her mother was expecting her. Something. She didn't know what she was saying. She rose and swept past him on reluctant legs, darting out of his office towards the shadowy stairs. She paused long enough to shed her clogs: too clunky, too dangerous, on a dark, winding staircase. He had never let her leave in the evening without accompanying her downstairs, lantern in hand. Once or twice, he'd offered to have a soldier escort her home, but she had turned him down: she was perfectly safe in her own village.

She would not go back for a lantern. She began her escape down the staircase, feeling as she had only once in her life, when an earthquake had made the floor in her room heave, threatening to pull the ground out from under her. The marble stairs seemed icy under her feet. A moonbeam came in through a small window, but the darkness, the stillness, seemed dense with obscure menace. She ran down, clutching a wooden clog in each hand, ran towards the exit, the moonlight.

It was only when she arrived downstairs, after she had crossed the foyer and was about to open the portals, that she realised she'd left her bag in Umbreit's office. Her hand-loomed satchel, containing her journal!

The realisation made Calliope stop mid-stride. For a moment, she stood twisted with indecision. Finally, she turned and began to climb the staircase again, berating herself for her incorrigible forgetfulness. She muttered to herself like an old woman, but there was no one to hear her; even Ourania the cleaner had gone home. The only sounds were those of rats scratching behind the walls. The sentries were no longer positioned at the front entrance, but at the garden gate. She couldn't hear them, or any sound from Umbreit's office. Perhaps he was back at work, she thought, sitting at his desk, shuffling official papers as if nothing had happened.

And had anything happened? Had she just overreacted as usual? And would he see her now for the provincial she was: a twenty-seven-year-old woman behaving like a frightened hen? Her father had occasionally warned her against surrendering to emotion, but he never told her what to do should she ever find herself caught between two conflicting voices. And, yes, she had been caught! She hadn't known what to do. And so she'd fled, like a hysterical schoolgirl. Oh God!

All this was still whirling in Calliope's head as she reached the second landing. Umbreit was indeed back at his desk, but he was not working. He sat alone in a pool of light, his elbows on his desk, his face buried in his hands. He was unaware of her return, did not see her pause on the threshold, her hands with their clogs once more dangling at her sides. She could have gone in and snatched her bag and fled again. Instead, she waited silently in the shadows, aware of her own pulse, watching the moths flutter around the oil lamp.

This moment, too, seemed interminable, but suddenly he became conscious of her presence, had perhaps sensed her scent, her breath. Slowly, he let his hands slide down from his face. And then just sat there, staring at her in hopeless silence.

She saw that he had been weeping.

VI

She had never allowed herself to contemplate touching him, being touched by him. To entertain such thoughts, to acknowledge the possibility of physical contact, would have been more terrifying, more fraught with danger, than any Resistance activity. Of course, they could discuss literature and philosophy, could exchange books, the occasional joke. What harm could there be in that? There was, as she'd told her mother, little enough pleasure to be had nowadays.

If only he hadn't touched her. If only she hadn't seen him weep!

But hadn't she been warned? Hadn't her own mother tried to tell her that she was not playing with ideas but with fire?

Yes, her mother had said all this, and more. And, truly, she had felt scalded back in his office, his brief touch like a drop of hot wax on unsuspecting skin. If only she had listened! Now, there was no holding back the truth any more. Neither the truth nor the inner keening. To think of him weeping... alone in a foreign village.

She had gone back only to retrieve her bag, had been about to snatch it off the chair, when he suddenly rose, knocking over the bottle of ink with his elbow. What had he meant to say? She supposed she would never know. The bottle had gone flying off the desk, splattering purple ink over the sea urchin, the whitewashed wall, the scrubbed pine floorboards. It rooted Umbreit to the spot. It transfixed Calliope in mid-stride, her hand on the back of the chair, eyes riveted to his face. She had let out an involuntary gasp, then stood, dazed, two unbidden words rolling off her tongue.

'I'm sorry... sorry.'

He muttered something she didn't quite catch, for by then she was wheeling about, once more dashing towards the exit. And then she was running again, every cell in her body surrendering to despair.

To think that, against all odds, through some random decision in Hitler's bureaucracy, she was made to cross paths with an exceptional German. What for? What were they supposed to do about it, a Greek Resistance member and a Wehrmacht officer?

The question tormented Calliope. She did not sleep. She did not go to work for three days, sending a message to say she was sick.

And she *was* sick, all her internal organs feeling battered. She had been offered a glimpse of him, of the flower of possibility, only the better to know what she was apparently destined to be deprived of. She thought of Kimon, of how little she had been willing to settle for, how unaware she'd been of the depth of her own marital compromise.

She knew its full depth now.

And something else as well: she was a woman for whom love was as much a matter of admiration as of physical attraction. She had not admired Kimon. That she could admire a man engaged in thwarting her own people seemed like perversity. But, yes, she admired Umbreit – not just his competence and intelligence, but the delicacy suffusing every look, every gesture, with a sort of benevolent grace. He seemed interested in everything, capable of observing things in the blink of an eye. A soldier who might have been a philosopher, a novelist, an explorer. She had long since noted his virtues, but it took her much longer to concede that he had his flaws.

Perhaps hoping to bring about a change in her internal weather, she paused to contemplate Lorenz Umbreit's shortcomings. She had not lived with him, could not imagine his German life. But after fifteen months of working with him, she realised he was rather complicated. He might have steely nerves, but he could be moody and prickly and stubborn, a man who did not find it easy to admit that he might be wrong.

Now and then, she had heard him pace in his office, his boots thumping back and forth between desk and windows.

Calliope herself was given to grappling with her dilemmas either while taking solitary walks or lying awake in bed. But after three sleepless nights, she knew that neither Umbreit's approach to problem-solving, nor her own, could ever generate an answer that would come to the surface shining with the light of unequivocal truth.

And, perhaps, in his own way, Lorenz Umbreit had reached the same conclusion. For when she finally returned to the town hall, when she arrived upstairs to report for work, she found Umbreit's office door locked. A pinned note said he would be in Mytilene for the next few days. Sergeant Reis would be at the office every evening, between six and nine.

And that was all. A handwritten note, a closed door, a surfeit of emotion that left her feeling paralysed.

She remained standing outside the German office, clutching pen and notebook. Beyond the door, the room seemed to be vibrating with something. She put her ear to the solid door. A rock bee seemed to be trapped in Umbreit's office, buzzing incessantly. The sound was so close, so loud, it might have been issuing out of her own feverish brain.

But there was something else behind that locked door: a faint, familiar smell that was just beginning to tug at her heart. Ink. The whiff of spilled ink. Three days had gone by, but the acrid smell still wafted through the keyhole and under the door, gradually invading her nostrils. Vaguely, Calliope supposed that Umbreit hadn't had a chance to get the wall whitewashed and the pine floor bleached. For reasons she could not have explained, the thought made tears flood her eyes all over again. She turned away from the office door, but the odour of ink went on clinging to her nasal membranes.

She began to make her way down towards her own office.

VII

In mid-November, Lorenz Umbreit was transferred to Mytilene, ostensibly to replace a senior officer wounded by partisans after leaving a local brothel with his adjutant. The visit to the brothel was quickly hushed up by the German authorities; the swift reprisal was widely publicised. Ten Mytilene natives had been rounded up at random, then publicly executed. One happened to be a friend of Calliope's uncle, but she was less interested in the coincidence than in her own ongoing turmoil.

Although, with mutual resolve, she and Umbreit conducted themselves as if nothing had transpired between them, she assumed that he had personally requested the transfer. She admired him all the more for his decisiveness, his masterly discipline.

But the transfer, it turned out, was not meant to be permanent. Umbreit informed the Molyvos council that he would likely be reassigned once the wounded officer was back on his feet. Meanwhile, Lieutenant Franz Dwinger would be overseeing operations in both Petra and Molyvos. Sergeant Reis would remain to carry on routine business; Umbreit himself would be back for occasional inspections.

All these changes left the Molyviates' nerves jangled, but Calliope and her Resistance colleagues had at least one reason to feel a measure of guilt-tinged relief: Makis Kouches, the Petra farmer caught negotiating for hand grenades, had committed suicide. He'd been hauled off to Gestapo headquarters and thrown in jail, where he reportedly consumed pellets of rat poison. It was unclear how much

Kouches had known about the Molyvos connection. The only thing Dhaniel could ascertain was that the farmer had poisoned himself *before* undergoing interrogation.

Calliope had fallen into the habit of dropping in at the clinic after taking Sappho for a walk. Now that there were no medicines left, many chose to call on Sultana the herbalist; those who still wanted to consult Dhaniel usually came in the morning.

One late-November afternoon, while Calliope and the doctor sat talking in the surgery, Molyvos's dispirited men were beginning to gather in Rozakis's *kapheneion*. Odysseus the beekeeper was seated by the window with Michalis the sexton and the blacksmith brothers when the village baker went by with his stout, rosy-cheeked wife. Petros Morales was rumoured to be a German collaborator, though he had always been known as a 'domestic cat', a man who preferred to stay home with his family. It was a preference that occasionally rankled, but not as much as Morales's smugness. His appearance was not imposing, but he strode with the air of a pasha venturing out with his wife for an evening stroll. Elektra had long since lost her beauty, but she'd passed it on to her three daughters, the youngest of whom was still unspoken for. The eldest had married a Mandamados merchant, the second the harbour master's son. It was to the latter's house that Petros and Elektra were heading that day.

The beekeeper, who lived in the baker's neighbourhood, knew the family better than anyone at his table. When Paraskevas the blacksmith asked whether the baker really was a German collaborator, the old man looked up from the cigarette he was rolling and gave a reluctant shrug.

'What can I tell you?' He made a show of lighting his cigarette. 'I don't know this for sure and, well, you know me, I never believe what I ain't seen with my own two eyes. But…' Odysseus lowered his voice, going on to speak of a recent night when he heard strange noises coming from the bakery.

'It was after two and I was still awake, scratching away like a flea-bitten dog. How a man's supposed to get any sleep with this eczema, I don't know! Still, I know what I heard. Though, mind you, I ain't saying I know what it means, I ain't—'

'Ach, get to the point, will you?' snapped Natis, the bachelor blacksmith.

Odysseus shifted in his chair. He let his voice drop another octave. 'It was very late and quiet as a tomb, see? And… well, there I am, tossing in my own bed, when I suddenly hear a noise – someone going into the bakery!'

'At two in the morning?'

'Around two.' Odysseus took a long sip of tea. 'So I ask myself, I ask, what would a man be doing in his shop at such an ungodly hour, eh? What with the curfew and all… you tell me! He hasn't baked so much as a crust in months!'

The four men toyed with their worry beads, chewing on all this.

'So, d'you see anything or not?' asked Paraskevas.

'How could I see anything? You expect me to run out in my pyjamas?' Odysseus paused, hacking. 'Anyway, you know what they say… they say—'

But this thought, too, was to go unvoiced because Michalis the sexton suddenly decided to have his say. He was clutching his jaw, talking through a toothache. 'Ach, people say all sorts of things!' He gestured dismissively. 'If you ask me, we're all getting too suspicious. If you believe everything you hear, everyone's father or brother or cousin is a collaborator and—'

'Yeah, yeah, we know.' Paraskevas patted the sexton's shoulder. 'The devil might be boiling human flesh under your nose and you'd say it was *stifadho* cooking!'

This statement generated splutters of mirth, for it was perfectly true: the sexton was a man who, even with an asthmatic son and an infected molar, tended to see only the best in people. Tall and gangling, with protruding eyes and an exceptionally long neck, he was known for his resemblance to an ostrich, and a fondness for salacious jokes.

'Well,' he was saying now, 'who knows, maybe he had a rendezvous, like, with some dishy wench, eh?'

'Petros? With eagle-eyed Elektra watching him day and night?' Odysseus chortled, scratching away. 'You don't know—'

'That's just it: we don't know a thing,' Michalis ventured, only to be stopped by a jolt of pain. There used to be an itinerant dentist who would come to Molyvos once a week, but all that had ended with the Occupation. 'I think,' he persisted, 'I think—'

'Ach, go on with you,' Paraskevas interposed. 'Where there's smoke, there's fire. Why doesn't anyone accuse *me* of being a collaborator?'

The sexton tried to argue, but the more he protested, the more strident the men became in defending their own suspicions. Soon, they were railing not only against the baker but against other villagers who did not seem diminished by the Occupation. By now, men at other tables had jumped in, each new voice fuelling the debate. Natis, the bachelor blacksmith, did not say much, but anyone who cared to glance at him would have seen the nerve pulsing in his forehead.

Suddenly, he banged his huge fist on the table, making the glasses rattle.

'I say, why don't we go to investigate?' he boomed, twisting in his chair. A tailor known as Fat Dinos was seated nearby with his two cousins. 'What d'you say, *phile*?' the blacksmith called out. 'Shall we go see what the baker's been up to?'

'That puffed-up bastard?' The tailor's button-like eyes flashed in his sagging face. He was no longer fat but seemed as stuck with his name as he was with the memory of his humiliation. It was not by chance that Natis the blacksmith had turned to Dinos. Everyone knew that the tailor had once asked for Morales's eldest daughter and had been spurned. He had finally married chatterbox Evgenia's daughter, whom he was given to taunting in public.

'Well, what are we waiting for? Let's go!' Dinos hollered. 'Let's all go and see!'

VIII

In subsequent days, the police chief would be able to establish only that the blacksmith brothers had been the rabble-rousers. No one wanted to talk, not even the *kapheneion* owner, who insisted that he'd been washing dishes when the trouble started. The police chief seemed to believe Rozakis but, as Mirto would eventually point out, his elder daughter, Dora, had been jilted by the baker's brother, so how was anyone supposed to know the truth?

It was a tragic muddle, there was no doubt about it. This was what Mirto would say later that night, after Calliope returned home. She had been on her way from the clinic, had just reached her own neighbourhood, when she first heard the commotion on the baker's street. Sappho was sniffing the evening air, straining towards the hubbub. Calliope followed, tense but curious.

By the time she arrived on the scene, a dozen men had rushed up from the *plateia* and were surging towards the bakery, joined along the way by others swinging pitchforks, axes, shovels. Calliope recognised Eleni Bastia's father and uncle at the head of the pack, their eyes bloodshot, the veins in their necks bulging. She drew back, scolding Sappho, who kept trying to leap into the fray. Petros Morales was nowhere to be seen, but the frenzied mob pressed on towards his shop, forgetting about the curfew.

A shiver ran through Calliope's bones. The wind was snarling over the men's heads, snatching at their hair as they converged on the shuttered bakery, chopping, hammering, jeering. It was almost dusk now. Fragments of metal were flying towards the roof when a triumphant cry rose from the maddened throng, followed by whoops of delirious joy.

'Ach, the bastard!' someone yelled from the entrance. 'Look at these shelves, will you? Coffee, sugar, jam—'

'The jam's Bulgarian!' someone piped up. 'How did the pig-fucking bastard manage to get jam from the Bulgarians anyway?'

'How? It's clear as day, you muttonhead: the Bulgarians are Hitler's allies... oh, look at that: cigarettes!'

It would not take the police long to work out that the baker had been in cahoots with the harbour master, who must have bribed some German soldier in charge of foodstuffs. The harbour master had an office on the waterfront; the baker, whose daughter was married to the harbour master's son, had ample storage space. It all made perfect sense.

The mob, however, had no interest in such speculations. Within minutes, dozens of men were storming out of the bakery, gleefully clutching packages, boxes, jars; a handful of women had elbowed their way in, egging each other on.

'Don't just stand there!' the beekeeper's wife shrieked at Calliope. She stooped down to retrieve an accidentally dropped package. 'Leave your dog and go grab something before the Germans get here!'

Calliope did not budge, but it would later occur to her that had she been as hungry as her neighbours, she might have been tempted to join in the looting. As it was, the only other person who remained empty-handed was Hektor the fool, who kept jumping up and down beside her, hooting with excitement. Finally, Calliope headed home, but she'd barely rounded the corner when Hektor began to scream.

'Fire! Fire! Fire!'

Calliope spun around, tugging on Sappho's leash. Flames were darting out of the bakery windows, snapping at the thickening dark. Several looters were jostling to get out: coughing, shouting, clutching packages.

'*Aman, aman*, they've set fire to the bakery!'

'Oh, the saints preserve us! My husband's still inside!'

The women were still shrieking, the crowd still gabbing, when a high-pitched wail rose from within the bakery. Calliope recognised the voice instantly. The woman was their neighbour, the *hamam* caretaker's widow. In the frantic rush towards the exit, her sixteen-year-old daughter, Melpo, had been trampled down. Skinny little Melpo, with her potato nose and big goofy smile!

All at once, everyone's interest shifted away from the burning shop towards the unconscious girl. A neighbour shrilled at her son to run for the doctor. 'Hurry, *kale*, hurry! Tell him to come at once!'

In the terrible excitement that had gripped the crowd, no one noticed the wild-eyed baker. Morales had finally turned up, had briefly stopped on a shadowy corner, then taken to his heels. It was later said that he must have been fleeing to his daughter in Mandamados. The last man to see him alive was *Papa* Iakovos, who had been ministering to the gravedigger on the outskirts. The priest would later report that the baker had been running for all he was worth. But as the *papadhia* would later say over and over, 'When your fate's chasing you, neither God nor the devil can save you from its clutches!'

The baker's fate was to be blown up by a German mine. Molyviates had learned to recognise the danger signs, but it was dark by then and Morales had not been in a state to exercise caution.

Eventually, both the police and Lieutenant Dwinger arrived on the scene. Some of the men who had participated in the looting were now trying to stop the flames from spreading. By midnight, everyone had heard about the torched bakery.

Only two men seemed indifferent to these goings-on: Michalis the sexton, whose toothache was to torment him all night, and Stamatis the headmaster, who had his ear pressed to his wireless, intent on far more momentous events. For while the bakery was going up in flames, General Montgomery's troops were fighting a triumphant battle in Egypt, finally forcing the Germans to retreat.

It would turn out to be the first decisive Allied victory.

IX

'I told them!' the fortune teller croaked from under her crumpled bedclothes. 'I *tried* to tell them, but no one would believe me!'

She was speaking to Mirto and her sister, Elpida, who had stopped for a bedside visit. Old Zenovia was down with shingles but, back on Good Friday, she had predicted a sudden turn in the tide of war. 'No later than the end of the year!'

It was not yet Christmas, but Zenovia's prophecy seemed to be coming true, even as her own condition appeared to be worsening. Back home in her own kitchen, Mirto declared that old Zenovia might benefit from some boiled cod soup; the latest news from Russia, she added, might even provide an instant cure!

The Germans were losing the battle in Stalingrad. This provided a modicum of hope around the world, but the dying in the village continued.

The baker and poor Melpo were not the only ones to die. Fanis the gravedigger had also passed away, as had Athena Bastia, Eleni's mother. The blacksmith's wife had grown passive after her son had run off to join the guerrillas, but the arrest of her husband and brother-in-law must have seemed like the last straw. Still, who would have expected a herbalist's daughter to mistake a destroying angel for the common button mushroom? Was it possible that Athena's death was no accident? That she had simply had enough of the bone-wearying struggle?

Such were the snatches of conversation Calliope caught wherever she went. The villagers mourned Fanis, Athena, and poor, backward Melpo, but none had grief to spare for the baker's widow. With no one to provide for herself and her youngest daughter, Elektra had been forced to exchange Marika's dowry house for a winter's supply of flour and potatoes. Farmers could name their price these days. After all, you couldn't eat mortar and stones, could you?

Elektra had lost the house, then shut herself up with poor Marika. And, no matter how people had felt about the baker, it seemed as if the torching of his shop had roused some pernicious spirits threatening to slip across every threshold. This, at least, was Calliope's feeling as she passed Elektra's house, bearing her mother's fish soup for the fortune teller.

There was no response at Zenovia's, but most villagers didn't bother locking their doors during the day if they were inside. Thinking that the old woman might still be napping, Calliope decided to leave the soup on the kitchen table. It was just after six o'clock. She opened the door, recoiling from the cat stench. As always, there were cats everywhere, most of them gathered in the hallway, around the kerosene stove, which did not seem to be working.

'*Kyria* Zenovia?'

Calliope had stopped at the foot of the stairs, her skin prickling. She thought she'd heard something: an odd gulping sound. Had she imagined it? She took off her wooden clogs and set her basket down.

'*Kyria* Zenovia?'

She began to ascend, certain now that the intermittent gasps were coming from upstairs. She followed the sound all the way to the master bedroom, pausing at the half-open door. She gave it a slight push, holding her breath.

The old woman's bedroom had four large windows, but all the shutters were closed. There was a faint smell of lemon geraniums and stale urine, but also some other, vaguely familiar odour Calliope couldn't identify. She took another step, casting her eyes about until she made out the large murky bed. Was the old woman trying to bury her sobs in the pillow?

'Are you all right, *Kyria* Zenovia?' Calliope padded across the room, accidentally stepping on the tail of a cat curled on the bedside rug. The cat snapped at her ankle, hissed, then vanished under the bed. '*Panaghia mou!*'

Spinning, Calliope threw herself at one of the windows, flinging the shutters open. She stood leaning out, filling her lungs with air. When the nausea subsided, she turned, took a step towards the bed, then shrank back with a hoarse exclamation.

In the tangle of blankets lay Hektor the fool, his arms wrapped around Zenovia, his head pressed against hers on the embroidered pillows.

'Hektor?' Calliope whispered. 'What are you doing here?'

No answer. Calliope stepped closer. She repeated the question. Hektor raised his head, his face blotchy with grief. He was dressed in his outdoor clothes, but his hair stood up as if he had spent all night tossing and turning. All around him, all around Zenovia's inanimate hump, lay a dozen or so cats, some dozing, some languidly turning their heads to blink at the intruder.

Hektor went on sobbing. Fresh tears kept spurting out of his eyes, gushing down his stubbly jaws, while Calliope stood transfixed, her stomach knotted with intense but not quite coherent emotions. An early-evening breeze came up from the sea and was stirring the fetid air. The stench came from a chamber pot underneath the bed.

Hektor seemed to have forgotten all about Calliope. He was touching Zenovia's face: her parchment-like cheeks, her withered mouth, her broad, furrowed forehead. His own face wore the reverent expression a priest might wear while unwrapping a religious relic, or the most ordinary of men on first stroking the face of his newborn child.

Another moment passed. Hektor raised himself up, letting his eyes travel from the old woman's face towards Calliope's. He had finally stopped sobbing and was now gazing at her imploringly, his mouth jerking with the effort of conveying an impassioned message.

'She... she...' he kept sputtering with a sort of hoarse hiccup. 'She...'

But Hektor could not quite bring out the fact of Zenovia's death, and it didn't matter, for by now Calliope knew all there was to know. She padded closer to the bed, then reached out to the quivering, blubbering man, who had for years lived in the old woman's shed.

'It's all right, Hektor,' she said. 'It's all right. I understand.'

TWO

I

Lorenz Umbreit was still in Mytilene when the troubles in Petra started. The island had by then been occupied for nearly two years. Calliope would eventually say that had Umbreit still been in charge, the tragic events would never have happened. There were many Petrans who shared this view; others said that had their schoolmaster's wife not been sleepwalking the night before, had Makris had a proper night's rest and had less weighing on his mind, he would have surely used the brains God had given him and not stuck out his neck for the Germans to axe.

Petra's schoolmaster was a heavyset man who had spent his life avoiding physical exertion. He had turned thirty-eight that spring, but there was something comical about him – the ruddy complexion perhaps, or the bulbous nose. Achilleas Makris was nonetheless esteemed for his wide-ranging knowledge, as well as his evident affection for his charges. If he chanced to see a mother berate her child, or a father box his son's ear, the schoolmaster was sure to intervene with all the authority vested in his position. Molyviates who had married into Petra families said he reminded them of Philippas Adham, God sanctify his soul. Their Petra relatives grumbled but took Makris's meddling in their stride. A childless man could not be expected to understand anything about raising children, much less keep his nose out of people's business.

But Makris had his own worries. Soon after Lieutenant Franz Dwinger had been posted to Petra, his wife, Alkesti, had started sleepwalking. The night before the events leading to her husband's death, she had left the house around midnight and went strolling along the beach. There were those who thought there was something suspicious about these nocturnal walks. It was a well-known fact that Achilleas Makris, fourteen years older than Alkesti, was even more besotted with his lovely wife than with the schoolchildren. It was equally well known that no good ever came from immoderate love for one's spouse, especially one who had been talked into marrying against inclination.

Makris found his wife sometime after midnight. He ushered her home and put her to bed, singing her to sleep as one would a child. But he himself could not sleep, and spent half the night reading Babylonian myths. In the morning, he went to school, doing his best to impart knowledge to his young charges. School attendance had improved in the past year, thanks to the relief programme organised by the Red Cross. With flour flown in and soup kitchens set up, island children were no longer in danger of starving; some even seemed hardy enough for occasional mischief.

The schoolmaster permitted himself only one indulgence: one glass of ouzo on his way home. The day after he found his wife on the beach, Makris locked the school door, waved to the children playing in the yard, then headed to the *kapheneion*. A housewife painting her fence later recalled his asking after her ailing parents; a young mother joggling her infant in the doorway remembered his pausing to pinch her son's cheek, commenting on the delicious smells wafting from her kitchen. Makris said something about hungry bears not being able to dance, and continued on his way.

As he turned the corner, the schoolmaster spotted two schoolboys crouching next to a German motorcycle. The vehicle had a sidecar and was routinely used by the Germans for the Petra–Molyvos commute. As a rule, it was parked outside the Wehrmacht's well-guarded headquarters. But Dwinger and his adjutant had just learned that Lakis the hunchback might be a Resistance member, and had gone in to investigate. Old Lakis was no more than fifty, but he was a sickly man who had been talked into helping the Resistance, only to be denounced by an aggrieved neighbour.

Dwinger and his adjutant could not have expected to stay very long, but it was long enough for the schoolboys to spot the parked motorcycle. They looked like children retrieving a ball or chasing a kitten, but something about them stopped the schoolmaster in his tracks.

'*Yassas, pedhia!*' Makris lumbered down the alley, but the two boys took to their heels, accidentally dropping the knife they'd been using to slash the motorcycle's tyres. One of the boys managed to escape, but his classmate, a local fisherman's son, tripped and went sprawling across the cobblestones. For a second or two, he lay in the alley, stunned, then scrambled to his feet, reaching for the abandoned penknife.

At that precise moment, Dwinger and his adjutant emerged, dragging the chalk-faced hunchback between them.

The boy was attempting to flee when the shot rang out. It reverberated beyond the alley, followed by a child's scream, then the schoolmaster's cry of protest.

'Do not touch him!' Dwinger's voice answered. *Fass ihn nicht an!*

The command pinioned Makris in mid-stride, his face wobbling like a drowning man's. The fisherman's son lay crumpled in the dirt, clutching his leg.

Makris had fallen silent, but the fracas had drawn a knot of men out of the *kapheneion*, their fists hanging like dead birds at their sides.

The schoolmaster was doing his best to control his body. Dwinger had let go of the hunchback and was shoving his pistol back into its holster, calmly, deliberately. He regarded Makris through half-closed eyes, his mouth lifting at one corner. Even without the sneering expression, Dwinger's was not an endearing face, his flinty eyes suggesting intimate knowledge of everybody's worst secrets. He knew Makris better than he did anyone else: the schoolmaster was the Germans' interpreter in Petra.

'He's a child… just a child, for God's sake!' Makris's voice quavered, speaking the enemy's language. He made a frantic motion towards the bleeding boy. 'He needs help… he needs medical attention!'

The German regarded the gesticulating man for a moment, bared his teeth in something resembling a grin, then slid his whistle into his mouth, and blew.

Instead of reinforcements, a young man in a dark suit was shouldering his way through the crowd. 'I'm the doctor!' he kept repeating. 'The doctor!'

In fact, the closing of Greek universities had left Panos Gazetas short of obtaining a medical diploma, but the villagers had welcomed him with open arms when he arrived from the capital, to be betrothed to the mayor's daughter.

But Gazetas, too, was motioned away. There was a bleat of dismay from the crowd, promptly silenced by a threatening gesture from Dwinger. A gust of wind blew someone's hat off, but the hat went unclaimed, lying on the stones between the crowd and the whimpering child.

The aspiring doctor took a decisive step forward.

'*Halt!*' Dwinger spat out. '*Halt!*'

When Gazetas ignored the order, the German pulled out his pistol. He smiled his fiendish smile, took careful aim, then shot the writhing child into abrupt stillness.

'*Eeeegh!*' The onlookers lurched forth, then stopped with their mouths open, like an impassioned chorus arrested in mid-song. The doctor's face had lost its colour; Lakis the hunchback went abruptly limp.

Dwinger whipped around to face the restive crowd. He shouted out a warning, then turned to help his adjutant haul the hunchback up to his feet.

Makris, meanwhile, appeared to be drowning in a sea of loathing. His face working, he flung himself at Dwinger, lunging for his bullish neck. For a beat, the cluster of onlookers froze, their eyes bulging. Then they all spun and scattered like cats fleeing a bucket of water. There was no telling what the authorities might do if Dwinger lost so much as a single hair.

The German escaped unscathed. The schoolmaster's attack had been foiled by the adjutant, who had let go of the hunchback, wrestling Makris into a headlock.

At that moment, three soldiers came barrelling down the alley. Dwinger was shaken, but less so than the fleeing villagers. If they had any doubts about what awaited Makris, it was only because of the schoolmaster's knowledge of German. His knowledge was not always adequate, but Makris was all the authorities had in Petra. And there were those who would later suggest that Dwinger had deliberately provoked Makris so as to get a better interpreter, maybe force the authorities to let him summon the Molyvos schoolmistress?

Petra's school was housed in an old Turkish mansion, with a spacious yard graced by an acacia tree. A couple of farmers came by just as Makris was being roped to the ancient tree. The children had been ordered off the school grounds, but stood watching from behind the fence, along with the dazed farmers. It was this cluster of witnesses that later reported on the schoolmaster's melancholy end.

The end would come with a single bullet to Makris's impetuous heart. But not immediately. Not until Dwinger himself strode to the schoolhouse, black boot viciously kicking at the entrance door. He stopped and peered into the dim interior. Glancing over his shoulder, he called to his adjutant, who strode away, returning with a jerrycan full of fuel.

Dwinger stepped aside, smiling a bit as the soldier splashed the fuel across the threshold. Then Dwinger himself struck a match, as smugly theatrical as a stage magician. The children let out a strangled gasp. A rooster poised on the roof flapped away, cackling dementedly. Dwinger and the bound schoolmaster stood mutely beside each other while the flames spread their arms, snapping up windows and doors, blackboards and desks and children's exercise books.

It did not take long. Seeing the windows burst into flames, Makris exercised his only remaining power. He squeezed his eyes shut, grief blotching his cheeks as black jets of smoke strove towards the sky. There was no shutting out the hissing and spitting and crackling of the spreading flames. Nor, for that matter, the sudden howl of a fisherman's wife who had just found her only son dead in a deserted alley.

Achilleas Makris died soon after. Old Lakis the hunchback was found in his jail cell, dead from cardiac arrest. Franz Dwinger was the only man in Petra who had any reason to celebrate that Easter, but the failed attempt on his life would eventually bring about significant changes in both Petra and Molyvos.

II

Calliope's personal life was among those destined to be touched by the Petra tragedy, but also, just as surprisingly, by the Lyras men's aborted escape.

The foreigner who had masterminded the fishermen's getaway was a mysterious Allied agent named Rupert Timothy Ealing. After the Turks had sent the fugitives back to Lesbos, Ealing was taken in by an elderly widow, an abbot's sister residing just outside Petra. When Dwinger's terror campaign began to intensify, the abbot had the Englishman moved to his monastery. The war was not expected to last much longer. The Germans had finally been defeated at Stalingrad. Japanese troops had been crushed in the Bismarck Sea. Axis forces had surrendered in North Africa. In Italy, Mussolini had at long last fallen from power.

In the summer of 1943, however, an earthquake shook the island, causing widespread devastation. The hilltop monastery of St Mathaios remained standing but would require repairs before winter set in. There would be church officials and municipal inspectors and workmen coming and going. It would be madness to let Ealing stay, the distraught abbot told his Resistance contact.

When he learned that Molyvos had escaped virtually unscathed, the abbot sent an urgent message to *Papa* Emanouil, who quickly offered to shelter the Englishman until his in-laws arrived for their annual visit. Yannis Rozakis agreed to keep Ealing until St Thekla's Feast, then someone else would have to be found. It was considered too risky for a fugitive to stay too long with any one family.

One stormy evening in early October, Dr Dhaniel stopped to have tea with Calliope and Mirto, stunning them with the disclosure that the Englishman was now in their midst. Ourania Nakou, the former seamstress, had promised to take the foreigner that week, but her house had just been searched, so it seemed that she, or perhaps her son, had fallen under suspicion.

'So, here I am,' said the doctor. 'Your company's as delightful as ever, but I confess it's not what brings me here on this dismal evening.' He sipped his tea, looking from mother to daughter, waiting for them to absorb the news. Would they consider sheltering the Englishman, he finally asked. That this was a risky proposition hardly needed to be stated, though their house was probably the safest in the village.

'We would take him in ourselves, but the children—'

'Of course, it's out of the question!' Mirto interjected.

Calliope hesitated, then turned to her mother. 'Are you willing to—'

Mirto made a disgruntled gesture. 'If you're willing, I'm willing!' she snapped. 'He'll have to stay in the cellar, of course.'

'Of course,' said the doctor. 'He speaks French, by the way.'

'Well, I can certainly use the practice,' Calliope said.

And so it was settled. Rupert Ealing moved in towards the end of November.

Mirto cleared out the storage room because the cellar had become damp. The storage space had a staircase leading into the cellar, where the thirty-four-year-old foreigner was instructed to disappear the moment he heard anyone at the front door. He was a quick, wiry man with a thick head of curly hair and the gleeful eyes of an adolescent who has just dreamed up some delightful prank. What with the religious texts in the monastery and Calliope's French novels, he joked, his education would be much improved by the time the war ended.

When he wasn't reading or sleeping, Ealing offered an occasional English lesson. Perhaps because he missed his children, he liked to amuse himself by teaching Calliope limericks and nursery rhymes. He sang or recited them, then wrote the words down with a French translation, instructing Calliope to memorise them.

I'd rather have fingers than toes
I'd rather have ears than a nose
And as for my hair
I'm glad it's all there
I'll be awfully sad when it goes!

That was the beginning of Calliope's acquaintance with English humour and grammar. She had never considered studying a third language, but was delighted to have Ealing's eccentric lessons, and be diverted by his jokes.

But the news that the former seamstress's house had been ransacked kept gnawing at her. She knew that, in the event of an arrest, Ourania would not be able to withstand Gestapo interrogation. She also knew that, should she herself become compromised, Umbreit would not have it in his power to save her.

He was back in Molyvos now, having been transferred after another failed attempt on Dwinger's life. Umbreit was now in charge of the entire coastal region, doing his best to placate the volatile Petrans. He divided his time between the two villages but, through some tacit agreement, he and Calliope continued to avoid being alone with each other.

Mirto was relieved that her daughter was now doing much of her work at home, but it wasn't long before her worries and misgivings gave way to an unexpected concern.

She readily conceded the pleasure of the Englishman's company. She especially enjoyed Rupert's imitations of Hitler, Churchill, Mussolini. But if she'd known that the foreigner was an intellectual who would be engaging Calliope in lengthy discussions, she would never have agreed to take him in. Never!

The Englishman was married, with three young children, but Mirto's anxiety erupted one Sunday, just before morning Mass. Calliope had stayed up late the night before, talking and laughing with Rupert. Mirto herself was about to go to church, leaving her daughter alone with a hot-blooded foreigner under her own roof. She didn't like it, didn't like it at all, she kept saying.

'How do you know he's hot-blooded?' Calliope asked.

'How do I know? How do I know? I know you'd rather stay with him than come to church with me!'

'But Mama!' Calliope puffed her cheeks. 'I stayed home Sundays long before Ealing arrived!'

'That's true as far as it goes, but now you have a much better reason!'

This was the sort of circuitous logic that used to madden Calliope, but now it only made her laugh, for Mirto's maternal intuitions had fallen wide of the mark: she was not at all attracted to Rupert Ealing, if only because her heart had long since declared its allegiance to another. Despite everything, she still felt that everyone in the world spoke one language, while she and Lorenz Umbreit spoke another.

But there was no doubt about Ealing being an exceptional man. They discussed everything, from the progress of the war to some of the philosophical questions she had been grappling with since she'd read Nietzsche. Ealing might have an irreverent side, but he, too, was a deeply curious man, as interested in Mirto's memories and Sappho's canine psychology as in the nature of power, truth, justice.

When, just before Christmas, the time came for him to move on, a forged ID was discreetly delivered by the mayor's brother. With his light brown hair dyed black and his jaws unshaven, Rupert Ealing could pass for a stonemason named Vassilis Roufos. Assuming he kept a low profile, he should have no trouble blending in with Mytilene natives.

The Englishman was to stay with *Papa* Ioannis. The only hitch was his paltry knowledge of modern Greek. Ealing had studied classical Greek, but had been advised to play a deaf-mute. He seemed evasive about his precise purpose in the Aegean, but was known to have studied history and linguistics before the war. On his last evening in Molyvos, he mentioned that he had also acted in amateur theatricals, back in his Oxford days.

'Well, my friend, here's your chance to put your talent to the test,' Dhaniel said, in his accented French. Ealing kept clowning for his hosts, cracking skittish jokes. It was evidently easier to do this than to contemplate tomorrow's venture.

The tension, alas, was allayed neither by jokes nor by the spinach pancakes Mirto had made with the recently donated flour. The efforts of the Red Cross had immeasurably eased villagers' lives, but Mirto herself showed little appetite. She kept biting her lips, wringing her hands, exchanging tense looks with the doctor. Dhaniel ate heartily, offering bits of advice to the Englishman, like an anxious father sending his young son out into the world.

Ealing would be travelling to Mytilene in the mayor's taxi, along with three passengers who had legitimate reasons for a trip to the capital. There would be Yannis Rozakis, whose brother was known to be terminally ill; Stella Gravari, the doctor's mother-in-law, who spent every Christmas with her elder daughter; and the doctor himself, who needed to consult a cardiologist. Dhaniel's occasional chest pains were real, but his trip to Mytilene was carefully timed: his presence made it unlikely that the car would be searched should they run into a roadblock.

Calliope had become so accustomed to living with dread it was hard to imagine a carefree existence. But then, there were so many things none of them could have imagined before the Occupation. Who could have foreseen that she and her mother would some day find themselves harbouring a British fugitive?

On the Englishman's last evening in Molyvos, after the doctor had gone home and Mirto to bed, Calliope and Rupert stayed up alone for the last time.

'We'll miss you,' Calliope said, ready for a final goodnight. She was holding a bowl of oil with a single burning wick. 'Write to us… when it's all over. Please?'

'I will… I promise.' Ealing crossed his heart. He apologised for having no gift to offer for their many kindnesses. 'I hope you come to London some day, though,' he said, kissing her cheek, 'and let us reciprocate.'

'I've always wanted to visit England,' Calliope said.

III

The doctor's mother-in-law had brought blackberry jam sandwiches and a bag of dry figs for the three-hour journey. Having passed safely through Kaloni, they stopped at a pinewood to answer the call of nature and to let Ealing out of the boot. The German interpreter in Kaloni was an inquisitive corporal, often present during random roadblocks. It seemed prudent to keep the Englishman out of sight until they left the region, and again just before entering Mytilene. If there happened to be a roadblock along the way, there would likely be only rank-and-file soldiers.

But there just might be someone with a smattering of French, some show-off chap who would want to know what a stonemason from the capital had been doing in Molyvos. Should this happen, the doctor would explain that the deaf-mute had come to the village hoping to do odd jobs for Stella Gravari, who had occasionally hired him back in Mytilene.

While all this was under discussion, Rupert Ealing was nestled inside the black Ford's boot. When they eventually stopped to release him, the Englishman clambered out, peering about with a long, theatrical scowl.

'Why aren't there any Germans when you need them?' he quipped in French. He had his hands at his waist and was rolling his head to relieve a stiff neck. 'I'm sure they would provide a more comfortable mode of transport!'

'*Certainement,*' said Dhaniel. 'All the way to Gestapo headquarters!'

They laughed. Dhaniel translated their exchange to his mother-in-law while the mayor and the *kapheneion* owner trudged into the woods.

'There are some things one should never joke about,' Stella Gravari said to the doctor. She was a woman who had been raised to conduct herself with good cheer and flawless decorum, but who had grown dour and anxious after her daughter's death in childbirth.

A gust of wind came soughing through the pines and she shivered dramatically.

'*Poh poh poh*, how cold it is suddenly!'

It was two days before Christmas. Kyriakos and Rozakis emerged from the woods to find Ealing standing in the pine-scented air, thoughtfully staring at a clump of trees while eating his sandwich. A bird was trilling somewhere in the wood. Ealing listened with an air of acute attention, soon identifying the melodious bird as a common crossbill.

'*Un bec-croisé des sapins*,' he said to Dhaniel. He swallowed the last of his sandwich, then sauntered into the woods, hands thrust into pockets. The doctor gazed after him with undisguised affection.

'This foreigner seems to know something about everything,' he said.

Kyriakos chortled. '*I* know he's going to get his nuts frozen if he takes too…' He trailed off, remembering the elderly widow. He apologised.

The Englishman came back, settling in between Rozakis and Stella. They were on their way. There were houses, fields, orchards, then the scenery became a monotonous silvery blur. Nothing but olive trees. The sky was as empty and bleak as if the wind had swept every ray of sun to some unknown realm. Ealing busied himself poring over Kyriakos's map. Soon, he drifted off, as did Stella Gravari and Yannis Rozakis. Only the doctor and the mayor remained awake, their eyes fixed on the perilous road ahead.

IV

The farmer, an old man riding a mule cart, was not from Mytilene but from Pamphylia. All the same, he'd heard that things were tense in the capital. Two days earlier, anti-fascist flyers had been distributed all over town and the Germans had failed to capture the culprits. The bastards were now clamping down on all Mytilene residents, the farmer told Molyvos's mayor.

Kyriakos had hailed the stranger on the empty road, hoping for news from the capital. This was not the news he had hoped to hear.

'May they drown in their own piss!' he spat out in parting.

He drove on, raising dust and gravel, speculating about the flyers. As they approached Mytilene's outskirts, Ealing sat up and glanced at his watch. Stella woke as well and began to burrow in her oversized bag.

'Better move the Englishman before we hit the checkpoint,' she counselled.

'Ach, *Kyria* Stella,' Kyriakos said from behind the wheel. 'What d'you take me for? I'm the mayor, for heaven's sake!'

'What, can't a woman express an opinion any more? You would think—'

'Please, let it go, Mother,' the doctor cut in. 'It's his nerves. Try to understand.'

'Well, I have nerves too, you know!' Stella retorted, powdering her nose. 'I'll have you remember that four children are dependent on my surviving this venture.'

'I remember, I remember.' Dhaniel sighed. 'Only—'

'Ach, stop, all of you!' Yannis Rozakis, awake now, gestured irritably. 'How can we keep our wits about us if we don't stop bickering?'

Everyone nodded at this, except for Rupert Ealing, who stopped to blow his nose, then tapped Stella on the shoulder, asking to borrow her compact. He sat scrutinising his own altered features, as if to reassure himself that his English looks had not triumphed over those of the putative stonemason.

'Not bad,' he said. His unwashed hair and stubbled jaws made Ealing look like a simple labourer. It took little effort to imagine him hefting stones and buckets of mortar. He was handing the compact back to Stella when Kyriakos braked on a side road. He was about to open the door for Ealing when the doctor stopped him, thinking out loud.

If the Germans were busy rounding up suspects, he said, their interpreters were almost certainly engaged in extensive interrogations. It was extremely unlikely they would run into any Greek-speaking Germans. 'On the other hand, they're probably hoping to find more of those flyers—'

'So?' Kyriakos said.

'So, they're likely to be inspecting boots today. Maybe we should let him stay with us after all.'

The doctor's idea was tossed back and forth until all agreed that he had a point. All except Stella, who feared that Ealing might give himself away.

'He may look Greek,' she argued, 'but he blows his nose like an Englishman!'

'Don't worry, Mother.' Dhaniel expelled a forbearing breath. 'We'll tell him not to blow his nose if the Germans stop us.' He said something in French to Ealing, who did his best to soothe Stella in his fanciful ancient Greek.

But Stella would not be soothed. 'And what if he sneezes?' she said, addressing the back of her son-in-law's head. The doctor had a way of rubbing the bridge of his nose whenever his patience was being sorely tested. He turned, and was about to say something, when Rozakis roused himself, bestowing a rare smile on the fretting widow.

'Now, now, *Kyria* Stella,' he said, leaning towards her across Rupert Ealing. 'If there's one thing an Englishman does like the rest of us, it's sneeze. Believe me, I heard him do it many times while he stayed with us.'

'Well…' Stella flicked him sceptical glance. 'If you say so.'

Ealing closed his eyes. He appeared to be dozing again when the dreaded barricade appeared in the distance. Three soldiers could be seen, attired in long winter coats, carabines slung over their shoulders. Stella shrank in her seat, muttering under her breath.

'Get a grip on yourself, Mother!' the doctor snapped. 'Try to act normal.' The mayor screeched to a halt, peering through the windshield.

'*Dokumente!*'

A soldier was leaning into the driver's window, his eyes sweeping the fumbling passengers. Perhaps because of Stella's perspiring forehead, or the capacious bag she was clutching, the soldier stopped to scrutinise her face, as if suspecting a male rebel in disguise. He gave the men's IDs a cursory look, but studiously examined Stella's. The old woman's face was drained of colour. She couldn't have looked more worried had hand grenades been stashed in her bag.

The corporal threw the driver's door open. 'Out!' he ordered. 'All of you!' A young man with cornflower-blue eyes, he moved in a jerky, self-conscious way, like a disgruntled adolescent determined to assert his independence.

'Relax,' Rozakis said to Stella, in the tone of voice a father might use to calm a child at the dentist's. 'They just want to inspect the car… it's normal.' For all his size, there was something delicate about the *kapheneion* owner. He managed to get Stella to collect herself, while a tall, reed-like private busied himself searching the car's interior.

The corporal ordered Kyriakos to open the boot; the second private stood looking on, carabine at the ready. A few feet away, the passengers clustered on the edge of a ravine, doing their best to look bored.

Suddenly, an old woman came toddling out of a farmhouse, gesticulating wildly. She was shouting as she crossed the road, her voice scratchy, as if from excessive use.

'What's she yattering about?' the carabine-brandishing private asked, scowling ferociously. He was a good-looking young man whose expression said he would rather be anywhere in the world than on this foreign, windblown patch of earth. For all they knew, though, this could be a Resistance plot. The old peasant might be there as a diversion; the passengers could be guerrillas waiting to strike.

'She's lost her lamb,' Dhaniel said, forgetting he was not supposed to know German. The crows in the tree shrieked, as if in sudden glee – *krrah, krrah, krrah.*

'Her lamb?' The soldier gave the crone a sceptical going-over. Dressed in black from head to toe, she was wringing her hands, tearfully demanding whether any of them had seen the straying animal. Getting neither help nor clues, she turned away, peering into the ravine with her cloudy eyes. She was muttering to herself, alternately appealing to the Virgin and calling to her straying lamb.

'Where are you, where are you, my little rascal?' There was a bleating from within the ravine. 'Ach, there he is, the trickster!' The old woman's face broke into a toothless grin. 'Come, you little rascal!' she shrieked, scurrying off on her crooked legs. 'I can see him now! He's there!' she cried. 'Come—'

'Tell her not to go into the ravine,' the German private cautioned. Dhaniel translated, but the woman blundered on, flapping a reassuring hand.

And then, both the soldiers and the passengers became distracted.

The corporal was slamming the boot door, his disgruntled expression leaving no doubt: he had fully expected to find contraband in this village taxi. He glanced at Stella Gravari, then ordered the private to frisk the passengers, starting with the lady. In the distance, they could still hear the bleating of the lamb, the old peasant's voice calling, calling.

When Stella understood that the soldier meant to search her person, she uttered a wail of protest. The doctor let out a martyred sigh. The soldier looked tense, waiting for him to persuade his mother-in-law to calm down and let him do his job.

Stella wasn't going to make it easy. She was still protesting when something exploded in the ravine, sending blasts of smoke towards the wintry sky.

'Ach, *Thee mou*, a landmine!' Rozakis's fingers were tugging at his jowls.

'A landmine?' Stella crossed herself, then began to jabber away. The air was thick with smoke and dust but, all at once, the lamb was heard bleating again: a faint, plaintive sound rising from the bed of the seething ravine.

The soldiers were still peering down, still scratching their heads, when a second explosion was heard – a deafening sound drowning out the crows' cacophony, the lamb's pitiful bleat, the Greeks' cries of dismay, the Germans' confused exclamations. Both passengers and soldiers had flinched back from the edge of the ravine, muddled by stench and dust. For a moment, no one uttered a word, until the corporal turned to speak to the private. Dhaniel was the only one paying attention.

'Don't worry,' the soldier was saying. 'Her family will thank us... one mouth less to feed.'

He was about to add something but, catching Dhaniel's look, stopped and cleared his nose, fidgeting with his cap. For a short spell, perfect silence hung over the dust-shrouded roadside. The entire universe seemed to be holding its breath, as if waiting for some divine power to wash it all away and make it new again.

V

Yannis Rozakis and Kyriakos the mayor had been drinking for two hours when the gypsy entered. They had come to celebrate their successful mission, and to pass secret documents to Orestes Fotiadis, who'd owned the Molyvos pharmacy before the Occupation.

The Mytilene *kapheneion* was pleasantly warm, tantalisingly scented by roasting chestnuts. There was a constant hubbub, a spirit of bonhomie sharpened by the dropping temperatures. Rozakis had never shed his forlorn air after his son failed to return from Albania, but Kyriakos was in high spirits, especially after Orestes joined them with a carafe of ouzo.

With the shortage of medicines, the pharmacist was no longer working, but he belonged to a landowning family and, in the third year of the Occupation, was still fat-bellied, still had the soft, plump hands of a complacent bishop.

But there was nothing complacent about Orestes. His small eyes might resemble raisins pressed into a fresh bun, but they were as keen and alert as a spy's.

He was facing the entrance when the gypsy came in, tossing her plaits. He recognised her immediately, recalled buying a yo-yo from her back in Molyvos.

Rozakis remembered her as well, but the mayor didn't.

'Glykeria, eh?' Kyriakos was ogling the stranger. 'Good name for a dishy wench,' he said, belching into his ouzo.

The gypsy had come to peddle holiday chocolates. She was offering them to two well-dressed men when Orestes and Kyriakos rose to relieve themselves. Rozakis stayed behind to keep their table. The *kapheneion* was packed. Rumours were flying that a German ammunition truck had been blown up near the port.

Kyriakos and Orestes disappeared behind the utilities door. The secret documents quickly passed from the mayor's hands into the ex-pharmacist's. The urinals stank, but the mayor seemed determined to share every detail of that morning's mission. Orestes listened, looking a little bored, or perhaps just tired.

By the time Kyriakos finished his story, the gypsy had worked her way towards the back of the room, where Rozakis sat smoking. She cast a casual glance in his direction, paused, then sauntered towards him, a yelp of recognition escaping her throat.

'I remember you!' she crowed. She stood scanning his features, her head canted as she strove to place him. The *kapheneion* owner had aged since the Albanian draft, but there was still the prominent nose, and the birthmark above his eyebrow.

'You're from Molyvos, aren't you, my friend?' The gypsy stood beaming. 'You own the *kapheneion*, don't you?'

'I do.' Rozakis dragged on his hand-rolled cigarette, then tapped off the ashes, barely glancing up.

'Sure, I remember you,' the gypsy went on. 'You were… you offered my boys a plate of beans.'

Rozakis shrugged.

The gypsy remained standing, a box of chocolates pressed below her breasts. 'So, what brings you to Mytilene?'

'Family matters.' Rozakis swished the ouzo in his glass. He watched Orestes and Kyriakos squeeze their way back among the marble-topped tables.

'Well, sir,' said the gypsy, 'how would you like to buy a chocolate or two? Pure milk chocolate, top quality and—'

Rozakis cleared his nose. 'No, thank you. I don't like sweets.'

'But didn't you just tell me you had a family?' The gypsy had stepped back to make room for Kyriakos and Orestes. 'A wife, children? St Basil's Day is just—'

'Here, I'll buy one,' Orestes said, reaching into his pocket. 'For my grandson. How much?'

'For you, sir, one thousand drachmas.'

'Ach, go on with you!' Orestes's flaccid cheeks shook with merriment. 'Here, this is as much as you'll get from me. Take it or leave it.'

They finally settled on five hundred drachmas. The gypsy stashed the bills between her breasts, winking at Kyriakos. The mayor might occasionally drink too much, but women were nonetheless drawn to his flashing eyes and leonine head of hair. Rozakis rose from the table.

'Where are you going?' asked Orestes. 'It's still early—'

'A friend of my brother's just walked in. I want to say hello.' Rozakis's brother had died several months earlier, but his death had gone unreported so that the family could benefit from the extra food coupons issued by the Red Cross.

'How 'bout you?' the gypsy asked Kyriakos. She had slid past Rozakis's chair and leaned forward, thrusting the chocolate box out towards the mayor.

Kyriakos appeared indifferent to the sweets. His gaze was riveted to the gypsy's breasts, which were pushing out roundly against her brick-coloured sweater.

'I don't care for chocolates,' he said, reaching for his glass.

'Huh? What is it with you Molyviates?'

'There's a war on, lady,' Orestes said irritably. 'Not everyone can afford to blow money on sweets, you know.'

The gypsy turned, her tongue darting over her lips. 'True enough, sir,' she said. 'But it's holiday time. Even in wartime, there must be a little sweetness, no?'

Orestes made an ambiguous gesture. 'You're wasting your time, lady.'

'Ach, what's time, sir, when you're in good company?' The gypsy cackled, turning to smile into Kyriakos's eyes. 'Aren't I right?'

The Molyvos mayor sat grinning foolishly, like a tipsy, tongue-tied adolescent.

All at once, the gypsy reached into her box. She plucked one round chocolate, peeled back the silver wrapper, and popped it straight into Kyriakos's mouth.

'You might think you don't care for sweets, sir, but you've never tasted Glykeria's!' She held out a finger and flicked a tiny speck of chocolate off Kyriakos's chin.

Orestes drained his glass and pushed away from the table. 'I'm going home!' he announced. The shop owner was beginning to roll down the blackout blinds.

'Don't worry, this one's on me,' the gypsy told Kyriakos. Neither she nor the mayor took any notice of Orestes's departure. Other men were leaving as well, though in recent days the Germans had become lax in enforcing the evening curfew. Rozakis was threading his way back to the table.

'Believe me,' the gypsy was crooning in Kyriakos's ear. 'I could make your life much sweeter, dear sir.'

'Is that so?' Kyriakos grinned, glancing up as Rozakis approached.

'I'll be here until curfew.' The gypsy smiled back. 'If you like, we could leave together.'

Kyriakos slapped the edge of the table. 'Well, why not? See you later,' he said, shifting to make room for Rozakis.

'That… that was a damn good chocolate!' he declared, his eyes on the gypsy's retreating backside. 'Where does she get chocolates like that anyway?'

'Where do you think? She's probably fucked half the German army.' Rozakis waved away a cloud of smoke. 'Be careful,' he said. 'Remember Manolis the barber?'

'Yeah? What about him?'

'She fucked him too, years ago. He let her stay in the back of the shop and, guess what, she ended up pinching his money.'

'Well,' said Kyriakos, 'I'm not a fool like Manolis, am I? Keeping money with a floozy around!' The mayor belched. 'You're forgetting that I… I've been around the world, whereas Manolis… Manolis never even made it to Athens!'

'So?'

'So, I've got experience, my friend! You name a place and I've probably been there!'

'Still and all,' said Rozakis. 'I'm telling you—'

'Japanese, African, Melanesian, you name it!' Kyriakos was going on. 'I've had them all, but you know what?'

Rozakis rose with sudden resolve. 'Come on, let's go!'

'Wait!' Kyriakos picked up his ouzo glass. 'I'm not ready yet!'

'Come on,' said Rozakis. 'It's almost curfew time. We're meeting Dhaniel at six a.m.'

'So? There's almost… almost twelve hours yet!'

Rozakis puffed his cheeks. He pushed his iron-grey hair back from his forehead. 'Are you coming or not?'

'They say gypsies are real hot-blooded.' Kyriakos paused, shooting Rozakis an appraising glance. 'Maybe we could all—'

'Forget it!'

'Well,' said Kyriakos. 'You go then. Go to sleep. I'll see you in the morning.'

'No.' Rozakis spoke calmly, like a sorely tested but unbending parent. 'I'm going to the toilet, then we're leaving… before they start patrolling.'

Kyriakos made a vague gesture, watching Rozakis make his way towards the urinals.

The *kapheneion* was more than half empty now. Rozakis crossed the room, absent-mindedly tousling the hair of the *kapheneion* owner's son, who was sprawled under the counter, reworking a cat's cradle.

He ended up having to wait for a urinal, listening to two men argue about the recent sabotage. It wasn't a long wait, and Rozakis was as fast as a man with a full bladder could possibly be. When he came swinging through the utilities door, however, Kyriakos was gone.

'Fuck!'

Rozakis dashed out, but the street was dark and empty and cold. He stood slightly hunched, swearing under his breath. The moon was high, but the neighbourhood looked deserted. A few languid snowflakes were drifting down, melting as soon as they hit the pavement.

Suddenly, a woman's laughter rang out from around the corner; a bright, echoing laughter, eloquent with a playful, exuberant intimacy.

Rozakis sprinted across the street, but all he could see in the moonlight was an old drunk shambling towards him, his head thrown back, his mouth wide open, intent on swallowing the snowflakes whirling around his head.

VI

'Is your name really Glykeria?'

'Sure. Why? Isn't yours Kyriakos?'

'Kyriakos Himonas. I'm the Molyvos mayor.'

'Is that so?' The naked gypsy rolled on to her side to study Kyriakos's face in the candlelight. Her huge eyes were shadowed. 'Mayor, eh?'

'What, you don't believe me?'

'Sure, I believe you. But you bargain like a Turkish camel trader.'

Kyriakos made a small noise between his teeth. 'I've been around.'

'Oh yeah? Where you been to?'

'All over the world. You name it, I've been there.'

'Ah, you're a sailor then.'

'I was a sailor,' Kyriakos said. 'I told you: I'm a mayor now.'

The gypsy chuckled. She shot an ironic glance towards Kyriakos's thighs. He was slumped against the pillows, bloodshot eyes ranging over the whitewashed bedroom. It was a small room, divided from the kitchen by a hanging grey blanket. Glykeria's old mother slept in the kitchen but was said to be stone deaf.

Kyriakos sat up, shook his massive head, as if trying to clear it, then reached for a cigarette. The room smelled of burning coal and unwashed socks but seemed clean enough, and pleasantly warm.

'Where's the toilet?' he drawled, his gaze seeking out his clothes. The garments were lying in a heap on one of the chairs, next to an old vanity table.

'Outside. Across the courtyard.' Glykeria sat on the edge of the bed, appraising herself in the mirror like a bored princess.

Kyriakos muttered under his breath.

'There's a jar in the corner. Use it if you like.'

Kyriakos hoisted himself off the bed. It was a large iron-framed bed, creaking under his shifting weight. At the foot of the bed stood the brazier, which in his haste he almost stumbled into. Staggering backwards, Kyriakos hit the bedside table, all but upsetting the burning candle. 'Ach, *sto diablo*!'

'Watch you don't singe your *popo*!' Glykeria tittered. She slid a pocket watch from under a pillow and consulted it, then glanced up at the mayor, indulgently amused, like a mother watching a clumsy child.

The mayor shuffled across the room, muttering to himself. The pine floor squeaked under his feet as he reached for the empty jar. Finally, he turned his back on the gypsy and urinated as best he could, a cigarette clamped between his teeth.

'Where are the children?' he asked, getting back into bed.

'Children?'

'Rozakis said you had two boys with you… when you came to Molyvos.'

'Ah, those were my nephews.' Glykeria drew a slow hand down Kyriakos's thigh. 'My sister got sick that year,' she said, falling silent as German soldiers went by, arguing in garrulous voices.

'I drank too much,' Kyriakos said. He spoke to the ceiling, his eyes half-closed, the tin ashtray set on his hairy chest.

'It's all right.' Glykeria patted his arm. 'Take your time. You've got until nine.'

'Why? What happens at nine?'

'Nothing. At nine thirty my man comes from his evening shift.'

Kyriakos turned to face her. 'You mean to tell me you're married?'

Glykeria cleared her nose, making a non-committal gesture.

Kyriakos eyed her for a prolonged moment. 'Well, are you or aren't you?'

'Oh, what business is it of yours?' Glykeria snapped. 'You paid me for two hours. That was the deal, no?'

'I could pay you a little more,' Kyriakos said.

'No, you have to leave. At nine sharp, Mr Mayor.'

He cast her a sidelong glance. 'You making fun of me or what?'

'Nah,' said Glykeria. She had loosened her plaits, as he'd asked, and now lay scrutinising her split ends with a vague sort of interest. Kyriakos continued to watch her.

'How can you sleep with half the men in town if you're hitched?'

'Half the men in town?' Glykeria hooted. 'Where d'you hear that?' She swung a leg over Kyriakos's thigh. 'I only sleep with men I fancy, and there aren't that many. I wouldn't have slept with that fat friend of yours, for example. Not even for a gold-stuffed chest.'

'But in that case... in that case, why ask for money?'

'Why not?' Glykeria stroked his moustache, but there was something taunting in her manner. 'I fancy men, but I fancy money too. What's so strange about that?'

'Hm.' Kyriakos rubbed his gums.

'Anyway,' she went on, 'I support my mother, I support my sister's children. She can't work any more.' Glykeria sighed. In the kitchen, the old woman snored on, muttering in her dreams.

Suddenly, as if to alter the tenor of their exchange, Glykeria rolled over and straddled Kyriakos, her hair surrounding him like a tent. Kyriakos raised his arms and twined them round the gypsy.

He went on embracing her, his mouth sliding down from her neck, his huge hands squeezing her buttocks. The only problem now was a minor one: Kyriakos's body had got pushed back and his head was pressing uncomfortably against the bed frame. He tried to slide down, to roll into a dominant position but, at that precise moment, a mouse came scurrying over the bedclothes – a little grey mouse, disappearing towards the floor.

Kyriakos groaned. 'You've got mice here!'

'What? Oh...' Glykeria laughed. 'Well, you didn't pay for a room at the Grande Bretagne, Mr Mayor.' She sat up and glanced at the floor, then shrugged and gave his genitals a playful poke. 'Ach, ach, ach, Mr Mayor,' she cackled. 'Looks like you've burned yourself out sailing around the world.' She let her head drop back towards the pillow. 'I once knew a sailor from Plomari—'

'Ach, what do I care about your damn sailors?' Kyriakos reached over and put another cigarette to the candle. He'd rolled them earlier, arranging them carefully on the bedside table. 'I wanna celebrate. You got something to drink?'

'No. You've got only fifteen minutes left.' Glykeria yawned. 'What have you got to celebrate anyway?'

Kyriakos chuckled. 'If only you knew.'

'What?' She turned to him. 'What does a mayor do these days anyway? Aren't the Germans in charge in your village?'

'They like to think they're in charge.'

'Aren't they?'

'Yes and no.' Kyriakos laughed. He began to toy with Glykeria's nipples.

The gypsy shifted her weight. 'So, you haven't told me. What are you celebrating?'

'Ah, if you only knew,' he said again. 'If the Germans knew!'

The gypsy's lips tightened. 'The bastards killed my brother-in-law,' she said, staring at the ceiling. 'Picked up a bunch of men because of some brothel incident, and… *bang!*'

'Is that a fact?' Kyriakos scratched his chest. 'Well,' he said thickly, 'in that case… you'll be glad to know we're working on it.'

'Working on what?'

'That, *Kyria mou*, I'm not at liberty to say. But take it from me: I'm no pen-pushing bureaucrat.' He let out a small scoffing sound. 'The men here, your men in the capital, may be stuffing themselves with chocolates, but we… we're doing something to get rid of the bastards.'

'Oh yeah?'

'Better believe it, lady!' Kyriakos went on blustering in this manner, until Glykeria slid her hand under the pillow and consulted the pocket watch again.

All at once, she heaved herself up and swung her legs off the bed.

'Time to go home, Mr Mayor.' She sat for a moment, hugging herself as she looked about, vaguely disgruntled. Kyriakos stirred and reached out for her, but the gypsy shook herself free, laughing, and lowered her feet to the hand-loomed rug.

'It's five minutes to nine.'

The mayor lay watching her get ready. She had her back to him now. All he could see from the bed was her narrow waist, with the taut buttocks blooming out between the dark curtain of hair and the slender legs planted on the rug. 'What's time when you're in good company?' he chortled, echoing Glykeria's own words earlier.

Glykeria spun round. 'Ach, you're finally waking up!' She stood regarding him for a moment, wryly amused. 'The company might be good, but a deal's a deal. Come on, mister.' She made a short whistling sound, cocking her thumb towards the front door. 'Time to go!'

There was a pegboard hanging near the kitchen entrance. Glykeria yanked off her clothes, wriggling into her panties, then into her striped skirt with its elastic band. Naked from the waist up, she picked up her sweater, then stood sniffing it for a moment, her nipples seeking the ceiling. Kyriakos sat perched on the edge of the bed, his pupils dilated with longing.

'But if he's not a real husband,' he ventured suddenly, 'can't—'

Glykeria's eyes flashed. 'I told you, it's none of your business! You've got to go! Now!' Her hand shot out, pointing towards the door.

Kyriakos eased himself to his feet. He was a powerfully built man and, now that his reluctant member was reasserting itself, there was a gleam in his eyes.

Glykeria had pulled on her socks and was beginning to draw a comb through her hair when Kyriakos sidled up to her and tried to cup her breasts. The image was reflected in the vanity's spotty mirror: the fully dressed gypsy and the naked, hirsute man with his large hands splayed over the prominent breasts.

'Ach, you!' Glykeria slapped Kyriakos's hands, wagging a jaunty finger. She snatched up the pocket watch and shoved it under his nose. 'There's no time!' She let out an exaggerated sigh. 'Come back another time and—'

'No,' said Kyriakos doggedly. 'I don't get to Mytilene very often. Why—'

'I said no! Get dressed!' She put on one of her shoes and began to look for the other, plaiting her hair with swift, practised fingers.

She had all but finished when she spotted her shoe behind the curtain. She snapped it up and put it on, tying up the laces. When she looked up again, it was to find Kyriakos slumped back on the edge of the mattress. He was staring at his own tie, which had slipped off the chair and lay across the floor like a silky, striped snake.

'Ach, you're still sitting?' Glykeria hissed.

'I… I can't leave… not now!' Kyriakos protested. He was about to add something, but the gypsy was no longer listening. Chin resolutely thrust out, she headed straight for Kyriakos's clothes. She snatched the tangled garments from the chair, gathering them into a slipshod bundle: the coat and trousers, the shirt and cardigan, the shoes and socks and cotton underwear. Muttering to herself, she marched in the direction of the bed, hugging the clothes to her chest, as if meaning to fling them at their owner. Instead, with one swift movement, she threw open the window and tossed out the rumpled clothes with a little triumphant cry. Kyriakos had sprung up from the bed, but it was too late.

'*Aaaach!*' he bellowed, watching his clothes fall towards the moonlit pavement, coins and bills flying every which way. Kyriakos cast the gypsy a venomous look.

'You better hurry up, Mr Mayor, before someone grabs your stuff, and then what?' Glykeria threw back her head, going off into peals of laughter.

Kyriakos waved a threatening fist. Then he spun and tore across the room, flinging the front door open.

The gypsy laughed and closed the window. Braiding her second plait, she went to the door and was about to lock it when Kyriakos reappeared: a naked, menacing giant frothing at the mouth like an enraged bull. Glykeria tried to slam the door in his face, but Kyriakos kicked it open, dropping his pile of clothes. He stood breathing hard, a ferocious look twisting his face.

'Fucking whore!' he hissed, smacking the gypsy's left cheek. He was about to slap the right, but stopped abruptly, like a man recalling something of great importance. Spinning around, he dashed out again, pausing just long enough to collect his scattered clothes.

The gypsy locked the door, an angry flush rising on her cheeks. She picked up the jar of urine, holding it carefully as she hastened across the room. For the second time, she threw the window open and stood waiting. When Kyriakos appeared, still buttoning himself, the gypsy rose on her tiptoes, then flung the jar out, aiming it straight at the mayor's back.

Kyriakos was bending down to snatch up a folded note from the ground, but somehow, the jar of urine fell wide of the mark. It landed on the pavement with a crashing sound. The gypsy swore.

The mayor, momentarily frozen, glanced over his shoulder, as if expecting another assault. Then he straightened up, wheeled about, and thumbed his nose, hooting like a gleeful boy.

Glykeria stared down for one baleful moment, then slowly closed the window. She was no longer laughing.

VII

One look at Dhaniel's face and Calliope knew he had heard the news, probably from Rozakis, who was just leaving as she approached the clinic. The doctor was going home early. Seeing him come through the gate with his Gladstone bag, Sappho began to wag her tail. She shook her rear end. She raised her head. She barked.

Dhaniel ignored her antics.

Calliope had been on her way to visit her friend Eleni, who was pregnant again, but her husband, Tomas, had stopped her in the *agora*, whispering in her ear. There was a rumour that Yorgos Lyras had been captured in Mytilene. At the cinema.

'The cinema!'

'So they say. It could be some other Lyras.'

Sadly, the doctor confirmed it was indeed Captain Yorgos.

'Can you believe it?' he asked, plodding away from the clinic.

'He's supposed to be lying low and goes to see a Hungarian melodrama, then gets involved in some petty squabble. In the capital!' Dhaniel shook his head, a weary man groping for comprehension.

Two German soldiers were striding towards them, carabines slung over their shoulders. Calliope waited for them to pass, reflecting that Molyviates seemed increasingly indifferent to their own fate. A few had gradually gone mad. The building contractor's mother had begun to eat paper; the *hamam* caretaker's widow had stopped bathing and cleaning her house, but continued to conduct conversations with her dead husband and daughter. Others, like Eleni's mother, had grown apathetic.

'Sometimes I get the feeling that people want… that they deliberately court danger, just to get it over with,' she said to the doctor.

'Ach, I don't know.' Dhaniel heaved a sigh. He thought that men, fierce men like Yorgos, could not tolerate constraints. 'I don't believe they're indifferent to their fate. But this need, this compulsion to assert their independence – it just gets the better of them.'

There was a long, thoughtful pause. It was getting windy. Dhaniel placed a hand over his flapping tie, going on to tell Calliope about the mayor, another hothead, getting himself entangled with a seductive gypsy. 'He and Rozakis almost came to blows over it in Mytilene.'

'Really?' said Calliope. Kyriakos was unpredictable when drunk, but the *kapheneion* owner had always been the village peacemaker. She sighed, glancing at the sea. The sun was starting to set now, sliding down like a giant egg yolk.

'Did you ever meet her, by the way?' asked the doctor. 'She's been here a few times, selling tablecloths and stuff.'

'Oh!' Calliope cut in. She had first seen the itinerant gypsy after school one day, selling yo-yos outside the barbershop. 'A good-looking woman, with a beauty spot on her cheek?'

'She's called Glykeria.' Dhaniel chuckled. 'Queen of Sheba in rags.'

'I thought she looked like a tropical bird,' Calliope said, recalling the first time she had seen the stranger, standing outside the barber's with two little boys. She recalled how quick people had been to blame her children for the subsequent lice outbreak. As if they'd never seen head lice before! Recently, there had been reports that the Germans were sending gypsies to labour camps, along with European Jews.

'Doctor, Doctor!'

Dhaniel glanced over his shoulder. Michalis the sexton was running after them, wild-eyed; his son was having one of his asthma attacks.

'It's a bad one! Please come right away, Doctor!'

'Coming. I'll see you tomorrow,' Dhaniel said to Calliope.

And then he was gone, leaving her on a windy corner, halfway to Eleni's house.

Calliope hesitated, then decided to see her friend another day. It was getting dark, and she had forgotten to bring her night pass. And so she headed home, Sappho trotting at her side. She had gone to the clinic in the vague hope of finding reassurance, only to have her worst fears confirmed. Dhaniel had said nothing about the captain's prospects, but they both knew that Yorgos was bound to be tortured. For one brief moment, the knowledge rose and hissed in her face. But then she resumed breathing and slowly, cautiously, began to back away from the portentous news, as one might do with some slumbering but reputedly vicious beast.

THREE

I

He was known as the Lizard. He had heavy-lidded eyes set in a narrow, pockmarked face, but his voice could be as seductive as a lover's. Seated across from Yorgos Lyras, Heinrich Volkmann gazed at the prisoner with his reptilian eyes. During their first meeting, the interrogator appeared chummy, almost voluptuously relaxed, offering the prisoner a cigarette, plying him with personal questions.

The interview took place in a turn-of-the-century mansion built by a local judge. The Germans had turned the cellar into a jail, where Lyras had spent several days surrounded by little piles of dry bones. The guards were Greek policemen appointed by the Germans. It was they who would eventually tell the story of the captain's imprisonment, how he had scoffed entering his cell for the first time.

'If they think they can scare me with such childish tactics, they don't know who they're dealing with!' he blustered. There were several gaps between his teeth, where the gold crowns had been before the attempted escape to Turkey.

The guards were grimly silent. They remained silent when they heard the captain curse that night, after the resident rats had emerged, scurrying across his prone body, scouring for fallen crumbs. Lyras had eaten a thin broth at noon and two dry slices of bread in the evening. He spent the rest of the night awake, falling asleep only after dawn glimmered in the cell window.

There was nothing to do but sleep. And battle the rats. And watch the weather change in the tiny barred window. A rainy spell gave way to a week of sunshine. Out in the garden, mating doves were beginning to coo; now and then, a starling might flutter by, or a stray cat stop to peer through the grimy window. Winter seemed to be ebbing, but the scents of spring could not penetrate the thick, musty walls.

One overcast morning, two German soldiers appeared in the cellar. They let Lyras wash and shave, then led him upstairs to a stark room, where Volkmann sat waiting. There was a long table with a writing pad and a vase holding a branch of pink almond blossoms. An interpreter stood waiting.

Lyras was uncuffed and offered coffee, bread, jam. Volkmann looked on with the indulgent air of a father watching his son wolf down a favourite treat. But finally, the food was gone, the tray was whisked away. Lyras stirred and belched. Volkmann rose from the table and began to pace. 'Is it true that you're a member of the Greek Resistance?'

Lyras looked into the interrogator's face. 'Yes,' he said, 'it's true.'

'And are you willing to sign a confession to that effect?'

'I am.' Lyras turned to the interpreter. 'Tell him not to waste his time. I'm ready to sign at once. I want to get it over with. Understand?'

The interpreter rendered the request into German, making the Lizard's lips stretch in a thin smile. 'Everything in good time, *Kapitän*,' he said, sitting down. 'We're not in any particular hurry. Are you?'

Lyras muttered something incoherent.

'Would you like to share your thoughts with us?' Volkmann asked, tapping his fingers on the edge of the table. He looked like a bored school principal addressing a churlish pupil.

Lyras was silent, but his right leg had begun to jerk. The room was bare except for the table and chairs. A light bulb was aimed straight at the prisoner's face.

'It's wise of you to be so forthcoming,' Volkmann was saying. 'But we've known about your Resistance connection for a while, *Kapitän*.'

Lyras lifted a shoulder.

'And, well, you seem like a reasonable man. You'll surely understand that we're not offering our hospitality just so you can tell us what we already know!' He laughed, his heavy eyes inviting Lyras to share his joke.

Silence. The fisherman kept his gaze fastened to his helplessly tapping foot.

'So...' Volkmann heaved himself out of his chair and resumed pacing, hands clasped behind his back. 'The first thing we'd like to know is your son's whereabouts. Your elder son, Takis. Would you tell us what happened to him?'

At this, a black spark flashed in Yorgos Lyras's eyes. 'I don't know where my son is. We went our separate ways months ago!' He waited for the interpreter to translate the statement. 'Anyway, I wouldn't give up my son even if I knew.' He looked scornfully into the heavy lizard eyes and said: 'Maybe a German could do something like that. A Greek father, never!'

'Very well.' The German sat down again and steepled his sausage-like fingers. 'We'll try to respect your paternal sentiments, *Kapitän*, but there are some things you can surely tell us. Something about the Englishman, for example?'

'The Englishman,' Lyras echoed, shifting in his chair.

'Yes. The one the Turks sent back with you and your son. Remember him? He goes by the name of Roufos, but I'm told his real name's Rupert Ealing.'

'Sure, I remember him.' Lyras made a vaguely disgruntled gesture. 'But I told you: we all went our separate ways.'

'And you have no idea where the Englishman's been hiding?'

'No!' The captain's calloused hands flew up. 'Look, we're not stupid, you know. We make sure no one has more information than necessary.' He stared at the German squarely. 'For all I know, he's back in England now.'

Volkmann weighed this, studiously examining his nails. 'All

right,' he said. 'What can you tell us about the truck that got blown up just before Christmas?'

'I can tell you this: the first time I heard about the truck was just before the cinema. In fact, I only went *because* I wanted to find out more about it.'

'Why?'

'Why? Why? I'm a curious man! Ask anyone: I always have to know what's going on!'

'Is that so?'

'I swear! I had nothing to do with the explosion. I wasn't even in the capital!'

'And where were you, please?'

'I was... underground.'

'Someone was hiding you?'

Silence.

'Who? Who was hiding you?'

'I can't tell you that!' Lyras let out a loud Turkish curse. 'Hang me if you like, but I can't denounce people who risked their lives for me!' He turned his face towards the interpreter. 'What does he think we are?' He cursed yet again.

Volkmann looked at him for a moment, then pushed back from the table. 'Very well,' he said with abrupt resolve. 'That's all.'

Lyras levered himself out of his chair. He stood rubbing his jaw.

'That's all for today. But I want you to think about my questions, *Kapitän*,' Volkmann added sternly. 'Because I'm going to have more of them and, you know, we're not stupid either.' He grinned, exposing yellow teeth. 'I'm willing to show some understanding where your son's concerned, but I'm not prepared to believe that you can't answer any of our questions.'

He paused and stared at Lyras: his droopy eyes and stubbly jaws, the swollen veins in his neck. 'Now that we've got to know each other, perhaps you'll permit me to be blunt, *Kapitän*: we'll expect greater cooperation from you. Is that understood?'

Lyras remained silent, his huge fists hanging at his sides.

'Take him away,' said Volkmann with sudden pique.

The soldiers led the prisoner back to his cell. They had him strip down. They left him alone. Hours passed. After supper, an officer returned with the interpreter and told Lyras he could get dressed, but would have to spend the night upright, his arms raised over his head. 'It's said to improve memory function.'

Lyras scrambled to his feet. He lifted his arms and stood with his chin raised and his barrel chest thrust out. The window grew black. The rats emerged from their hiding holes. The captain went on standing. Now and then, he lifted a foot and kicked at a rat sniffing around his toes. His arms began to slide down, as if supporting some great invisible burden.

Finally, the beatings started. That evening, there was the butt of a revolver whenever his arms weakened. The following night, a whip made of ox sinews lashed across his back. He appeared at his second interrogation with one of his eyes puffed shut and his lip split in two. There were numerous welts and bruises, invisible under his prison garb. Asked whether he had anything to say, Lyras reiterated his willingness to sign a confession. He was presented with a document attesting to his clandestine activities, along with a formal statement. *Every word was translated for me by the Greek interpreter. I understood everything and hereby confirm this to be an accurate record. The entire interview was translated for me before I signed.*

He signed the same statement day after day. He signed it after his nails were ripped out and his soles scorched with burning cigarettes. He went on signing it after his testicles had been squeezed, but had nothing new to say.

This went on for a week, then suddenly stopped. Lyras was left to languish in his cell. When he began to recover, he was made to lie prone, his feet bound with a heavy rope. A rifle was set between his feet, then slowly twisted, tightening the rope. It was rarely necessary to resort to this measure, but some men were born pig-headed. That was what Volkmann said, watching Lyras through the prison bars.

The following night, a Greek doctor was summoned and attempted to help the prisoner recover from his injuries. Lyras was a stalwart man and he recovered enough to recognise the two shackled men who were brought into his cell a few nights later. Lyras had just finished eating when the men were hauled in. It was dark in the cell, but one of the guards waved a torch in front of the new prisoners' faces.

The two men were Kyriakos Himonas, Molyvos's mayor, and Yannis Rozakis, the *kapheneion* owner, whose younger daughter, Anna, was married to Yorgos Lyras's son.

The captain of the *Eleftheria* buried his tortured face in his hands and let his tears spill over. It was the only time anyone had ever seen Yorgos Lyras weep.

II

The almond trees were vaunting their finest blossoms when the soldiers came for the doctor. They arrived late in the afternoon, as if out of consideration for Dhaniel's professional commitments. There had been no military jeep screeching to a halt in the *agora*, no arrest squad sent over from the capital. The mayor and *kapheneion* owner had been promptly dispatched to Gestapo headquarters in Mytilene, whereas Elias Dhaniel was summoned by two of Captain Umbreit's men to await Major von Herden's arrival the following morning. It was the day scheduled for von Herden's monthly visit; he was not coming expressly to question the doctor. Nevertheless, there was an air of courtesy to this particular arrest, perhaps even a whiff of apology on Captain Umbreit's part.

But none of this was known to Calliope when she first heard the news. She heard it from Hektor, who had come looking for her at the fortress, where she was letting Sappho have her daily run. It was St Theodoros's Day, and the sun was just beginning to set. There were children playing hide-and-seek below the fortress. Somewhere in the distance, a donkey was braying.

Suddenly, Calliope spotted the village fool, with his absurd yellow turban, clambering uphill with the agility of a mountain goat. The moment he made out the schoolmistress, Hektor began to flail his arms. He cupped his hands around his mouth and shouted something, but the wind snatched his words. Soon, he was bounding across the fortress grounds, blubbering: '*Kyria... Kyria!*' He stopped, gasping for breath. '*Kyria*, the doctor, the doctor—'

'What is it, Hektor?' Calliope assumed Dhaniel was needed somewhere.

'The do... the doctor's in t-t-trouble!' Hektor stammered, blinking furiously.

Calliope stared. 'What do you mean, Hektor?' Dhaniel had occasionally complained of chest pains, but the cardiologist had assured him the pains were due either to indigestion or stress. 'Is it his heart?'

Hektor shook his head, vigorously.

'It... it's the Germans... the so... soldiers...' He swallowed hard, desperately hunting for words. 'They... they came to... to get the doctor. He... he's in jail, *Kyria* Calliope!'

'In jail!' Calliope reached out and planted her hands on Hektor's shoulders. She peered straight into his swimming eyes, willing him into greater clarity. 'Have they taken him to Mytilene?'

Again, Hektor shook his head. He turned and pointed towards the town hall, whose pink shutters could be discerned in the distance, among the tiled rooftops. 'He... he's there! The s-soldiers came to get him!' he repeated with urgent emphasis.

'The soldiers came to take the doctor to the town hall?'

Hektor nodded, flailing. Sappho was sniffing something along the stone wall.

'Hektor.' Calliope gestured towards the dog. 'Please take Sappho home for me, will you? Tell my mother I'll be home later. Can you do that for me, Hektor?'

'Y-yes, *Kyria* Calliope. Yesyesyesyesyes!'

'Thank you,' she muttered. And then she whipped around, the wind slapping at her as she fled the fortress, street after street sweeping by while she ran towards the town hall. It was only as she passed the clinic that her suppressed dread finally exploded, sending forth heart-wrenching images of her closest friend – a handcuffed, grim-faced Elias Dhaniel – being led to jail like an animal to the slaughter.

She stopped and retched into a bush. Just a few days earlier, *Papa* Konstantinos, St Mathaios's abbot, had been arrested. As soon as the news had reached Molyvos, *Papa* Emanouil had sent an urgent message to Mytilene. Finally, just yesterday, they'd learned that both Rupert Ealing and *Papa* Ioannis had been transferred to a safe house.

Calliope crossed the village, dimly aware of curious villagers stopping to watch her dizzying progress through the winding streets. She turned a corner. She was close to the town hall now, but still running, fragmented voices wafting her way from doorways and courtyards.

At the town hall, Ourania had come out to fill a jug of water, then paused to greet the midwife and her daughter, who had been paying a name-day visit to Sergeant Theodoros Floros. The three women were exchanging pleasantries when Calliope flashed by, like a breathless animal escaping its predator. She was about to open the heavy portals, but just then Alfred Reis emerged, adjusting his officer's cap. Calliope brushed past him. There was only the indoor staircase now. Just one flight of stairs. She stormed into Captain Lorenz Umbreit's office without knocking.

'Is it true?' She halted in front of his desk, her heart thudding. 'Have you really arrested the doctor?'

Umbreit had risen the moment Calliope appeared in the doorway. He came around with his hands spread in a vaguely helpless gesture. He glanced at her face and his jaw tightened. 'We've brought him in for questioning.'

'Why?' Calliope asked in a strangled voice. 'What's he done to you?'

'To me personally, nothing. Von Herden's coming tomorrow morning and… well, it seems he has questions.'

Calliope weighed all this. 'Can I see him, please?'

'You know I can't do that.' Umbreit thrust his hands into his tunic pockets. 'I… I'd do it if I could,' he added. 'You know I would.' *Du weisst ich wurde.*

Calliope swallowed. 'Will I be present at tomorrow's interview?'

'I… don't think so.' His eyes veered away from her. He stopped and busied himself lighting an oil lamp. 'I believe they're bringing the Mytilene interpreter.'

She made an ambiguous sort of gesture, at once impatient and entreating. 'But he… he's a good man!' she cried. 'He wouldn't harm a fly, let alone a German!'

'I know.' Umbreit stood with his back to the window, fingers rubbing the back of his neck. The early evening's shadows were thickening now. In the back alley, two cats yowled and screeched, courting under the office windows.

At that instant, something seemed to snap in Calliope's head. She stood for a moment, holding out her arms in a vaguely beseeching gesture. Then, seemingly moving of their own accord, her hands drew her forward, coming to rest on Umbreit's forearms. It was the first time she had touched him.

'Please,' she said quietly. 'Please… I beg you to release him. I beg you!'

Although her voice faltered, Calliope's body went on inclining forward, her glittering eyes stating the terms of a bargain she might have come across in some long-forgotten novel.

'I'll do whatever you want,' she said, barely above a whisper. *Ich tue was immer du willst.*

At this, Umbreit stiffened. He compressed his lips and gave her a steady look, searching and bewildered. There was a moment of silence, during which his expression grew stern. He let out a long sigh, then raised his hands and gently – gently but firmly – lifted her palms off his own arms.

'Calliope.' His voice was more strained than ever. 'I understand the doctor's a close friend. I appreciate that you're doing your best to help, but…' He paused, his hand rubbing across his brow, his mouth. 'Do you really think I'm the sort of man who would take advantage of such an offer?'

Calliope averted her gaze.

'I'm sure you know how I feel about you,' Lorenz Umbreit said, relenting a little. 'Nothing… nothing has changed there, but…' He held out a finger and placed it under her chin, forcing her to meet his eyes. 'When… when you offer yourself to me, Calliope, I want it to be because you want me, not… not because—'

'But I do want you!' she heard herself blurt out. 'I do!'

And she did still want him; had become so accustomed to her suppressed desire it had come to seem like just another facet of her perpetual hunger. The prolonged deprivation was so familiar she could hardly remember how it felt to go to sleep sated.

What she could not forget was the doctor's friendship. She thought she would do anything to save Dhaniel. Still, she loved the truth well enough to ask herself later whether she would have been quite so willing to throw herself at Major von Herden.

But she did not ask herself this, or any other question, that day. Her mind, her capacity for thought, had been subsumed by dread. All she could do was stand in the office, trembling, every nerve in her body feeling exposed. She wanted to fling herself at Umbreit, refusing to take no for an answer, but simultaneously longed to make him forgive her manifestly offensive offer.

'I've tried and tried to repress my feelings,' she heard herself say in a defeated voice. 'I thought… I thought you must have known.'

At this, Lorenz Umbreit stopped. He stood staring at her with slow, reappraising eyes. Calliope was motionless, listening to her own heartbeat. Finally, Umbreit shook himself, an inarticulate sound escaping his throat. He reached for her hand. He held it for a long moment, gazing into her eyes.

'If… if you are sincere,' he said, swallowing hard. 'If you are sincere… we must, for both our sakes, wait a little longer. After the war… after the war—'

All at once, abandoned by words, Umbreit reached out and silently wound his arms around Calliope. He held her close to his chest, his lips brushing her ear. 'It can't last much longer,' he said in a barely audible voice. *Es kann nicht mehr lange dauern.* He opened his eyes, drawing back slightly to scan her face, as if to impress upon her the truth of his ardent message. *Es kann nicht…*

But then he stopped, his look flying over Calliope's shoulder, landing at the entrance.

'*Mein Gott*,' he let out, stiffening.

On the threshold to the office stood Ourania the cleaner, her hand clutching at her chest, her eyes pools of horror.

III

'I was so happy when they threw him in jail!' Eleni said, speaking to Calliope. She was not referring to the doctor but to her own unmarried uncle, who had started molesting her during puberty. Natis had stopped short of rape, but there was no telling where things might have gone had he not been drafted for Albania. 'I know it's a terrible thing to say, but it's true: I really hoped he'd rot behind bars!'

Both Eleni's uncle and her father were serving time for the torched bakery, but this was the first time she had shared her childhood secret with Calliope.

'Do you think I'm a bad person to be speaking like this?'

An incredulous little sound escaped Calliope. 'You, a bad person? *You?*' she said, taking her young friend's hand in her own. The hand was small and soft, the fingers swollen by pregnancy. The girl was barely nineteen. 'It's not you who should be feeling remorseful, my dear!'

Eleni was silent. She had a curious habit of rubbing her thumb and forefinger together, as if rolling a tiny wad of chewing gum between her fingertips. She sat pondering Calliope's words, her eyes casting about the kitchen. The eyes were dark and melancholy, set in a round face on which some complex question seemed to be perpetually etched.

It was Easter Tuesday. Calliope sat in Eleni's kitchen, staring at the rain pelting the windowpanes. In the firepit, a boiling kettle was hissing.

'Did you ever tell your parents?'

Eleni rose to make tea. 'He said he would poison my food if I told anyone.' She was in her sixth month and growing ample.

Everyone seemed to be feeding Eleni this time around. 'He said my father wouldn't believe me anyway.'

She made mountain tea, set the laundry cauldron back on the fire, then went on with her story. After her uncle had come back from Albania, as soon as he learned that she was engaged, he threatened to tell Tomas that she had seduced him.

'He said Tomas wouldn't want to marry me, and neither would anyone else.'

Calliope shook her head, sour with her own impotence. She placed her arm around Eleni's shoulders. 'You never did tell Tomas then?'

'No!' Alarm flickered in Eleni's face. 'You're not going to tell him, are you?'

'No, my dear… of course not.'

They sat sipping tea. There was the burbling sound of boiling laundry, the steady patter of rain. Calliope could find nothing else to say.

The conversation had come about because Eleni's imprisoned father and uncle were scheduled to be released just before her baby was due. Eleni and Tomas had moved into her parents' home. Lazaros, one of Eleni's twin brothers, had been working in his blacksmith father's workshop, fed and cared for by his devoted grandmother. After his mother died, he had only occasionally slept at home, but as soon as Eleni and Tomas moved in, he decided to reclaim his old room. When Eleni's father and uncle returned, she would have four men to look after, in addition to a newborn.

'What if he comes after me again?'

'Ach, Elenitsa. He's an old man now,' Calliope said. He would be fifty-one on being released. Not quite an old man, but what could she say? She was still chastising herself for failing to probe when the incorrigibly mirthful child had suddenly grown moody during adolescence. 'I'll make sure you are safe,' Calliope heard herself say, though she had no idea how to go about it. 'We'll work on it together.'

The laundry went on bubbling, gently rattling the aluminium lid. It was an oddly comforting sound, though not nearly as comforting as it might have been.

IV

By the time Calliope's visit to Eleni took place, over a month had passed since Dhaniel's arrest. The doctor was still in Mytilene, awaiting trial. Captain Umbreit had assured Calliope that he was being treated well, but what did it mean to be treated well by the Germans?

She began to dream about Dhaniel: a skeletal, shackled doctor dressed in prison garb, plodding towards the torture chamber. Two weeks before Easter, she finally decided to brazen it out with Umbreit. He might not want to respond, might not know the answer, but she didn't think he would lie to her.

'Is he being tortured?' Calliope asked, the last word pounding her brain.

'No. Rest assured he isn't.' Umbreit gazed at her for a moment, then tried to lift her spirits with a lame stab at humour. 'Von Herden wouldn't let them touch the doctor. What if his back goes out again?'

Several months earlier, stumbling on a cobblestone, the major had twisted his back while visiting Molyvos. If Dhaniel hadn't happened to know a trick an old Armenian had taught him back in Constantinople, the major might have found himself bedridden for weeks.

Umbreit attempted a smile. He and Calliope had been on edge since the day she had thrown herself at him, like stage actors arrested by a fire or earthquake, unable to get back into the spirit of the play.

One day, he appeared in her office for no apparent reason. Calliope looked up from her desk and found Umbreit looming there, as if about to convey something of dire importance. He said nothing, and neither did she, but her eyes welled, and her throat filled with longing.

And yet, the underlying resentment was still there, throbbing alongside her wayward desire. Their one and only embrace had been brief, but it had left the air around them charged with significance. It was as if, the moment he had taken her in his arms, Umbreit succeeded in breaking through the mental buffer she had been zealously guarding for months. *Es kann nicht mehr lange dauern...*

He had begun to spend most of his time in Petra, supposedly to deal with Dwinger's turbulent legacy. Reis had taken over many of Umbreit's former duties; the village council was handling urgent affairs. Calliope went on teaching. She went on liaising for the Germans. She helped Stella care for the doctor's four children. Consumed by work, she had gradually succeeded in distracting herself from the dread kindled by Ourania's intrusion. There was still, somewhere, a small knot of anxiety, but the haze of doom that had come over her in Umbreit's office began to fade when it became apparent that the shocked witness, possibly fearful of losing her job, had opted for discretion. What Ourania would do if and when Hitler's army ever left the village was another question.

Finally, Calliope's body began to revolt. She was starting to suffer from a chronically painful neck; sores appeared on her inner cheeks. And then her periods stopped for two months. Nor was she the only woman to whom this was happening. Something to do with stress and privation, the doctor had explained. Calliope was relieved to be spared the monthly ordeal, but one day she registered that her mother was looking at her askance.

Mirto made no attempt to deny her suspicion.

'*Pregnant?*' Calliope cried, stiffening. 'Whose child would this be, Mama?'

Mirto was hemming one of Calliope's skirts and would not look up from her thread and needle.

'Whose then? Umbreit's, Ealing's—'

'How am I—'

'Maybe Pericles's – he's old enough now... Or even the doctor's – why not? I've spent more time with him than anyone else...'

Mirto cast her a baleful look. She opened her mouth to speak, but Calliope was not done.

'There's also the headmaster, you know. I—'

'Ach, stop... please stop!' Mirto rubbed her eyes. 'How am I supposed to—'

'You're supposed to trust me! You're supposed to believe me

when I say I've never had relations with anyone besides Kimon!' Calliope paused, a small, bitter sound escaping her mouth. 'Anyway, I'm supposed to be barren, remember? Isn't that what everyone's been saying?'

Mirto gave a sigh. 'It wouldn't be the first time people were wrong.'

'Well, you're wrong too! I could not possibly be pregnant! Please believe me,' Calliope added, softening.

She knew her mother's nerves to be as frayed as her own, though in recent days they had both withdrawn deep into themselves. For days after the doctor's arrest, Mirto had stopped cleaning, and barely touched her food. And although Calliope herself was not fastidious about housekeeping, she had gradually begun to notice the dust angels clinging to room corners, the bird droppings left unswept on windowsills. Hoping to provide a little cheer, she had brought a sumptuous bouquet of roses from the town hall and placed it in a vase. Her mother thanked her. A week later, the wilted roses were still there in their onyx vase, the odour of fetid water hanging in the dusty air.

She decided not to share Eleni's secret with Mirto. But she was still brooding on it – her own culpability – as she made her way home on that drizzly Easter Tuesday. The streets looked deserted. The rain had gradually ceased, but black clouds were still floating across the evening sky. It was getting dark. She had not quite reached the *plateia* when she spotted several dogs sprawled on the wet cobblestones. Two German guards were pacing in front of the barber's. What were they doing here? What was there to guard? Every shop in the *agora* was shuttered now that the merchants had run out of stock.

Calliope strode on, fidgeting with her slipping head-kerchief. She was about to pass the *pantopoleion* when, all at once, the entire rainwashed *plateia* seemed to blur, then abruptly darken. Another moment and she would start howling, but in that brief black spell, all she could do was whimper, her shoulders hunched, her fists pressed against her mouth, like a child recoiling from an imminent blow.

Suspended from the dripping mulberry tree were the sagging

corpses of Yorgos Lyras and Kyriakos Himonas, former fishing captain and erstwhile mayor. The third hapless man was Yannis Rozakis, the *kapheneion* owner, who, bruised and bloodied, was dangling between them, as if ever hopeful of making peace between the two fiery colleagues.

V

It was turning out to be another bitter spring. Herakles the cobbler had recently died, but not without shedding unexpected light on the brutal, almost forgotten, crime he had secretly committed back in 1935. He had, he confessed to his priest on his deathbed, just learnt that he had contracted syphilis, had spent an entire evening getting drunk in the *agora*. When he passed the Adhams' gate on his way home, their dog went into a barking frenzy. Only two days earlier, Socrates had defecated on the main street, just outside the cobbler's own shop. The schoolmistress had quickly collected the droppings, but Herakles had other reasons for feeling cross anyway. He had heard people say that Johnny the Australian had asked for his sister's hand only after Calliope had turned him down. Stupidly, drunkenly, he had taken his rage out on the barking dog.

That *Papa* Iakovos had shared the secrets of the confessional with his wife surprised no one who knew St Kyriaki's priest. But the man himself fumed on learning that Olympia had spread the gossip in the *agora* – all because of some trivial quarrel over shoe repair!

But the week in which all this had come to light soon brought far more distressing news. The doctor had been shipped off to a labour camp, along with St Mathaios's abbot. It was by then June, but full understanding was just beginning to penetrate Calliope's mental barricades: Dhaniel was not going to be released. He was not about to return home.

Although the truth about Nazi camps was as yet a well-guarded secret, Dhaniel's arrest and the death of their colleagues had left Calliope floundering.

Ironically, despite all the years she had spent railing against the clergy, she was beginning to find occasional solace in *Papa* Emanouil's company. It was St Pandeleimon's priest who had passed on the news about the doctor, who then tried to comfort her, pointing out that a labour camp was, after all, a relatively merciful fate.

Papa Emanouil was an autodidact, a former tailor who had one day decided to join the clergy so as to better feed his family. The family kept growing and *Papa* Emanouil remained a poor man – until recently, when he found himself a beneficiary of Zenovia the fortune teller's will. That Calliope was a co-beneficiary was what had brought them together.

Two days after receiving the news about the labour camp, Calliope returned to the priest's house. The *papadhia* was busy laundering clothes, but *Papa* Emanouil took Calliope to the courtyard, where, over small cups of ersatz coffee, he made an astonishing revelation: Rupert Ealing and *Papa* Ioannis had found asylum in a Mytilene brothel! Calliope, who had been hunting in her bag for a handkerchief, looked up, her eyes widening.

'*A brothel?*'

'So I've heard.' *Papa* Emanouil's grin was as mischievous as a boy's. Someone in the Mytilene Resistance apparently had a connection to a local madam.

'I'm having trouble imagining this, *Papa* Emanouil.'

'That's life, *koritsi mou.* You never know where it's going to take you.'

Calliope chuckled into her coffee, but before long, an obvious question began to scratch in the back of her head. If the Germans arrested the doctor and the abbot, why not her or *Papa* Emanouil? Were the Germans just playing games, biding their time in hopes of catching more fish in their net?

It was a question she had done her best to suppress. There was no suppressing it any more.

VI

The very next day, Calliope was summoned to Petra.

Umbreit had adopted a conciliatory attitude in Molyvos's sister village. He was far more effective at dealing with the natives than Franz Dwinger had been, but he had made little progress with his Greek. Most of the time, he used the interpreter from Kaloni; only once did he send for Calliope. It was possible that her professional services were required again, that the Kaloni interpreter was ill or away on leave.

And yet, zooming down in the Germans' sidecar, wave after wave of dread kept washing over Calliope's brain. The motorcycle raced on, raising clouds of dust. There was a whiff of hot fuel, the cloying scent of oleander. Halfway down, she made Reis stop so she could scramble out and empty her roiling stomach.

'I'm sorry,' she muttered, settling back into the sidecar. 'Sorry.'

Mortified to the point of tears, she was taken aback by Reis's show of sympathy. His eyes were still watchful, still icy blue, but something had changed in them. He was offering her a clean handkerchief. Could he possibly be pitying her? Was it because he knew what awaited her?

Both Umbreit and Reis appeared to be going through some sort of internal crisis. At first, Calliope had taken Umbreit's melancholy air to be related to matters of the heart. By summer, however, even the least observant of villagers had noted that the Germans seemed to be growing dispirited. The Allies had recently begun bombing German cities. They had triumphed in Rome, had invaded Normandy. But none of these victories succeeded in arresting Calliope's grief whenever she thought of the doctor. Should she have thrown herself at von Herden? Would he have accepted the bargain she had so thoughtlessly tried to strike with Lorenz Umbreit?

These questions had been gnawing at her ever since the doctor's arrest. But on the way to Petra, fear for her own safety began to pierce Calliope's marrow. What if they had finally found out about her own involvement? What would Umbreit do about it? With a part of her heart, she almost felt sorry for his predicament, for if there was one thing she did not doubt, it was Lorenz Umbreit's love.

She supposed she loved him too – loved him still – though it could not be denied that something had begun to sour within her after she'd stumbled upon the three corpses dangling in the *plateia*. Umbreit had been in Petra for two days, but on the third, Calliope spotted him from her desk, bounding up the town hall's stairs.

She followed him to his office, then stood at the threshold, pulsing with hostility. He motioned her to sit down, his eyelid twitching. Calliope slid into a chair. Grappling for self-control, she went on to ask the question clawing at her heart. Was Umbreit responsible for hanging the three Molyviates?

'No.' There was the familiar gesture involving tense hand and flaxen hair. 'They died in Mytilene... all three of them.' He sighed.

Calliope made an impatient gesture. 'But weren't you the one to hang them, in the *agora*?'

He picked up his map pointer, held it for a moment as one might a whip, then put it down, staring at his decorative pebble jar.

'I was not the one to hang them.'

'But you must have been the one to give the order?' Calliope insisted, still hoping to be proven wrong. 'Weren't you?'

Umbreit stirred in his chair. Ever so slightly, he drew himself up. 'They were already dead. I was merely following orders.' He sat gazing at her, mute for a moment. Suddenly, he said, 'They didn't manage to get anything out of them. I thought you might like to know.'

'What? Are you saying they didn't manage to break them? Not one of them?'

Calliope was conscious of a flicker of pride. But in that case, how had the Germans found out about the doctor's involvement?

Umbreit admitted the men had been interrogated by the Gestapo. He did so with his eyes averted. 'I'm sorry,' he said humbly.

Calliope was less surprised by Umbreit's apology than by his sudden willingness to discuss confidential matters. She sat still, confused, trying to prevail over her inner tumult. A part of her wanted to shake him, slap him, the other to throw her arms around his neck and comfort him in his manifest sorrow. Furious with herself, with the absurdity of pitying the enemy, she sat up with a bitter grimace.

'It's no good, is it, being a sentimental soul?' she said, sarcastically echoing his own words. 'You don't go around killing men, then feel sorry for them!'

'Calliope,' he said. 'I do feel for them. I do, but…' He stopped. He let out another sigh. 'I'm a Wehrmacht officer, Calliope! We are at war. I can't just—'

'Yes, I know: you can't risk your career for a handful of Greek peasants!' she said, cutting him off icily. She knew perfectly well she was being spiteful, yet something in her insisted on punishing him.

Umbreit looked stung, his features sliding downwards. 'This is not a career I've chosen, Calliope,' he said quietly. 'I thought you understood that, yet… oh!'

He broke off, his palms declaring the hopelessness of it all. 'It's… I can't possibly make you see! You don't know, you can't understand what it means to be a soldier!'

Calliope studied him for a moment. Suddenly, she rose. 'You're right. I can't understand it.' And then she turned and strode out to unleash her sorrow.

All this had taken place in Molyvos, shortly after Easter. It was summer by the time she was summoned to Petra, but her inner weather remained unpredictable.

VII

The first thing she noticed on entering the Petra office was a file resting dead centre on Lorenz Umbreit's desk. It was a manila folder stamped *GEHEIM* in square black letters. SECRET. Calliope was transfixed by the German word, dimly aware that Umbreit had risen from his chair, his right hand limply extended towards her.

'*Wie geht es dir?*'

He was asking how she was, sounding gently solicitous, like a man greeting a colleague who'd suffered a death in the family. Despite the friendly greeting, Calliope reminded herself to tread carefully. If she slipped today, she might compromise not only herself but her colleagues too.

'How do you think I am?' she demanded, ignoring his proffered hand. 'I assume you know the doctor's been sent to a labour camp? You must—'

He cut her off, gesturing towards a chair. 'Sit down, Calliope.'

That he hadn't reverted to formality was vaguely reassuring, but something about his manner confused her. He had a large stone he had picked up somewhere. It was very smooth, very pale, the size and shape of a small child's foot. Umbreit kept toying with it; his eyes queried her, as if trying to diagnose her precise mental state.

That Umbreit had changed since arriving on the island had been clear to Calliope for months. Every time she saw him, there was something new he had found in his solitary wanderings. Little by little, he was surrounding himself with souvenirs from her own island: sea urchins and shells, pebbles and driftwood.

Calliope drew herself up. 'Why am I here?'

He gazed at her sadly. 'I wanted to be the one to tell you about the doctor,' he finally said. 'I didn't realise you'd already heard.' He kindly refrained from asking how the news had reached her. 'I know how much he means to you.'

So the grim scene she had been dreading was not about to be played out after all. She was relieved, grateful. At the same time, some belligerent facet of her mind insisted on holding him responsible for Dhaniel's transfer to a labour camp, for not having prevented it.

'What's it to you?' she flared up. 'One Greek more or less. It's—'

'Calliope!' He half rose from his chair, then slumped back, looking defeated. It was impossible not to note that his face was sallow; his eyes had gradually lost their clarity. 'I want you to know I did everything in my power,' he said at last.

There was no mistaking his inner torment, yet each uttered word only served to further scrape Calliope's nerves. It was as if she had unconsciously resolved to adopt the most negative interpretation of his every statement. Was she trying to pick a quarrel?

'You did everything in your power,' she heard herself echo. 'You mean you made sure he got sent away?'

Yes, she was trying to provoke him, if only to vent her own impotent rage. But as the hostile words came tumbling out, something struck her. Was it possible that Umbreit had in fact been jealous of her attachment to Dhaniel? That he thought the patriotic doctor might try to talk her out of her unseemly friendship? Dhaniel had, in fact, come close to doing so, had alluded to recent rumours but, finally, had stopped short of reproaching her.

'Why was he sent to a labour camp?' she asked after a long pause. Her churlishness, she realised, was beginning to test Umbreit's patience.

'Would you have preferred to see him executed?'

'Why would he be executed? The man's innocent!'

Umbreit studied her. 'Are you sure?'

Calliope was floundering. 'He's a good man. You said so yourself.'

'A good man, but not an innocent one – at least not where we're concerned,' he said, making Calliope shrink into her chair. His eyes might have lost their freshness, but they seemed no less penetrating.

'Why? What's he done?'

There was a sigh, a tense raking of the hay-coloured hair. 'You know I can't go into that,' Umbreit said. 'But believe me: it's all been carefully investigated and documented. There's not a shred of doubt about the doctor's involvement.'

'Involvement in what?'

Umbreit gave her a faintly admonitory look. *What do you take me for,* his eyes seemed to say.

Calliope shifted her weight, fresh apprehension flooding her heart. For if they really had proof of Dhaniel's activities, was it possible they did not know about her own role? Was Umbreit merely waiting for her to fall into his trap?

'But if they're so sure of his guilt,' she blurted, 'how is it he's still alive?' She tossed the question at him boldly, as if to subdue the chill seeping through her bones. 'Well?' she said when no answer seemed to be forthcoming.

'I… both I and von Herden intervened.' Umbreit averted his eyes.

'Is that true?' she asked, looking at him intently. She knew he was not a man who would ever claim unearned credit; nor was he the sort who could utter an outright lie. The knowledge, as much as his silence and mournful eyes, made a spark of love leap back into her chest. 'Thank you,' she said after a moment.

Umbreit stirred, passing a nervous hand over his jaw. Calliope shifted her eyes. She let them travel around the room: over the two sunny windows, the Führer's portrait, the daybed neatly covered in a grey wool blanket. She supposed Umbreit slept on this bed whenever he was in Petra. Someone had placed pots of fresh basil on the windowsills. It crossed her mind that if the Germans stayed much longer, they might well end up more Hellenised than the Greeks had become Germanified.

Umbreit observed her small smile and perhaps concluded that a change in her inner state might be taking place. He rose from his chair and came around the desk, his right hand briefly thrust into his pocket. Stopping before her, he unfurled his fist and reached for her hand. Her hand was at rest on the edge of the desk, but he turned it gently, dropping the green stone into her open palm.

'In the sun, it glows just like an emerald.' He smiled.

Calliope said nothing. She was staring down at the stone, as if trying to decide what she was meant to do with it.

'I keep wanting to give you things,' he let out after a moment. 'Hardly a day goes by that I don't feel this… this urge to bestow something on you.' Saying this, he reached out and tenderly stroked her face, as if trying to memorise the shape of her cheekbone, the texture of her skin.

Calliope sat breathing quietly, less surprised by Umbreit's intensity than by his apparent indifference to the possibility of being caught in such an intimate pose. The door to the street was kept locked in Petra, but the office door had been left ajar. Reis could be heard stirring in the adjacent office. Umbreit was a cautious man. Why was he being so careless today?

'What's going on?' she heard herself ask. 'You – both you and Reis – are behaving strangely. Reis is like… a different man.'

Umbreit smiled wanly. He was about to answer when Lieutenant Reis himself appeared at the door, as if sensing he was being discussed. Crossing the room, he passed a note to Umbreit, then turned to leave, saying he would return at two o'clock, ready to take *Frau* Alexiou back.

Umbreit glanced at the note. 'My poor adjutant is in love.'

'Reis?' Calliope stopped toying with the pebble. 'With whom?'

Umbreit folded his arms, leaning against the edge of his desk. 'A local widow named Alkesti.' He sighed. 'I'm told her husband was a schoolmaster here.'

'What? The one Dwinger killed?'

Umbreit's smile evaporated. He nodded.

'*She* is seeing Alfred Reis?'

Umbreit shrugged. Calliope went on staring, shrinking back from the news as if she'd been slapped. Her dismay was all the more acute for being unreasonable. Why should a Petra widow's relationship with Reis seem more shocking than her own with Umbreit? Was it because Alkesti's husband had been executed by the Germans?

That must be it, she decided. But the truth, she soon realised, was somewhat more complicated. For one thing, she had instantly assumed Reis's relationship to be intimate, whereas hers…

Hers, after all this time, was just a hopeless muddle. She had no idea what she wanted any more. She wanted Lorenz Umbreit not to be German – that was all she wanted unequivocally. Everything else was subject to contradiction, anger, doubt.

Although there was no denying their mutual attraction, Calliope's feelings towards Umbreit had grown so jumbled that when he suddenly took her hands and held them, she felt half her body respond to his touch, while the other half stiffened, as if sensing danger. She was grappling with the vision of Dhaniel lugging rocks or digging ditches – whatever it was they made prisoners do in a labour camp. She felt herself starting to recoil again. 'I…'

But this time, Umbreit refused to retreat. He drew her to her feet, his arms finding their way round her waist. He held her for one intense moment in which her surprised senses began to open up like flowers. She was acutely aware of the trees sighing outside the windows, the banner of light dancing across the Führer's portrait. At the same time, a scathing chorus was starting to make itself heard in her ears.

He would not let her go. There was the familiar smell of ink and coffee and leather as his lips touched her hair. 'It cannot last much longer,' he whispered, exactly as he had the day Ourania had barged in on them. His breath warmed her neck. *Es kann nicht mehr lange dauern.*

'It's lasted much too long already.' Calliope spoke bitterly – because it was true, of course, but also because he was still exploring her neck, shoulders, arms, raising one of them to put his lips to her pulsing wrist.

'Yes,' he conceded. 'It has lasted much too long.'

There had been a time when Calliope would have given a great deal to hear Umbreit utter these words. Now, she registered them with only one corner of her mind because the rest was intent on his warm, purposeful hands. The hands looked alien on her flesh, yet she seemed incapable of extricating herself.

A moment went by. She was – gently but resolutely – being propelled across the room. She was vaguely aware of this, though she had closed her eyes, listening to her own heart, to the foreign voice murmuring in her ear. When she opened her eyes again, it was in the full knowledge that her body was now dictating the terms, and that she was finally about to submit to its blind imperative. On the wall above them, over the narrow daybed, the Führer gazed at them severely, all but irrelevant.

VIII

Seraphim Lemos's wife spat the moment she saw Calliope. Their paths crossed on St Elias Day, as the contractor's wife was walking home from church, accompanied by her daughter. Going past the

Adhams' house, she briefly hesitated, then turned her head slightly and spat, the way old men were prone to do, clearing their throat of phlegm. The gesture expressed both contempt and loathing but had the merit of being unambiguous. Two days later, at Eleni's house, Veroniki the midwife's hostility was less explicit.

The old woman's eyes were becoming cloudy, but the accusation in them burned as brightly as the fear and excitement in Eleni's eyes. Calliope's protégée had gone into labour one day after her herbalist *yaya* had come down with dysentery. Dysentery was another infection rampant around the island. Calliope's aunt, Elpida, had also contracted it.

Eleni's contractions were coming and going. Veroniki kept reaching into her linen basket, wiping Eleni's flushed face, rubbing her legs with oil. She had given her raspberry tea and mallows to speed up labour, but the baby seemed loath to relinquish the comfort of its mother's womb. By evening, Tomas's eyes were beginning to grow hollow. His mother, who was caring for Eleni's *yaya*, came down for a spell and, fearing an epileptic fit, ordered her son away.

'Go, *pedhi mou*, go wait in the *kapheneion*!'

Eleni's mother-in-law was a short, grey-haired woman whose small, gapped teeth gave her the slightly goofy appearance of an eager-to-please child. Eleni was deeply attached to Nitsa, who was airing about, boiling water and tea, getting cobwebs ready to staunch heavy blood flow.

'It's going to be a while,' Veroniki declared halfway through the evening. A scrawny woman resembling a furled umbrella, the midwife had directed her comment at Nitsa, who looked worried, stroking a strand of damp hair away from Eleni's cheek. It was a sultry evening and, though the windows were open, the air in the room felt sodden, smelling of oil and sweat and the decaying-flesh smell of birthwort. After a while, assured that Calliope would stay, Tomas's mother decided to check up on her own patient.

'I'll be back later,' she promised her daughter-in-law.

Calliope went to sit at the bedside. She took Eleni's hand. She muttered vaguely soothing words, doing her best to ignore Veroniki's coldness. Eleni was panting between contractions. Her damp hair was drenched in sweat, her face contorted as pain gripped her uterus.

After a while, Veroniki made Eleni pad around the room, stopping her now and then to insist on the foul birthwort juice. 'Drink, drink some, *koritsi mou*,' she murmured. 'It'll strengthen the contractions, my child.'

Eleni drank, her face warped by disgust. She sat. She stood. She kneeled down. She got up. She returned to bed. Veroniki began to slap her belly, her sallow face beaded with perspiration. It was midsummer now. Attracted by the smell of birthwort, swarms of flies had come in, buzzing around the lamps.

There were two oil lamps burning by the bed, and in their meagre light, Eleni's eyes were beginning to have a glazed look. The old midwife's skin was a crumpled parchment, but her movements remained brisk and assured and faintly condescending: this was her realm, her kingdom. Speaking to Eleni, her voice was velvety with solicitude.

'Everything's fine,' she mumbled to the quivering girl. 'Everyone's fine, but it's going to be a while yet, *koritsi mou*.'

'How long?' Calliope heard herself ask, haunted by the knowledge of her young friend's previous losses.

'A while,' the midwife snapped. 'Get me more light if you want to make yourself useful!'

Calliope hesitated, then went to the neighbours to borrow a lamp. She was beginning to worry about Sappho, who was accustomed to being walked in the evening. It was by now past ten and Mirto would be at her sick sister's house. Sappho was locked up in the storage room, probably whining with distress.

Soon after the extra lamp had been lit, Nitsa returned, bustling in with her usual vigour. Calliope told Eleni she must run home and let Sappho relieve herself.

'I'll be back as soon as I can,' she promised.

At about the same time, some of the *kapheneion*'s regulars were starting to go home. The Germans had finally given up enforcing the curfew, retreating to their quarters to listen to their wireless broadcasts. Two days earlier, there had been an assassination attempt on Hitler's life. The Führer was virtually unscathed, but his troops appeared more demoralised than ever.

Calliope had her own reasons for feeling discouraged. While Sappho leaped and barked and ran circles around the garden, her mind kept returning to the mounting evidence that Ourania the cleaner had tattled after all. The villagers, Aunt Elpida had reported, were becoming divided into those who believed the spreading rumour about her and Umbreit and those who defended her. Her supporters were quick to point to Calliope's close friendship with the doctor. Would a man who had risked his life to fight the Germans, a man as upright as Elias Dhaniel, have remained friends with a Nazi whore?

All this was still torturing Calliope as she headed back to Eleni's house. She was almost there, had reached St Pandeleimon's, when she found herself gripped by an atavistic impulse. Darting into the deserted church, she lit a votive candle for Eleni. And then another one for the doctor, astonished to find herself muttering an impassioned prayer.

'No human being can be rational all the time,' she recalled her father saying.

She was leaving the church, chuckling to herself, when a knot of men sauntered by the gate. They had been singing rowdily but broke off the moment she emerged from the churchyard. As she closed the gate behind her, Calliope suddenly recognised her older brother-in-law, Vangelis. Another moment and she made out the olive-mill owner's son, who was flanked by Ourania's son and a shadowy man she had yet to identify.

'Well, well, well, look who's here!' Dimitris Stephanides spoke with mock heartiness, his voice slurring. 'If it isn't our little schoolmistress!' Dimitris had been Kimon's best man; they'd gone through school and army together, but the showy, devotedly waxed moustache was new. It reminded Calliope of a trapeze artist she had once seen at an Athens circus.

'My own sister-in-law!' Vangelis threw out his arms, as if to greet a long-lost relative. He placed himself in Calliope's path, resolutely blocking her way.

'Let me pass!' Calliope snapped. She stepped sideways, only to find her way barred again. The fourth man was someone named Nilos, who lived next door to Ourania and whose son was among Calliope's pupils. The men reeked of ouzo.

'Is this where you meet your lover then?' Vangelis demanded, unsteady on his feet. 'A Nazi lover in a Greek church!'

'Don't be ridiculous!' Calliope snapped. 'I went to light a candle for Eleni. She—'

'You, lighting candles?' Vangelis hooted. 'Since when have you got religious?' he said, bumping her with his shoulder.

'I… oh, what business is it of yours?' Calliope bristled.

'Naturally, it's my business! You're my brother's widow!'

'Exactly! So, please cut out the nonsense and let me pass. Eleni is—'

'Ach, let her pass,' interposed Ourania's son, who seemed more sober than his drinking buddies. 'She's going to squeal to her lover and get us all in trouble.'

'Is that so?' Kimon's best man chortled. 'So it's true what they say… he's your lover then?' He stood tugging at his flamboyant moustache, contemplating Calliope with the curiosity of a fisherman who has just found a new species of fish caught in his net.

'You're all drunk!' Calliope heard herself exclaim. Ourania's neighbour was watching her closely, his hands in his pockets, his face immobile as stone. If only his son were a better pupil…

'Oh, come on, admit it!' insisted Kimon's best man. He had spread his arms wide, barring her way.

'Admit it!' echoed Vangelis, his eyes slitted with menace.

'There's nothing to admit!' Calliope was still trying to muscle through, but the men only laughed, like children who had suddenly grasped the point of some complicated game.

Calliope whipped around, hoping to see someone who might intervene. To think that a bunch of drunken louts could stop her from getting back to Eleni!

All at once, she pitched ahead, thrusting her arms forward to sweep Vangelis out of her way.

'Let me go!' she shrilled as her brother-in-law's hands clamped on to her wrists. She was thrashing from side to side, struggling to extricate herself. 'Let me go, you stinking idiots!'

At this, Dimitris made a faux-astonished sound. 'Did she just call us idiots? This… this Nazi whore is calling us—'

'Come on now, let her go,' said Ourania's son, his voice growing tense.

Vangelis's fist came swinging out, like a rock dislodged by a sudden landslide.

Calliope staggered, a cry escaping her throat. She was still trying to recover from the blow when Nilos struck, hitting below her breasts. This time, she went reeling backwards, crumpling onto the cobblestones as though the bones in her legs had been abruptly shattered.

'You're calling *us* idiots?' Vangelis hissed at her. 'You, who… who dishonoured my brother's memory as if… as if…' Unable to find the right words, he raised his leg and brought it down viciously. 'I'll give you idiots!'

Groaning, Calliope rolled over, tasting blood and dust. There was a shock of pain as Dimitris's foot assaulted her ribs. The blows kept on coming. The blood went on thudding in her ears. She was being bludgeoned by a ruthless horde, battered by a thousand colossal boots. After a while, everything grew black. The men's voices reached her across a vast, turbulent sea. She was drowning, drowning.

Then, all at once, the blows ceased. Calliope became aware of a distant shout, then the sound of receding footsteps. She attempted to get up. Dimly, she knew that she must get up. With a valiant effort, she succeeded in rolling on to her back, only to lie there, heaving, the sky throbbing above her, a chorus of maddened crickets shrieking in her ears.

Hektor the fool was bending over her.

'*K-k-Kyria… Kyria…* Calliope,' he was stammering. His face was suspended above her, its contours swaying like some water-blurred marine creature's. '*K-Kyria…*'

'Hektor…' Groaning, Calliope raised herself slightly and spat out a mouthful of blood. 'Go… run to my aunt,' she croaked.

Then she flopped back, and the icy stars shot out of the sky and came striking her flesh like bullets.

Hektor raced to Elpida's house, somehow managing to convey to Mirto that her daughter was in urgent need of help... that she was to be found just outside St Pandeleimon's church... that they'd better hurry.

He did not wait for her. While Mirto wriggled into a dressing gown and rushed out into the night, Hektor flew to the town hall, where he attempted to get past the two sentries, possibly meaning to alert Lorenz Umbreit. The captain was spending the night in Petra, but Hektor could not have known this, even had he not been drunk, which he was.

'*Kyria* Ca-ca...' Thwarted by his own impediment, Hektor began to gesticulate towards St Pandeleimon's, his eyes rolling in their sockets, his raspy voice hissing into the two guards' faces. '*K-k-ky-ria...*'

He blubbered on and on, standing his ground, while the sentries sniggered, trying to ward him off. Amused at first, they were becoming vexed by Hektor's foul breath and flying spit. They swore. They told him to scram. They kicked and threatened and swore yet again.

But Hektor was not giving up. He tried to insinuate himself between the two sentries, still drooling, still trying to communicate. But the only person capable of interpreting his desperate appeal was just then lying in a bloody heap on a deserted street, dimly aware of her own surroundings. She was on the verge of losing consciousness when a shot resonated through the slumbering neighbourhood. A single gunshot, followed by prolonged silence.

Suddenly, a woman's voice rose in the night. A twisted, disembodied howl that happened to be the maternal cry accompanying a difficult birth, but could just as easily have been the sound of an older mother's erupting grief.

And then silence reigned again, broken only by the roar of the sea, the bark of a dog, the rhythmic sound of a woman's feet slapping the cobblestones.

Mirto ran and ran, limping through the sleeping village.

FOUR

I

There were two Germans in deaf-mute Zoe's ink drawing: two helmeted soldiers leaning side by side over a balcony, their expression and posture suggesting hilarity. On the pavement below, three boys were engaged in a scuffle. They looked like ordinary children wrestling over a football, but were in fact fighting over dinner scraps thrown down by the soldiers.

'They made us into animals,' Olga Samiou said, speaking to Calliope. It was the summer of 1945. The Occupation was finally over. Calliope was leafing through Zoe's drawing pads. The Molyvos carpenter's widow and her deaf-mute daughter had just arrived from Athens, where Olga had lately worked as a char, saving money for the journey home.

'You should have let us know. We would have sent you money,' Calliope's mother said, not for the first time.

Back in the early 1920s, she had taken Olga under her wing, nursing the traumatised refugee and her husband in her Molyvos home. But now Olga's husband was dead, and she was on her way back to Molyvos with her deaf-mute daughter. Mirto was preparing dinner. Through the open window came the voice of a hawker selling courgettes and peppers; a neighbour's radio played an Édith Piaf song.

Calliope went on leafing through Zoe's drawings, while the

twenty-one-year-old artist slept upstairs, in a house belonging to Dr Dhaniel's mother-in-law.

There were three sketch pads in all, their dog-eared pages chronicling every heart-rending aspect of the Occupation. There were drawings of Athenians camped around the subway's warm air vents, of soldiers stopping civilians to confiscate jewellery, of corpse-littered pavements and skeletal children queuing up for soup.

'That's the last one she did,' Olga said, dabbing at her eyes. 'After that, she drew only on pavements and pillars.'

Poor Zoe had run out of art supplies, but had kept on drawing until the day her father died, just before the end of the Occupation. He had been shot along with old Fotini's son, both of them hunting for food on the outskirts. No one knew who the killer was. Perhaps some farmer they had tried to steal from?

'Don't ask what we had to do to survive,' said Olga.

At a loss for words, Calliope wrapped her arms around the carpenter's widow. Her own well of tears had by now frozen over and might, she felt, never thaw out again. City dwellers' hardships had been known for some time, but the truth about the Nazi camps had emerged only recently. For months, Calliope had tried to tell herself that Lorenz would never have participated in the gassing of prisoners. But then his own words would come back to taunt her:

'You don't know, you can't understand what it means to be a soldier!'

It was by now common knowledge that virtually all Salonika's Jews had perished at Auschwitz; an ancient community wiped out in a single season. Calliope was haunted by the black-and-white images, tortured by the tragic fate of poor Hektor, shot while trying to save her life. Gradually, her ribs had healed, her body had learned to function without a spleen, but it was still impossible to imagine the village of her birth without poor, addled Hektor.

'Ach, those were black years,' Mirto put in with a heavy sigh. She waved away a fly, then stopped to taste the aubergine casserole simmering on the stove. 'But at least we're eating again,' she added.

II

For months, Calliope had tried to put the Occupation years behind her; had done her best to suppress all thoughts of Lorenz Umbreit even after learning that he had done everything possible to save her life. He and, incredibly enough, Alfred Reis as well. It was Reis who had contacted Umbreit on that fateful July night, after Mirto had found him outside the town hall, bent over Hektor's body.

The village fool had been killed by one of the sentries, but Calliope was found in the nick of time. She was whisked by the Germans to Mytilene, where she underwent emergency surgery.

Mirto had quickly moved to the capital. She stayed with her brother and sister-in-law, then arranged to rent Stella Gravari's house on learning that her daughter would need prolonged medical care. Calliope was young and sure to regain her health, but it would take time, the doctors kept saying. It would take time.

Ten months after surgery, Calliope was becoming impatient with her own body. Her joints still ached, and her bones felt fragile, as though she were her mother's age and not a young woman who had just turned thirty. It was impossible not to contemplate the bitter irony that it was Molyviates, her own people, who had almost killed her, while the enemy she had fought finally saved her life.

And yet, the hospital staff had not allowed Umbreit near her while she was in intensive care; had not even told her of his subsequent efforts to gain admission. Now, the Wehrmacht troops were gone, but Calliope could not believe that Umbreit had sailed away without so much as a farewell note. Perhaps he had left a letter with her Molyvos aunt? Elpida had recently lost her younger son to bone cancer. Perhaps she had been too distraught to bother with mail?

Whatever the answer, the letter that finally reached Calliope that week had been sent care of Tomas Kafatou, Eleni's husband. The telegraphist had passed it on to his wife, who brought it with her when she came to the capital for a paediatric check-up. Ten-month-old Athena, Calliope's second godchild, was thriving, and so was

Eleni. Her wayward uncle had recently married Dora the weeper, moving into her dowry house, solving Eleni's problem.

But Lorenz Umbreit's letter had yet to be opened.

The envelope had been stamped in Zürich, in late April. Since then, Mussolini had been executed by Italian guerrillas, Hitler had committed suicide, Germany had formally surrendered to the Allies. Calliope had yet to decide whether to read Umbreit's letter. Somehow, while Olga and Zoe were there, she felt resolute enough to avoid it. For months now, she had lived like this, warding off the past, keeping the future at bay. But then, Olga and Zoe left for Molyvos and, unable to sleep, Calliope found herself irresistibly curious about the letter's contents.

It had come in a blue airmail envelope, bearing a Swiss stamp but familiar handwriting, familiar purple ink. On the back of the envelope, across the glued flap, a monogram had been added, possibly intended to discourage tampering.

And still, Calliope dithered. It was over between them. Over! She cautioned herself against slipping into the quagmire of her recent past. She did so again and again.

It was midnight before the foreign envelope was finally slit open. Sitting up in bed, Calliope slid her hand inside, hesitated for a moment, then extracted a sheet of white onionskin. Just a single sheet, which she was soon unfolding with shaky fingers, vaguely disappointed by the brevity of the German letter.

27 April 1945

My dear Calliope,

I am writing this not knowing whether my letter will ever reach you. I've been wanting to write for some time but could not find the words with which to ask your forgiveness. I have finally come to realise that forgiveness may be too much to expect from you and your people. All the same, I desperately want to say one thing, and I beg you to believe me: I had no knowledge whatsoever of the death camps, though now that I do, I frankly don't know how to live with it.

I've had a nervous breakdown and am still convalescing at a

Swiss sanatorium, but should be going home soon. I hope with all my heart that you have regained your health, and that the years ahead will make it possible for you and your beautiful country to recover from the devastation we have wreaked upon you.

As ever, Lorenz

P.S. Should you decide to answer this letter, perhaps you won't mind satisfying a trivial but nagging curiosity. The day Reis and I ran into you and your mother on the Eftalou road, there was more than wild mustard in your baskets, yes? I ask this not because it's of any consequence now, but because I have always wondered whether I was able to read you as well as I thought I could.

'*Panaghia mou!*'

Calliope sagged against the pillows, feeling something turn over in her chest.

Almost a year had passed since she had last seen Umbreit, but it was his note – above all, his astonishing postscript – that seemed to dissolve the stone lodged within her heart. She wept half the night, then drifted off with the light on, bolting awake just before dawn.

There was no going back to sleep. She rose to use the toilet, then returned to bed and read the letter all over again, finally allowing herself to contemplate a subject she had suppressed for months: she had been pregnant the night of the beating, had lost the baby in hospital, never suspecting that she had, against all odds, conceived on that chaotic spring day in Petra, during her one and only sexual embrace with Umbreit.

She replaced the letter in its envelope, then lay staring at the purple monogram: *LFU*. The father of her lost child and she didn't even know his middle name. After all these months, she was still hard-pressed to explain how she had allowed herself to be swept away in Petra's German office, with Adolf Hitler staring down at them!

She was still brooding on all this when Mirto came in to wake her. She came earlier than usual because it was the day before St Calliope's Feast. Calliope was still indifferent to name days, but this year she had good reason to celebrate: Dr Dhaniel was about to return from Dachau, along with *Papa* Konstantinos, St Mathaios's abbot. Dachau had been liberated in late April, but the survivors had only recently started to return. Dhaniel was scheduled to arrive tomorrow, his safe return the only event promising to dissipate the melancholy mists hovering over their days.

The sleepless night had left Calliope with a throbbing headache. She must stop at the pharmacy later, pick up a painkiller, as well as sleeping tablets. She wanted to ensure a restful sleep tonight, wanted to feel and look her best tomorrow.

The pharmacy was no longer owned by the Fotiadis family, who had recently moved to Patras. Orestes himself was no longer among the living, having been executed by the Resistance after it was discovered that he had been a Gestapo double agent, responsible for the arrests of the mayor, doctor, *kapheneion* owner, abbot. There were, of course, others involved in what had come to be known as the English Spy Case but, fortunately, Orestes Fotiadis had not had their names.

Incredibly, Calliope had learned about Fotiadis's execution from Rupert Ealing, who had left for England in the wake of the Germans' departure. Eventually, he wrote to her, repeating his hope that she might come to England some day. Pericles, who was in Mytilene preparing for university, was taking English lessons and had talked Calliope into sharing his private teacher. Calliope could not begin to imagine herself strolling along the Thames, visiting Shakespeare's birthplace, but she was happy to find distraction in the amusing English lessons. German was resolutely in the past; English might be the future.

III

Finally, Friday morning arrived. Calliope, Mirto, and Pericles were joined by the doctor's children and mother-in-law, as well as by the ageing *Papa* Emanouil, who had travelled to welcome the doctor and St Mathaios's abbot. Yannis Rozakis's widow and daughters were also at the port; Pavlos, the missing son, had turned out to be alive after all, though he had been seriously wounded in Egypt.

'Ach, if only my husband could be here today!' Rozakis's widow kept saying, craning her neck. 'If only he could have lived long enough to see our Pavlaki alive!'

The white ferryboat was quickly advancing towards the port, its foghorn blasting. It was nearly noon. The boat was two hours late, but ferries had always been late, can't blame the Occupation for that, people kept saying.

The little joke seemed immensely funny to everyone. There was wild applause as the boat eased its way into the harbour. Then a tall priest came elbowing his way through the jostling crowd, having spotted *Papa* Emanouil's stovepipe hat among the waiting Molyviates. It was *Papa* Ioannis.

'The Resistance priest!' Dora the weeper whispered in her mother's ear.

The two priests embraced; excited greetings were exchanged amid a cacophony of chattering relatives, droning hawkers, clamouring porters. The porters kept trying to push their way through the thickening crowd; the hawkers went on peddling sesame rolls, roasted peanuts, miniature flags.

At least two of the hawkers were gypsies and, for a moment, Calliope thought she recognised Glykeria. But no, this woman was older and plainer, though she too resembled a tropical bird, dressed in turquoise and red and orange. Calliope bought a flag for her seven-year-old godson, then Pericles lifted him onto his shoulders so Aristides could see the passengers starting to queue up on the lower deck.

Now that the ferry had docked, there was pandemonium on the quay. The crowd was surging forward, reluctantly parting for disembarking vehicles. The trucks came rattling down in clouds of exhaust fumes and dust, but could barely make way through the pressing crowd. There were shouts and protests as uniformed officials attempted to keep back impatient relatives. Drivers honked horns. Policemen blew whistles. Porters quarrelled while waiting for custom. Then, at last, the gangplank was lowered, and the first dishevelled passengers came shuffling off the boat.

At this point, the crowd became an unstoppable torrent. Dora the weeper let out an excited yelp. 'Look!' She pointed, waving frantically. 'There he is, Mama, look – no, not there: *there*!' Pavlos Rozakis had turned up at the top of the gangplank, flanked by Dr Dhaniel and *Papa* Konstantinos. 'Yes, of course it's him, Mama! He's just grown a beard, *kale*!'

'I see the beard,' said her mother, frowning. 'But look... look how thin he is! A regular scarecrow. Are you sure it's him?'

'Of course it's him, Mama!' Dora's sister jumped in. '*Panaghia mou!*' Anna crossed herself with theatrical fervour; then she, too, began to wave, while Dora burst into uncontrollable sobs.

Calliope witnessed all this in silence, her own eyes blurring. She braced her feet against the surging crowd, batting at her wet cheeks with the back of her hand. Dhaniel's daughters and mother-in-law were weeping silently. The doctor was still too far off for Calliope to see whether he had changed. Not for the first time, she thanked a god she did not believe in that the doctor had been arrested toward the end of the war. Who could tell how long he would have lasted otherwise?

'It's a miracle!' *Papa* Ioannis was babbling excitedly. 'Three of the finest men ever born on the island and all three come back alive! It's a miracle!'

No one bothered to correct the priest. No one seemed to remember that the doctor was actually one of the *Turkospori* from Asia Minor. The three men were still shouldering their way through the crowd when Aristides spotted his father.

'I see him!' he shrilled, his sandalled feet kicking the air. 'I see my *baba*!'

'Your *baba* is a hero! A real hero!' *Papa* Emanouil stated sententiously. Caught up in the joyful spirit, the elderly priest announced they must all go and celebrate together: have a festive meal on the waterfront, drink some local wine.

'What, you mean today? Right now?' The doctor's mother-in-law looked sceptical. She pointed out the passengers would be exhausted after their long journey, but *Papa* Emanouil waved her doubts away.

'We have to drink to the future today! The future!' he reiterated, reaching out to pat Calliope's shoulder. 'Ach, *koritsi mou*, this is not a day for tears, but for celebration,' he stated. 'Celebration, *koritsi mou*!'

Everyone in the party nodded in agreement, but Calliope was no longer listening. She and Dhaniel were gazing at each other across the shrinking distance, tears streaming down their faces. In an hour or so, they would all sit down and repudiate the past, as one might repudiate the memory of some boorish, disruptive guest. Calliope's godson had clambered down, his matchstick arms flung towards the fleecy clouds, as if trying to capture them.

'*Baba, Baba, Baba!*'

Calliope kept laughing through her tears, ruffling the child's hair. She did not know what to do with her own impatient arms. So she tugged at her belt, and straightened her skirt, and then just stood there, holding her godson's hand, waiting for the future to begin.

1947-1959

'The World is like a drunken peasant, if you lift him in the saddle on one side, he'll fall off on the other.'

Luther

ONE

I

One windy October night, two famished guerrillas clambered down the balding hill slopes, as agile as mountain goats prancing through rocks and brambles. It was two days after St Dimitrios's Feast, but the smell of winter swirled in the air, spurring the men on through the whispering darkness. They had been living outdoors for months, sleeping in caves and forests. Now and then, the national army soldiers would march right by their hideouts, singing their allegiance to king and country. A day earlier, there had been a skirmish in the Argheno hills, and the older man had been slightly wounded.

'I hope the old hag knows how to change a bandage,' he muttered.

The old hag was Mirto Adham, who was believed to be a royalist, but whose daughter was known to harbour leftist sympathies. The communist guerrillas had their informers. They knew that Calliope spent every Sunday night with her lover in the late fortune teller's house, and that she brought her dog along. It was one reason they had chosen this widow, this particular night.

The two men entered the sleeping village through a back road, as furtive as pine martens stealing into a poultry shed. It was by now well past two a.m. St Kyriaki was the younger man's own neighbourhood, but Kostas Kapellas kept his eyes averted from his family's shuttered windows. His decision to join the guerrillas in

1947 had been a surprising one for such a diffident, pampered boy, even one whose postmaster father had threatened to disown him if he didn't stop attending the communists' clandestine meetings.

Gentle but famously mulish, Kostas had left home for the hills, welcomed by the new communist commander. Nikos Antipas was a steely leader. Fearing entrapment, he forbade his men any conjugal visits, setting an example by staying away from his own young wife and child. In no time at all, he had established an intelligence network along the coast, with shepherds and fishermen reporting on the movements of government soldiers. By mid-August, the authorities had placed a twenty-five-million-drachma bounty on Antipas's head, but the new leader remained as elusive as an octopus.

The two young partisans marched on, shivering against the wind. In the silence of the night, Kostas's stomach began to rumble.

'I could use a bowl of *trahana* right now,' he said, his hand seeking the grenade in his pocket the way an anxious child's hand might mechanically seek a familiar toy. He was barely twenty. His comrade, Christos, was more experienced, having fled to the hills when the island had still been under German occupation.

'We're almost there,' he said.

They were approaching the widow's residence, a two-storey house looming on a windswept corner. In the moonlight, the two men could make out the outline of a high stone fence, a wooden gate that squeaked on being opened. Behind them, the moon floated in the murky sky, intermittently obscured by clouds. The interlopers glanced at the shuttered windows, then stole towards the back entrance.

II

She stood framed in the doorway, clutching an oil lamp, eyes dilated less with fear than with a sort of arrested amazement. She had on a flannel robe and long, woollen stockings. Her hair had been gathered into a wispy plait, but a few grey strands had escaped in sleep, framing her withered features. The blacksmith's son was clearly visible in the kitchen but, in her confusion, the old woman muttered something about rats, then began to pluck compulsively at her belt.

'But what do you want?' she finally asked, her entire being focused on the eye of the rifle aimed at her chest. There was a burning candle on the pine table; a faint smell of melting wax hung in the air.

'What do you think we want?' Christos spat out, reaching into the bread box. 'Food. Food and blankets.'

'Food?' The widow stood blinking for a moment or two. Suddenly, she recognised him. She said his name twice. It came out sounding like a question the first time, but barely more than a sigh the second. 'Aren't you ashamed, *pedhi mou*? Wouldn't I have given you food if you'd asked for it?'

'Why should I be ashamed? It's others who should be ashamed!' Christos's eyes bore into the widow's face, his mouth warped in a contempt so deep it seemed to border on pleasure. All the same, he had relaxed his grip on the rifle, shifting his feet under her gaze like an errant boy being called to task by a stern grandmother.

'I think you—'

'What's it to me what you think?' Christos cut in. 'We're not here to listen to your ideas, are we?' He gave 'ideas' an ironic emphasis. 'Come on, now. Where d'you keep your *trahana*?'

The old woman limped towards the kitchen table. She set down the lamp and blew out the candle. There was something deliberate in all her movements, as if every step she took caused her physical pain. Now that she had identified the intruder, her face had relaxed. She turned and lit a fire, making the shadows dance.

'The *trahana*'s in the pantry. I'll gladly give you some,' she answered at length, 'but only… only if you put down your…' She trailed off, having suddenly registered the beam of light flickering outside the pantry.

'We're not here to negotiate!' Christos barked. 'We do the fighting, you do as you're told!'

The widow was silent, picking at her fraying robe. Kostas Kapellas had emerged out of the pantry, holding a candlestick. With his clothes rumpled and hair in disarray, he might have been a boy awakened by the call of nature.

'Please, *Kyria* Mirto,' he said earnestly. 'Do as he says and everything—'

'Ach! You, Kostaki?' Mirto Adham stood gaping, face furrowed with a sort of stunned reproach. The postmaster's son was a stocky young man raised by a gaggle of women. He had three sisters as well as two maiden aunts and a besotted mother, but in recent months, his plump features had acquired a lean, faintly bewildered mien.

Christos had taken off his pullover and was rolling up his sleeve to expose his bicep.

'*Panaghia mou!*' The old woman crossed herself, blinking at the blood seeping through the bandage.

'Why don't you take care of my arm?' Christos barked. 'Instead of standing there like a ghost. Go on, get a bandage or something!'

'I – I don't have a bandage. I'll have to find something upstairs.'

'Well, get it!' snapped Christos. He bit into the leftover bread. 'Let's go!'

Mirto picked up the lamp with a martyred air. 'It's a good thing your mother's not alive to see how you treat old women.'

'Leave my mother out of this!'

The widow paused in her tracks. 'If you want me to change your bandage, you'd better behave like a human being.' She began to climb the stairs. Christos followed, gripping the rifle.

He set it down in the bedroom, stopping to peel off his vest. A brazier was whispering at the foot of the bed, and this was where he planted himself, a sudden look of childish glee suffusing his face. He had just discovered a wilted cigarette in one of his shirt pockets.

Mirto Adham was rummaging through a trunk. She seemed maddeningly determined to take her time, examining one garment after another, finally bringing out a long, gauzy nightgown, which she carefully inspected, while Christos stood unwinding his stained bandage.

The old woman appeared to have forgotten all about the intruder. Muttering to herself, she went about shredding the old nightgown into long, uneven strips, stopping to cast a worried glance at the rattling shutters. The room was spacious but draughty. It smelled of mothballs and smouldering olive pips. At last, she hobbled over and began to examine the wound. 'I'll have to wash it.'

'Never mind, it's clean enough, just—'

'It has to be washed, *pedhi mou*!' she remonstrated, as if addressing an impetuous child eager to run out and play. 'It could get infected.'

'Well, hurry up then!'

But she was already shuffling towards the enamel basin, lifting the jug and pouring water onto a fresh cloth. She swabbed the injured arm as gently and efficiently as a nurse, silent at last in the shadowy room, with the brazier hissing and an owl calling somewhere in the distance.

'There!' she finally said, tying up the strips of cloth around the thin arm. Christos was long-limbed, like his father, and had the same face, as alert and impassive as a bird of prey's.

'Now, get us some blankets!' he snapped, dropping his ashes onto the pine floor. 'Go on! It doesn't have to be your bridal quilts. Just get us something warm. Quick!' He settled into a stuffed chair, alternately dragging on his cigarette and poking in his mouth.

There was an old pine wardrobe standing against the wall. Leaning into it, Mirto pulled out two grey blankets, muttering about what the world was coming to: village boys dragging old women out of bed, dropping ashes onto clean floors. The blacksmith's son listened to this litany in silence, his eyes following the plume of smoke curling towards the ceiling. The tobacco seemed to be calming him; his voice, when he finally spoke, had lost some of its edge.

'Your sleep's not important,' he said, fixing Mirto with a long, didactic gaze. 'The revolution's what's important... your helping patriots like me is—'

'Patriots!' She ceased folding the blankets and swivelled to face him, her eyes flaring within their web of wrinkles. 'What makes you a greater patriot than me? Didn't I do my bit during the Occupation?'

'What makes me a greater patriot is that I sleep in a cave and fight the fascists, while you snuggle up in your warm bed!' This reply seemed to give the blacksmith's son inordinate satisfaction. He rose and picked up his rifle, the cigarette dangling between his lips. 'Go on, get moving!' He gestured towards the door. 'Bring the blankets with you!'

Downstairs, Kostas was seated in a pool of light, hunched over a plate of cold fish. Christos stood glaring at him from the threshold.

'She's a good cook!' Kostas blurted, lurching out of his chair.

Christos's eyes were two chips of coal. 'A good cook?' he flared up. 'We're not here on a social visit, with compliments to the hostess, eh, putty-face?'

Kostas wiped his mouth with the back of his hand. He had a cowlick which, in tense moments, he compulsively tried to push off his forehead.

All at once, Christos seemed to relent. 'Did you find the *trahana*?'

The postmaster's son gestured towards the divan. '*Kritharaki* too.'

At this, the old woman let out a croak of protest. 'And what are we supposed to eat all winter?'

'Don't you worry, *Kyria*. I'm sure your daughter won't let you starve,' Christos retorted. The candle was guttering on the kitchen table, about to go out. 'Go on – give Kostas the blankets.' He gestured with his head. 'Hurry up now!'

The kitchen was dimmer now, its hanging pots and drying vegetables hardly discernible on the murky walls. Kostas was picking his way towards the old woman, holding out his arms, as if in anticipation of an embrace.

'Ach, ach, ach, Kostaki *mou*!' Mirto said, relinquishing the blankets.

'Remember to keep your mouth shut, eh?' Christos patted his rifle, as though to make it clear it was a real weapon, not a toy. 'You will remember, won't you?'

'What I'll do is pray to the Virgin for you!'

'Ach, don't bother!' The blacksmith's son slung the jute sack over his shoulder. 'The Virgin helps those who help themselves!'

Kostas was heading out, muttering goodnight.

'Goodnight!' Christos echoed ironically. He cast the widow one final glance, then stalked off into the night, slamming the door behind him.

Alone in the kitchen, Mirto Adham shivered, clasping her robe about her. For a moment, she stood by the dying flames, rubbing her hip and peering into the night. The wind was still wailing, swallowing the men's footfall.

Suddenly, the old woman crumpled to the floor, like a puppet whose string has abruptly been snapped. The cats, which had briefly and hopefully trailed the two men's bulging sacks, returned to the window, yowling and hissing in each other's faces. On the kitchen table, the oil lamp continued to burn, making protesting noises. Soon, it too went out, leaving the old woman lying in a heap on the kitchen floor, clawing at the darkness, as if to grasp something that kept eluding her.

TWO

I

The last time he asked her to marry him had been on St Basil's Day, 1947. She had said no once before, but he must have hoped to find her more amenable after her mother's death.

She had not been amenable, but he had been right in sensing that she was feeling as bereft and bewildered as an orphaned child. For weeks, she had rattled around in the empty house, able to perform only the most essential tasks. She was incapable of making a responsible decision – how could he expect her to? She begged him to ask again on her birthday, by which time she hoped to have greater clarity.

And now her thirty-third birthday had come around, and though she knew Eli Dhaniel well enough to be sure that he had not forgotten, Calliope also knew that he would not raise the subject today – not while they were all reeling from the news of the Lyras family's latest tragedy.

Mimis, Calliope's old classmate and erstwhile football champion, had just hung himself. That he had not done so after his leg had been amputated, but did after a lengthy police interrogation, shocked and puzzled both rightists and leftists; that the authorities had chosen to arrest the handicapped Mimis rather than his brother seemed more understandable. Takis, the captain's elder son, was known to be as pig-headed as his late father, unlikely to break under interrogation.

No one doubted that both brothers were communists. They had been too vocal for their own good during the Occupation. The authorities must have hoped they would know something about the communist commander's whereabouts, though Nikos Antipas was related to them only by marriage.

Such was the buzz of speculation flying all over the village in the wake of Mimis's suicide. No one would ever learn the reasons for his detention. All anyone knew was that Captain Yorgos's younger son had finally signed the abhorrent Declaration of Repentance. There was no doubt about this because the confessors' names were broadcast in church during Sunday services. Everyone was aware that such signatures were obtained under duress, yet most confessors avoided being seen in public after the announcement.

That Monday, the evening of Calliope's birthday, the doctor arrived late, looking more rumpled than ever. Mimis, he told Calliope, had stopped at the clinic on Saturday after being released, complaining of a persistent cough. Dhaniel had examined him, given him cough syrup, and sent him to bed. An unremarkable visit. Yet he couldn't shake the feeling that he'd missed something.

The doctor, too, was known to be a communist, though no one ever complained, as they did elsewhere, that he neglected patients if they happened to support the opposing side. If he was criticised, it was only for never setting foot in church, and for spending too much time with the widowed schoolmistress. On his occasional visits to the *kapheneion*, Dhaniel had heard both Calliope's supporters and detractors speak of her with equal authority. There were those who accused her of having been a German collaborator; others insisted that she had been in the Resistance. That both the doctor and *Papa* Emanouil were among Calliope's staunchest defenders might have silenced critics, but couldn't she have been a double agent, like Orestes Fotiadis, their erstwhile pharmacist?

All this Eli had occasionally shared with Calliope, but today all they could think about was Mimis's unlucky family. They were sitting in the small room off the kitchen, where Mirto used to rest of an evening, knitting or mending socks. In the corner, there was still a basket containing skeins of multicoloured wool.

Calliope was about to offer dinner, but Eli requested brandy.

'Don't you want to eat?'

'Later.' He was hunched over, his elbows on his knees, his face between his hands. Sappho padded in, wagging her tail, then flumped down at the doctor's feet. The clock in the foyer chimed eleven times.

When Calliope handed Eli his glass, he shifted and drew her to him, absently trifling with her hair. His own hair was almost silver now but still abundant, his face more gaunt than it had been before Dachau.

Calliope reached for an ashtray, then sat for a while, smoking desultorily. In her head surfaced the image of the Lyras brothers in short trousers, one fair, one dark, both given to picking at scabs, their limbs perpetually covered in bruises of various hues and sizes.

'I don't know what it is with our men,' she mused out loud. 'When they don't have Turks or Italians or Germans to fight, they go after each other.' Ever since the Civil War started, the entire country had become divided into rightist and leftist camps, pitting neighbours and family members against each other. 'Do you suppose we've just forgotten how to live in peace?'

Eli gazed into his glass as if it might miraculously provide insight. 'I think we've forgotten how to live without suspicion and rage.'

'So, how are we to go on?' Calliope asked after a moment's silence. 'When will it all end?'

'God only knows.' The response was as automatic as Calliope's occasional invocations of the Virgin Mary. She had long since stopped being surprised by human contradictions. Her own conflicted feelings for Lorenz had made one thing clear: she was no exception. Her love for Eli Dhaniel might seem unimpeachable, but it was no less surprising given that, for years, she had thought of him as an older mentor. If anyone had ventured to tell her before the Occupation that some day she would be waiting for her mother to fall asleep so she could sneak out for a tryst with the doctor, she would have either laughed or slapped such a person's face.

Of course, her mother must have guessed that she had a lover, staying out as she did till the crack of dawn. Did she know who the lover was?

Calliope had felt an occasional flash of resentment at having to steal out like a wilful maiden, though she could have easily solved the problem by marrying Eli. She loved him, she had no doubt about that, though at first, she could not help comparing her feelings to her wayward wartime passion.

She seldom compared any more, but could not help herself the other day, after receiving birthday greetings from Heidelberg. Lorenz Umbreit wrote without fail twice a year, but Calliope never answered. Her pain over their relationship had gradually become muted, but she would never understand how it was that men – intelligent, decent men – could serve despicable causes. There were times, she wrote in her journal, when she felt herself turning into a misanthrope.

Eli's idealism, on the other hand, often left her shaking her head. That a doctor could support communism, while in the north, communist rebels slaughtered every educated man they could ferret out, seemed beyond comprehension. It was one of the things they quarrelled about, finally resolving to steer clear of politics.

In time, Calliope understood that for Eli to lose faith in communism might cause some sort of inner rupture. It would, she thought, be no less heartbreaking than the life of a priest robbed of his faith in God.

Eli Dhaniel was no longer the infallible man he had once seemed to be, but – and this truly astonished her – she had discovered that a man's flaws and foibles could actually bring about a deepening of feeling. In retrospect, being with Umbreit seemed tantamount to feeling perpetually intoxicated, as though the Occupation had forced her to subsist not on beans and dandelions but on wine and cherry preserves. By contrast, being with Eli left her feeling thoroughly sated, a woman who had just consumed a crisp, freshly baked roll, lavishly spread with honey. Her anguish now was for her divided homeland. She still recorded her feelings in her journal, but it fell to her talented brother-in-law to make art of the Civil War.

There had been no news from Pericles, not since he had been

expelled from university and sent to Makronisos, a notorious prison camp for leftist dissidents. Just before his arrest, however, Pericles had sent Calliope two poems. One of them, his latest, depicted a veteran soldier who, demented by the Occupation, wounds himself with an old Turkish sword. Standing in the lush countryside, the soldier slashes his own arm, then watches his flesh bleed into a spring meadow – drop by drop by drop, tormented by the pain, unable to chuck the sword away.

II

The Civil War had brought a new headmaster to the village. A staunch royalist, Leandros Tsouras had been transferred from Kaloni to replace Stamatis Miltiadis, who had been jailed after a policeman had overheard him humming a subversive song. The song, in which the King was likened to a mule, was a popular one in Aghiassos, Stamatis's home village. He had gone there for a wedding; had, he was to claim later, picked up the catchy tune without meaning to.

The headmaster had been the first communist jailed in Molyvos. He was released after signing the Declaration of Repentance, but his teaching days were over. A signature was a signature, the authorities had argued, but who could tell what ideas a schoolmaster might take it into his head to plant in impressionable children's heads? Calliope, who had gradually arrived at a reasonable working relationship with Stamatis, found herself doubly vexed by his successor.

Tsouras was a widower in his mid-forties, a man devoted to his books, his garden, his two magnificent peacocks. Tall and erect, he had prominent blue eyes and a heavy chin that had over the years become submerged in his neck, giving him a smug, supercilious look. He had a son at university and a daughter married to an Athenian civil servant and would have much preferred a transfer to

Athens. Alas, even his son-in-law's connections had so far failed to secure the desired post.

All this the headmaster had shared with Calliope early on, bent on establishing a congenial footing. He kept a respectful distance after Mirto's death, but when spring arrived, he finally declared his interest, as bashful as a smitten adolescent. He knew there were rumours about her and the doctor, but he didn't believe them, he said. Not for a single moment.

'Well, this rumour happens to be true.' Calliope's eyes smiled.

At this, Tsouras coloured and began to fiddle with his necktie. He seemed on the verge of speaking, but then succumbed to a spate of ferocious sneezes. Calliope waited for him to stop. The headmaster claimed to be suffering from allergies.

There were no further indiscretions, but at some point, Calliope became aware that Tsouras had grown hostile. He was a man who prided himself on his fair-mindedness. She was a good teacher, he conceded in one of their school meetings, but surely he could not be blamed for objecting to her smoking and wearing scent in class? Surely he was not alone in thinking that such habits ought to be renounced by a woman entrusted with children's education? People talked, he told her. A schoolmistress could not afford to be indifferent to public opinion.

'I am not indifferent to public opinion,' Calliope said. 'I care deeply how people feel about my teaching. And, by the way, I never smoke at school.'

'A respectable teacher must behave like one at all times.'

Calliope sighed. 'I won't wear scent any more,' she said.

It had occurred to her that Tsouras might be allergic to her perfume. Yet there he was now, ambling through the playground, beset by another sneezing storm. He sneezed explosively, again and again and again, oblivious to the children's laughter.

When, at last, the sneezing spell was over, Tsouras resumed his stroll, surveying the playground with the air of a victorious general attending a celebratory parade. A recently engaged teacher was also out with his class, but Tsouras's gaze kept returning to Calliope.

Suddenly, on a half-spiteful, half-impish impulse, she decided to play Slap the Donkey with her pupils.

The children were mostly eleven-year-olds, but the butcher's grandson was almost thirteen, having been kept back two years in a row.

'Slap the donkey!' Calliope was crouching on all fours, her knotted hair loosening, her rump catching the sun.

'Slap the donkey!' the children echoed, leaping over their laughing teacher.

She had instructed them to slap between her shoulder blades, but the irrepressible Manos slapped her bottom, then remained astride, bouncing like a demented jockey. Reminded of the rules, he finally hopped off, bumping into the even more backward Apollon. If the sailor's ill-fated son was allowed to attend school at all, it was only because of people's compassion for his mother, whose husband had abandoned the family, starting a new one in America.

Calliope, too, pitied Apollon's mother; had repeatedly resisted the headmaster's efforts to expel the poor child. In the classroom, Apollon was usually subdued, dreamily picking his nose, or doodling in his notebook. But in the schoolyard, feeling his backside bumped, the boy slid into hilarity. Soon, both he and the butcher's grandson were whooping with savage glee.

'That's all! We've played enough for one day,' Calliope said. She stopped to straighten her blouse and pin up escaping strands of hair. Only then did she become aware that Tsouras was watching from a distance, like a large, expectant, venomous spider.

III

The school year was almost over when Calliope knew without any doubt: the headmaster had taken to spying on her.

By the late 1940s, the school had four classrooms, each with two windows, each facing a long expanse of silvery olive groves. Below the windows, oleander had been planted, pink and white bushes that had over the years matured into flowering trees. The only creatures normally seen through the classroom windows were the somnolent sheep grazing under olive trees, the occasional roving cat.

But now, perhaps once a week, there was also Leandros Tsouras, probably thinking himself invisible through the oleander. The man was a fool, but quite possibly a dangerous one. Calliope had spotted his disembodied head that morning during class dictation, had found herself fighting a childish impulse to stick out her tongue or waggle her fingers over her ears.

'The Marathon victory galvanised the Greek nation because it demonstrated that the Persians were not invincible.'

She went on with the dictation, but thoughts of the headmaster came back to taunt her later that day, on her way to Petra. She had an early evening appointment with a notary; had, at the last moment, decided to bring her godson along so they could enjoy home-made ice cream at a seaside sweet shop. It was an exceptionally hot day for June.

The appointment with the notary was meant to settle financial matters stemming from the late fortune teller's will. Zenovia's land and olive orchard had been bequeathed to *Papa* Emanouil, her large Molyvos house to the schoolmistress, 'who would be sure to put it to good use'. A codicil stipulated that Hektor be allowed to keep the garden shack, and that he be paid for feeding the cats and picking olives.

Zenovia's will had dumbfounded Calliope: had the old woman lost her marbles? In time, both surprise and unease faded, giving way to an occasional ripple of guilt. Hektor the fool was gone but, five years after the fortune teller's death, it was impossible not to feel that the old woman's faith had been misplaced: all Calliope had ever done with the house was use it for her weekly trysts.

The notary had suggested that Zenovia's house be rented before it fell into ruin. He had sent several reminders, making Calliope wish that Zenovia had left the house to someone else, or at least that she had said nothing about putting it to good use. She recalled a pre-war conversation in which she'd told Zenovia that the village children were in need of a library. Had that been the bee in the old woman's bonnet?

The sun was sliding towards the horizon as Calliope and her godson went strolling along Petra's seaside promenade. Aristides, who was not yet ten, stopped to watch a local man beat a freshly caught octopus. The Petran beat it against a rock, stopping only when some of the spurting ink splattered on to his nose. Aristides went into peals of laughter, reaching for Calliope's hand. In the *kapheneion*, men were beginning to gather, rightists clustered on one side of the room, leftists on the other. The sweet shop was just opening up.

'But are you sure you really want ice cream?' Calliope asked, tweaking her godson's nose. The child smelled like freshly picked berries. 'Absolutely sure?'

Aristides nodded, chin bobbing up and down. 'Suresure-suresuresure!'

They were strolling along the sea, eating their treat, when Aristides's attention was snagged by a legless man selling roasted seeds and nuts from a handmade cart.

Calliope didn't know the former army officer, but she had heard about him in the early days of the Civil War, after communist guerrillas had reportedly set off an explosion in the Argheno hills.

Aristides was looking over his shoulder, speaking in an urgent whisper. 'But how... how does he get around?'

'Did you see his muscles?' Calliope blew smoke into the balmy air. 'He pushes himself up and down with his hands and arms.'

Aristides's chin was starting to quiver.

'Look!' Calliope pointed, hoping to distract her godchild. 'Look at the kids.' Two barefoot boys were jogging by, rolling a metal hoop. A little girl toddled after her mother, clutching a jar with a trapped jellyfish. The mother stopped, and waited, then reached out to brush a stray curl away from her daughter's eyes. The tiny maternal gesture was barely worth noting, yet it filled Calliope's chest with a sudden longing for her late mother.

The feeling was nothing new.

IV

The storm started on an early-September afternoon, sending everyone home during shopping hours. Because of the storm, because her son was afraid of thunder, the communist commander's wife put the boy to bed later than usual, after she had trimmed his hair and fed him a snack, and the rain had finally slackened.

They had been using the chamber pot, but once the rain stopped, Ermione threw a shawl around her shoulders and padded to the outhouse. The privy was cold and damp as she lowered herself over the Turkish toilet, hands clutching her bunched-up skirts. She then hurried back with the empty chamber pot, had just put it away and bolted the door when she heard the crunch of footsteps on the gravel path. There was a rap at the door.

'Nikos!' Ermione darted back to the entrance, fumbling with the bolt. 'Ni—'

The man who came hurtling out of the dark was not her husband but Dimitris Stephanides, the son of the late olive-mill owner. He was hissing at her to be quiet.

Ermione sprang back. The intruder had a flick knife. His eyes darting about, Stephanides took in the large, cluttered kitchen: the basin of dishes waiting to be washed, the dying fire, the shadowy corners beyond the range of the oil lamp. It was only nine o'clock, but the storm had caused a power outage. A laundry line was suspended from two long nails, hung with a child's underwear. On the table, next to a flower vase, lay a hand mirror, a comb, a pair of kitchen scissors.

'Where's your husband?'

Stephanides crossed the room, walking with a slight limp. He reeked of ouzo.

'He's not here.' Ermione had backed away, intent on Stephanides's every movement.

'I know he's not here! *Where* is he, I asked!'

Ermione's face quivered. 'I haven't seen my husband in months!'

'Oh, go on! He couldn't stay away from you this long.'

Stephanides snickered. He was a balding, thickly built man with eyes that seemed to be in perpetual search of some misplaced item. He was only in his mid-thirties, but the extravagant moustache looked like it would have to compensate for quite a lot. Years ago, he and Nikos Antipas had been classmates.

'I hear you're such a good wife too,' the intruder said, 'washing your husband's feet and all. Isn't that right?'

Ermione raised a shoulder, as if deprecating her own wifely devotion. She seemed about to say something when lightning filled the windows. She was a beautiful young woman, with honey-coloured hair tumbling over her shoulders. Her parents had died in Skala Sykaminias during the Occupation; her in-laws did not approve of their son's choice of bride any more than they did of his politics.

'I suppose you're hoping to collect the reward?' she blurted out.

Stephanides cleared his nose. 'I'm *planning* to collect the reward,' he stated, looking at her with a crooked smile. 'Now, for the last time, where is he?'

'I have no idea!' Ermione tossed out. 'But I know you'll never catch him!'

'You think so? You think he's too smart for us, eh?' Stephanides chortled. 'Funny thing is his own father doesn't think he's so smart, does he?' Nikos Antipas's father was a staunch royalist; he'd been heard to laugh in the *kapheneion*, hearing of the twenty-five-million-drachma reward placed on his son's head. 'He's not worth so much as a drachma, that's what his father said!' Stephanides's eyes gleamed with irony. 'What d'you say to that?'

'What do I say? I say a single one of his fingernails is worth more than the whole of you put together – moustache and all!'

At this, a black spark appeared in Stephanides's eyes.

'You bitch! Who do you think you are? You who came here with nothing but the rags on your back! You stupid, arrogant bitch!' Saying this, the intruder gave Ermione a violent push, watching her stagger backwards. She managed to right herself, only to trip on a bird whistle and go reeling to the floor, her slipper flying off her foot. 'A communist bitch opening her sewer of a mouth! At Dimitris Stephanides!'

Ermione sat hunched over her foot, her face scrunched with pain.

'What's the matter? Has the lady hurt herself?' Stephanides tilted forward, mock-solicitous. He was about to add something when Ermione leaned forward, spitting straight into the taunting face.

'You!' Stephanides looked stunned for a moment, but quickly rallied. He put away the knife. He extracted a handkerchief from his pocket, then a pair of handcuffs. He swiped at his cheek with the rumpled cloth, then stuffed it into Ermione's mouth. He grabbed her wrists and bound them with the handcuffs.

'So, where's that clever husband of yours now, eh? Let's see how quickly he comes to your rescue!'

It was raining again, the storm blowing gusts of water against the windowpanes. Ermione was weeping now, kneeling with her mouth gagged and her hands shackled, eyes wildly sweeping around the room. Stephanides stood stroking his moustache, like a military strategist contemplating his next manoeuvre.

All at once, as if inspired, he lunged towards the table and pounced on Ermione's scissors. With a swift, brutal gesture, he swept away the drying underwear. Then he cut down the laundry line, which was made of butcher's twine.

She began to jostle from side to side, resisting his efforts to bind her. Soon, he had her all trussed up, hunched over in the pool of flickering light, with the dying embers hissing in the hearth and the rain spitting on the tiled roof. There was a rip of lightning, a ferocious roar of thunder that seemed to shake the house to its very foundations. In the absence of the customary dowry, Nikos and his family lived in an old rented house, standing all alone on the way to the harbour.

Seizing a clump of hair, Stephanides began to hack, the scissors flashing through Ermione's thick tresses. He gripped an ear, letting the golden coils drop around the defeated body like flowers from a dying bush. He chopped on the left and on the right, on top and on the bottom, in front and in the back, never so much as glancing at Ermione's face until he was done. The young wife's head resembled the shorn skulls of female prisoners in wartime newsreels.

Only then did Stephanides stop to look into his victim's eyes. He lowered himself to Ermione's level and poked his face at hers, his tobacco-stained teeth bared in something between grin and grimace. 'So! Are you going to tell me now?'

The response to this was a choked sound, a toss of the violated head.

'No?' He stood up, letting his hand travel to his belt. There was a momentary hush. He let go of his buckle, then began to fumble with his fly buttons. He undid them slowly, deliberately, ignoring the muffled sounds coming out of Ermione's constricted mouth. His absorption was such that a moment passed before he registered that her eyes were fixed not on him, but somewhere beyond his shoulder.

There was no doubt about it: the child gave him pause. He stood on the threshold, a six-year-old boy dressed in a flannel robe, his bare feet peeping from under the hem, his eyes huge with terror. As the man's gaze fell on the boy, his mother let out a choked sound and appeared to grow limp, a look of pure entreaty filling her eyes.

The child was whimpering. He took a step forward, arms raised in frantic appeal. 'Mama!'

'Stay where you are!' Stephanides barked. 'Don't budge, or I'll kill your mother, understand?' He gave the child an arresting look, then shifted his attention back to Ermione. He appeared, all at once, almost conspiratorial, as if the two of them shared a secret beyond the child's ken. 'So, you ready to tell me now?'

The response this time was a strangled sound, a slow, defeated nod. Stephanides leaned forward. He yanked the gag out of Ermione's mouth, waiting, while she fought a spluttering cough. Finally, she stopped. She remained silent.

'Well?'

'He's in the hills... somewhere around Vafios.' The young mother looked doomed, her eyes darting towards her son. The boy's whimpering had turned into gulping sobs; a worm of mucus was sliding from his nose.

Stephanides ignored him, searching the mother's face. Unable to decide whether she was telling the truth, he reached into his trousers and whipped out his penis. The air in the room grew dense with menace. For a moment, Stephanides seemed to hesitate; then, squaring his shoulders, he began to urinate all over Antipas's wife. He aimed the stream at her neck, her face, her raw scalp, like a gardener bent on watering every corner of a neglected garden. Ermione, whose face was streaked with tears, now had urine coursing down her cheeks. She kept her head angled to one side, her eyes squeezed shut, her mouth twisted with disgust.

'So, is there anything else you might like to tell me?' Stephanides had taken out his knife and was sliding it across his own cushioned palm, as if testing its sharpness. 'Where can we find your husband?'

Slowly, Ermione's eyes blinked open. She glanced at her son, then at the knife, trembling violently. She looked straight into her captor's face and shook her head. There was, her gesture said, nothing else she could tell him. She was at his mercy. For another moment, Stephanides stood staring at her with restless eyes. The boy was clutching at his groin, his sobs turned to hiccups. The man looked fleetingly at a loss, like an actor groping for forgotten lines.

'Look here!' He had picked up the mirror and was thrusting it at Ermione, whose eyes were screwed shut. 'Look, I said: I want you to see yourself!'

And at last she did. She glanced at her own reflection, then raised her gaze, the sea-green eyes shimmering with accusation.

'Don't look at me like that! You're lucky it's me or you'd be losing something more precious than your whorish hair!' Stephanides rose and tossed the mirror into the sizzling hearth. The shattered glass made a shriek escape the child's mouth, but the intruder shot him another look and the shriek faded into a whimper.

Stephanides was about to put his knife away when something seemed to strike him. Bending forward, he narrowed his eyes and held the blade to the young mother's throat. 'If you're ever tempted to talk, remember this!' he said, gazing at her creamy neck like a lover. 'Understand?'

Ermione was silent. The child sobbed, a puddle of urine forming at his feet.

'Do you understand?'

Ermione dropped her gaze. She nodded.

Stephanides let out a long, heavy breath. He snapped the knife shut and returned it to his pocket, then went about freeing Ermione's wrists. Outside, it was raining again. Stephanides hesitated, then finally turned to go, pausing only long enough to pat the child's head, as if to reassure him that all would be well.

V

There were those who said that Dimitris Stephanides must have finally lost his reason. He was not, after all, a stupid man. But something seemed to have snapped in him during the black years. Jailed for the drunken assault on the schoolmistress, Dimitris was released after the Occupation, only to find his father imprisoned for wartime profiteering. He quarrelled with his uncle, who had taken over the olive mill. He began to beat his wife.

Ermione reported Stephanides, then took her son back to Skala Sykaminias. Everyone knew it was only a matter of time before Antipas got wind of his wife's ordeal. The village, as usual, was divided, the leftists choosing to believe Ermione – what reason did she have to lie after all? – the rightists supporting Stephanides's denials. The authorities kept a close watch on the communist commander's home, as well as on Ermione's relatives' residence. Stephanides was out on bail, pending trial.

Calliope didn't doubt Ermione's story, but she had her own worries that autumn, suspecting she might be pregnant, but above all uneasy over Leandros Tsouras's growing hostility. Was she perhaps imagining things? He was a man who criticised everybody, but with her, it seemed personal.

One night, smoking in bed next to Eli Dhaniel, she found herself voicing her concern. Holy Cross Day had come and gone, but the night was still almost as warm as summer. Sappho was sleeping by the balcony; Eli's foot was absently toying with Calliope's toes. He thought that she was probably fretting unnecessarily. Everybody said she was a superb teacher.

'I'm sure the Ministry of Education knows it as well as anyone.' Dhaniel was able to say this with some confidence because, once a year, a government watchdog appeared without warning in the nation's classrooms, monitoring teachers.

'Ach, I don't know,' Calliope said. 'I just hope you're right.'

Was she making too much of the conflict? Was she blowing it out of all proportion? She thought of a lame joke Tsouras had recently cracked in the teachers' room, hinting that she, too, might be a communist.

'As if I would ever support a party capable of organising a *paidomazoma*!' she had said to Tsouras. For several months, there had been reports that communist guerrillas were abducting children from right-wing villages, sending them to be raised by Eastern-bloc families.

Unthinkingly, Calliope went on to share this recent exchange with Eli, instantly stopping his flirtatious toes.

'So you, too, believe that nonsense.' Eli sighed, shaking his head. 'I never thought *you* would fall for their propaganda.'

'How do you know it's propaganda?' Calliope flashed out. Ever since the reports had begun to circulate, her mind kept conjuring up the alleged horror in northern Greece: the screaming children plucked out of their beds, the wailing mothers, the trucks trundling across the border, packed with terrified children on their way to strangers.

'Ach, the things people dream up these days.' Eli shook his head. 'If there's one thing I'm sure of it's that no Greek would ever abduct another Greek's children.'

Calliope agreed that the *paidomazoma* sounded far-fetched. On the other hand, would he have believed communists capable of burning villages, of burying their own people alive?

The question made Eli sit up, his voice swelling. 'You talk as if it's only the communists who commit atrocities! What about—'

'Ach, *Panaghia mou*! You sound like my pupils. *He did this to me, Kyria... yes, Kyria, but he started it, it's his fault!*' Calliope said all this in a falsetto voice, piqued by the ease with which he dismissed her views. Because he was older, because for years she had been an adoring, naive protégée, he had a tendency to be patronising.

'You should have been there to hear Petros scream when they pulled out his nails,' he was saying now. 'Pulled them one by one, the bastards!'

Petros was the son of a fisherman coerced into collaborating with the Germans. As if to redeem his family's reputation, the son had become a staunch communist, nabbed for painting a subversive slogan on the long sea wall: *BREAD AND OIL FOR THE PEOPLE!*

Calliope had seen the slogan, but she didn't have to hear Petros's screams to know that the authorities were torturing leftist suspects.

'What I want to know is what makes us different from the Germans,' she said, stubbing out her cigarette. The question had reared its head before, but she had never dared air it. 'We're doing the same things they did, the very same, though—'

'The Germans!' Eli rounded on her. 'If it weren't for the British and the Germans, we wouldn't be where we are today!'

'Yes, and before that it was the Turks. Everything was the Turks' fault!' She paused and ordered Sappho to quiet down. The dog had been roused by a passer-by playing a harmonica. 'The Germans, too, had their scapegoats, you know.'

'Calliope!' Eli stared, a vein pulsing in his temple. 'We're nothing like the Germans! We're just a poor nation others keep manipulating for their own ends!'

Calliope was silent, her mind calling up Greek battalions marching across Turkey before the Great Catastrophe. Well, she wasn't going to reopen *that* can of worms.

'I've had a letter from my French cousin,' she said instead. 'She's trying to understand what's happening here. I don't know what to tell her.'

'Tell her what I once said to your father,' Eli interposed. 'When two bulls tussle, it's always the grasshoppers that suffer.' He lay scratching his chest for a moment. 'By the time the British and the Americans and the Russians are done toying with us, we—'

'You're forgetting Tito,' she put in, faintly ironic.

'Indeed! And our other neighbours! That's what foreigners can't understand: it's not our fault we don't trust anyone.'

'Not even each other.' Calliope sighed, thinking of the Greek factions struggling for power, each accusing the other of having collaborated with the Germans. All at once, she was tired of it all; tired, as well as sorry to have provoked a political argument in bed.

She leaned over and lightly bit Eli's earlobe. 'I trust you!' she said.

This was true but had nothing to do with her flaring desire. Banishing her worries, she let her tongue run down Eli's chest, flirting with his navel. Hairless men were generally considered unmanly, but she much preferred Eli's smooth torso – Eli's and Lorenz Umbreit's – to her late husband's hirsute chest and back. In recent months, the doctor's body had begun to thicken, but his torso was still firm, his limbs youthfully muscled. She was deeply attached to his body's growing complexity. The skin around his neck, with its hint of old age, moved her in inexplicable ways; the flesh of his abdomen made her want to weep, as if all the sorrows of his past had found shelter within its tender cave. She and Eli might be politically opposed, but their bodies never failed to sing in harmony.

THREE

I

In late October, Calliope received a letter from Pericles, distressed to learn that he was in an Athens hospital, undergoing treatment for tuberculosis. Smuggled out by a leftist nurse, the letter was seven pages long, including three new poems about the Civil War.

That evening, taking Sappho for a walk, Calliope decided to stop at the clinic to share the poems with Eli. The clinic was closed. A note was taped to the door, scribbled by Olga Samiou, the late carpenter's widow, who was now assisting Dhaniel in the surgery. The doctor was attending a council meeting, the note stated. In case of an emergency, he was to be found at the town hall.

It was the evening before *Ohi* Day. Calliope headed home, Sappho trotting beside her through the shuttered *agora*. She had the dog on a leash because Sappho was prone to pounce on anything edible: dead rodents, mangled birds, other dogs' droppings. Pericles's news had left Calliope's heart feeling bruised, but the season, with its intimation of winter, had always tugged at her soul.

They had just passed the old bakery and were approaching a neighbourhood alley when Sappho came to a sudden halt. Sniffing the air, she began to whine, pulling on her leash. Calliope had become aware of strange, fuddled sounds issuing from beyond the stone wall running along the alley. At first, she thought it must be cats. Then she heard muffled thumps and a faint moaning sound.

Sappho let out a volley of barks, then bounded ahead, tugging Calliope along.

She stopped at the entrance to the alley, peering into the dark. There was a street lamp nearby, and the alley wasn't long, but it took Calliope a minute to make out a blurred figure clambering up from the ground. Sappho went on barking, straining on her leash.

There were, it turned out, two other men in the alley. One by one, they lurched into the night, their footsteps echoing on the cobblestones. Calliope took a tentative step forward. A few feet away, she made out the contours of a body lying in the shadows, making odd gulping sounds, the sound water made penetrating a densely clogged sewer.

Ach, Thee mou!

Growing resolute, Calliope tethered Sappho to a nearby tree. What she saw by the wall made her bones shudder, as if reliving the sensation of walloping boots and hammering fists on her own cringing flesh.

The battered man was Dimitris Stephanides. She would never have recognised him without his flamboyant moustache. The face and chest were awash in blood, the stomach clobbered so savagely that, Dhaniel would later testify, his bowel had been punctured. It had been too dark to identify the assailants, but they were almost certainly communists, avenging the assault on Antipas's wife.

The victim was making little agonised sounds, as though trying to squeeze some urgent message out of his mangled throat. Then, all at once, he stopped, growing still among the trampled weeds.

Calliope thought Stephanides was probably past help. She was about to check his pulse when Sappho let out a hair-raising howl. A tingling sensation rose at the back of Calliope's neck.

I must get out of here, she thought chaotically. *I must go to the police.*

II

The cramps started the next morning. In the hazy interlude between sleep and wakefulness, Calliope yawned, stretched, plumped up her pillow. The clock struck seven times. The neighbour's rooster began to crow. A few minutes passed, during which Calliope became aware of wetness between her thighs. There were two stains on the white cotton sheet, one small and round, the other elongated: a bright red exclamation mark issued by her own body. Gingerly, she shambled across the room, extracting a cotton rag from one of the drawers. She stuffed it into a pair of knickers, then plodded downstairs, Sappho nosing at her heels.

She was not pregnant after all. Her periods had always been erratic, but the only time she had stopped menstruating for over three months had been during the Occupation. Could this be a miscarriage? Her mother had had two early in her marriage. To her surprise, Calliope was simultaneously relieved and disappointed. She had not shared her suspicions with Eli, but finally did so that night, over an evening meal in her own kitchen.

'Why didn't you tell me?' Eli's voice carried a reproachful note. He stopped eating the fish soup she had cooked for him. It was one of his favourite dishes.

'I suppose I knew what would happen if I did tell you.'

'What would have happened?'

She gave him a slow, melancholy smile, as though responding to one of her godson's naive questions. 'You would have insisted I marry you.'

'No doubt. I might have even persuaded you.'

Calliope sat for a moment, poking her fork at a leftover fish bone.

'Eli,' she said, speaking with tender resolve. 'I've tried to make you see. I don't think I'm meant to marry, to have children and all that.'

He studied her for a moment, rubbing his jaw. He'd told her, when he came, that he had a toothache. 'What do you think you are meant to be doing?'

'I'm not sure, but…'

He reached across the table for her hand. 'Please level with me, darling.'

'I don't know!' She snatched her hand away and began fumbling for her pack of cigarettes. She struck a match. 'I don't know.'

'But what do you want?' Eli demanded with quiet tenacity. 'What is it that—'

'I don't know, I tell you!' She looked away, feeling the way she imagined her pupils did when called upon to give an answer they did not possess. 'I keep hoping I'll find out one of these days, then maybe—'

'Find out what, exactly?'

'Why I can't be like other women,' she said, her mother's words echoing in her ears. *We shouldn't have pushed you to marry… you were not born to be a wife and mother.* She stubbed out her cigarette, then rose to clear the table, her eyes stinging. 'I'll tell you one thing,' she said after a moment. 'I wouldn't want to have a daughter like me.'

'No?' He looked at her with the hint of a smile. 'I would!'

'You think so?'

'Absolutely!'

She smiled at him sadly. 'I don't think we would have been happy, married to each other,' she heard herself say at last.

'Why not?'

'Oh, my dear!' Calliope averted her gaze, then reached for an apple and began peeling it, her eyes fastened on the curling skin as though the task demanded all her attention. Not for the first time, she found herself trying to imagine a life with Eli's children and mother-in-law. Although Eli's daughters were virtually grown, the mental picture refused to gel: waking up to breakfast with husband and children, having to satisfy everyone's daily demands, never having any time to think, to read, to daydream. She believed she was not cut out for this particular challenge; she probably was too selfish but couldn't say so. He might think she didn't love his children, which was far from the truth, though she did love Aristides best.

Calliope offered Eli half a cored apple. She said, 'Sooner or later, you would have started bossing me around. Isn't that a husband's prerogative?' The words were accompanied by a small smile, fond, yet vaguely ironic.

'Is it?'

She was being frivolous, his gaze told her. She had picked up the apple peel and was winding it around her forefinger, like a bandage. Although the last statement had been meant in jest, it came to her that it might nonetheless be true.

'You don't really believe I'd boss you around, do you?' Eli was saying.

'Yes... yes, I think I do,' Calliope answered, admitting the truth. She looked at him with unflinching eyes. 'You would have forbidden me to smoke in bed, to keep Sappho indoors, to—'

'Calliope!' he broke in. 'I'm not some kind of... of tyrant! I would not have been issuing orders. You should know—'

'Maybe not orders,' she allowed, growing obstinate, 'but you would... oh, please, let's drop this subject once and for all, darling, shall we?' She turned toward the window, feeling the threat of tears.

Mirto's cat was loping across the garden, a newborn kitten clamped between her teeth. The day Mirto was buried, Loula had sneaked into the house and tried to jump into the open casket. There had been mourners coming and going. Calliope threw Loula out time and again, but the cat kept stealing in. When the pall-bearers came out with the casket, Loula followed them all the way to church, alongside the mourners.

'Please don't cry.' Eli held Calliope's fingers, his nut-brown eyes mellow with solicitude. 'I'm just trying to understand, my love.'

But the words only made fresh tears spring into Calliope's eyes. 'Oh, why must life be so complicated?' she said, swiping at her cheeks.

'Life's not that complicated,' he said patiently, as if explaining some elusive concept to one of his children. 'It's people like us that needlessly complicate it.'

'You think so?' Calliope paused, mulling over her late husband's observation that she thought too much. Beyond the

229

fence, she could hear a neighbour feeding her chickens, addressing the stupid creatures as tenderly as some mothers did a beloved child. This particular mother, though, was often heard screeching abuse at her children, saving her tenderness for her hens. No, Calliope decided, Eli was wrong. Life *was* complicated. Even the simplest human beings were complicated.

Finally, Eli changed the subject, going on to talk about the men responsible for Dimitris Stephanides's murder. One of the men had managed to escape to the hills, but the second man, a Petra barber, had been quickly nabbed. The third man, Fat Dinos, had just been arrested that day.

'They say it was Marina who denounced him,' Calliope put in. She had heard the rumours in the *agora* but was finding them hard to credit. Marina was Fat Dinos's timid wife. 'Do you think it's true?'

It was. Chatterbox Evgenia had been to the clinic, confiding the story in tedious detail. How Dinos had come home, splattered with blood. How, the very next day, Marina went straight to the police. Evgenia was Marina's mother. She suffered from occasional hives, and from a chronic inability to keep anything to herself.

Calliope sat thinking of poor Marina, mocked in public by her own husband, sometimes in their two sons' presence. 'I wouldn't have thought she had it in her to seek revenge,' she said.

'Oh, I don't know about revenge. I suspect she just saw an opportunity to get rid of the bully, and grabbed it,' Eli said and sighed. He looked pensive for a long moment, then raised his eyes, smiling a little.

'What?'

'I was just thinking: poor Marina may be the only one in the whole country to benefit from the Civil War.'

Calliope laughed, planting a kiss on Eli's neck. She loved his neck. She loved his melancholy air and his sense of humour. Above all, she loved his inability to keep a grudge.

III

Three days before Christmas, Odysseus the beekeeper was caught red-handed, aiding and abetting the rebels. He had been arrested once before, after a mule-riding farmer had spotted a guerrilla huddled under Odysseus's cow's belly, sucking on her udders like a greedy calf. The beekeeper was suspected of having deliberately let his cow loose, providing nourishment for the rebels. He had been interrogated but quickly released. Some believed this was because his daughter was married to the new mayor; others said it was probably due to his advanced age. Odysseus himself believed he had succeeded in outwitting the police. He had, after a drinking binge, confided this to Calliope. His children might think he was growing dim, yet somehow he'd managed to convince the chief of his innocence.

The beekeeper had lain low for several months, devoting himself to his beehives and his youngest grandson, who was recovering from polio. The assignment he eventually accepted entailed carting hand grenades to the outskirts of nearby Petri. Twice a year – at Easter and at Christmas – he travelled to surrounding villages to peddle his famed thyme honey.

On that fateful December day, he stuffed the bag of grenades into the bottom of a large jute sack, piled jars of honey on top, and clambered onto his rickety mule cart. He left after the midday meal, taking a shotgun along, ostensibly to ward off a potential guerrilla attack on some mountain road.

The men who ambushed Odysseus were not partisans but gendarmes. They had sprung out from behind a clump of trees, brandishing guns, shouting at the old man to halt. Despite the care he had taken to conceal the grenades, the flustered Odysseus lost his wits and reached for his gun. He was aiming it at the gendarmes when two shots rang out, shattering the bucolic silence. One of the bullets went into Odysseus's left cheek and out the other; the second hit his shoulder.

Eventually, the old man was transported to the *agora*. It was

Saturday afternoon and the streets bustled with shoppers and idle old men ambling about, their hands clasped behind their backs. The moment the gendarmes tossed the beekeeper out of his cart, a crowd gathered around the *plateia*. Odysseus had been dumped under the mulberry tree, his spotted skull exposed, his turban uncoiling on the cobblestones. By the time Sergeant Floros arrived on the scene, blood was streaming from Odysseus's shoulder.

'Ach, *Panaghia mou*, is he dead?' *Papa* Iakovos's sister asked, bouncing out of the *pantopoleion*, a wicker basket swinging from her arm.

'Nah, he's not dead,' the butcher answered. 'They caught him, though, smuggling grenades to the guerrillas.'

'Old Odysseus?' The priest's sister shifted her basket. 'Impossible! He's been our neighbour for years, *kale*!'

'Ach, Marianthi! These days you can't trust your own mother, let alone your neighbours,' the butcher countered.

The wounded man groaned, as if in feeble protest.

This was when Calliope, who had been at the pharmacy, hurried to join the crowd. One day, when she was an adolescent, the beekeeper had found her crying after school, had taken her to his farm to see a litter of newborn puppies. That was the beginning of the comfort she still found in dogs' company. It was Odysseus who had given her Socrates.

The moment Calliope understood who the victim was, she attempted to push through the crowd, only to find her way blocked by Sergeant Floros. The policeman was a heavyset man with small ears and a large, florid face resembling a wilted cabbage.

'In God's name, what are you doing?' Calliope spurted. 'Are you going to let him bleed to death – your own compatriot?'

'Compatriot! The bastard would sell us all to the Russians if he had his way!'

'But he… he's just an old man!' Calliope pleaded.

'An old man he is, *Kyria* Calliope, but even a geezer can kill, you know!'

'Has he shot anyone? Odysseus?' Calliope's mind was working feverishly.

She knew that Eli was in Kaloni, getting a tooth extracted, but her eyes went on scanning the crowd, until she spotted one of her pupils. She beckoned the child over, instructing him to run and fetch the mayor, Odysseus's son-in-law.

Floros grabbed the boy's arm. 'There's no point.'

'What do you mean there's no point?' Calliope bristled. 'Even a communist's entitled to medical care!'

Floros opened his mouth to say something, but the crowd's jeers made his response redundant.

'He deserves to hang from this here tree if you ask me!' someone said, spitting. 'First, he lets the guerrillas have milk, then he gives them arms!'

'Ach, *Thee mou*,' Calliope murmured, still casting about for someone willing to intervene. At the back of the crowd, she spotted the headmaster, but dismissed any thought of appealing to him. She stood craning her neck, hoping to see one of the village councillors.

'Please... I beg you to do something!' She was once more addressing Sergeant Floros, whose parents had moved to Molyvos from the Peloponnese to care for his young daughter after his wife died in childbirth. 'You have an old father yourself,' she implored. 'What if—'

'My father's not a communist!'

'All right, so Odysseus is a communist! But you, all of you, are Christians! How can you all—'

'We may be Christians,' Makis the postman hollered, 'but communists have no use for religion. They don't even believe in God, *Kyria* Calliope!'

Calliope did not answer. The police sergeant was her one chance, if only because she had taken his daughter under her wing after the mother's death.

'Look, you can put him on trial if you have to. I just want to stop his bleeding!' Calliope pleaded. She made another attempt to push through, but Floros stopped her again, a defensive note creeping into his voice.

'I'm under orders, *Kyria* Calliope.'

Calliope rounded on him. 'Under orders to do what? Let an old man bleed to death just because you're too cowardly to act like a man?' She pointed towards Odysseus. 'He may be a communist, but at least he wasn't too cowardly to risk his life for what he believed in!'

'Let him die for his beliefs then!' the postman shouted. He was exceptionally tall and bony, with a small head and long neck that made him look like a giraffe looming over the heads of the crowd. Beside him, Calliope spotted poor Apollon, his backward nephew. As she glanced their way, her pupil raised a catapult, aiming it down at Odysseus. The stone went whistling in the air, landing on the beekeeper's blood-soaked shoulder.

'Apollon! What in God's name are you doing? Stop!' Calliope shrieked, seeing the boy fiddle with another stone. 'Stop it right now, I said!'

The way the child dropped the stone, it might have been a hot chunk of coal. He buried his chin in his chest and began to blubber, his thick brows knitted together. The wounded man's moaning was growing more feeble.

At that moment, as if inspired by the backward child, several men started to pick up stones, hurling them at the beekeeper's contorted body.

'Death to all Bolshevik traitors!'

'Down with communism!'

'Here's to King and country!'

'Please stop!' Calliope's voice was starting to crack. 'We're supposed to be a civilised nation, not a tribe of barbarians!'

'Even civilised nations execute traitors, *Kyria* Calliope,' Floros put in. Calliope made another attempt to slide past him but was stopped again, this time rather roughly. Shaking herself free, she whipped around and was about to address the crowd when she caught the headmaster staring straight at her. Tsouras's expression was only slightly more supercilious than usual, but Calliope's body recoiled from the loathing in his prolonged gaze. And at that moment, she briefly forgot all about the dying Odysseus, feeling as if her own cringing flesh had just been assailed by bullets.

FOUR

I

Just before Easter 1949, there was an outbreak of chicken pox among Molyvos's children. With half her pupils away, Calliope decided to scrap her lesson plan: she would spend the last hour or so on a little-known chapter from their own history. Perched on the edge of her desk, she told her class how, back in the fifteenth century, Molyvos had been rescued by a princess named Onetta d'Oria. In those days, the island was still ruled by the Genoese; an Italian prince had built the fortress still crowning their village.

'But the prince was away, the Turks were coming and, well, something had to be done, right?' Calliope paused dramatically, then went on to speak of the villagers' fear and d'Oria's despair, of people's prayers for a divine miracle.

There had been no miracle but, just as the Turks approached, the princess astonished the crowd, appearing in full armour, shouting: 'Let's teach those marauders a lesson they'll never forget!'

The children sat listening, alert and still, speechless when Calliope reached the triumphant ending. The classroom was so quiet two flies could be heard buzzing at the windows. At that moment, a knock came at the door; a note from the headmaster was handed to Calliope, requesting that she drop in at day's end.

The request was not unusual. Tsouras often found excuses to detain his teachers. But that afternoon, Calliope felt her skin tighten as she entered the headmaster's office. The moment Tsouras invited her to take a seat, she knew that she was about to be caught in a web as fatal as that of a deadly tarantula. Tsouras was running his hand over his face, as if ensuring everything was in place.

'*Kyria* Calliope,' he said, speaking formally. 'As you know, I've always done my best, my very best, to be fair-minded. Strict, I admit, but fair-minded.' He paused with a conscious sort of delicacy, as if offering her a chance to refute his gambit.

Calliope was silent.

'Well, as I was saying, I've done my best to fulfil my duties as far as—'

'Oh, please! Spare me the preamble, will you?'

'I beg your pardon?' Tsouras hesitated. 'Very well. As you wish, *Kyria* Calliope. It is my duty, then – my unpleasant duty – to inform you that the Ministry of Education has reached a unanimous decision to relieve you of your duties at the end of the school year.' The words came out sounding rehearsed. 'There will, of course, be an official letter, but I thought… I thought it only—'

At this point, Calliope shook herself out of her mental stupor. 'Relieve me of my duties?' she echoed, her demeanour hiding her anxiety. 'On what grounds?'

'On what grounds?' He stared at her with arch surprise, as though she were an unruly pupil foolishly defending herself in the face of incontrovertible evidence. 'You're a fine teacher, *Kyria* Calliope,' he continued. 'I know we've had our differences, but all the same, I'd be the last person to deny your skills.'

This speech, too, had a rehearsed quality, but when the headmaster opened his mouth again, Calliope's skin suddenly proved too tight to contain her outrage.

'What have you done – told them that I'm not a suitable role model?' It was something he had said during one of their recent clashes.

'There is that,' he said after the briefest hesitation, 'and, well, truth to tell, there have been complaints—'

'Complaints!' she scoffed. 'From whom?'

Tsouras let out a forbearing breath. He steepled his fingers. 'As

I say, there have been complaints, but that's not the issue now. The issue is your current political dossier. As you—'

Once more, she didn't let him finish. 'My political dossier!' she erupted. 'I'm a centrist, as you know.'

Tsouras offered a forgiving smile. 'I know that's what you've told us. It isn't what the authorities have been led to believe.'

Calliope stared, doing her best to subdue the fluttering in her chest. 'Go on.'

'The authorities have received reports that you've been listening to Sofia broadcasts. I'm sure I don't have to tell you—'

'Sofia!' she broke in. Radio Sofia was a clandestine Greek communist station broadcasting from Bulgaria. 'That's a ridiculous lie!'

He stirred a little. 'It's not what your neighbours say.'

'My neighbours?' Calliope stopped, her lower eyelid twitching. 'It's a lie,' she repeated, striving for composure.

'Are you accusing your neighbours of malice?'

'I don't know what anyone told you,' said Calliope. 'I know I'd never waste a single moment listening to Radio Sofia.'

'No?'

'Absolutely not. I know the communist broadcasts can lie just as shamelessly as our own government stations!'

The headmaster's lips twitched in what might have been a smile or a warning. There was a rap on the door.

'Come in!' Tsouras swivelled towards the entrance, a squeak of surprise escaping his lips. He sprang out of his chair, beaming. A young man had just thrust his head through the open door.

'*Yassou, Baba!*' Timolis Tsouras stopped in his tracks, his gaze sliding towards Calliope. 'I'm sorry. I'll—'

'Come in, come in, my boy! Let me greet you properly!' The headmaster held out his arms. He introduced his son to Calliope, who registered the young man's beauty despite her inner turmoil. Timolis Tsouras resembled his father in height and colouring, but whereas the headmaster's eyes were pale and supercilious, his son's were almost violet, as alert and curious as the eyes of a puppy exploring a new domain.

The headmaster studied his son, eyes crinkled with unbridled pride. 'I wasn't expecting you for another hour!'

'I found a taxi. I'll wait outside.' The young man spoke in a warm, sprightly voice. 'Nice meeting you!' he tossed out towards Calliope.

'Please excuse me for a moment.' Tsouras followed his son and stood whispering outside, while Calliope watched the afternoon light dance on the desk, the blackboard, the shelves holding attendance records and students' report cards. The windows were open, letting in the scents of spring, the cry of a distant cuckoo.

Re-entering the room, Tsouras strode towards his desk and sat down energetically, pushing up his sleeves. There was a moment when something unexpected, some spark of human sympathy, glimmered between them, but was quickly lost, like a dying ember.

'I am sorry,' he said, composing his features into an expression of professional gravitas. 'I wasn't expecting him.'

Calliope offered a minimal shrug, her eyes fixed on a desktop globe standing on Tsouras's desk. The room, the whole universe, seemed too cramped to contain her dread. What would she do if Tsouras wasn't bluffing, if he really had the Ministry of Education behind him?

She stared at him, grappling for composure. 'Let me make this clear,' she finally said. 'I'm not a communist, or even a leftist. I am a centrist,' she reiterated.

'A centrist,' he echoed, as if essaying a word whose precise meaning eluded him. 'A centrist is someone who could go one way or another, depending on—'

'A centrist,' she broke in, 'is someone who believes in democracy, who—'

'Democracy?' he said, with the same querying, slightly bewildered air.

'Democracy!' she repeated. 'It's the one thing I believe is worth fighting for. The one thing neither the left nor the right is offering us.'

'Indeed!' He cocked an ironic eyebrow, lips stretched in something resembling a smile. 'And yet,' he said, 'your close friend, the doctor, is a well-known communist.' He crossed his arms over his chest. 'Isn't that so?'

'I have friends who are communists, others who are royalists,' she said with calm certitude. 'I don't necessarily share their political views.'

'Hm,' he said, 'I've been led to believe that all your friends are… if not communists, then at least strong leftists.'

'Well, you've been misled,' Calliope retorted. 'Olga Samiou, one of my oldest friends, happens to be a royalist, so—'

'Olga Samiou, the doctor's aide?'

'Yes.'

Tsouras continued to look sceptical, perhaps because he could not conceive of a communist doctor hiring a royalist who not only cleaned his surgery but served as a de facto nurse. 'All the same,' he said.

'All the same, my friends' political views are beside the point,' Calliope stated. 'The point is I am being dismissed for the wrong reasons.'

'And what would the right reasons be, might I ask?'

'The only legitimate reason would be incompetence or abuse of my charges.' She paused. 'Which even you can't bring yourself to accuse me of.'

'My dear *Kyria* Calliope.' Tsouras let out a martyred sigh. 'I am not an unreasonable man,' he said, looking at her with a new expression, at once reproachful and faintly wounded. The look seemed familiar somehow. It reminded Calliope unpleasantly of someone, but whom?

And then it came to her: Seraphim, the building contractor! He, too, had gazed at her with this air of injured pride. And though years had gone by since the German roof repair, the memory sent forth a sudden spasm of hot indignation.

'You're not an unreasonable man,' she echoed ironically, 'but you are a spiteful one!' She was beside herself now, seething with the realisation that the battle had been lost long before she entered the office. All that was left to her now was the sour satisfaction of venting her rage. 'You tried to seduce me and did not succeed. That's what this is all about, isn't it?'

'*Kyria* Calliope!'

'This has nothing to do with my politics but with your wounded pride,' Calliope continued. 'If I'd let you have your way, you wouldn't give a button about my politics!'

'*Kyria* Calliope, if you please!' Tsouras massaged his chin, staring at her from under his bushy eyebrows.

'What?' she said. 'You think it's wrong to breach professional decorum, but acceptable to spread malicious lies?'

'Ach, *Kyria* Calliope.' Tsouras sighed, a sorely tested man growing resigned. 'You seem to think that I'm out to punish you, whereas the truth…' He hesitated, then judiciously corrected himself. 'Or let's just say the fact… the fact is I wasn't the only one to witness your outburst over the beekeeper.'

'Odysseus was an old man and a good neighbour. My outburst had nothing to do with politics!'

'Maybe so, maybe so.' Tsouras glanced at her, then consulted his watch. 'I might be willing to believe you, but the decision, as I said, is not in my hands; it's the Ministry's.'

There was a beat of silence, during which a sheep was heard bleating beyond the window. 'Certainly, you'll be given a chance to contest it in due course, *Kyria* Calliope.'

He waited. When she failed to respond, Tsouras reached for a sheaf of papers and began to slide them into his open briefcase. He rose then, ostentatiously clearing his throat. 'I thought it only fair to prepare you. Now, if you'll please excuse me…'

He stood waiting, stiff with courtesy, fingertips drumming on his briefcase.

And, at last, Calliope stirred. Placing her hands on the chair's arms, she hoisted herself to her feet, then stood facing Tsouras, speechless with loathing.

'You bastard,' she said at last. Her hands longed to scratch his smug face, but she spoke quietly, neutrally, as if this were a secret only the two of them were entitled to share. 'You hypocritical bastard.'

II

Was Heraclitus right, then, saying character was destiny? If so, was her reluctance to acquiesce and conform, her inability to curry favour with the likes of Tsouras, responsible for her predicament? She remembered reading Stendhal, asking herself whether it was possible to live in society and still be true to oneself, without hypocrisy, without the need for perpetual compromise?

Questions. Nothing but questions in the aftermath of her ignoble dismissal. Enough questions to last an entire summer, with nothing to look forward to. By now, the letter from the Ministry of Education had been received, read, and answered, in the full knowledge that nothing was going to reverse the bureaucrats' decision.

Once the term ended, Calliope set herself the stupefying challenge of getting out of bed every morning, mustering the wherewithal to wash, make breakfast, and find a pair of fresh knickers and something with which to cover her useless bones.

She had no ambitions, no aspirations, other than to get through the day. She was, she allowed, luckier than the former headmaster, who had been arrested for humming a subversive song. But what was she supposed to do with the rest of her life – scour pots and polish cutlery? Eli had his patients, he had his family, so Calliope read more voraciously than ever, and slept more, and wrote longer letters. She wrote to Rupert Ealing, who was still working for the British government. She wrote to Pericles, who was still in recovery. She was, on at least one occasion, tempted to write to Umbreit, but what would be the point?

She fought off the impulse by writing to her Parisian cousin. She had never met her French uncle's daughters, but felt close to the elder one, a Comparative Literature professor named Alexandra Sorel. The younger one, Marianne, had married an American and was living in Massachusetts, working as an interpreter.

One day, having received a letter from Pericles, Calliope impulsively sat down to translate two of his latest poems into French. Thrilled by the results, she sent them to her cousin. There was welcome distraction in all these activities but inadequate consolation. When her name day came around, she went to the cemetery, where she unburdened herself at her mother's grave.

One of the things she could not bring herself to confess to Eli but did while communing with her late mother was the weight of shame she carried that summer, as if she had been caught committing a crime and couldn't bear to show her face in public. She walked Sappho late in the evening, or in mid-afternoon, when most villagers rested. She paid a neighbour's son to post letters and buy groceries, though she had few needs and little appetite.

One afternoon in August she went back to the cemetery and encountered Stavroula Houmi, the local kiosk owner's wife and the late Captain Yorgos's sister. She was a middle-aged woman with a square body and frantic eyes, one of which stared at Calliope from within a mound of grotesquely swollen flesh, like an insect caught in a clump of fresh dough.

'Stavroula!' Calliope, who was sitting at her mother's graveside, sprang up, trapped between solicitude and a wrenching need to flee. 'What happened to you?'

Stavroula had lost both her brother and a young son during the Occupation and had yet to shed her grieving, distracted air.

'Ach, *Kyria* Calliope!' Stavroula's face crumpled. 'Only the *Panaghia* knows my sorrows.' She had left home wearing her apron and was nervously burrowing in its pocket, the sun taunting her greying head.

'Come.' Calliope patted Stavroula's shoulder. 'Let's sit in the shade.'

There was a bench near the entrance, under a leafy tree. Calliope steered Stavroula towards it, the air around them pulsing with heat and insects.

'Ach, ach, ach, *Kyria* Calliope!' Stavroula flumped down, clutching a handkerchief, her knees wide apart. She was barely coherent, but Calliope gradually gathered the problem had to do with Stavroula's husband, who had been caught with a stash of *Orizospastis*, the underground communist paper.

'I would have stood by him, would have died with him!'

Stavroula said with feeling. 'But to think he betrayed his customers! To think he would agree to sign the Declaration!'

'Ach, don't be so hard on him, Stavroula,' Calliope ventured. 'It isn't easy to say no when—'

'My brother said no to the Germans!' Stavroula flashed out. 'The bastards pulled out his nails and crushed his *ameletita*, but he didn't give in, did he?' She faced Calliope with her wild eyes, one swollen, the other glinting with hot indignation. 'How can you sign something renouncing what you've spent all your life believing?'

Calliope sighed. 'Not everyone is born to be a hero, Stavroula.'

'Well, I wasn't born to be a coward's wife!'

What was there to say?

Stavroula blew her nose, mulling things over. 'Fine,' she allowed after the briefest pause. 'So he couldn't help being spineless, but what am I supposed to do? How can I show respect to a man like that?'

'Maybe you should just try to pity him?'

'I do pity him! I do! What I can't do is wash his feet and share a bed with a jellyfish! He's lucky I've been willing to cook his dinner!'

'Ach, Stavroula.'

'It's true. I served it to him like always, but when I got ready to sleep on the daybed, he flew into a rage and...' She pointed at her swollen eye. 'You can see for yourself!'

Calliope shifted her perspiring thighs. 'What are you going to do?'

'I don't know... but I'm not going back to him!' Stavroula cleared her nostrils. She wanted to go to her married daughter in Athens, but didn't know whether her son-in-law would allow it. Also, she didn't have the money for a ticket.

'I can give you money,' Calliope put in, glad to be able to help. 'But are you sure—'

'I'm sure!' Stavroula insisted. She was, Calliope thought, as bullheaded as her late brother. She even looked like him, with her jutting chin and blazing eyes. 'It's not just the Declaration,' she went on, kneading her soggy handkerchief. 'He's been beating me ever since the Occupation. You'd think it was my fault our poor Manolaki died.'

At this, Calliope began to massage her temples. It was one thing to reject a man because he was no hero, but if he beat his wife? She wasn't sure what she, or even Stavroula, ought to do. The last thing she wanted was to meddle in others' private affairs.

'I could lie down with a man who beat me while drunk,' Stavroula was saying. 'I've done that! But with a sober man... a coward who whips me like a dog? Never!'

Suddenly, perhaps recalling the purpose of her flight to the cemetery, she fumbled in her pocket and whipped out a photograph. A young soldier had been captured leaning against a eucalyptus tree, smiling at the camera.

'That's the man I married!' she declared, pride and bitterness vying in her voice. 'I rue the day we exchanged marriage wreaths,' she said, spitting at the snapshot. 'I'm going to put a curse on him!' she announced. 'Maybe the *Panaghia* will hear my prayers.'

She began to scratch in the moist earth, first with her nails, then with a stick she found lying in the dirt. She seemed to have forgotten all about Calliope as she crouched in the afternoon dazzle, muttering under her breath like some demented witch. Calliope watched with an inner shiver. Stavroula was tearing her husband's photo. She ripped it into tiny bits, then hunched over and, breathing harshly, buried the annihilated image in the cemetery's earth. Calliope became acutely aware of the vibration of insects, the hiss of the wind taunting the tree branches.

Finally, Stavroula scrambled to her feet and clapped away the dirt on her hands, shooting a defiant glance over her shoulder. It was going on four o'clock. The battered woman's features quivered, then collapsed into a mask of sudden defeat.

'Stavroula!' Calliope was still fighting the compulsion to flee, but found herself offering the comfort of her own arms. 'Come. Don't... please don't cry, Stavroula.' She began to make soothing maternal sounds, as if the distraught woman were her own daughter and not someone easily old enough to be her mother.

'But what am I going to do, *Kyria* Calliope? Where—'

'Don't worry. Come. It'll be all right,' Calliope said, growing decisive. She took the trembling woman's arm. 'First, we're going to send a telegram to Athens, then we'll sit and wait. You'll have to be very patient, Stavroula. Let's wait and see what your daughter has to say, shall we?'

III

Inspiration, Calliope would some day tell an Athenian interviewer, is like an apricot or a cherry pip, spat out and lying ignored on the wayside, until some sudden change in environmental conditions makes it sprout and grow into a fruit-laden tree.

The metaphor would be offered by way of explaining a life-altering idea inspired by the chance encounter with Stavroula Houmi. The change in her own circumstances was, of course, due to her lost teaching post, but there was also the nagging guilt over the fortune teller's neglected house. She had, she would say in the years to come, been obsessed with the need to atone for her innate selfishness.

She had certainly felt selfish at the cemetery, thinking she ought to take Stavroula home with her, yet recoiling from the idea. It was, she argued with herself, like asking a solitary monk to host some garrulous sailor washed up after a shipwreck.

And yet, she was not indifferent to Stavroula's plight. Plodding down towards the telegraph office, Calliope recalled the distressing stories she had heard from her friend Eleni, who was now working as a midwife, privy to married women's woes. And here was one of these secretly wretched women, shuffling downhill with her apron on, her face blotched by tears. The kiosk owner was a tense but mild-mannered man. Who would have thought he would turn out to be a wife beater?

It was sheer happenstance that the road from the cemetery to the *agora* led past the fortune teller's house, that recent inertia had not blunted Calliope's native resourcefulness. As she walked past Zenovia's entrance, mechanically glancing at the shuttered windows, her mind was still groping for a solution to Stavroula's dilemma. The house was large and still empty. Why not let Stavroula take refuge there, at least temporarily? Maybe the daughter would talk her husband into taking her mother in; or the chastened kiosk owner, having to fend for himself, would beg his wife to return, and swear never to lay a hand on her. At the very least, poor Stavroula would have gained time to reflect on her situation.

That Zenovia herself would have thoroughly approved of the invitation made it seem not only fitting but almost preordained. Not that Calliope had any desire to sway Stavroula either way. Having wired Athens, she hurried home and got the key to Zenovia's house. She showed the hand-wringing woman where bedding was kept, then beat a hasty retreat.

Within a week, the kiosk owner's wife was settled with her daughter in the capital. Calliope felt both gratified and relieved, yet more aimless than ever. Before her expulsion from school, she had worked on the idea of starting a children's library, a project she'd planned to pursue during the summer break. If she had done nothing about it, it was only because of the lassitude that had come over her in the wake of her unexpected dismissal.

Stavroula's daughter had sent her thanks, but Calliope continued to flounder on her bleak mental island, comforted by Eli and his son, distracted by books and letters. In early September, there was a letter from Pericles, whose health was finally on the mend. Calliope, who communicated with him through his devoted nurse, was delighted by the medical prognosis, all the more as she was able to write back with exciting news: her cousin Alexandra had sent Pericles's poems to a French journal and its editor was eager to publish them!

Alexandra's surprising letter so lifted Calliope's spirits that she sat down that very evening to render Pericles's latest poem into French. All at once, she understood how a shipwrecked sailor might feel, spotting a flickering light on an alien shore.

IV

And then, one Saturday morning, the most surprising letter of all arrived. Calliope had become accustomed to receiving Umbreit's greetings around Christmas and her birthday; had felt secretly gratified that he had not forgotten her, though she resisted the temptation to write back, and was not sure why he went on writing. Perhaps it was his way of expiating his guilt?

But it was only October now and, this time, Umbreit was writing to request a favour. He was teaching literature at Heidelberg University, as well as trying his hand at writing a novel. The plot was set in wartime Molyvos. He had, of course, done research but still had questions only a Greek could answer. He would certainly understand if Calliope declined to reply but was hoping that her love of books might persuade her to oblige him by answering some questions.

Calliope read the letter but postponed making a decision because she was helping her eleven-year-old godson with his homework, then taking him for a swim.

It was nearly noon when Aristides finished his assignments, dashing out to fetch a classmate named Fanny Dimou, hoping she might be allowed to join them.

The Dimous lived nearby, so Calliope knew the family well. She thought it a great pity that Fanny's father would not let his clever daughter attend Petra's middle school. Knowledge was a fine thing, the father had conceded, but sending a young girl out of the village was asking for trouble.

Such attitudes had rankled with Calliope ever since Eleni Bastia's educational ambitions had been thwarted, but Fanny's parents often kept her brother home as well: to pick olives or do farm chores. Calliope, who was just then reading *Jude the Obscure*, found her thoughts drifting sadly to Gavril Dimou, who, at that very moment, was probably tending to farm animals, while his father sat in the *kapheneion*, drinking and arguing over politics.

All through the summer there had been talk of the split between

Tito's Yugoslavia and the USSR. While Fanny sought her father's permission to go to the beach, Calliope eavesdropped on the men's rehash of the political fallout. Yorgos Roumeliotis, the new schoolmaster hired to replace her, was taking part in the discussion. He was somewhere in his mid-thirties, pale and skeletal, with the vaguely resigned look of a man married to a shrew. Calliope had yet to be introduced but noted from a distance that he had a slight speech defect, making his 'r's sound like those of a Frenchman trying to recite Homer.

'My name is Yorgos Roumeliotis, and I am from Ksirokambi.' Aristides was soon aping the new schoolmaster. 'From Ksi-ro-kam-bi!' he said, spluttering with mirth. The boy had a gift for mimicry, delighting Calliope with his acute observations. Halfway down to the beach, he paused to inspect a fly trapped in a pine tree's sap, and then a crab spider that, he told his classmate, could change colour on moving from one plant to another. Calliope had lived in the village all her life but had never noticed this. And what would she do in a year or two, when Aristides was no longer interested in his *Nona*?

The moment they arrived on the beach, the children sprinted into the sea, while Calliope stood clutching her parasol, shouting after them to stay near the shore. She then sat in the shade to read, dimly aware of the squawking seagulls, the rhythmic slap of waves on the pebbly shore.

By the time her god-daughter found her, Calliope was fully absorbed in Hardy, but looked up to see Athena giggling, about to squirt water from a fat sea slug. The child had her late father's observant eyes, her mother's round face and luminous skin.

Eleni had been one of the prettiest girls in the village. She was still only in her twenties, but already resigned to having been born into an unlucky family. Not only had she lost a young husband, but her mother had died of mushroom poisoning, her father of cirrhosis. Her Uncle Natis, on the other hand, seemed to be thriving, having quickly fathered two robust sons with Dora the weeper.

Tomas had died during an epileptic seizure, leaving behind an inconsolable widow. Eleni was mute for days and might have remained in a state of prolonged mourning had it not been for her daughter, and the pressure from the doctor to take up midwifery. Veroniki, the old midwife, had finally passed away and Dhaniel was barely coping with all the new births and ailments in the wake of the Occupation. Eleni was persuaded to go to Mytilene and train as a midwife.

The two friends sat chatting under the tamarisks, but Calliope's mind kept wandering in private directions. Eventually, she mentioned Umbreit's letter.

Eleni stopped and regarded her keenly. 'Are you going to answer?'

'I don't know. I haven't decided.' Calliope tapped her cigarette. 'But just think, Elenitsa: a novel about our village!'

Eleni chewed on this for a moment. 'But do you really think he'll find a publisher? Why would anyone be interested in a backward Greek island?'

Calliope's eyes had come to rest on the three children, who were now playing together at the water's edge. 'I don't see why not,' she said, sounding vaguely miffed. 'Why are people interested in Thomas Hardy's primitive villages?'

'Hm.' Eleni looked pensive. 'Good question, I suppose,' she said.

And then the two women sat side by side, staring out at the swelling sea, thinking their own thoughts.

V

Having lost her own pen somewhere in her wanderings, Calliope had the nib replaced on her father's Waterman. She began to use it as winter set in, surrounded by his old books, translating poetry. If only he could see her now! If only she had known sooner the pleasure to be had in ferreting out the perfect word, the way each image followed another, forming a string of words as exquisite and inevitable as olives ripening on a branch.

Although she sometimes wished she had the gift to write her own poetry, it was the unexpected success of her literary translations that pulled Calliope back from the shores of despair. Her translations of Pericles's poems had been praised by her French cousin, as well as by Rupert Ealing. The Englishman had urged her to keep on translating until there were enough poems for a collection. He was sure a foreign publisher could be found some day.

The very day she received the letter from London, Calliope sat down to reply, waiting for Eli to arrive. Rupert was keen to know how the Civil War was playing out in the village, though he was sometimes in possession of facts even before they reached the northern Aegean. Tito's break with Moscow had splintered the Greek left. What with Yugoslavia and Albania withdrawing their support of Greek communists, Rupert thought the Civil War had probably run its course.

It was in this letter that the Englishman confirmed what Calliope had long suspected: Greek children had indeed been transported across the border to be indoctrinated by communist families. Some thirty thousand children were said to have been snatched from their homes, but there were counter rumours of children from Greek orphanages being shipped off to America, for adoption by right-wing families. The latter reports, Rupert wrote, were as yet unconfirmed, but Queen Frederika was said to be a prime mover in this covert campaign.

The news about the Queen's role was so astounding that the doctor had hardly come through the door when Calliope thrust Rupert's letter at him. He sat down to shuck off his shoes, fumbling for his slippers while he read the letter. A few minutes passed. He was still clutching the letter as he padded into the sitting room, his jaw working tensely.

Although months had passed since the argument over the *paidomazoma*, Dhaniel had never wavered in his belief that the rumoured abductions were merely government propaganda. Now, as he sat rereading the letter, a baffled look spread over his features: Rupert Ealing was well placed to know what was what.

'Unbelievable,' he muttered, staring at the floor. He sat for a moment, pinching the bridge of his nose. 'Unbelievable!'

Calliope had settled into an old chair, keeping her thoughts to herself. There was the sound of rats scuffling through walls, of Sappho's wheezing breath. The dog lay dozing at Eli's feet, as she did whenever he came. Sappho's devotion was bewildering, given the doctor's apparent indifference. He did not like to have animals indoors.

When Eli declined to eat, Calliope sighed and didn't press him. That their German-born Queen might be involved in dubious operations was upsetting but believable to someone of Eli's political persuasion. The communists' *paidomazoma*, on the other hand, he seemed incapable of processing.

Having fetched the brandy, Calliope tried to distract Eli with talk of her personal projects. Eli knew about the children's library she was setting up in Zenovia's house, but not about the tutorial service she hoped to offer. She had been meaning to tell him for weeks, but feared some unforeseen obstacle, dreaded another failure.

The new idea had germinated the day she had taken Aristides and Fanny down to the beach. Listening in on their chatter, she had marvelled at their lively imagination. She thought bright children like Aristides and Fanny desperately needed a library, but less gifted children might also thrive, given tutorial help. It was a well-known fact that even clever children sometimes failed to pass Kaloni's high-school entrance exams. Calliope was especially troubled by Molyvos girls' arrested education. Most men didn't want their daughters leaving the village for school, but surely they couldn't object to their attending informal study sessions at the library?

She was beginning to share these thoughts with Eli, but all at once stopped, scanning his face intently. 'What is it?' she asked. 'You think I'm just dreaming, don't you?'

Eli looked startled. 'I'm sorry, darling!' He reached out and drew her from her chair and onto his lap. 'I think it's a brilliant idea,' he said, stroking her hair away from her face. 'Zenovia will be dancing in her grave!'

'I hope so. I do hope so,' Calliope murmured. She started to add something, but then stopped herself, not yet ready to share an even bolder idea she had been contemplating ever since she'd run into Stavroula Houmi at the cemetery. She was reluctant to voice it because she herself could foresee several obstacles. She had, in any case, sensed that Eli was merely making conversation. He was clearly still grappling with Ealing's letter.

With dinner over and the dishes done, Calliope hauled Eli out of his chair and steered him upstairs, Sappho pressing in after them. She slept in her own bed when she was alone, but in the matrimonial one when Eli spent the night. In truth, she slept little in either bed, having resolved to kick her growing dependence on sleeping tablets now that she no longer had to get up for class.

So she lay awake in the double bed, while Eli drifted off, his legs entangled with hers. She knew she would likely stay awake until the neighbours' rooster began to crow, but was resigned to it. She nestled against Eli's warm body, listening to the peaceful breathing of man and dog, the shrieking of a night bird. The air around the bed was beginning to grow chilly, so she sat up and fumbled for her nightgown. It was nearly three thirty before she felt herself being towed towards sleep.

Suddenly, a moan escaped Eli's throat and his eyes snapped open. He sat for a moment, rubbing his eyes, muttering incoherently. At length, he grew lucid, sliding towards the edge of the bed. He scratched his head, then reached for the bedside torch. The power in the village was still being cut at midnight.

Calliope stirred. 'Bad dream?'

'Mm.' He thrust his feet into his slippers, pulled on his dressing gown, then shambled across the room. Sappho had scrambled to her feet and was sluggishly padding after him.

'Bring me a glass of water, will you?' Calliope murmured. She was by now accustomed to Eli's nightmares, which had plagued him ever since his return from Dachau. She burrowed deeper under the covers. Warm and sleepy, she heard the toilet flush, then the sound of slippers shuffling towards the kitchen. She heard the faucet being turned on, and then the sound of Eli's footfall approaching the staircase. There was a brief pause, as if he had just realised he had forgotten something.

Calliope was finally dozing off when she heard a sudden thud. Had the flowerpot on the newel post been knocked down, she wondered drowsily.

But then she was fully awake, listening. She sat up in bed, throwing off the blankets.

'Eli?' She went swishing out of the bedroom, heading for the stairs. 'Are you all right, darling?'

But even as she asked the question, Calliope could taste dread rising in her throat. She blundered towards the stairhead, every mental cell abruptly alert. *Why isn't he answering? What's happened to the torch?*

'Eli?'

She was still fumbling her way down the shadowy stairs, hand gripping the banister, when Sappho let out a tentative little bark, and then a sudden howl. It was a sound that Calliope had heard only once before, on the night Dimitris Stephanides was beaten to death.

'Eli!' she screamed. 'Eli!'

And still there was no answer. Calliope's panic seemed to reverberate through the nocturnal silence. Another moment and her voice joined the dog's, howling together in the predawn dark. In the foyer, the clock's pendulum struck four times – *boom, boom, boom, boom* – as it had every night for almost half a century.

FIVE

I

29 August 1952

Dear Rupert,

I am sorry I have been such a poor correspondent lately, though I did send you a note after getting your invitation and was dismayed to learn that it never reached you. In any case, it was great to hear from you again, and to see your grown-up son and his lovely bride!

The photos are beautiful. I wish I could have been there for the wedding, even if I am something of a cynic when it comes to marriage. And I truly appreciate your concern. I am quite well but busier than ever. The kentro *continues to take up most of my time, and the rest just seems to fly away. I can't believe almost three years have passed since we lost our dear Eli. The older I get, the more I understand the villagers' fatalism. How it used to infuriate me! I'm beginning to see, though, that in many cases, this is all we human beings can do: accept the cards fate has dealt us and limp on as best we can.*

What I still have trouble accepting are the villagers' entrenched attitudes, which sometimes maim and kill through sheer ignorance. I believe in education as others believe in the Virgin's powers. It's the only thing that will take us out of the Middle Ages.

I was sorry to hear that you don't much like your new job, but will be very interested to read your memoirs. It seems the older we get, the more compelling our own past becomes, and the less time there is for all the things we still hope to accomplish.

I started out with the modest hope of improving our children's education but have willy-nilly become something of a social worker. Not that I can always provide solutions. Much of the time all I can do is validate women's grievances. It's not much, I know, but in the absence of laws, in the absence of a social support system, in the absence of financial independence, validation is often all there is. There are days when I despair of it all. What do you say to a woman whose brother has raped her adolescent daughter? What do you say to a young bride whose husband has beaten her up for not having dinner ready when he came home from work?

We have a new doctor, but he is not well liked, even if he does keep icons. We also have a new priest, but most women prefer to consult either me or my friend, the village midwife. Some used to like talking to Papa Emanouil, but now that he, too, is gone, the villagers seem a little like orphaned children. I had no idea there were so many unhappy women around. I suppose I had just been too wrapped up in myself. You'll be glad to know that I have become less self-absorbed and may finally be starting to atone for all my omissions and commissions.

Sappho died just before Christmas. She might have lived longer, but never quite regained her spirits after Eli's death. Pericles is back, but there is no doubt that Makronisos and his long illness have left their mark. He is moodier now, and sometimes appears inexplicably restless. But he is immensely excited by the acceptance of his book, and dreams of seeing it published abroad.

Speaking of books, Umbreit's novel is about to be published in French. I think that writing it has helped him come to terms with his role in the Occupation, though it's to his credit that he never tried to whitewash the past. I didn't think I'd ever speak to him again, but having such an ambitious novel dedicated to me has, I suppose, softened my heart – or maybe just tickled my vanity? But there is something else. Having seen the abominable things Greeks did to each other, I've come to regard all human beings with an equally jaundiced eye. Incredibly, some facts about the Civil War *are only now coming to light. Did you know that more Greeks were killed by other Greeks than by the Germans? It is mind-boggling! To think that a quarter of a million people have been left homeless, on top of those imprisoned or exiled! That Greeks could shove their compatriots into burning ovens, could rape and kill children in front of their parents. To think that ordinary men could chop off women's nipples and turn them into worry beads!*

All these atrocities took place far away from here but, three years after the end of this stupid war, we also remain bitterly divided. A leftist who needs a table would rather eat off the floor than go to a rightist carpenter. My friend Eleni's brothers won't speak to each other. And so on. Lesbos has come to be known as The Red Island, while the government continues to discriminate against leftists. A man wishing to start a business still needs a document attesting to his never having been a member of the Communist Party. I thought that, with time, things might improve, but the country is so unstable, both economically and politically, that the end doesn't seem to be in sight. This is why thousands of Greeks are emigrating to the four corners of the earth.

Our government, meanwhile, seems to see everyone as a potential spy. Let this be a warning to you, should you decide to return to Greece some day, as you keep promising. Not that I'd want to discourage you. It would be a great pleasure to see you, Rupert, even if it means getting my ears boxed for forgetting most of the English you taught me. I had some English lessons while I was in Mytilene, but the only thing I remember from you is the limerick about the loss of hair. I assume you still have your nose and your toes (one of my neighbours recently had his nose bitten off by a rabid dog), and if you've lost your hair, well, it doesn't really matter. It's what's under the hair that counts.

I hope this letter finds you well. I won't be travelling to Athens for a while but will try to get you Elytis's poems when I go.

Yours, Calliope

II

It was late February, but she was overdressed, waiting for a taxi. Athens had been cool the previous evening, but the ferry docked in Mytilene on a morning as bright and balmy as spring. Calliope had taken off her jacket but was still too warm in her new pullover and trousers. The outfit had been purchased in Kolonaki. She had never before considered buying trousers, but the moment she spotted this pair in a shop window, she impulsively decided to go in, if only to try them on.

The trousers were made of a soft tweedy fabric, cinnamon-hued, with tiny reddish spots in the weave. Cuffed at the ankles, they had a pocket on each side and buttons in front, exactly like a man's. Only she had never known a man's trousers to have such an elegant cut and feel. Certainly, none would have hugged her hips and bottom as these trousers did.

'Imported from London.' The boutique owner had come up, her head canted, an ivory cigarette holder clamped between her ruby-coloured lips. 'They look like they were made for you, don't they?'

'Mm.' Calliope contemplated her own reflection while the shop owner waited, looking archly doubtful. The doubt may have had something to do with the price, which was exorbitant.

Calliope thrust her hands in the trouser pockets, intrigued by the fact that a stylish garment could alter more than one's outward appearance. The trousers were nothing but an expensively tailored piece of cloth, yet somehow the new image was generating a peculiar sense of empowerment. The reflection in the boutique's mirror resembled the women Calliope had seen in the foreign journals in Akademias Street. She had come to buy books for the children's library but ended up leafing through some American magazines while waiting.

There had been photographs of women riding horses and waving from convertible cars. Women in tapered skirts with breasts poking through tight sweaters. Women in jodhpurs. Women in striped vests and trousers.

Meeting her own eyes in the mirror, Calliope felt, for the first time, like a modern woman, ready to take on the world.

The thought made her smile. The boutique owner had briefly disappeared but was now coming back with a leather belt. She hastened to thread it through the tweedy loops, but then frowned a little, staring at Calliope's lilac-hued blouse.

'You would probably want to wear a crisp shirt or a sweater with these trousers,' she suggested, stepping back in her patent-leather shoes.

'Yes, maybe a sweater,' Calliope said, though she had not quite decided whether to buy the trousers. 'Do you have anything in this colour?' She pointed to the reddish spots, feeling like a child plucking off daisy petals. If they had a sweater in this colour, she was meant to buy trousers; otherwise, she would walk out as she'd come, dressed in skirt, blouse, jacket.

'I have something beautiful in angora, though—'

'May I see it, please?'

The Athenian clicked away, coming back with the most luxurious piece of clothing Calliope had ever held between her hands: a long-sleeved top, the colour of persimmons. Its price was equally shocking, but the only time Calliope could remember experiencing a similar leap of love for a piece of clothing had been back in the late 1930s, when she'd impulsively bought a French jacket in Mytilene.

She ended up spending an average Greek's monthly salary, buying the trousers and belt, as well as the angora top. She had put them on just before she left Piraeus and was still wearing them the following morning. The taxi driver dropped her off at the *kentro*, helping her with the books and suitcase before heading back to Mytilene.

Calliope picked up her jacket, then a small red valise she had bought in Athens. She'd thought it would be useful, since she occasionally had to spend the night in Mytilene and all she owned was a large leather suitcase. One of the porters would have to bring that one, since her house was not accessible on wheels. The little red valise was empty, except for some toiletries.

By the time she made her way through the *agora*, men were beginning to gather outside the *kapheneion*, drinking their midday ouzo. They had been discussing union with Cyprus but fell abruptly silent, watching Calliope pass with her chic valise, her spring jacket folded over her arm. She was feeling inexplicably buoyant, like a woman returning from a restful holiday in some European spa instead of a few hectic days in the capital.

Crossing the *plateia*, she stopped to greet a former pupil on leave from the army, then caught her elder brother-in-law and his mother staring at her from the *pantopoleion*'s threshold. Both Vangelis and Martha had their mouths open, like children gawking at a gypsy coppersmith or knife sharpener passing through the village.

'They're only staring at you because of the trousers,' the young man said, as if to reassure her there was nothing else anyone could possibly find fault with.

'I know.' Calliope smiled, patting the young man's arm. Then she turned and began to climb the village steps, chuckling to herself.

III

There are many ways to break a man, but at Makronisos, the most dreaded torture had been inspired by an ancient punishment once reserved for adulterous women. Pericles himself had never personally experienced the barbaric treatment, but one day he told Calliope about a notorious communist leader who had been stuffed into a sack with two cats, then dumped in the sea, ostensibly to be drowned.

'Just imagine this… imagine the sack beginning to sink to the bottom of the sea, the crazed cats scratching every which way, the poor bastard trying to breathe, to protect his eyes, even as he feels himself beginning to drown. But, at the last possible moment, a reprieve! The sack is hauled out of the sea, the hissing cats are released, and the prisoner, streaming with blood, is given the Declaration of Repentance and asked to sign. Would you, or wouldn't you?'

The question had come up in the wake of a philosophical

discussion regarding heroism. Perhaps because he hadn't experienced it personally, Pericles never attempted to write about this particular torture until one day a letter arrived from Samos. He was sitting in Calliope's kitchen, reading his former cellmate's letter, when one of the cats leapt into his lap. And it was at that moment, as he felt Tigris's claws dig into his flesh, as he tried to slap the six-toed cat off his thighs, that he found himself reaching for his notebook.

He worked on the poem for the next two weeks, but it did not take the village that long to discover that Calliope Adham and her young brother-in-law had at some point become lovers. She was by then thirty-seven years old; Pericles was a decade younger. Somehow, having survived Makronisos, having triumphed over tuberculosis, he had succeeded in making her forget that she had been his teacher when he was still a schoolboy in short trousers, obsessed with world capitals.

At first, Calliope had feared that her involvement with her late husband's brother might sabotage her work at the *kentro*, but she quickly discovered that where there is a potential advantage, most people will find grounds for turning a blind eye.

By the summer of 1952, when Pericles returned, both the children's library and the tutorials were considered an unqualified success. Molyvos children planning to attend high school were passing entrance exams with distinction; grade-school children received free instruction after school hours.

The most challenging programme, however, was designed to help adolescent girls whose education had stopped at primary level. When Calliope had first aired the idea, Mathaios the mayor warned her that most parents would consider it a waste of time. Calliope thought it over, then proceeded to publicise the programme as highly selective: only ten girls would be chosen to participate in the free study sessions.

Mathaios laughed when he heard about it. She was as cunning as a man, he said.

It quickly became a matter of prestige to have a daughter selected for the *kentro*. Having engaged former pupils to help with young children's homework, Calliope devoted herself to the study sessions, meeting two groups on alternate days to discuss history, poetry, logic. She had been careful to schedule the sessions in the late morning. This had placated the mothers, who needed help with domestic chores, while the absence of boys stole the fathers' thunder. Before long, Molyvos mothers could be heard boasting that their marriageable daughters could not only cook and embroider, but were also among 'Calliope's girls'.

Calliope's girls were known to be clever and diligent, and too busy to succumb to temptation, as the late baker's daughter was rumoured to have done with a young Athenian. The mayor had recently brought in a construction crew to restore the crumbling Genoese fortress; the baker's daughter had been spotted alone with one of the workers. The only place Calliope's girls ever went unaccompanied was the *kentro*. Two years after its inception, the new enterprise was functioning so smoothly that Calliope was able to devote her evenings to her own literary pursuits.

Calliope's aunt was impressed by her niece's achievements but scandalised by her private life. When she found out that Calliope had taken Pericles for a lover, Elpida saw it as her duty to intervene on her late sister's behalf. The village might be willing to turn a blind eye, she said, but what about Mirto?

'Your poor mother will be tormented in heaven!'

But this warning only made Calliope sigh and kiss her aunt's sagging cheeks. After all these years, she said, her mother surely knew better than to believe that playing by the rules and praying to the Virgin offered any sort of protection.

'From now on, I'm going to live by my own rules!' she stated.

'From now on?' Elpida chuckled, rueful. 'You always have, *koritsi mou*. Always – as far back as I can remember.'

IV

By 1954, Pericles had all but recovered from his recent ordeals.

One Sunday, they decided to have a picnic in Eftalou. It was a brilliant spring day. They spread a blanket next to a blossoming almond tree, in a meadow spotted with poppies, anemones, daisies. Calliope had prepared taramosalata and stuffed tomatoes. She had also brought cheese pies and stuffed vine leaves sent by the late beekeeper's daughter.

It was generally believed that Calliope had lost her job because of her public support for the beekeeper. Though she had staunchly refused to discuss her expulsion, the family's gestures of gratitude did not go unappreciated.

She had little time to cook, and Pericles could barely make a cup of coffee. Although he had studied literature with the intention of teaching, Kimon's brother seemed content to let his mother and lover look after him, while he wandered in Eftalou, and read, and wrote poetry.

When they had finished their picnic, Pericles rose and stretched, then plucked an almond blossom from Calliope's hair. 'Race you down to the beach?'

Calliope wiped her hands, scrambling up. 'Only if you don't mind losing!'

'One, two, three, go!'

They romped on the water's edge, chasing and tickling each other with snakes of dripping seaweed. She was a carefree girl again! She could roll in a sunlit meadow, amid drifting pollen and thrumming insects, could forget all about abused wives and deprived children – forget to think altogether, though Pericles never seemed to. He was like a spider, perpetually spinning the web that would catch the brilliant butterflies fluttering through his inner landscape. There was nothing that, sooner or later, did not find its way into his incandescent lyrics.

He was much the same as a lover: intense and watchful, as if committing every flicker of the eyelid, every explored patch of skin, to his greedy memory.

That Sunday, they made love in an Eftalou cove, where Pericles sometimes napped during his wanderings. The seagulls shrieked, circling the rocks; the sea murmured in the blue distance. And all the while, his eyes would be on her, finding rare pearls, discerning improbable rhymes. Her body, Calliope felt, did not belong to her but to some desperate creature struggling to be rescued. It bit and scratched and shrieked along with the raucous seagulls. In time, it landed on its private island: depleted, astonished, blessed.

V

A month later, the long-awaited copy of *Sacrifice* finally arrived. The book had come in the morning mail and, the moment he opened the package, Pericles raced across the village to share it with Calliope. She was in the wisteria arbour, reading, when he stormed through the gate. It was two days before Easter. Breathless, he stopped and held out the book, gazing at her mutely.

'Oh!' Calliope reached for the book, breathing in the heady smell of freshly printed pages, running her fingers over the smooth sea-blue cover. She opened the book as an exiled scholar might open some precious manuscript after decades away from the printed word. Pericles remained standing, watching her thumb the pages.

'You've missed something,' he said after a moment's pause. 'Go back to the beginning.'

She went back. She read the inscription. She was incapable of writing a single memorable line, but standing before her was yet another writer who had dedicated his book to her. *For Calliope, my contrary muse.*

He seemed, all at once, on the edge of tears, gazing at the volume in her hands with the expression a man might wear on watching his wife nurse a newborn. Soon, he was hoisting Calliope to her feet, delirious with joy. Makronisos had left him moodier than he had been before the Civil War, but still given to occasional rapture.

'I want you to marry me!' he blurted, eyes bright as sapphires.

'*What?*' Calliope threw back her head and laughed. 'Just because I've inspired a poem or two?'

'Of course not!' Pericles said. He was the same height as his brother had been, but leaner, more sinewy. 'I've loved you my whole life.'

'Ach, don't be silly!' Calliope spoke in the tone of voice she might have used in the old days, when she was his teacher. 'I'm ten years older than you!'

'So?'

'So, I'll feel like your mother in a few years.'

He shook his head. 'You're in the prime of life!' he stated. 'Ask anybody!'

She plucked a leaf and tickled his nose. He was a man who never stopped to think of the future. 'So what happens when I'm past my prime?'

'Oh, I'll probably be dead by then. All great poets die young,' he stated breezily.

'That's not true! Anyway—'

'Anyway, you're my brother's widow,' he put in, nibbling her earlobe. 'Hindus and Muslims have laws requiring a man to marry his brother's widow.'

'Really?' Calliope pondered this, breathing in the odour of Pericles's youthful sweat. 'Then you must thank God you're not Hindu or Muslim.' She extricated herself from his embrace and reached for her pack of cigarettes. 'You should marry a young woman one of these days. Marry and have children.'

All at once, Calliope could feel her mouth starting to twitch. The thought of having a child with a man she could vividly recall as a boy in shorts seemed too funny to contemplate, but one thing she was determined to make clear once and for all. She would not allow marriage to become a bone of contention again, especially not with a young man, no matter how talented.

Half of *Sacrifice* was devoted to the Occupation, the second half to the Civil War. Pericles didn't like to talk about Makronisos, but the poems spoke for themselves. He had been tortured in the prison camp. His tuberculosis had been diagnosed only after he collapsed one morning, cleaning the prison latrines. Calliope had no doubt that some day the book would be published in France or England, maybe even America.

Over the weeping shores of invaded dreams, the sun, captive, refuses to shine.

She finished the first poem, then went on to read a much older one, inspired years ago by the sight of a hungry child trying to shoot down a dove.

She leaned over and kissed Pericles.

'May there be many more where these came from!' she said with feeling. 'Dozens – hundreds – of them!'

VI

Dear Lorenz,

What a wonderful surprise – thank you so much! I believe I enjoyed the French edition even more than the original, partly because I didn't have to keep using the dictionary, but also because I noticed some things I'd missed the first time.

I was sorry to hear that you are not entirely happy with the translation, but letting some stranger take over your work must be, I imagine, a little like passing a newborn infant to a wet nurse without being sure of the quality of her milk. Anyway, just for the fun of it, I took the first page of the original and translated it into French, then compared my own version with that of Madame Desrosiers. It's astonishing, isn't it, the degree to which the translator's own sensibility informs the translation? I confess I prefer my own version, but no doubt that's sheer conceit on my part!

Your fictional Penelope is also occasionally conceited, but has virtues I cannot claim to possess. For one thing, she is far more heroic than I, even if you've made her resemble me in some obvious ways. You may find it hard to believe, but I really am a coward. If

I joined the Resistance, it was only because I have always found impotence more difficult to tolerate than fear.

The Nightingale's Silence *made me marvel again at how well you have captured our wartime agony. Not every writer can so persuasively portray a foreign culture or enter a fictional woman's skin.*

I was very glad to hear about the sequel and am longing to know what it is about. If you go on like this, you may come to be regarded as a German Hellenophile, though I suppose some might consider this an oxymoron. I am tempted to press you to tell me more, but understand your reluctance. I, too, am occasionally surprised to find that I am not altogether free of superstition. I spent years poking fun at my poor mother, but the older I get, the clearer it seems to me that superstition is just a universal expression of human impotence. An illiterate villager panicking at the sight of a black cat might be unable to articulate his real fear, but he somehow knows that he can no more stop an earthquake or an invading army than he can a black cat crossing his path or an owl hooting on his own roof. One of the things I especially appreciated in your novel was the Destiny leitmotif. My French cousin, who teaches Comparative Literature, says your philosophical background is evident in your writing, though you manage to raise serious philosophical questions without sounding didactic.

I recently read Moby-Dick, *intrigued to find that Melville, too, was preoccupied with Fate. Do you know his work? I also found* Billy Budd *extremely moving. I'd never stopped to consider how helpless inarticulate people must feel, especially when confronted with a silver-tongued opponent.*

I don't know whether this is what is meant by wisdom, but I am slowly becoming more sympathetic to my neighbours' foibles. I imagine that inside every uneducated villager is a voice desperate to be heard, unable to express itself with the longed-for eloquence, just as I am unable to find the words for the poetry I feel glimmering within me. Pericles says I am too greedy, and he may be right, though he himself seems to fluctuate between thinking himself another

Seferis and wanting to burn his entire oeuvre whenever he feels he has failed to capture some elusive image.

I think about such things whenever I am alone, which is not that often. My husband used to say that I thought too much. Sometimes I agree with that, other times I feel I don't think nearly as much as I'd like to. Still, I am very glad to have found something worthwhile to do with myself. There are days when I can't help thinking that Zenovia Antoniou really did have a clairvoyant gift, though I've always been sceptical of such claims. But I'd better stop here. I wish you great success with your new novel, and a happy Christmas to you and your family.

Sincerely, Calliope

VII

In future years, Calliope would insist that she never considered rendering Lorenz Umbreit's work into Greek – not until he wrote back later that winter, urging her to try translating a couple of chapters, which his German publisher would then send to an Athenian colleague.

Although deeply flattered, Calliope found the very thought daunting. Translating German prose into Greek might be easier than translating Greek poetry into French, but she was not sure that she was up to the challenge.

Umbreit, however, had not lost his powers of persuasion. He pressed Calliope to have a stab at the prologue, but Easter had come and gone before she finally sat down to try it, and even then, rather reluctantly.

Pericles had won a Greek poetry award. The day after the Burning of Judas festivities, he sailed to Piraeus for interviews, leaving Calliope to her own devices. By Friday afternoon, she was out of excuses. She spent all day working on Umbreit's prologue, almost forgetting her appointment with the mayor's ten-year-old son, who needed help with schoolwork after his bout with polio.

Sotiris was usually tutored by Fanny Dimou, Aristides's child-hood playmate. Calliope's godson was by now in high school, but Fanny had been forced to leave school at thirteen, forbidden to keep company with boys. She eventually started attending the study sessions and, more recently, helping *kentro* children with homework. Calliope paid a modest salary to her young tutors, ensuring regular attendance.

That Friday, however, Fanny Dimou was being betrothed to Pavlos Rozakis, the late *kapheneion* owner's thirty-four-year-old son. Pavlos was now the owner, and though Calliope liked him well enough, she could not subdue a certain sadness, knowing that Fanny's and Aristides's childhood attachment had no future now.

The sadness was still with her when the maths session was over. Sotiris had gone home and she, too, was ready to leave the *kentro* when the front door opened and in sauntered Timolis Tsouras, son of the man responsible for the loss of her teaching position. He was passing by, Timolis explained, and hoped she might be willing to recommend a book for his niece's name day. He was going to Mytilene tomorrow.

'She's a real book-eater, that one... not like me,' he added disarmingly.

'Well, you've come to the right place,' answered Calliope. She was intrigued by Timolis's decision to consult her, given that she and his father were not on speaking terms. The young man had by then finished both his studies and military service. He would be somewhere in his mid-twenties. 'I'll make you a list.'

He was almost androgynous in his beauty, though there was no vanity in his manner, only the hint of some deep need for friendship or understanding. It might have had something to do with his mother's premature death, or perhaps the recent falling-out with his father. There had been the usual village gossip, but Calliope had never learned the details. Was he trying to spite his father?

Having established the niece's age and interests, Calliope jotted down several titles, then rose from her desk, making conversation while preparing to leave for the day.

Timolis had recently qualified as a notary.

'What are your plans now?' she asked, locking up the *kentro*. They were both heading towards the St Kyriaki neighbourhood.

'I don't know – I'll stay here for a while, then decide.' He had hoped to go to America for a year, but it hadn't worked out, he eventually said. He had a simple, forthright manner, a fetching way of tilting his head and casting sidelong looks as he spoke, smiling ever so faintly. He would have been the sort of boy who brought flowers or cherries for the teacher and found excuses to linger after class.

'So, what made you decide to stay in Molyvos?' she asked after a while.

'My father,' Timolis said. He had remarkable eyes: black-rimmed blue irises and dark lashes, as curly as a girl's. 'He thinks I should open an office here. In Molyvos.'

'Oh yes? It would be great not to have to go to Petra,' Calliope said.

Timolis smiled a little. 'He's afraid I'll marry an American and stay there.'

'Well, it's been known to happen,' Calliope said, on a wave of sympathy. It would not be easy to get out from under Leandros Tsouras's thumb, she thought, then quickly cautioned herself: *Do not meddle!*

They had reached the parapet overlooking the sea and paused to watch the sunset. Calliope's mother-in-law lived in this neighbourhood, halfway up the hill. As the day waned, the primroses began to unfurl, their scent fusing with the smell of tar from the newly constructed road. The road was finally paved, cutting travel time to the capital in half.

Timolis took out a pack of cigarettes and held it out to Calliope. They leaned against the parapet, smoking companionably, watching children play. Two of the boys were chasing a ball; the youngest frolicked with a stray puppy, crowing happily. With his light eyes and pale hair, the child reminded Calliope of Aristides, just before his hair had been cut for the first time. To think that her godson was almost eighteen now!

They were still watching, laughing at the child and the dog, when Pericles suddenly came around the corner, on his way down to the *agora*. Spotting Calliope, he froze, then sauntered towards the lookout, smiling uncertainly. His mother had run out of sugar and sent him to get some before the shops closed, he explained. There was, Calliope noted, a flicker of unease in Timolis's eyes. She stood watching the two men with interest: two sets of blue eyes assessing each other in the golden dusk.

'What were you doing with him?' Pericles was soon asking, having decided to get the sugar from another grocery. Timolis had gone his own way by then.

'He stopped at the library.'

'The library? What, the man reads fairy tales?'

Calliope smiled. She explained about the niece, the name day, the book. 'He's going to Mytilene tomorrow.'

Pericles was silent.

'*What?*' she flared up. 'What's the matter with you? Don't tell me you're jealous!'

'Me, jealous?' Pericles scoffed. 'What have I got to be jealous of?'

'Exactly!' Calliope could never decide whether her lover's occasional flashes of arrogance amused or repelled her. She cast him a sidelong glance. 'But you *are* jealous. Look at you!' She reached out to touch his pulsing jaw, but Pericles jerked back, brushing her hand away.

'What's he doing here anyway?' he demanded. 'Is he planning to stay?'

'For now,' Calliope said, pausing to crush her cigarette. 'He wants to go to America, but his father won't let him.'

'I see.'

The grocer scooped out sugar into a paper bag and gave Pericles his change.

'See you later,' Pericles said.

It was almost dark when Calliope arrived home. She flicked on the lights and headed up to her bedroom. She was about to change and start preparing supper but suddenly stopped and, fully dressed, turned towards the vanity mirror. There were, Eleni had told her, those who said it was having a young lover that kept her looking so youthful. And, well, perhaps they were right?

During his stay in Athens, Pericles had seen a film with a young Italian actress named Sophia Loren, who reminded him of Calliope. Calliope had never heard of Sophia Loren, but, appraising her own reflection, she shook her head a little, thinking of the two young men running into each other at the lookout. And then she smiled to herself.

She had recently turned forty.

SIX

I

8 September 1955

Dear Alexandra,

Your letter arrived on the same day as the announcement that Pericles's book won the National Prize for Poetry! He is thrilled, of course, but I worry that all this acclaim is going to his head. Perhaps it's to be expected. He is still young and will, I hope, acquire some humility once he can take his success for granted.

As for my own humble endeavours, most villagers seem to appreciate our efforts, but it's much easier to make progress with children than to change adults' mindsets. This is especially maddening with village women, who could certainly benefit from occasionally breaking with tradition. I realise this is easier said than done. Only among young women do I see the promise of eventual change. Last week, a sixteen-year-old girl threatened to take poison if her father forced her to marry a man twenty-two years older. He insisted she was bluffing, though a Petra girl had poisoned herself under similar circumstances only two years ago. I reminded the father of this, and he finally relented.

My success rate is not nearly as high as I'd like it to be. Several of the girls in my study groups complain that their own mothers treat them like slaves while their brothers sit playing cards. So, you see, women themselves perpetuate the problem. I can't tell you how proud I am that I taught Aristides to help me around the house when he was a child. But now that he is at university, I see him only in the summer and, briefly, at Christmas and Easter. He has a girlfriend (ironically, one from a prominent right-wing family) and seems to be flourishing, studying architecture like his sister, but suddenly thinking about going into politics some day. He has always been interested in social issues, but I can't imagine such a high-minded person entering politics without having his spirit crushed. But what young man has ever listened to his Nona? He is still young enough to think he can change the world.

Political change is very slow here, but at least the Marshall Plan is helping our economy recover. We finally have a paved road! It now takes only an hour to get to the capital. This will make our lives much easier, especially with medical emergencies. Last month, a local woman set a precedent by giving birth at a Mytilene hospital, albeit only because her cousin had recently had 'a blue baby'.

Finally, some good news: Eli's eldest daughter works at a prestigious architectural firm in Athens, the second is expecting another child, and the youngest, who has been helping me at the kentro, seems to be keen on our new doctor. I am hard at work on Umbreit's novel. The Greek publisher liked my extract, so I took a deep breath and signed a contract under my maiden name. I am going to be using Adham from now on because that's who I feel I am. The work, though slow, is immensely satisfying. Umbreit is planning a trilogy and is hoping to come back to Greece to pursue research in the Peloponnese. For obvious reasons, he won't come here, but I may see him in Athens in spring. The publisher wants to meet me, and I am looking forward to it, though I have mixed feelings about seeing Umbreit after all this time. As for seeing you, I can only reiterate my invitation. I understand your situation, of course, but still hope you will find it possible to come one of these days. Until then, bon anniversaire! I hope my gift will give you years of pleasure.

Yours, Calliope

II

Pericles was sitting at Calliope's kitchen table, working on a new poem. He had written the first stanza in just half an hour yesterday. Now he was struggling with the second, stopping every now and then to shoot a baleful glance towards Calliope, who was at the sink, scrubbing a copper kettle.

Calliope ignored his black looks. She went on cleaning, driven by manic energy. She always knew when her *periodos* was coming on: it was the only time she approached domestic chores without her habitual reluctance.

Pericles rose to get a glass of water. Despite his generally superb concentration, he had been restless all day, pacing the floor, scratching his head, shooing the cats away. He downed the water in silence, then returned to the table, lips hardening with fresh resolve. He had rather thin lips, which looked as stern as a monk's, except when something amused him. His smile then was as radiant as it had been in childhood. When he smiled, Calliope felt she could forgive Pericles almost anything.

He was not smiling now. When the poem continued to elude him, he sprang to his feet, crumpled the sheet of paper, and tossed it into the kitchen hearth. The fire shot out a few surprised sparks, then blazed on, making hissing sounds. When Calliope failed to react, Pericles wheeled about, gave his trousers a nervous little hitch, and finally spoke.

'How long will you be gone?'

'About a week,' Calliope said, going on with her chores.

Some twenty-four hours earlier, she had informed him that she was going to meet Lorenz Umbreit in Athens, but Pericles hadn't asked any questions then; he had merely withdrawn into himself, silently nursing his grievance.

'What are you going to do?' he was asking now. 'Take your German friend to the Acropolis? Show him where the swastika used to fly?'

Calliope ignored the sarcasm. 'No. I might go with Aristides, though.' She spoke nonchalantly, wiping the glass jars with unprecedented diligence.

'Is his wife coming?

'Umbreit's wife? I doubt it.' She stopped to think it over. 'Actually, I don't know.'

'Why wouldn't she come?'

'I didn't say she wasn't. I said I didn't know.' Calliope sighed. 'He's coming to do research. It's not a holiday.'

'So why does he want to see you?'

'Oh, for God's sake!' she finally erupted. 'I'm translating his book, remember? I have a list of things I need to review with him.' She glanced at him balefully. 'You, of all people, should understand!'

'Will you be going with him?'

'To the Peloponnese? Don't be ridiculous! I'm going to see him in Athens, at some restaurant. We're supposed to have lunch with the publisher.'

'The publisher,' Pericles echoed. He was silent for a while. 'I want you to know I'm not at all happy about this,' he finally said. 'I don't like you going alone to Athens, publisher or no publisher.'

She glanced up, feeling her eyelids flicker. 'Well,' she said, 'I'm going anyway.'

He went on eyeing her sullenly. 'Does it mean nothing to you that this makes me unhappy? I haven't been able to write a single stanza today!'

'You'll get over it.'

Pericles raked his hand through his hair and let it stand stiffly, like a cockscomb. 'If I were your husband, I would stop you from going,' he said.

'There you are then. I always knew marriage was not for me.'

'You turn everything into a joke,' he said, 'but the truth is—'

'The truth is I wasn't joking,' she interposed. 'Why should I need your permission to go to Athens? Did you ask my permission when you went?'

'I wasn't going for a rendezvous with another woman, was I?'

'How would I know what you were going to do? Did I question you?' She stopped and passed her forearm across her forehead. 'For all I know, you spent every night with your adoring little nurse.'

Pericles blew into his cheeks, watching Tigris chase a cricket across the kitchen floor. The insect scuttled under the hutch and Tigris kept slapping at the wooden edge with his fat paw.

'Just tell me this,' Pericles said after a moment's hesitation. 'Was there anything to the rumour about the two of you?'

'Which particular rumour?' Calliope asked the question in a breezy tone, but suddenly stopped, replaced the sugar jar, and inhaled deeply. 'Look…' She spoke forbearingly. 'I'm doing my best not to lose my temper. I know you're jealous. I know you can't help it, but—'

'I'm not jealous!' he interjected. 'I just don't like my woman gallivanting all over Athens with a former Nazi!'

'So that's what this is all about – patriotism?'

'Among other things. Do you know any man who would let his woman—'

'I'm not *your woman*!' Calliope snapped. She regarded him for a moment, striving for equanimity. 'Look. Why can't you understand? That's one of the reasons I never wanted to marry. I can't stand anyone telling me what to do!'

Pericles detached himself from the table and went to wash the coffee cup, as she had trained him to. He rinsed it and set it on the counter. 'Would you have gone if Dhaniel had forbidden it?'

'Eli wouldn't have dreamed of dictating to me!' she said. 'But, yes, I would have gone anyway.'

Pericles weighed this for a moment, then sidled up to her and placed his hands over her breasts. 'You're so beautiful,' he muttered in her ear. 'I can't bear…' He stopped; she had extricated herself from his arms, reaching for a candlestick. 'So now you don't even want me to touch you?' He sounded like a petulant adolescent.

'Not when you're trying to manipulate me.'

'Manipulate you!' he said. 'You talk as if I never touch you on other days!'

She let out a little puff of exasperation. 'Have I ever told you how much I hate it when you shout at me?'

'Was I shouting?' He glared at her for a moment, then whipped around and stood staring at a fly beating against the window. Tigris had been joined by one-eared Loula, who was assiduously licking his underside. 'Funny how there are all these things you suddenly dislike about me,' Pericles said. 'Do you even like my poetry?'

'I think your poetry is sublime.'

'But?'

'But right now you're behaving like a bully.'

'A bully? Me?' Having been bullied in childhood, Pericles liked to think of other men as the bullies.

Calliope went on calmly picking wax out of the candlestick. 'Would you be happier if I said you were a child having a temper tantrum?'

He regarded her with steely eyes, something new flickering in his face. 'I'd be happier if you could stay home and behave like a decent woman.'

'What did you say?' she hissed, rounding on him at last.

'You heard me.'

'Well, now you hear me! I'm not only going to Athens, I'm going to do whatever pleases me! And if that includes jumping into bed with a German, then that...' *That is what I'm going to do*, she was about to say. She knew she was taunting him; of course she knew it. And yet, when Pericles reached out and slapped her face, Calliope's mouth shaped itself into a small oval of mute amazement.

The surprise lasted no more than a second, just long enough for the memory of Kimon's slap to go hissing through her brain. Then, as if of its own accord, her right hand flew out and slapped Pericles right back, on his sharp, visibly pulsing jaw. She stood trembling with rage, thinking: *You're just like your brother!* Thinking: *I swore no man would ever lay a hand on me again. I swore it!*

But these thoughts remained unvoiced.

'Get out.' She strove to speak quietly, but flared up when he showed no sign of budging. 'Go!' she shouted. 'Go back to your mother! Tell her she was right all along!'

She waited, pointing towards the door, until at last Pericles roused himself, shot her an embittered glance, and strode towards the garden. Loula stopped licking Tigris and twisted her head to

277

watch him leave. The buzzing fly abandoned the windowpane and hastened to flit towards the fresh air.

III

He had brought her gifts: an exquisite Murano sculpture of a nightingale, as well as an illustrated 1904 edition of *Madame Bovary*. The first he had bought in Venice, the second in Paris, where, passing a Left Bank stall, he recalled Calliope's wartime longing to read Gustave Flaubert.

Calliope had hoped to avoid speaking of the Occupation, but Titos Stamoulis, the publisher, had brought up the subject at lunch, albeit only in connection with Umbreit's novel. To judge by their French conversation, by her own outward composure, they might have been discussing *War and Peace*; the woman to whom Umbreit's novel was dedicated might have been a stranger, known only to the author.

The lunch had taken place at the Grande Bretagne, where Lorenz Umbreit was staying, and in whose emptying dining room he and Calliope lingered after Stamoulis left, planning to go over passages she had copied for consultation. But then, just as she was about to reach for her notebook, Umbreit offered his gifts and, speaking German now, they became engaged in a literary discussion unrelated to the work in progress. Calliope had read *Madame Bovary* soon after the end of the war but, she was soon telling Lorenz, it was still resonating with her. 'Sometimes I think that if it hadn't been for the war, if Kimon survived Albania, I might have easily become a Greek Madame Bovary.'

It was something she had occasionally pondered over the years, but the statement only made Lorenz Umbreit smile. He was now approaching his mid-forties. His hairline was beginning to recede, his cheekbones were less prominent, but his gaze, his voice, penetrated Calliope's body like an all-but-forgotten refrain.

'Emma Bovary was a foolish, frivolous woman,' he said.

'Ah, but you yourself said I was a sentimental soul. Remember?'

Lorenz smiled. 'There were some crucial facts I didn't have when I made that statement,' he said, shifting to cross his legs. She supposed he must be alluding to her Resistance activities.

'It's true I never shared Bovary's longing for glamour and luxury,' she conceded. 'But when I read the novel, I suddenly remembered my father cautioning me against confusing novels with real life.'

His smile broadened. 'I suppose one could read *Madame Bovary* as a cautionary novel about the danger of reading novels.'

'Indeed.' She, too, smiled. She took a drag on her cigarette, waiting for a clanking tram to go by. 'Speaking of novels, did you ever get to read *Steppenwolf*?'

'I did.' He gazed at her sadly, watching her tuck a strand of hair behind her ear. She saw him take in her earrings, round garnet jewels that had belonged to her mother and that she had put on to match her new suit. He was still interested in everything, still registering everything. Calliope thought of her late husband, who would have had to be shaken to notice anything that did not have a profit potential.

She said, 'Kimon was nothing like Charles Bovary, but I did feel trapped in my marriage, just like Emma. Not just the marriage, the whole social milieu, with its stupidities, its brutalities.' She waved away a puff of smoke but might have been thought to be dismissing her own youthful folly.

Lorenz looked thoughtful. 'Madame Bovary and you might have a thing or two in common,' he said, 'but she totally lacks your virtues.'

'Hm.' Calliope smiled vaguely but said nothing, tapping her cigarette into the ashtray. Every response she could think of would have sounded like false modesty.

Lorenz called for more coffee. He drank too much of it these days, though he had given up smoking during a bout of bronchitis. He shared all this with Calliope, then leaned back in his chair and gave her a long appraising look.

'So you think you've changed since the war?' He looked rather wistful.

'I know I have.' She looked away, eyes hazy with recollection. 'I think my mother was right all along,' she said. 'I was – before the war, before I met you – a spoiled, self-centred girl afflicted with excess imagination.'

He gazed at her for a moment. 'You're too hard on yourself,' he said as the waiter returned, bearing a coffee tray. 'Much harder than Flaubert would have been.'

'You think so?'

'You always were,' he went on. 'You may have been a little naive when you were young, but then, we all were.' He brushed his flaxen hair off his brow. It was the closest he would come to speaking of his own monumental error. 'Anyway, you sound happier with your lot these days – judging from your letters.'

Calliope stared into her coffee. 'I'm not *un*happy. I think happiness is often a matter of simply accepting your destiny.'

He looked at her with unabashed affection, like a doting uncle. 'Still grappling with destiny, I see.'

'Not really. I think I've just about arrived at the point where I'm ready for total surrender.'

He smiled, but with such exquisite sadness that, all at once, she was desperate to change the subject. She reached for her bag, glancing up as a Dutch couple went by: a bald man wearing a natty grey suit and saddle shoes, and a fair-haired woman with round, laughing eyes, as blue as a child's marbles.

The woman wore a sky-blue outfit and a hat with artificial cherries. Under the hat, yellow curls framed the pretty face. It flashed on Calliope that Lorenz's wife might resemble this sort of woman, but all she knew was her name: Alicia.

Lorenz had wanted to come to Greece before Christmas, but Alicia reminded him that his sons were in a school play. He did most of his writing in the summer but was looking forward to his sabbatical. The current, exploratory trip was made possible by an Easter break. Stamoulis had found an interpreter who would drive him to the Peloponnese.

'Where exactly are you going?' Calliope asked, toying with her pen.

'Kalavryta. I was stationed there before getting transferred to Lesbos.' He hesitated, then relented, saying that the plot of his second novel had been inspired by historic events in the Peloponnese, but also by the wartime execution of Petra's schoolmaster. All he needed right now was a few days to poke around town. He planned to come back at the end of summer.

'As for your questions...' He glanced at his watch. 'How would you feel about discussing them over dinner? We could both rest for a few hours, then—'

'I'm sorry...' Calliope began an apology, but he quickly waved it away, as if he couldn't bear excuses. 'I'm expected at my godson's house around eight,' she said all the same. She was not only seeing Aristides but meeting his mother's relatives. She had a sudden, fleeting vision of the young Lorenz Umbreit urging her to take the Nietzsche book she had just declined with a lame excuse. For some reason, she needed him to know that she wasn't lying now. 'I would be happy to have dinner with you,' she said, 'but I honestly can't... there are other people involved.'

He gazed at her for a moment. 'How about tomorrow then?' he asked, as if testing her sincerity. 'I was planning to go to the Acropolis, but I can do that in the morning. You can come with me, if you like... we could have lunch in Plaka. I promise to answer all your questions then.' He sat watching her closely. 'I really am very tired right now,' he added, faintly apologetic. He had flown in early that morning, had been talking non-stop all day. 'Please say yes.' He smiled disarmingly. 'I was also hoping to see the changing of the guard. I'm told it's on at eleven?'

'I think so.' Calliope had last seen the *Evzones* in Kimon's company. The parliament building had still been the Royal Palace then. They had watched the ceremony, then found themselves embroiled in a fierce argument over the monarchy. 'All right,' she said to Lorenz. 'I'll come with you.'

The delighted look on his face reminded Calliope how, years ago, his smile had seemed like a precious gift. 'Shall I come to fetch you?'

'It's not necessary,' she said. Her hotel was within easy walking distance; the parliament was just across the street from the Grande Bretagne. 'I could meet you here around ten thirty?'

'Splendid!' He beamed at her again, motioning to the waiter.

She had gradually become aware of the urban rumble outside the landmark hotel. Did Lorenz know that the Grande Bretagne had been the Nazis' headquarters during the Occupation? He must know, she thought, letting her eyes range over the glittering chandeliers, the sumptuously curtained windows.

It was going on six o'clock. The waiter accepted payment and shuffled away. In the corner, the Dutchman said something to his pert companion, who threw back her head and laughed. Calliope lowered her eyes, warding off a mental picture of Alicia Umbreit laughing at one of her husband's jokes.

IV

Lorenz Umbreit had left the Grande Bretagne's dining room and was crossing the marble-floored lobby to greet Calliope. It was Sunday morning, the first day of April. A cluster of Italians had just trooped in, prattling in front of the reception desk. In the distance, church bells were pealing. It was not yet Easter for Orthodox Greeks, but it was for Lorenz Umbreit.

'*Frohe Ostern!*' Calliope shook his hand, offering the traditional German greeting. 'Ready for the *Evzones*?'

'Ready! I promise not to play any April Fool's pranks, but I can't speak for the weather,' he said, gesturing towards the sky. It had started out to be a fine spring day, but all at once, dark clouds were starting to swallow the sun.

'I should have thought to bring my umbrella,' Calliope said.

'The Acropolis with umbrellas?' He laughed at the very thought, then stopped and glanced at his watch. 'I have a big one upstairs. Shall I run and get it?'

It was ten forty, but there would be a crowd; they were just going across the street.

'You can always get it after the ceremony,' Calliope said. 'It lasts barely twenty minutes.'

'All right then. So, tell me about your *Evzones*,' he said, waiting for a tram to pass.

Greeks, Calliope said, adored the *Evzones*, but they also liked to poke fun at their attire. The uniforms had been inspired by the garb of anti-Ottoman rebels during the War of Independence. 'They are called *Klephtes*.'

She offered all this over the urban roar, but soon a traffic policeman's whistle brought the bustle to an abrupt stop, and a military band was heard, marching towards Syntagma Square. Then the *Evzones* themselves appeared, a theatrical parade of rifle-bearing men dressed in kilted tunics and red garrison caps with waist-long tassels swishing about like black horses' tails.

'In summer,' said Calliope, 'the *fustanellas* are white and have four hundred pleats in them.'

'Four hundred!'

'One for every year of Ottoman rule.'

The *Evzones* were approaching the Tomb of the Unknown Soldier. They wore white stockings with black knee tassels, their flamboyantly kicking feet clad in red clogs sporting black pompoms. There was a handful of foreigners, mingling with natives in their Sunday best, the children nibbling on sweets and pink candyfloss. Umbreit was taking photographs. His sons, he said, would be keen to see them.

When the ceremony was over, they went for a closer look at the Tomb. The inscriptions surrounding the marble relief included quotations from Pericles's ancient funeral oration. Calliope translated, wrenching her mind away from the thought of Pericles Alexiou, whom she hadn't seen since their recent quarrel.

Syntagma Square was where Athenians traditionally held their political demonstrations. It was where the first shots of the Civil War were fired. Churchill had come to mediate and was almost assassinated during his short stay at the Grande Bretagne. A bomb had been placed in the hotel's sewer on Christmas Eve.

'But don't worry,' Calliope added. 'The only danger right now is our getting caught in a downpour.' They laughed. She pointed out that it didn't seem to be clearing up. They should probably go and get the umbrella.

Umbreit glanced at the sky, but he had just spotted an organ grinder with a monkey and wanted to take a picture. The gypsy was as tiny as a ten-year-old but had the wizened face of a crafty old man recalling some youthful prank. Calliope waited, imagining Lorenz Umbreit back home, sharing the photographs with his family.

The gypsy was playing 'La Vie en rose' when the monkey began to squeal. A pack of dogs was approaching the corner, trotting alongside the traffic with an air of singular purpose, as if rushing to some momentous rally. A plane was flying overhead. Calliope, who had barely seen an aircraft since the Occupation, tilted her chin up. At that moment, as if the shifting of her head had triggered some divine signal, the surly skies opened and rain began to pelt the strolling families, the organ player and his monkey, the moss-green café awnings across the street.

Umbreit snapped his camera shut, shooting a quick glance towards the packed café. He gestured with his head. 'Back to the hotel?'

'Yes!' She began to laugh as they darted back, though the rain was starting to come down in sheets, sizzling down on the historic square. She entered the hotel lobby, plucking at her clinging georgette dress with one hand, mopping her streaming face with the other. Umbreit began to fuss with his camera. He glanced at Calliope, then cast about with his eyes, as if in search of inspiration. He gazed down at his own soaked shoes, then turned to look at hers.

'*Mea culpa.*' He sighed, looking undecided. 'If you like, we could go to my room,' he finally said. 'I have a suite... I could perhaps...' He made a vague gesture suggesting the possibility of somehow drying up.

Calliope hesitated but could not think of a better option.

'We can see the Acropolis from my room.' He achieved a smile.

'In that case... I accept.'

He ushered her to the lifts and down the corridor, then unlocked the door to his suite and stepped back with an ironic little bow.

She remembered the mock bow, was beginning to remember other things she had forgotten over the years. There was the scent of fresh freesias and, faintly, of furniture wax.

All at once, he grew as brisk as he had been in uniform, hastening to point out the bathroom, offer his dressing gown. He picked a towel for himself, then headed towards the bedroom.

Clutching gown and handbag, Calliope stepped into the marbled bathroom, marvelling at the opulence. She pulled off her sodden shoes, rolled off her stockings, then unbuttoned her clinging dress, hanging it to dry over a towel rack. Her bra, too, was damp. She hesitated but finally removed it and hung it up as well. It seemed somehow disingenuous to feel so ill at ease in the room of a man she had been intimate with, a man whose unborn child she had carried.

It was pleasantly warm in the bathroom. Calliope mopped herself thoroughly, then struggled into the paisley dressing gown, detecting a vaguely familiar scent. She combed her hair, then reapplied lipstick. Leaning in to the mirror, she rolled her lips, tightened the belt on the dressing gown, then stepped out of the bathroom, barefoot.

Lorenz was seated on the edge of the sofa, opening a bottle of CAIR champagne. He had changed into a fresh pair of trousers and a shirt with blue and dun-hued stripes. He glanced up and appraised her appearance briefly with a vaguely humorous spark in his eyes but without comment.

'Stamoulis arranged this to welcome me,' he said, pouring out the champagne. She accepted a glass, then went to stand by the window.

Only the back of the Parthenon could be seen from this vantage point, though construction laws dictated that the Acropolis be visible from anywhere in the capital.

'Pity they couldn't come up with a law governing the weather,' Calliope quipped.

Lorenz laughed, watching her settle into a wing chair. She set her glass down on the coffee table and brought out her notebook. She crossed her legs. She carefully adjusted the silky gown over her knees, groping for a modicum of professional dignity. Her hair was still damp, curling loosely just above her shoulders.

She had several questions stemming from her imperfect

knowledge of German; she wanted to ensure that she had not misunderstood his intentions. When she read the copied passages out loud, he smiled a little, as if the sound of his own words coming out of her mouth both delighted and slightly embarrassed him. She asked a question that had to do with his protagonist's state of mind. When he said *konfus*, did he mean muddled or bewildered?

Lorenz Umbreit answered her questions, interjecting an occasional comment. They sipped their champagne. They exchanged thoughts on the German text. She had several pages of scribbled notes, but it took less than two hours to review them all. Halfway through their discussion, he stopped to ask whether he might call room service and order lunch. Once more she hesitated; once more she agreed.

The decision seemed perfectly reasonable until, looking up from her notebook while he spoke on the phone, she became aware of a flash of lust. She hastened to quell it by setting the glass down and going to stand by the balcony. She had meant to buy cigarettes, but the rain had thwarted their plans.

What are you going to do, take your German friend to the Acropolis? Show him where the swastika used to fly?

She was still resisting Pericles's echoing words when Lorenz replaced the receiver and sat down again, tugging at his trousers. By the time lunch arrived, all her questions had been answered, but the rain showed no sign of abating. They could hear it patter on the balcony, muting the urban rumble. The suite was well-heated and, what with the good food and the wine, the awkwardness of the situation gradually dissipated.

They began to talk about personal matters. She told him about her mother's death, which still haunted her. Lorenz's mother had also died tragically, a year after learning that her youngest son had been killed on the Eastern Front. When she heard the news, he said, his mother went instantly blind and never recovered.

'The news of his death made her go blind?'

'It's a hysterical syndrome.' Lorenz sighed. Some people regain their sight; his mother never did. There was, he thought, something sadly symbolic about it all. 'She died believing in the Führer… died, I sometimes think, because she could not bear the truth.'

Calliope reflected that the same might be said of Eli Dhaniel, a thought she soon found herself sharing with Lorenz.

And then they both fell silent, sipping coffee, staring at the waning afternoon. She said freesias were her favourite flowers; he said the Greek champagne was excellent. They talked, then, about the Civil War, the *kentro*, Pericles's blossoming career. Lorenz must have gathered she had lived with the doctor, and perhaps guessed about Pericles as well. The longer they talked, the more vividly she recalled the feeling he had always given her: of seeing more, knowing more, than seemed humanly possible.

It became impossible, at a certain point, not to realise that she hadn't asked about his family. It seemed rude not to do so as they sat there, surrounded by the cocooning silence, the ceaseless pulsing of rain.

'Do you have a photograph of your family?' Calliope smiled across the coffee table but instantly regretted her question. She had, she would eventually admit to herself, spoken from a desperate need to subdue her aroused senses. She should not have drunk so much.

He was holding out a Christmas snapshot of a handsome family: a smiling, fair-haired man and his two young sons, seated in front of a blazing fire. Both boys were as blond as their father, but the mother was as dark as a Greek. Alicia.

Calliope studied Lorenz Umbreit's wife, contemplating the fact that she bore no resemblance whatsoever to the Dutchwoman downstairs. If there was anyone she resembled, it was Calliope herself. With a suffocating feeling, she took in the dark, curly hair, the dimpled smile, the steady, forthright gaze. *Ach, Thee mou.*

Calliope knew that she, too, should smile, should offer some banal comment. But even as the thought flitted through her mind, her throat felt constricted. She raised her gaze and looked into his eyes.

He did not flinch before her scrutiny, but she was still floundering. And in that chaotic moment, desperate to break the charged silence, she suddenly found herself telling him about her pregnancy.

'I lost the child at the hospital,' she said and averted her gaze. 'I didn't even know – not until much later.'

At last, it was out. But then, as if in response to the mention of pregnancy, Calliope felt her tongue thicken. Lurching from her chair, she bolted to the bathroom, where she hunkered over the toilet, heaving and retching, her very teeth aching with unleashed grief.

Her stomach was soon empty, but the blood was still beating in her ears as she rinsed her mouth, applying toothpaste with her finger, then dousing her face with water. *I must leave*, she thought, *must borrow an umbrella and return it later.*

She opened the bathroom door. She watched Lorenz turn away from the window and gaze at her across the room with a complicated expression in which doubt and confusion and anguish were all evident. She felt a stab of pain but remained standing, pinioned by his gaze. A room-service cart went trundling down the long corridor. There was a knock on the adjacent door, the murmur of voices.

She was about to speak, intending to say something about leaving, when he hesitated for the briefest moment, then took a brisk step forward. He was holding out his hands, like a supplicant before an unexpectedly opening door. Calliope's own hand was resting over her breast, in a gesture unconsciously mimicking her mother but merely intended to placate the unruly beating in her chest. There being no laws to govern the weather, the rain went on falling, as if it might never cease.

V

It was her own scream that woke Calliope on Monday morning – the scream and the dream that had generated it and that left her heart pounding as wildly as she imagined it would have if she had indeed been a Makronisos prisoner, about to be dumped into the sea with a pack of crazed cats.

The scream had woken Lorenz as well, though barely five minutes before his wake-up call. Another sixty-five minutes and she would be alone in this posh hotel room, her heart no longer beating in terror but already resigned to pain.

'It's all right.' He was cradling her in his arms. 'It was just a dream.'

'Yes.'

He sighed. 'I'm being picked up in an hour.'

'I know.'

He drew back a little and looked into her eyes. 'Would you like to have breakfast with me?'

She shook her head. The rain had stopped sometime in the night.

'We could have it here if you like,' he said.

She rubbed her eyes. 'I'm not hungry. Thank you.'

'Are you sure you won't come to Kalavryta?' he asked, not for the first time. She was sure, though already she could feel his absence, his body beginning to drift away from her. It was a body whose movements had always expressed purpose; not a single gesture was ever wasted. Even now, in peacetime, this was a man of prudence, efficiency, foresight. That she was the one person for whom circumspection had been cast to the wind somehow seemed humbling.

She lay watching him stride towards the bathroom. No matter that he was reluctant. No matter that he would have preferred to take her in his arms and stay. She knew this was so, had never known anything with greater certainty. But there was a shower to be taken and teeth to be brushed, and all the other rituals he presumably performed at home. A chauffeured car would be waiting for him at seven. She would leave the Grande Bretagne alone, making her way to the kingdom of the damned.

'Why don't you go back to sleep?' he was soon asking, pulling on his trousers while she lay watching him drowsily. 'I'll be back on Friday.'

'Shall I stay in bed until then?'

'Why not?' A smile was accomplished. He leaned over and put his lips on hers. 'Friday night at eight,' he stated decisively.

Well, he was German after all. Not having been raised on steady doses of Greek mythology, he would make no allowances for divine caprice. He would be ready exactly as planned, would leave Kalavryta on Friday, knowing how long the trip would take but never stopping to consider the possibility of hailstorms, stalled engines, road accidents.

'Will you be here?' he asked, sitting beside her when it was time to go.

'I'll be here.'

For the moment, she, too, had forgotten all about the prankish gods.

VI

The message was waiting for her at the Attikon: *Please phone mayor as soon as possible. Important.*

The mayor! She had left the hotel's number with Mathaios in case something unexpected came up at the *kentro*. And something apparently had, though it took an agonising hour for the call to go through. Only then did Calliope learn that the news had something to do with the late baker's daughter, who had just eloped.

'Marika? I don't believe it!'

As a child, Marika had been a goody two shoes; she had also been bright and diligent, never skipping school even after the bakery had burned down and classmates became cruel.

Calliope sat down, thinking of the note the distraught girl had written one day, pleading for her support. She had been in virtual house arrest after her mother got wind of the rumours about the fortress restorer. But the rumours were unfounded, Marika insisted. All she had ever done with the stranger was chat. She begged to be allowed to attend the study sessions and, somehow, Calliope had persuaded Elektra to let her come.

'Don't tell me she was supposed to be at the *kentro* when—'

'No.' Mathaios cleared his throat. 'They eloped on Saturday night. In a fishing boat.'

'Ach... poor Elektra,' Calliope muttered.

Marika's Athenian restorer had turned out to be a fisherman's son from Chios. It was impossible not to pity the late baker's widow, but why was Mathaios calling her?

'It's Elektra. She went crazy when she found Marika's bed empty.'

'Well, can you blame her?'

'No, I mean really crazy. There's talk of sending her to Daphni.'

'Daphni!' Calliope gripped the receiver. Daphni was a notorious insane asylum. 'What did she do?'

At first, after everyone had left the *kentro*, all she'd done was throw stones at the windows, but this had apparently failed to provide relief, so, possibly inspired by the torching of her husband's bakery, Elektra set fire to the *kentro*.

'The *kentro*! Why the *kentro*? Didn't you say it was Saturday night?'

Mathaios sighed. 'She kept saying it was your fault, putting notions into the girls' heads.'

Calliope was silent for a long, dizzying moment.

'How bad is it?' she finally brought out, breaking the crackling silence.

'Well, it's a stone house… she couldn't burn it down—'

'But?'

'There's damage, naturally.'

There was another long silence as Calliope sat contemplating her options. 'Is there a ferryboat today – do you know?'

'There's an overnight one leaving at four.'

Calliope glanced at her watch. 'I'll see you in the morning,' she said.

She went downstairs and had a quick breakfast, then sat down to write a note to Lorenz. She would drop it off at his hotel on her way to Piraeus. That, it seemed, was what the fickle deities had decided. That was what she was meant to do.

2 April 1956

Dear Lorenz,

You may think a ploy on my part, but I give you my word of honour: it isn't. A village woman set fire to the kentro *yesterday, all because I wouldn't stop sticking my nose in other people's affairs.*

I have thought of myself all this time as a women's advocate, but it seems I am nothing but a meddlesome fool. I am beside myself with worry and must return to Molyvos at once. I'll write at greater length shortly, though I doubt I'll be back on Friday. Perhaps I should have taken a talisman when I left the village, or lit a candle to St Christopher. May he be with you on your way home, my dear.

I hope your trip to Kalavryta went well and promise to write as soon as I can.

Yours, Calliope

VII

Excerpt from Calliope Adham's journal – 2 April 1956

It is almost sixteen hours since we said goodbye. I have started to write to him three times but have destroyed all three letters. For once in my life, I don't know what to say. I keep thinking he must regret what happened between us and who can blame him? I blame myself. I have, it seems, not changed as much as I liked to think. I may be forty-one, but I am still the selfish girl polishing off a jar of cherry preserves. Wartime deprivation might have exculpated me, but what can I say to absolve myself now?

Nothing, except perhaps this: the force that keeps propelling me towards him is a blind force, a force of utter madness, beyond will or reason. How else can I explain ending up in bed with another woman's husband? I remember telling Elpida I would henceforth live by my own rules, but this is not what I meant. Never. That I have broken the golden rule makes my heart cower, the way Sappho used to do after gobbling up something forbidden but utterly irresistible. Perversely, I keep trying to imagine him at home, with his family. Strange, but the thought of his making love to Alicia is less distressing than imagining him calling her name, caressing her cheek, laughing over dinner. I think of her, her indisputable entitlement, and the pain is scarcely describable. I imagine him bringing flowers for her birthday, kissing her neck while she stands at the stove. I imagine him calling her 'Liebling' and I long for something my hands might pounce on and reduce to ashes.

And so, of course, I am to be punished. My punishment may be less drastic than being drowned with wild cats, but I can't help wondering whether a part of me did not know, on that last afternoon with Pericles, what might happen in Athens. Pericles certainly seemed to know. Could I have been lying to myself?

I don't know the answer, but I now realise something I was not ready to admit to Eli, or even to myself. One reason I have always been reluctant to marry is the fear that people might be right about me; that I am more like a man than a woman and might find it impossible to be monogamous. How can anyone, man or woman, promise to love another human being – love one and only one – forever?

I ask this question even though I feel sure I will love Lorenz to the day I die. So am I really less foolish, less ludicrous, than Emma Bovary? Lorenz seemed amused by the comparison, but, sooner or later, love makes fools of us all, in literature as in life. Lorenz's middle name, it turns out, is Friedrich, which apparently means 'peaceful ruler'. It made me laugh when I wanted to cry.

I don't feel like laughing any more. I don't know what to say, what to write to him.

'This is not the end,' he said to me, just before leaving the hotel this morning. Then he went off to Kalavryta, leaving me to grope my way out of a place where I never expected to be. I wish I believed in prayer. I wish I knew what to pray for.

VIII

The fire that had devastated the *kentro*'s first floor spelled the end of the study sessions. The children's tutorials would eventually resume, but the news of Marika's elopement brought about a permanent change in parental attitudes. It was as if, Calliope was to write to Lorenz Umbreit, sending adolescent girls to the *kentro* would expose them to some moral contagion, as if, sooner or later, they were all bound to elope, or do something equally rash.

By autumn, the library had reopened its doors, but Calliope herself was like one of the refugees from Asia Minor, who couldn't stop lamenting the day on which Constantinople had fallen to the Turks. That the fire had taken place while she had lain in Lorenz's arms made the catastrophe seem, at first, like a cruel April Fool's prank, then like some punitive deity's message. Although many villagers had pitched in to help restore the *kentro*, there had also been those who could not help expressing a smidgen of satisfaction. 'When the head gets too big, it can't escape punches,' Calliope's aunt had overheard someone say after Sunday Mass.

The statement about putting notions into the girls' heads made Calliope want to scream from the hilltop. Over and over, she reflected on how careful she'd been never to say anything that might encourage the girls to behave recklessly in their private lives. Even while reviewing the War of Independence, discussing the legendary Bouboulina, she had not so much as breathed a word about the Greek heroine's tempestuous love life. All for nothing! She was being blamed anyway.

At the searing height of her misery, the unfairness of it all only served to intensify Calliope's longing for Lorenz Umbreit. Repeatedly, she called on God without any expectation of being heard. Her heart lacerated by guilt, she resigned herself to small consolations: letters from Heidelberg, expressing solicitude, respect, understanding. Not trivial in themselves, they seemed so when examined in the resplendent light of what had been relinquished.

The inner struggle continued for months.

One day, after a sleepless night, Calliope surrendered, agreeing to meet Lorenz Umbreit again. It was by then late October. He was back in Greece on his sabbatical, going on with the research for the sequel to his novel. He had finally talked Calliope into accompanying him to Kalavryta, where the 1821 revolt against the Ottomans had started.

But this was not where Lorenz's interest lay.

In December of 1943, the Wehrmacht had torched the town, killing every male over fifteen – over a thousand men! – in reprisal for Resistance activities. One of the first things Calliope had seen on arriving in Kalavryta was the clock on the town's cathedral, its hands fixed at two thirty-four, when the slaughter began.

The hands of the clock had been arrested but, visiting the local Martyrs' Monument, Calliope could not stop her thoughts from straying. It was mid-afternoon and the hillside was deserted because of preparations for St Dimitrios's Feast. She was standing next to Lorenz, surveying the monument.

'There's something I've been meaning to ask you,' she said after a lengthy silence. 'That day in Eftalou… the day you and Reis ran into my mother and me. What would you have done if you'd found out I was not carrying mustard greens in my basket but live ammunition?'

The question made Lorenz pause, casting Calliope a quick sidelong look.

'But don't you see?' he finally said. 'I didn't look into your basket because I didn't want to know what you had in it.'

Calliope turned this over in her mind. 'Those bullets could have killed you,' she said after a moment. 'Just one of them in a guerrilla's gun and—'

'I suppose I was willing to take that risk.'

Calliope was silent. He had been prepared to die rather than have his suspicions confirmed and have to arrest her in Alfred Reis's presence. The thought made something stir in her chest. Walking away from the memorial, she stopped, rose on her tiptoes, and put her mouth to her lover's lips.

IX

Alas, nothing could stop her mind from wandering. December 1943, just before Christmas, was when Rupert Ealing had left Molyvos.

At the time, Lorenz was stationed in Mytilene, but what if he had never been transferred away from Kalavryta? What if he had been ordered to set the town ablaze?

'What ever happened to Alfred Reis?' she suddenly asked.

'Reis?' He shot her a quick glance. 'Didn't you hear?'

'What?'

There was a heavy sigh, a moment's hesitation. 'Reis came to see Alkesti in Athens after the war, and her brother shot him.'

Calliope stopped dead in her tracks. 'Her brother—'

'You didn't know?' He looked fleetingly baffled, but then awareness dawned. 'It was right after the war. You were probably still in hospital.'

Another moment went by. 'What happened?'

'The brother found them in bed. He—'

Calliope's hands flew up to her ears. She did not want to hear any more.

'It's in my novel,' said Lorenz. 'You'll have to read it sooner or later.'

Silence. So he had moved the Petra love affair to Kalavryta, raising the fictional stakes by setting the story around the destruction of a historic town, the slaughter of its entire male population. At that moment, Calliope felt herself starting to recoil, as she had after seeing newsreels of the Nazi death camps. A decade had passed since the end of the war, but the images had not yet lost their gouging power.

Yet here she was, an erstwhile Resistance member, strolling through this blood-soaked landscape, arm in arm with a former Wehrmacht officer. They were heading back to the centre, towards one of the town's resurrected hotels. It was late October. They walked slowly, the grim historic facts vying over Calliope's head with thoughts of Lorenz's wife and children.

He had not spoken of them, except to say that he would be going back for his son's birthday, then returning to Greece after Christmas. It had been agreed that Calliope would act as his interpreter. She had led Molyviates to believe that she was in Athens, visiting Aristides and her cousin Grigoris. She had never thought of herself as a liar, let alone an adulteress. Yet here she was. Here they both were, as if the rest of the world had ceased to exist.

On the way back to their hotel, they stopped at a fruit stall. Lorenz loved pomegranates, which he had never tasted before the Occupation. Calliope liked eating the seeds but lacked the patience to extract them. She also disliked having her fingers stained.

'I'll peel them for you,' Lorenz said back at the hotel.

'You're going to spoil me,' Calliope said.

She ran a hot bath, trying to silence her whispering mind. Soon, Lorenz came in, bearing a white bowl full of glittering pomegranate seeds. He sat on the edge of the bathtub and began to pop the tiny gems into her open mouth. Calliope chewed on them slowly. She reached for a bar of soap. She smiled.

'I feel like the abducted Persephone.'

'Ha! I had exactly the same thought,' Lorenz said, filling her mouth with more crimson seeds, while Calliope marvelled at how often their minds meandered in the same direction. She thought of Hades's love for Persephone; his consenting to see her for only three months a year, letting her spend the remaining nine on earth, where she clearly belonged.

She did not belong in Kalavryta. This much Calliope knew. Leaving Molyvos, she had almost instructed the taxi driver to turn back, but then changed her mind, deciding to take the wind as she found it.

She was finding the wind predictably stormy, though she managed to keep the internal tumult to herself, as she had her wartime suffering all those years ago. She was careful not to allude to the future, or ask any questions, least of all of herself.

All the same, when, after three weeks, it was time for Lorenz to leave, she handed him a symbolic sprig of basil she had plucked during their last evening stroll in Athens.

'This will ensure your return,' she said, trying for a smile.

He stopped in the middle of the sidewalk and peered into her eyes.

'My return?' he said gravely. 'No charms needed, my love.'

Calliope was silent. She watched him slip the sprig of basil into his buttonhole and saw his eyes mist over. There was a sudden ache in the vicinity of her heart, but she allowed him to take her arm, and they quietly resumed walking along the moonlit sea.

X

The Owl's Cry, the novel Umbreit had been researching in the Peloponnese, was scheduled to be released in Berlin in the spring of 1958. The Greek edition would not be out for another year. Calliope was still polishing the last segment of her translation. She had brought the manuscript to Athens, where Lorenz was researching the third novel in his Aegean trilogy. *Morning Doves* was set during the Civil War; that's all he would say about it. He had been spending hours at the National Archives, while Calliope sat in the shady courtyard, working. They had rented a furnished villa in a seaside suburb. But that late-March morning – her last day in Athens – she had gone into town to buy summer shoes and pick up some books to take back home.

There had been several secret meetings since that first reunion in Athens, but Lorenz was flying back to Germany the following day. Again. They had fallen asleep in each other's arms after a long swim and an excellent lunch at a nearby taverna. Yet Calliope had woken from her nap feeling vaguely disgruntled. Lorenz was still dozing, so she picked up one of the books she had purchased and began to read, only to find herself arrested by a Villa-Lobos aria playing on Lorenz's transistor radio.

The broadcast was coming from Paris. Calliope lay perfectly still, listening to Victoria de los Ángeles's querying lament, the eight mournful cellos, the anguished voice rising towards an impassioned crescendo. The piece sent a shiver through her, but then a neighbour's dog began to bark, and Lorenz opened his eyes.

'What? What did you say?' he mumbled, rubbing his eyes.

'Nothing. Just cursing the dog.' Calliope sighed.

Lorenz sat up. The news came on. He turned off the radio and reached out lazily, drawing Calliope towards him. Her book tumbled off the bed. 'What are you reading?'

'*Anna Karenina*,' Calliope said. 'In French. I read the Greek version when I was much too young.'

Lorenz yawned again. 'How young?'

'Under sixteen,' she said. 'I was staying with my aunt and uncle in Mytilene and found it in their library. I filched it and read it. They never even noticed.' Calliope chuckled, her eyes on a spider crawling up the wall. She was still afraid of spiders, but this one was so frail its legs were like the filaments in a light bulb.

'Would you like me to get rid of it?' Lorenz asked, a smile in his voice.

'No, let it be,' Calliope said. He had obviously traced her gaze, but it never failed to amaze her, the things he noticed, the things he remembered. She thought of the huge hairy spider she had recently found in her toilet at home, of her neighbours' laughter when she ran out in her bathrobe, begging someone to get rid of it. They wouldn't laugh if they could see her now, she thought with an inner sigh. Even her French cousin was not likely to be amused.

A few minutes went by. It occurred to Calliope that people were far less judgemental about fictional characters' moral lapses than the transgressions of men and women they knew in real life. She was thinking of Anna Karenina, but when she tried to share this thought with Lorenz, he only shrugged, smiling a little sadly.

'*Tout comprendre, c'est tout pardonner*,' he said.

Then he consulted his watch and the small gesture suddenly irked Calliope. He seemed, as always, obsessed with time; *she* seemed, as usual, quarrelsome before his departure. She imagined him in Heidelberg: reading the morning paper over breakfast, getting rid of a house insect, kissing his wife goodbye. She had never known self-loathing before, but she knew it now.

'My father once told me I was high-minded,' she said, thinking out loud.

'You *are* high-minded,' he said. 'But, well, life can be a humbling experience.'

'Yes, indeed. And I'll admit it: I probably needed to be humbled.' She paused and mulled it over for a minute or two. 'When you think about it, though, there's no point in being humbled if you haven't learned anything, is there?'

Lorenz ran his hand through his hair but said nothing. It was getting dark. 'Why don't you say something?' Calliope turned and looked at him keenly. 'Do you think I'm wrong? Don't you feel guilty when you get home to Alicia?' It was the first time she had voiced a question about his family life. She still admired his steely reserve, yet she also resented it. She wanted to penetrate his inner fortress, to see it come crumbling down.

'I don't want to talk about Alicia,' he said, his jaw tightening.

'But why?' Calliope asked. Then, because she was angry at herself for not holding her tongue, and because she felt excluded from his real life, she went on, somewhat resentfully. 'You can lie to your wife, but you can't talk about her?'

'I talk to my psychiatrist,' he said curtly. 'My time with you is too precious. Please let's not spoil it.'

She gazed at him for a moment. 'You're very lucky,' she finally said.

'Lucky?'

'You get to fictionalise your experience. You don't have to share any of it.'

'I'm not writing about us, believe me.'

'No, you always write about things after the fact. You write when they're over.'

'That's true,' he allowed. 'I do.'

'So.' She let out a bitter chuckle. 'Some day, when this is over between us, this conversation will appear in some novel, and you… you will write a disclaimer saying it's all just the product of your imagination?'

He gave her a long, wounded look, his eyes the colour of a stormy sea.

'It's never going to be over between us,' he said. 'Whatever happens.' He reached out and stroked her cheek with infinite tenderness.

Calliope lay motionless, staring at the ceiling. When she failed to respond, he flung the blankets aside and reached for his trousers. The sight of him getting dressed twisted her lungs.

'Do you want to go get something to eat?' he asked after a while.

'I'm not hungry,' she said.

'I am. I'll go get something.'

He came back half an hour later, bearing stuffed vine leaves, taramosalata, tiny meatballs, and stuffed courgette blossoms, which he knew she loved. He sat down on the edge of the bed and began to slide morsels of food into her mouth, as if she were recovering from some illness and was too feeble to feed herself.

'I'm sorry,' she said. 'I seem to want to punish you for leaving me again. Will you forgive me?'

'Nothing to forgive,' he said, then resumed feeding her. He picked one of the delicate courgette blossoms, looked at it for a moment, as if to ensure its perfection, then leaned forward to slip it into her mouth. As he did so, Calliope experienced a current of love so powerful it threatened to crack her heart. But this moment, too, passed. She chewed. She swallowed obediently. She was silent.

XI

Calliope recognised her immediately. She would have had to be blind not to, having seen Alicia Umbreit's photograph, having quickly noted the physical resemblance. Lorenz's wife was a little shorter, her eyes were greener, her hair somewhat darker. If she perceived her own resemblance to her husband's translator, she gave no hint of it as she held out her hand.

'I've heard so much about you.'

Calliope felt the blood ebb from her face. 'And I about you,' she lied.

The German woman's eyes measured the Greek. She flashed a smile, saying something Calliope failed to absorb as she waited for the room to stop spinning. Lorenz, who had introduced the two women to each other, stood stiffly to the side, ignored by both. Calliope went on fighting the impulse to flee.

The 1959 book launch took place in an Athens university lecture hall, where rows of folding chairs had been set up, facing a long, draped table on which three microphones waited. Over by the wall, on a smaller table, was a pile of *The Owl's Cry*. The title had come to Lorenz after Calliope told him about her childhood fear of owls. For years, their eerie cries would send her shrieking into her father's arms and would, from time to time, reverberate in her dreams.

Calliope's mind was frantically wandering toward the distant past because the present left her desperately groping for anchorage. She became aware of Lorenz's eyes seeking hers, brimming with apology, yet indignation went on coursing through her veins. She suspected that Alicia had at the last moment decided to accompany her husband to Athens. A wife's intuition?

She would never know. She had been asked to arrive at the lecture hall early and did, hoping to have a glass of wine with Lorenz before official proceedings started. And there was Alicia Umbreit. Without any warning.

The programme called for introductions, bilingual readings, and a question-and-answer period, followed by book signings. Calliope herself was meant to read the Greek extract, as well as to translate the final questions and answers. Later, there would be a reception in the author's honour. Lorenz had planned to attend the reception, then spend the weekend with Calliope. Would he now be going to the seaside villa with Alicia? Would she guess that he had not been alone during his previous visits?

All these questions were still chasing each other through Calliope's head when she felt a pat on her shoulder. Titos Stamoulis, the publisher, had arrived.

Greetings were exchanged, cameras flashed. Someone offered Calliope a glass of wine, while she stood enveloped by haze, struggling with her inner upheaval.

In the year that had elapsed since the German release of *The Owl's Cry*, the book had become a bestseller, with translations into half a dozen languages underway. Among the guests was a Greek–German couple, friends of the publisher, who stopped to congratulate both author and translator. Calliope had felt proud of her own achievement, had looked forward to the book launch. She had not seen Lorenz since December; had never expected to find herself shaking hands and exchanging smiles, while her heart was being secretly slashed. *Alicia.*

She had just heard Lorenz say his wife's name, a name she had mentally heard him utter innumerable times, in dozens of imagined contexts. And yet, hearing him say the name now, in her own presence, made something snap in Calliope's brain. The sensation briefly paralysed every muscle in her body, but then she heard him speak her own name as well.

'Calliope,' he was saying. 'The photographer wants us to pose in front of the book display. Can we please…' He gestured towards the wall, abruptly reanimating her, like a puppeteer tugging on a puppet's strings.

'Yes, of course,' she said. 'Of course.'

She was wearing high heels, as was Alicia, but the wife seemed to be having no difficulty crossing the room. Hooking her arm through her husband's, she looked as self-possessed as a duchess, turning a neutral smile towards everyone in her path. At one point, Lorenz made a lame attempt at humour and Alicia flashed Calliope a complicitous smile, then leaned over and pressed her cheek to her husband's.

Despite his resolute air, Lorenz was beginning to show signs of strain, repeatedly raising his ink-stained hand to his perspiring hairline. Calliope observed the purple stain, and the smell of ink invaded her nostrils, as vivid as on the day he had knocked the ink bottle off his desk. She recalled the internal chaos. She recalled the pain. She was feeling it all over again now. Barely breathing, she let herself be steered across the room, a wine glass in her hand, a smile pasted on a face that, she felt, no longer belonged to her.

The photographer instructed Lorenz to station himself next to the pile of books. He positioned Alicia on his right and Calliope on his left, then stepped back and gazed at the three of them through the camera lens.

Lorenz had raised his long arms, looping one around his wife, the other around Calliope. Oh, how she hated him at that moment: his impeccable manners, his apparent sangfroid! He was smiling straight at the camera, while his left hand tried to convey the depth of his private anguish. She was sure about the sorrow, but could nonetheless feel her mind hardening against him. It came to her then that it was in her power to bring this slick performance to an ignominious end. Fleetingly, she felt he deserved it.

'I'd like one of Mr Umbreit alone,' the photographer said and, obediently, the two women stepped aside and stood together like sisters, watching the author pose before the pile of books, his arms crossed, smiling serenely.

Scrutinising the photograph in the years to come, Calliope would be hard put to say where the hint of inner despair lay in the captured image. Despite the smile, the carefully composed features, it was indisputably there, but where, exactly? In the steady Nordic gaze, the tender hollows framing the mouth – where?

She would never know. Steeling herself, she murmured an excuse and left the crowd before the formal proceedings started. The lecture hall was almost full as she picked her way towards the toilets, fighting the scream rising in her chest.

Opening the ladies' door, she darted into one of the stalls and bent over the trickling toilet, vomiting into its bowl. Trembling, she stepped out of the stall, shifting her gaze away from the mirror, as one instinctively would from another's shame.

Yet the shame went on roiling inside her. The trembling had stopped, but her cheeks were hot and prickly, as with the onset of fever.

Water. She must douse her face with water before sitting down to face the public scrutiny. There was no one else about. Pushing her hair behind her ears, Calliope bent over the basin and splashed cold water over her face. She straightened up to reach for a towel, her glance compulsively returning to the mirror. For a moment, she stood frozen, staring at her own image: the waxen skin, the dilated eyes, the mouth which Lorenz had said he could never get enough of. She was leaning in to the mirror, the way a woman might while examining teeth or nostrils.

There was nothing to examine. Everything had been examined innumerable times and found to be flawed beyond repair. Recoiling, Calliope watched a ball of spit come shooting out of her own mouth, besmirching the lustrous mirror. For a brief spell, she felt she might lose her bearings. She stood leaning against the sink, waiting for the moment to pass.

And the moment passed. There were footsteps approaching the toilet door. A restive audience was waiting.

1966–1974

'Of all human ills, greatest is fortune's wayward tyranny.'

Sophocles

ONE

I

Transcript of Athens Radio interview – 20 March 1966
Interviewer: Erti Papadimitriou
Guest: Calliope Adham

Calliope Adham is the recent winner of the Hellenic Award for Excellence in Literary Translation. She is also an educator, an advocate for battered women, and the author of numerous articles dealing with women's issues.

EP: Welcome to the programme, *Kyria* Adham, and congratulations on your recent award.

CA: Thank you. I'm glad to be here.

EP: *Kyria* Adham, you are considered to be the foremost Greek translator, but I gather you found your way into this domain by chance?

CA: Yes. I started out as a teacher, then I became a de facto social worker. I was in my mid-thirties before I started translating on a professional basis.

EP: You were born and raised on Lesbos, in the village of Mythimna – or, as you natives still call it, Molyvos. You began teaching several years before the war, at a time when women were kept at home and most villagers were barely literate. How did a village girl get from there to here?

CA: The short answer is: I had an exceptional father. He was the village headmaster but had been educated in Constantinople and was besotted with books. I—

EP (laughs): Besotted?

CA: Yes! Books and ideas. And, well, I was his only child. He began to read to me when I was barely out of nappies, then he taught me French and German. Somewhere along the way, he passed on his love of knowledge.

EP: So you began to teach. And then?

CA: Then I got fired. This was during the Civil War. My father had died back in 1935. There was a new headmaster and… let's just say we did not see eye to eye.

EP: The award you have just received was in recognition of your translation of Lorenz Umbreit's Aegean Trilogy, but you have also translated Ioannis Dimopoulos's novel into French and, of course, Pericles Alexiou's poetry. Do you prefer translating from or into your mother tongue?

CA: Well, each offers its own challenges and rewards. I like translating into Greek because it is my mother tongue, but also because it introduces my compatriots to books I admire. On the other hand, Pericles Alexiou's poems and Ioannis Dimopoulos's novel might not be known outside Greece if I hadn't had the time and contacts to pursue publication abroad.

EP: In a 1960 interview, you said that your knowledge of German was still spotty when you took on Umbreit's *The Nightingale's Silence*. That must have been quite a challenge?

CA: Yes… yes, it was, though translating poetry is actually harder, especially with two languages as different as Greek and French.

EP: Pericles Alexiou is known to have been your pupil, but how did someone with a limited knowledge of German get to translate an acclaimed German novel like *The Nightingale's Silence*?

CA: To tell you the truth, I wasn't at all sure I was up to it. I got talked into trying and, well, it seemed I could do the job, and so I did.

EP: You have said before that you met the author during the Occupation, while you were working for the Resistance. Are you the woman the fictional character of Penelope is based on?

CA: That you'll have to ask the author.

EP (laughs): Fair enough. But Mr Umbreit *was* a Wehrmacht officer stationed on Lesbos during the Occupation?

CA: Yes.

EP: And his first book is dedicated to you.

CA: Yes. And there are some Molyviates who will even tell you that I had collaborated with the Germans.

EP: Really? But you were in the Resistance!

CA: Exactly.

EP (pause): May I ask why you chose to stay in the village all these years?

CA: Well, I almost went to France when I was young, but then the war came, and the Civil War... there were personal factors, but I... I've come to believe that it was my destiny to stay in Molyvos and try to improve village women's lot.

EP: You opened the Zenovia Antoniou Centre in 1950, but you did not at first have a women's shelter in mind...

CA: No. All I knew was that the village needed a children's library and a tutorial centre. Some of my brightest pupils, mostly girls, had been prevented from leaving the village to go to middle school and I had nothing to do – I had just been fired – so I thought, *why not offer informal study sessions?* So I did and, well, the girls seemed keen to learn.

EP: Who was Zenovia Antoniou?

CA: Ah, Zenovia! (chuckles) She was a well-to-do village woman, a notary's wife, who had thrown out her womanising husband and lived alone for the rest of her life. She was a fortune teller. It was mostly a hobby, but she seemed to have some sort of clairvoyant gift. Anyway, she had no children, and for some reason decided to leave me her house in her will.

EP: And where did the idea of helping battered women come from?

CA: Well, you know, inspiration is like an apricot or a cherry pip, spat out and lying ignored on the wayside, until some sudden change in environmental conditions makes it sprout and grow into a fruit-laden tree. In my case, soon after I got fired, I ran into a woman who had been beaten by her husband, who had nowhere to go. The Antoniou house was empty, so I invited her to stay there and, well, that was the pip, you might say. Actually, the Molyvos *kentro* is seldom used as a shelter.

EP: But the one in Mytilene?

CA: The one in Mytilene was specifically founded to help battered women. I am only a consultant at this point; other women run it. Anyway, it's something someone would have done, sooner or later.

EP: Because of the prevalence of domestic violence?

CA: And because women in urban centres are beginning to get educated, and to question the status quo.

EP: In a recent magazine interview – I believe it was in *Zoe* – you said that doing away with domestic violence was your most serious ambition.

CA: That, and also encouraging women to get an education, to become independent.

EP: These are two admirable ambitions but, as you know, there are many who would argue that women's independence – women joining the workforce – will undermine the stability of the Greek family. What do you say to that?

CA: I think the stability of the Greek family has largely been paid for with women's silence... women's suffering. When you live in a society where women remain in abusive or exploitative situations because they have no other options, what you actually have is female enslavement. This is not a uniquely Greek situation, of course. Women all over the world are beginning to revolt.

EP: What do you think of the male-bashing that's beginning to take place in America?

CA: It just goes to show you that women can equal men in every way, including idiocy.

EP (laughs): But—

CA: I'm sorry to interrupt you – but to fully answer your question: I'm a strong supporter of women's rights, but I don't approve of militant rhetoric. I think that men are as much victims of social and historic forces as women. Both must be re-educated if significant change is ever to take place.

EP: But it's obviously going to be much harder to persuade men to change. I mean, it's never easy to relinquish power, is it?

CA: No, it isn't easy. People tend to resist change, but that's no reason to stop struggling, is it? Just because it isn't easy?

EP: No. You are right. Of course. There are those who say that you can be as tough as a man. How did you come to have such a reputation?

CA: Mostly by speaking my mind and refusing to compromise.

EP: But isn't compromise an essential part of learning to live with others?

CA: Yes. Yes, it is. I suppose that's why I live alone with half a dozen cats.

EP: Half a dozen?

CA: Yes! But to give you a serious answer: compromise may be an inevitable part of human coexistence, but I'm sure I don't have to tell you it's usually women who have to do all the compromising. In fact, I don't think compromise is the right word. Self-abnegation is probably more accurate. Most women who want to marry have to be prepared to humble themselves every day of their married lives.

EP: You were only in your late twenties when you were widowed. If I may be permitted to ask a personal question – did you make a conscious decision not to remarry?

CA: Well, you know, I haven't exactly been celibate since my husband died, but as for marriage, I think it debilitates women. I just turned fifty-one and I think that had I not been widowed, had I had children, I would not be sitting here with you today.

EP: So you—

CA: But – excuse me again – I don't want to give the impression that I think raising a family is not an important achievement. It may be the most important of all, but it's not for everyone. I think people – men and women – should have the option of choosing what to do with their lives. Greek family laws are, in my view, egregiously antiquated and must be revised.

EP: For example?

CA: For example, our laws permit a father to marry off an adolescent daughter without her consent. A social system that permits this, that makes it impossible for women to escape exploitation and abuse, is a system we must fight to reform if we are to evolve into a modern society.

EP: But don't you think that feminism is likely to bring about a backlash?

CA: So? Let there be a backlash! What do you expect from a revolution? Anyway, could things be much worse for women than they are already?

EP: Well...

CA: Look, it's like I said: people resist change. They always have. But when you really want to get somewhere, even a hay cart will eventually get you there.

EP: Or we would still be huddling in caves, I suppose?

CA: Exactly.

EP: All of which goes to say, I guess, that we must be prepared to deal with huge disappointments and setbacks. What has been the worst setback in your own professional life?

CA: Oh… probably the day a village woman decided to torch our *kentro*, holding me responsible for her daughter's elopement.

EP: What did you have to do with it?

CA: Well, I'm tempted to say 'nothing', but it wouldn't be quite true. I was responsible for getting the girl out of virtual house arrest and, in general, for encouraging young women to think more deeply about serious issues. And that came to include reflecting on their own lives, I suppose.

EP: So the *kentro* had to be rebuilt?

CA: Not from scratch, but restored, yes. All the books in the library had gone up in flames. It was very demoralising, especially as the girl's mother ended up in an insane asylum.

EP: What about village men? Has there not been any negative pushback from irate—

CA: Oh, to be sure. One fisherman whose wife sought shelter at the *kentro* several years ago tried to break down the front door, but this was one development I'd foreseen, so the door had been reinforced and barred. The husband stood on the street, screaming abuse, but even that backfired. He became a laughing stock and… well, no one tried anything like that again.

EP: *Kyria* Adham, you are clearly a woman of exceptional willpower and strength. I am sure many women will be wondering about both your resilience and… well, your youthful looks. What's the secret?

CA: Chocolates and young men.

EP (laughs): That's it?

CA: Well, it's not likely to be dusty bookstacks, is it?

EP (laughs again): I suppose you must know your way around bookstacks, but do you think that a plain woman could have accomplished as much as you have?

CA: If you're asking me whether appearance makes a difference in life, of course it does. Sometimes it offers an undeniable advantage, but it can also be a hindrance... even a source of pain.

EP: Really?

CA: Absolutely.

EP: Well, you seem, if I may say so, to wear both your suffering and your accomplishments very lightly, but I imagine the accomplishments give you enormous satisfaction. What are you proudest of? Is it the award you have just received or—

CA: I am proud of that – I love translating great books – but I am far prouder of the fact that today, most Molyvos girls remain at school past the primary level. My own god-daughter, whose mother was not even allowed to attend middle school, is about to graduate from university! I can't tell you how happy this makes me.

EP: So, what is the next challenge for *Kyria* Calliope Adham?

CA: It's the same old challenge – the struggle to end oppression: political, personal, educational. It's all part of the same process and it won't end in my lifetime.

II

One summer day, not long after the radio interview, Calliope was at her window, writing letters, when she heard *Papa* Iakovos's wife answer a Mytilene relative's question about the fine residence overlooking the public fountain: Calliope's house. Although the fountain had fallen into disuse, women continued to stop there on their way home, to rest or exchange gossip. Olympia, a woman bloated with virtue and secrets, could not resist an opportunity for a tantalising digression.

'She's had more lovers than pots and pans, that one!' she said, lowering her voice under Calliope's window. 'She's like a man. She takes whatever she wants!'

Ever since Calliope had put on her first pair of trousers, there were those who said that she was just a man trapped in a woman's body. It explained everything, especially her scandalous love life. After Eli's death, a rumour began to circulate that the doctor's death had been caused by sexual exhaustion. Eleni had heard it said that the poor man's heart had failed after making love seven times. One day, she could not resist sharing the rumour.

'Seven times!' Calliope burst out laughing. 'How do they know it was seven?'

Eleni grinned. 'They seem to think you're insatiable.'

'Not nearly as insatiable as they are for gossip!'

There was no lover in Calliope's life that summer, but there had been several after Lorenz Umbreit, chief among them Timolis Tsouras, the former headmaster's son. The headmaster was no longer in Molyvos; his son had married and emigrated to the United States. But there had been a time when the young notary provided Calliope with occasional, if not quite adequate, distraction.

That she had allowed herself to become involved with the headmaster's son had surprised Calliope no less than it had his father. There was Timolis's age. There was his indifference to books. But there was also the sour satisfaction of spiting both Leandros Tsouras's and the villagers' double standards. Pericles

– who finally married his Athenian nurse – had once told Calliope that his mother used to give him a brothel allowance, and that many women did likewise, even with married sons.

It was generally assumed that men's sexual appetites had to be secretly indulged, since no decent woman could satisfy a husband's baser needs. Could there really be an innate difference between the sexes? Calliope had found herself wondering. The foreign novels she read depicted men enjoying sexual encounters without suffering either guilt or regret, certainly without the tragic consequences of a Bovary or Karenina. Were women incapable of pure physical pleasure?

This question teased Calliope in her early forties, but years would go by before she acknowledged that her interest in Timolis might have had a whiff of the experimental about it. And yet, she had gradually grown fond of the young notary. When, after two years, he became the object of a visiting Greco–American's fancy, Calliope resolutely ended their affair. The young man was bound to marry sooner or later and this was an opportunity he must not forfeit.

By then, Leandros Tsouras had been transferred to Athens. Calliope began a tumultuous relationship with a fiery Mytilene journalist, then became briefly involved with a famous Athenian actor.

The last time she had seen the stage actor was in spring, the day after her radio interview. She had looked forward to visiting Athens, but her week-long stay was to mark the end of what she would thereafter describe as her 'hedonistic period'. It was as if broadcasting information about her private life had unexpectedly appeased some dormant rebellious spirit, she would some day tell Rupert Ealing.

Her English friend had arrived in Greece just before Easter. He was going through the final stages of a divorce – a rather civilised one, he had told Calliope in one of his letters. Once in Molyvos, however, he would put it differently: 'A goodwill divorce is like having all your teeth extracted and still having to smile.'

It was late March 1966. Ealing was in his mid-fifties – one of those average-looking men who somehow come to look more attractive with age. Over two decades had passed since he and Calliope had last seen each other. They embraced warmly.

'Well, your hair's still there!' She laughed, scanning his face.

He had a greying beard and shaggy hair, but had not lost the air of an adventurous boy preparing for some exciting field trip. His body was no longer wiry but retained an aura of perpetual eagerness, as if he might at any moment take it into his head to hop onto a mule's back or dive into the sea.

'Actually, you have more hair than before,' Calliope noted.

Except for the physical changes, Rupert Ealing seemed much the same, though he was beginning to contemplate early retirement. What he longed to do was travel and write his memoirs, he told Calliope. He had come to Molyvos for a holiday, with memories of a dispirited wartime village. The flamboyant beauty of spring on the island, the panoramic views and starry nights quickly cast their spell.

Calliope's house was undergoing renovations, but she had arranged for Rupert to stay with one of the foreigners, an artist friend of her French cousin. Thierry Brabant was renting an old mansion he called The Mausoleum. The house was neglected but had a beautiful garden and spectacular views. The Frenchman had fallen in love with a local boy. His enthusiasm, Calliope cautioned Rupert, must therefore be taken *avec un grain de sel*.

Greece was becoming a popular holiday destination but, in the mid-60s, Lesbos was still a largely bucolic island. After a month in Molyvos, Rupert returned to London, feeling no less enthralled than Thierry Brabant. He had, on returning home, decided he would like to write his memoirs in Greece. Why not? For the first time in his life, he was free to do exactly as he pleased and, right now, nothing would please him more than an extended Aegean sojourn, he wrote in his letter.

Calliope had no wish to discourage Rupert, but she did have doubts about his expectations. She wrote to remind him of the pervasive malice, the banality, the endless hypocrisy and gossip.

I suspect you would find all this in any village, even an English one, but I do think you should come here with your eyes open or risk being disappointed. To be sure, Molyvos is much more pleasant now than it was during the Occupation, but you have seen it at a ravishing time of year. It is not always spring here, and the sea, which you are so enamoured of, often swarms with jellyfish. If, after reading this, you still want to come, she concluded, *I'll be delighted to see you. Thierry says an American friend is thinking of coming, so who knows, this may be the beginning of an expatriate community. My French cousin will also be here in late summer. Her husband died last year, after a long illness, so she is finally free to travel.*

And with this, Calliope signed the letter, sealed the envelope, then stood up and stretched. She was going to post the letter, along with one to Paris. She had, over the years, trained herself to avoid dwelling on the past. But as she crossed the village, her mind meandered towards the long-ago winter evenings when she and Rupert sat singing nursery rhymes and reciting limericks. She recalled Mirto's fretting, her reluctance to leave Calliope alone with a married Englishman.

The memory made Calliope smile sadly. Some two decades after the end of the Occupation, she had not quite learned to resist the past's mysterious allure.

III

'I think Plato was absolutely right. Love is a grave mental disease,' Calliope said, smiling a little sadly. It was late August, and her French cousin was finally in Molyvos, ensconced in the guest room. 'What do you think?'

'I think it's a disease I wouldn't mind contracting again.' Alexandra laughed. Approaching fifty-five, the Parisian academic had the brave air of an ageing ballerina, a woman determined to be, if not quite a merry widow, then at least an upbeat one. Her hair had recently been tinted for the first time, her eyebrows plucked. She was tall and trim, with a long neck and an elegant carriage resembling Calliope's. She was chatty yet deeply observant, the sort of person whom nothing ever seemed to escape. In this, Calliope thought, she resembled Lorenz.

She had not seen him for seven years, and was surprised, soon after Alexandra's arrival, to find herself speaking of their affair. Almost at once, she regretted it, steering the conversation away from her own moral lapse to Greek politics. The country was still unstable, she told her cousin over a dish of stuffed aubergines. There were frequent strikes, demonstrations, riots. Leftists were still persecuted in the public sector; their children were denied university admission.

'You're talking about former partisans, I suppose?'

'No! The partisans – most of them anyway – have fled to Eastern bloc countries.' She was referring to ordinary folk with leftist leanings. 'There's a dossier on every Greek family; they know where each of us stands politically.'

Alexandra mulled this over. 'On the other hand, think where you'd be if the communists had won the Civil War. You'd be where your Bulgarian and Yugoslav neighbours are, and the rest of Eastern Europe.'

'No doubt,' Calliope said. 'Whoever won, Greeks were bound to lose.'

They were still talking, still finishing supper, when Eleni dropped in. She had been on her way to visit her mother-in-law but stopped to deliver a letter from Dimitra, Eli Dhaniel's eldest daughter. It was customary for the postman to pass on letters to friends or neighbours, saving himself the steep climb to St Kyriaki.

Eleni was spending the summer in Molyvos. She had been living in Athens for several years, partly because of her daughter's studies, but also because the new road to Mytilene had brought a virtual end to home births. As soon as it had been completed, most village women decided they wanted to be *moderni*. They began to have their babies delivered in hospital, though there were still men who forbade it, insisting on taking their wives to a Kaloni midwife. In the summer, when Eleni was back in Molyvos, there would still be an occasional request for her intervention.

It was almost ten o'clock when Calliope and her cousin finished washing up and headed upstairs. Calliope had discovered a young

French author whose short stories she had recently begun to translate. All she had so far was the title story, but she thought it brilliant. Would Alexandra like to read it, by any chance?

Alexandra was finishing Simone de Beauvoir but would be happy to read the story, she said, following Calliope into her study. The room had been Philippas's sanctuary but, except for a new bookshelf, remained much the same. It had a view of the sea and hills, and a large pedestal desk with a wingback chair.

Alexandra admired the view, then turned away, stopping to look at the photos on Calliope's desk. '*Oh la la*, how I wish I was young again!' she said, holding a recent snapshot of Calliope's godson.

Aristides Dhaniel had been captured with his fair hair flopping over one eye, his thumbs thrust into his jeans pockets. He was twenty-seven, completing his doctorate in Athens. His grandmother had passed away; his youngest sister had married a doctor and moved to Patras. The middle one lived in Mytilene and had three children.

'Only Dimitra is still unmarried,' Calliope said. Dimitra was the architect, much sought after in Athens. 'Greek men don't like their women to be quite so independent and successful.'

'Not only Greeks,' Alexandra said, abstracted. She was studying another photo.

Taken during the launch of *The Owl's Cry*, the framed photograph showed Lorenz Umbreit poised next to a pile of books. On the author's left stood a tentative-looking Calliope, on his right, a somewhat younger woman, smiling demurely.

'That's Alicia... his wife,' Calliope said, looking over her cousin's shoulder.

'*Really?* German?'

'Swiss. With an Italian ancestor somewhere down the line.'

'Hm.' Alexandra was still gazing at the photograph. 'She could be your sister.'

'I know. That was the last time I saw him,' Calliope said, her voice far away. Across the moonlit water, countless lights had been turned on in the distant hills. 'It's a terrible thing, you know. The heart is surely big enough to love more than one person, yet we're forced to choose. We must always choose,' she said with a sigh.

Alexandra replaced the photograph. 'Did she find out about you?'

'No.' Calliope sighed. 'I don't think so.'

Alexandra studied her for a moment. 'What happened?'

'I ended it.' Calliope pulled out a desk drawer and riffled through it until she found a carbon copy of a note she had sent Lorenz shortly after the Athens book launch. She had begun to keep their letters when it occurred to her that posterity might be interested in their correspondence.

'I couldn't go on with it after I'd met her,' she said quietly, as though explaining it to herself. She handed the carbon copy to Alexandra, then glanced at the book-launch photo. 'I've kept it here, where I can see it every day… just in case I'm tempted to stray again.'

Alexandra chuckled sadly. She handed the letter back. 'Do you think you'll ever see him again?'

'I doubt it.' Calliope sighed. 'I do hope we'll continue to write to each other, though,' she added after a moment. 'It means so much to me!'

'Really? I'd have preferred a clean break, I think,' Alexandra said.

'Well, to me it's a consolation… like a dummy offered to a hungry baby,' Calliope said, making her cousin smile.

'What about your English friend?'

'Rupert? He'll be here in October. I'm only sorry you won't be here to meet him,' Calliope added. She was back at the window now, pensively staring into the night. The lights went on flickering in the hills, like swarms of fireflies dancing in the murky distance.

IV

As if to signal the fact that life on a Greek island would not be the blissful idyll of Rupert Ealing's imaginings, the sea passage had been tempestuous. Rupert and Thierry Brabant's American friend had chanced to catch the same boat, the only foreigners sailing to Mytilene on that stormy October day. They had not known each other before boarding the ferry but fell to talking soon after their departure from Piraeus. Within half an hour, Rupert knew that Ed Bell – né Belinsky – was an aspiring writer with an advertising job; that his grandparents had been Russian aristocrats who'd managed to escape the Revolution; that he had met Thierry in Paris in the late 1950s; that he was in his mid-thirties and recently divorced.

The American liked to talk. He'd been sitting at the bar with *Newsweek* when Rupert walked into the lounge in search of a drink. As the Englishman approached, a small chortling sound escaped Ed Bell. He was reading an article on the newly founded National Organization for Women. The American, it seemed, blamed the women's liberation movement for the failure of his marriage. They tossed the subject between them for a while, then went on to discuss Vietnam. In the morning, Rupert introduced Ed to Calliope, who had come to meet the boat.

Calliope shook the American's hand, thinking he had the eyes of a child unable to decide whether to sulk or throw a temper tantrum. But he was catching the early bus to Molyvos; she and Rupert would be going back in the afternoon.

She had come to Mytilene to meet the ferry but also to see an optometrist about reading glasses. It was going on nine a.m. Having deposited Rupert's luggage at the taxi office, they picked their way through the *agora*, looking for a quiet café. It had rained much of the week, but by Saturday the sun had triumphed, bathing the capital in a golden autumnal light.

Rupert remembered Mytilene as a bleak provincial town, its twisted streets daily patrolled by soldiers. By the mid-1960s, hawkers' voices were wafting from pavements overflowing with fresh produce; farm carts trundled by, sending shoppers scampering away like pigeons.

Rupert kept glancing about him, as avid as a country bumpkin on his first visit to town. They were passing a fragrant bakery when he asked, 'Do they still make *rizogalo* here, with goat milk and pistachios?' He remembered having this pudding when he first

324

arrived on the island, before milk had become a luxury. 'I've got a sudden craving for it.'

'What modest cravings you have!' Calliope smiled. 'Come. I know just the place.'

She stepped aside to let an old man with a sesame-roll cart push by. Rupert pointed out the street where he had been sheltered by *Papa* Ioannis. The old priest had passed away, but the stalwart madam was still running her brothel. Rupert had brought a gift. Perhaps he could drop it off while Calliope had her eyes examined?

'Yes... yes, why not?' she replied vaguely. A fair-haired young man was waiting to cross the street. He reminded Calliope of her godson, whom she had not seen since July and would not see again until Christmas. She missed Aristides fiercely. Sometimes she wondered how generations of mothers had endured seeing their sons go off to war.

It was quieter on the seaside esplanade. A cluster of men in wool waistcoats were playing backgammon at an outdoor café. Rupert pulled out a chair, lit a cigarette, then turned to watch a ferryboat sail away. All around the port, rain puddles were drying up.

'It's been raining chair legs all week,' Calliope said, sitting across from Rupert.

'Chair legs?'

'That's what we say around here.'

'Really? In London, it rains cats and dogs.' Rupert grinned. He had small, gapped teeth; a child's teeth in the face of a bearded, middle-aged man.

'Are you going to insist on teaching me English all over again?' Calliope asked, withdrawing her elbows. Their waiter had arrived, bearing coffee and rice pudding.

'Of course. How else are you going to read my memoirs?'

A gypsy came threading her way among the tables, a bale of shawls draped over her arm. She stopped here and there, speaking in a slow, scratchy monotone. No, she didn't need a shawl, Calliope said, barely glancing up. When the gypsy stood her ground, Calliope looked up. The hawker was a middle-aged woman, round-shouldered, heavy around the hips, with a nutmeg-hued face going flaccid. Her long plait was filigreed with grey.

Some twenty-five years had passed since Calliope had seen Glykeria, but something about this ageing woman's eyes – the eyes and the beauty spot on her left cheek – made sudden recognition flood through her. The gypsy was still wheedling.

'Is your name Glykeria?' Calliope asked, cutting into the sales pitch.

The gypsy appraised her, her face revealing nothing. 'Do I know you?'

'You used to come to Molyvos. Before the Occupation.'

'Ach, Molyvos!' The gypsy beamed, a gold tooth glinting in the back of her mouth. 'Beautiful village, Molyvos!' Her eyes slid towards Rupert, who was smiling blandly; they returned to scan Calliope's outfit. 'You live there?'

'Yes,' Calliope said. There was something she wanted to say or ask, but what? She felt a vague sense of pity as the memory of the young gypsy, sprightly and colourful as a tropical bird, flitted through her brain.

After the Germans had arrested the doctor, Kyriakos Himonas told *Papa* Emanouil that the Mytilene whore must have ratted on them. Who would have thought that Orestes the pharmacist had been the one to betray them? Now, all three men were dead, and the cunning Glykeria was on the cusp of old age, probably unaware of Molyviates' suspicions.

'So, *Kyria mou*,' she was saying, 'are you going to buy one of these fine shawls? I'll let you have one for forty drachmas, since you are from my favourite village and have golden eyes.'

Despite herself, Calliope smiled. 'I'll give you thirty drachmas.'

'Thirty-five,' Glykeria said.

'Thirty-two. That's my final offer.'

The gypsy contemplated her for a moment. 'All right, I accept!' She began to peel a black shawl from the top of the batch, holding it out for Calliope's inspection. 'Handmade wool,' she said.

'Yes, it's nice.' Calliope was burrowing for her wallet. She had no need of another shawl but could give it to her housekeeper for St Basil's Day.

'The Virgin's blessings upon you!' Glykeria shuffled off, a stray dog sniffing at her heels.

Calliope stared at her retreating back, fighting an urge to run after her, as if the stranger had walked away with something that did not belong to her.

'I don't know what made me buy it,' she said, thinking out loud. It came to her then that, having left for England as soon as the Occupation ended, Rupert might not have heard of Kyriakos's encounter with Glykeria. She sipped her coffee, sharing the story.

'So that was her? The gypsy *femme fatale*?'

'That was her.' Calliope chuckled. She recalled Kimon telling her early on that he'd decided to ask for her hand only after a beautiful gypsy palmist stopping in the *kapheneion* told him that the girl of his dreams was waiting for him. All he had to do was ask.

'I sometimes wonder,' she said to Rupert, 'what if Kimon had not been in the *kapheneion* that day? What if she had read someone else's palm?'

'But my dear, so much of life is like that!'

Rupert put his spoon down. He went on to tell Calliope about his own brother, who had missed a train to Oxford, then took the next one, on which he met a Cypriot student who would become his wife, persuading him to study archaeology instead of law, as he'd planned to do.

Calliope sat shredding a paper napkin, pondering Rupert's words.

'What about you?' she asked after a while. 'What made you decide to become a spy?'

'I was never exactly a spy, you know.' Rupert's tongue picked up a stray bit of rice on his lip. He had actually worked for the Special Operations Executive, a secret British organisation whose mandate was sabotage and support to the Greek Resistance.

'But that's just as dangerous,' Calliope put in. 'You had a family. What made you want to do it?'

'Good question.' Rupert's glance wandered. 'I'd always thought I'd be an academic, you know. Act in amateur theatricals, have a family – a perfectly ordinary life. I certainly didn't think of myself as an adventurer.'

Calliope sipped her coffee. 'And then?'

'Then the war broke out and… well, by then I knew my marriage was a mistake. I also knew I wasn't brave enough to end it, not with three young children.'

'What was wrong with your wife?' Calliope asked.

'Nothing. Absolutely nothing. We were just wrong for each other.'

Calliope was silent. She found herself thinking of Lorenz Umbreit's wife, then stopped herself and glanced at her watch. 'Ready to go?'

'Mm.' Rupert took a final sip of coffee. 'Great *rizogalo*, by the way. Thanks!'

They were strolling away from the waterfront when Rupert asked whether she'd had a chance to look into housing. It was something he had requested in his letter, but after one or two enquiries, Calliope thought it best to let him choose for himself. With all the emigration in recent years, there was no shortage of houses.

'Don't worry, I'm not about to stick you in the cellar,' she said.

They walked on together. A beggar was sitting cross-legged on a street corner. Calliope took out her wallet and brought out a few drachmas for the blind man. They made a merry, jingling sound as they fell into the tin can, like the coins children received on singing their annual Christmas carols.

V

Evanthea, the housekeeper, reported that Calliope and the foreigner were *not* sleeping together. Their rooms were not even on the same floor, she informed the occasional sceptic. And, yes, both beds looked slept in, she was quick to add. The Englishman had all his clothes in his own wardrobe. He kept his radio and reading glasses on his own bedside table. Downstairs.

After weeks of feverish speculation, it was finally concluded that Ealing must be a homosexual. Everyone seemed to know he cooked and cleaned; he had, the postman reported, opened the door wearing an apron!

What the villagers did not then know was that Rupert had made himself so indispensable that, five and a half months after his arrival, he appeared to be permanently ensconced in Calliope's guest room. Being an early riser, and too restless to write for more than four hours a day, he was happy to tackle the domestic chores. He claimed they helped him think and offered more immediate rewards than his daily scribbling.

Calliope and Rupert spent many hours writing or reading in their respective quarters, but they usually dined together, and passed many an evening going for walks or chatting in the garden. The arrangement offered so much mutual satisfaction that, writing in her journal, Calliope was hard pressed to explain their strictly chaste relations. Only one thing seemed clear: her attachment to Rupert deepened in the course of that first winter. When he flew to London for Easter, she wrote in her journal that she could hardly bear the empty rooms and pervasive silence.

Rupert was gone for three weeks, but came back in time for Greek Easter, meeting up with Calliope's godson in Athens. The two men quickly took to each other, both being keen on history and politics, both given to playful mimicry.

Later, speaking to Calliope, Aristides marvelled at the Englishman's understanding of Greece and its history. But, knowledgeable though they both were, neither could have possibly predicted the long black era that still lay ahead.

VI

Preparing breakfast on the morning of 21 April 1967, Calliope turned on the radio, bewildered to hear nothing but military marches on both local and Athenian stations. No news. No announcements. Nothing but military marches. Rupert was out for groceries, so Calliope went into his room and turned on his short-wave radio to Deutsche Welle.

At two in the morning, while much of the country slept, a coup d'état had taken place in Athens. The conspirators – a group of army officers under the leadership of Colonel Yorgos Papadopoulos – had declared martial law. The official pretext was an imminent communist threat. There had been virtually no resistance.

The German news was soon confirmed by the BBC.

'They say leftists are being arrested all over Athens,' Rupert reported after listening to the English news. He was a man who usually found humour in any situation. He found none that day.

'I'd better phone Aristides,' Calliope said, ready to head to the telephone office.

Rupert consulted his watch. 'Yes. I should call London too.'

He managed to get through, but Calliope kept finding the Athenian circuits jumbled. After a dozen attempts, she gave up. She sat at home with Rupert, listening to speeches about a new social order, to promises of peace, stability, justice. *From now on, there will be no more rightists, centrists, or leftists, only Greeks who share a faith in Greece!*

'Stability and justice!' Calliope scoffed. 'I can't wait to see that.'

In the early evening, a child arrived with a message from the mayor, asking her to come to the town hall as soon as possible.

'Aristides called,' Mathaios said the moment Calliope entered the town hall. 'He asked me to tell you he's all right. He's gone into hiding.'

Calliope received the news with a sigh of relief. 'Did he leave a number?'

'No. He said you won't be able to reach him. He just wanted you to know he's safe.'

VII

That evening, Calliope and Rupert went for a stroll and found themselves hailed by Thierry Brabant. It was a beautiful night and the expats had gathered in the harbour, at what used to be the Germans' canteen during the Occupation. The nondescript building had recently been transformed into a small hotel, thanks to an inheritance from a childless Australian uncle; it was called Orpheus's Head Hotel. Legend had it that, having been severed and thrown into the Hebrus River, Orpheus's head had floated into the sea, eventually surfacing on a Lesbos beach.

The hotel had a modest restaurant facing the wharf. This was where the foreigners were now seated, served by Nikki Paschalou, Johnny the Australian's widowed sister, who had, years earlier, joined her brother in Australia, but was now living back in the village with her two daughters. Artemis, the younger one, was working the tables alongside her mother. She was in her early twenties and said to be as contrary as a crooked staff, having rejected a marriage proposal from a local policeman. Artemis's uncle, who had encouraged the suit, said he wouldn't speak to his niece until she came to her senses.

Calliope admired the girl's spunk, but, sitting with the foreigners on that late-April evening, it suddenly came to her that Artemis's decision might have something to do with Ed Bell. She had just seen the American wink at Nikki's daughter, while the jukebox played 'The House of the Rising Sun'. Swishing past their table, Artemis had smiled at Ed and tossed her head, theatrically mouthing the lyrics.

A wink and a smile didn't necessarily mean much. Artemis was a vivacious girl and Ed was given to flirting with attractive women. Still, glancing across the room, Calliope noticed that the silent exchange had not been lost on Artemis's uncle.

Mandras Paschalou was lounging against the wall, drinking with his police mates. They were discussing the new police chief, who had recently been transferred from Salonika. At the other end of the room sat several fishermen, among them Captain Yorgos's surviving son.

Although Takis Lyras was far from being the only staunch communist in the village, he had a way, especially when drunk, of provoking right-wing extremists. If people tolerated his occasional outbursts, it was only because an aura of patriotic martyrdom still hovered over the Lyras clan.

As soon as the foreigners stopped playing their American hits, Takis strode to the jukebox and punched in his own selections, including a popular Theodorakis song. Mikis Theodorakis was a renowned communist, but his music had yet to be officially banned. Nonetheless, the moment the rousing song began to play, Sergeant Floros leaned across the table and asked Mandras to stop it.

Artemis's uncle glanced up towards the fishermen's table. He was a middle-aged man who, like all the Paschalou brothers, had thick black eyebrows joined above the bridge of his nose. The eyebrows were knotted as he rose from the policemen's table. Hitching up his trousers, he crossed the restaurant, said something to his mother, then stooped and yanked the jukebox plug out of the wall.

'Hey, what d'you think you're doing?' Takis Lyras yelled, leaping from his chair. 'I put in—'

'Relax.' Mandras made a placating gesture. 'I'll give you your money back.'

'But you've got him in your jukebox! If you didn't want—'

'Am I supposed to know every song in the jukebox?' Mandras said, counting the change in the palm of his hand. 'Artemis is in charge of the music.'

'I don't want my money! There's no law against my listening to the music of my choice, is there?'

Saying this, Takis flicked at Mandras's extended hand and sent the coins flying. Old Fotini glanced up from the onions she was peeling and abandoned her task. She hobbled over from one direction, while Sergeant Floros, leaping out of his chair, approached from the other, his cabbage-like face pinker than ever.

'As of today, there's going to be new laws! You'd better learn to behave!' The policeman paused for effect, then ordered the fisherman back to his table. When Takis stood his ground, Floros clamped his fingers on the fisherman's arm, simultaneously urging Fotini to calm down. The old woman was shrieking through her toothless gums. The foreigners, who had been arguing about the likelihood of American involvement in the coup, had all fallen silent.

The policeman might have merely intended to lead Takis back to his own table, but his grasp made the fisherman swing out with a furious motion, catching Floros smack across his mouth.

And that was all it took on that momentous day.

Seeing the blood gush out of Floros's split lip, his two colleagues lunged for the fisherman. The sergeant remained standing, gingerly dabbing at his bleeding mouth.

Takis's own mouth was twisted with loathing. Struggling to extricate himself, he thrashed about, tossing out a string of profanities, while everyone watched in impotent silence. Calliope had half risen, but fell straight back, restrained by Rupert's hand. It was time to go home.

As they left the harbour, Rupert told her she could have easily found herself locked up along with the hot-headed Takis.

'I know,' Calliope said. 'Now you're starting to see the other face of Greece.'

'Well, you did warn me.' Rupert sighed.

A few hours earlier, he'd learned that his elder daughter, who had been trying to conceive for years, had suffered a miscarriage. He was still looking dispirited on returning home. Calliope considered a nightcap, but they had already drunk too much. Ready to head upstairs, she reached out on impulse, meaning to offer a comforting hug. An occasional embrace was not unknown between them, but on that spring night, some mysterious barrier came unexpectedly crashing down.

By the following morning, the village – the entire nation – began to absorb what it was in for under the new regime. Not even Evanthea the housekeeper would have been interested to know that the Englishman's bed had not been disturbed that night.

TWO

I

19 December 1967

Dear Lorenz,

One of our foreigners is posting this letter because I believe that my mail is passing through state censors' hands. Your last letter took over a month to get here, so I think you should write c/o Ed Bell until further notice. Ed is American, but he hates Papadopoulos even more than he does Lyndon Johnson (his brother is serving in Vietnam). It's hard to know whether the coup had CIA backing, as you suggest, but the Americans certainly have a hand in shaping our foreign policy. There are Greeks who accuse the USA of subsidising prison camps like Makronisos to promote American interests, which may well be true. But if there's anyone the authorities are not worried about right now, it's the Americans, so Ed will handle my mail from now on, in exchange for domestic olive oil.

A few days ago, some royalist diehards in the military attempted a counter coup but failed. The King has fled to Rome with his family, along with the Prime Minister. The cream of our intelligentsia has also gone into exile. Aristides is still underground but refuses to leave Greece. He thinks it's his duty to stay and work towards toppling the regime, though six thousand Greeks were arrested on the night of the coup alone. Captain Yorgos's elder son has been sent to Youra,

Pericles is in internal exile in western Greece, and I won't be surprised if they come after me too one of these days. Fortunately, our new police chief seems decent. Last month, he urged me to be more discreet about listening to Deutsche Welle. He has a daughter in Salonika who is a schoolmistress, he told me, as if to explain his unusual kindness. The extent to which the regime controls our lives is unbelievable. We are expected to attend church, but other public gatherings are prohibited. Last week, some parents took their children to a puppet show, only to have the room stormed by policemen. The only ones who protested were the disappointed children. People are afraid to speak up, especially those who need permits for a shop, a truck, a caique. Rozakis must be turning in his grave at having Papadopoulos's portrait hanging in his son's kapheneion. I am thinking of writing an article under a pseudonym. I think it's important for the world to know the full extent of the junta's reach. If I write it in German, would you be willing to edit it and see that it's published abroad?

I was interested to hear about the feminist magazine your friend is launching and am flattered that she wants to include me in the international women's series. My French cousin says that my life resembles a novel more than most novels resemble life! Two new women's shelters have been opened in Greece, inspired by our success in Mytilene. I am hoping to spend less time at the kentro and more at home, translating works that can no longer be published here. My god-daughter has recently graduated from university and works at the British Council library in Athens, so I have persuaded Eleni to move back and take over the kentro's administration. She never much liked Athens, so it was not difficult to talk her into returning. The hard part will be for me to relinquish control, but the junta has brought about an unexpected shift in my priorities.

Speaking of books, a German couple came looking for me one day, after reading your trilogy. They wanted to do an interview for some German magazine, but I told them it was up to you. A month later, two Frenchmen were also asking questions in the agora. Maybe we should put up a plaque outside my entrance?

I was sorry to hear Alicia has been unwell but trust she is back

335

on her feet by now. How is your new book coming along? I look
forward to reading it.

With best wishes for Christmas and the new year.
Yours, Calliope

II

In spring, Calliope's aunt contracted pneumonia. Calliope moved
Elpida to her own parents' bedroom, then nursed her with Evanthea's
help through two relapses. Towards the end of the year, Elpida died
in her sleep, aged eighty-one. It was a wonder she had lasted this
long, after losing her husband and beloved younger son. Grigoris,
her elder, had for years been at odds with his father, and had avoided
visiting Molyvos. By the time his mother passed away, he was in
his late fifties, a wealthy widower with two sons at Cambridge.
To Calliope, he seemed like a virtual stranger, despite the familiar
Mussolini jaw. He was nearly bald now, his mouth fixed in an
expression of perpetual irony. Calliope thought this might have
something to do with the political manoeuvres a shipping magnate
must have had to finesse under a right-wing regime. Papadopoulos
courted ship owners: extending concessions, demanding loyalty.

Grigoris had studied law, then married into a prominent shipping
family. He had to return to Athens two days after his mother's funeral
and needed to ask a favour. His parents' property had been seriously
neglected. It needed thorough cleaning as well as repairs. Could
Calliope possibly help with this, perhaps find someone interested
in renting the house?

Calliope said she could only try.

'I am deeply indebted to you – for everything.' Grigoris stood
scanning Calliope's features, as if searching for his childhood
playmate in the middle-aged face. It was the evening before his
departure. 'Is there anything I can do for you?'

Calliope thanked her cousin. There wasn't a thing she needed, except perhaps an explanation, she added, looking into his eyes. She recalled a long-ago conversation in which Grigoris said she was the only family member with whom he could have a frank political discussion. She was curious to know how a man who had once shared her own outlook could become a junta supporter.

'It's called survival, my dear.' Grigoris almost smiled. He was no longer so foolhardy as to think he could change the world – certainly not heroic enough. He had a deep, sonorous voice, a manner that made even trivial opinions sound like indisputable pronouncements. He regarded Calliope for a moment, as if trying to decide whether there was any point in continuing. 'My mother once said you had what she called "lofty aspirations". But take my advice, my dear, be sensible—'

'Ah, sensible! That I can't promise.'

Grigoris sighed. He held his hand inside his waistcoat, as if to keep it warm.

'Well, at least be careful.' He touched his lips gently to her cheek by way of goodbye. He said her eyes were still marvellously golden; they hadn't changed at all. 'Call me if you need anything. I'm always there for you.'

'Thank you,' said Calliope. He looked, she thought, worn out but sincere. She had invited him for supper, but Grigoris declined, saying he had things to do before his departure. Heading to Ed's house to pick up a letter, Calliope recalled her mother saying that Grigoris was not an unfeeling man, but one afraid of feeling too much.

Ed Bell was renting a house just behind the town hall. On her way there, Calliope ran into the mayor. Mathaios was widely admired, though some considered him a junta collaborator because he had chosen not to step down after the 1967 coup. Twenty months into the dictatorship, the mayor wore the look of a chastised child. Running into Calliope, he stopped and lowered his voice. He would have the forged ID by next week, he promised.

Calliope glanced over her shoulder, though it was Wednesday afternoon, and the shops were closed, their shutters rattling in the wind.

'Thank you… thank you!' she whispered. 'I'll leave as soon as it's ready.'

III

She came home to find Rupert whistling, busy preparing a wild mushroom dish. Calliope gathered his writing was going well. She could always tell because on such days he invariably wanted to try new dishes and make prolonged love, preferably under the stars. She had long since observed that when men felt pleased with themselves, they were often overcome by a possessive impulse. All the same, she was astonished to hear Rupert suggest that they might as well get married. The proposal was made in bed, when she was all but ready to be whisked away into the realm of sleep.

'But why?' she asked, abruptly awake. 'Why now?'

'Why not? We could get married at the British Embassy, or you could come to London and finally meet my family.' He knew she would never agree to be married in church. They had discussed the possibility of her coming to London for Christmas, but never of tying the knot.

'What's this all about?' she asked now, searching his face. 'Don't tell me your children don't know we're living in sin.'

'Of course they know.' He grinned at her, sheepish. 'They also know something you have yet to discover.'

'Which is?'

'Which is that deep, deep, deep inside, I'm both conventional and possessive,' he stated, smiling into one cheek. He had a way of disarming her.

'Full of surprises today, aren't we?' She regarded him for a moment. 'Give me one good reason why I should get married at the age of fifty-three.'

'Oh, you think that's too young? I suppose we *could* wait for a year or so.'

Calliope laughed. 'Seriously. I don't understand what it is with you men. Why—'

He didn't let her finish. 'I don't understand, either, but I do know it will make me happy to die knowing you were my wife.'

'Was it my aunt's funeral? Is that what this is all about?'

He lifted a shoulder, his eyes landing on Mirto's iconostasis. The wind was whistling through the trees in the garden, but the room was pleasantly warm. There was the smell of freshly washed bed sheets and burning charcoal.

'But why?' she repeated. 'Do you really think it will change anything?'

'I hope not.' He flashed her a quirky grin, then grew serious. 'I honestly don't know why it should matter,' he said. 'I do know that none of your objections to marriage apply any more.'

'You mean you no longer have to worry about my cuckolding you with some young Adonis?' Calliope smiled. She had, long ago, confided her suspicion that she was innately promiscuous.

'I mean you no longer have to worry that marriage will steal your thunder. You're your own person. Marriage is not going to change that now.'

She stopped to mull this over.

'Rupert,' she said. 'I haven't been so… so content in a very long time. Why can't you be satisfied with that? It's totally irrational, what you ask of me. It's—'

'Atavistic, I know, but can't I be irrational on occasion, like the rest of humanity?'

She smiled at that. 'Is it really that important to you?'

He nodded, still sheepish, like a child confessing to having eaten biscuits reserved for guests.

She reached out and stroked his beard. It was almost all grey now, yet his energy, his indomitable spirit, often humbled her.

'I'll think about it,' she finally said.

He kissed her, abruptly exuberant. 'Thank you!'

'Don't start celebrating yet. All I said was I'd think about it!'

IV

There were helmeted soldiers at Athens Airport, grimly alert, shouldering sub-machine guns. Rupert was flying to London but would be back in time for New Year's Eve. Calliope had decided against accompanying him. A few days earlier, she had been summoned for questioning by Molyvos's police chief. Louizos had been courteous, stopping her in the *agora*, asking her to drop in at her convenience. When she entered his office, he rose and shook her hand. He was, he said, under orders to enquire about her godson's whereabouts. 'Would you happen to know where he is these days?'

Calliope shrugged. She said she hadn't heard from Aristides in months, though his sister had written recently, asking whether it was true that Aristides had fled abroad.

'Unfortunately, I have no idea.' Calliope shifted her weight. 'But if you find out where he is, please let me know. I've been sick with worry.'

This much was true, but the letter from Athens had been sent as a ruse, after some of Aristides's classmates had been questioned by police.

Louizos seemed to believe her, but Calliope wasn't taking any chances. She arranged to meet Aristides at a party her publisher was giving on his wife's name day. There would be some twenty guests, but Calliope worried that she might be followed. Having seen Rupert off, she strode towards the airport toilets, carrying an old suitcase. She glanced into the mirror, then slipped into a stall, where she changed from her trouser suit and loafers into heels and a snug woollen dress. Inside the large suitcase nestled the small red valise she had bought in Athens back in the 1950s. She had also brought a hat to conceal her greying auburn hair. There was the cascading sound of flushing toilets, the hum of hand dryers. The arrival of a flight from Brussels was being announced. An elderly woman urged a child to hurry up and pee.

Calliope put away her travel outfit, adjusted her nylons, and slipped on a pair of sunglasses. She stepped out of the stall, dropped the battered suitcase behind the waste bins, and clicked away in her new suede shoes. All she had now was her red overnight valise and a large plastic bag. It was late afternoon. A few snowflakes drifted in the crisp air, melting on crawling taxis' roofs. Calliope raised a hand. She stepped off the kerb, glanced over her shoulder, then slid into the back of a cab.

'Kolonaki, please,' she said, peering out as the taxi lurched away from the airport. The day was quickly waning. She tugged at her dress, then leaned her head against the backrest with a long exhalation.

Nearly two years into the dictatorship, Athens wore an unfamiliar face. The soldiers were ubiquitous, as were the commercial billboards: American Express, Siemens, Coca-Cola. Sighing, Calliope yanked off her shoe and rubbed her arthritic toe, vaguely wondering how Rupert was doing, up among the clouds. The cab had stopped for a light, and she glanced out again, her eyes lighting on a large propaganda poster. *Long Live the Twenty-First of April!*

Her toe throbbed and throbbed.

V

She hardly recognised him, with his horn-rimmed spectacles and his hair dyed black. Gone was the blond lock of hair that had for years flopped over his eye. Gone, too, the moustache he had sported in recent months. But he was still quick and purposeful and deeply self-contained. There was a certain resemblance to his father – the chiselled, sharp-boned face, the luminous eyes – but something about his movements, his keen, attentive air, reminded Calliope of the young Lorenz Umbreit.

She had brought the promised ID, along with a new leather jacket. The name in the forged document was Konstantin Katranides. It was the name of a distant cousin on his mother's side. Aristides's hair had been dyed by his elder sister. It was still curly but was now cropped short. He was almost thirty.

Calliope reached out and impulsively ran her hand through the black curls. Aristides sipped his wine, then stopped to remove his spectacles. He kept putting them on, then taking them off, his fingers seeking the shaven moustache.

'Keep your spectacles on!' Calliope said. 'You have to look natural.'

'Yes, yes.' Aristides exhaled. 'I look like a natural book-eater, don't I?'

'Book-eater's good! What you don't want is to look like Che Guevara.' Calliope reached for an ashtray. They were seated in Titos and Anasthasia Stamoulis's living room, chatting in a quiet corner. It was a vast room, with Persian rugs and bookcases looming around the marble fireplace. Over by the kitchen stood a buffet covered with a white damask cloth. Aristides said there was enough food on the silver platters to feed a small tribe. Anasthasia – Tasia to her friends – was a busy doctor. She had a full-time maid from Crete, reputed to be an excellent cook. Aristides got up to replenish his plate.

'Why aren't you eating?' he asked. 'You should eat – it's great food.'

Calliope went on smoking. 'I'm not hungry.' She watched her godson chew for a moment. He was still eating like a lion, she said.

Aristides chuckled and went on devouring everything on his plate. He would have to be going soon, he said, then got drawn into a discussion of the recent referendum on the new constitution. From there, they went on to talk about Alexandros Panagoulis, a fiery dissident who had tried to blow up Papadopoulos's limousine. The attempt had failed. Panagoulis was arrested, tortured, and recently sentenced to death, amid international outcries.

Aristides set his plate aside and glanced at his watch. He really had to go, he repeated.

'Please promise me you'll be careful,' Calliope said, watching him zip up his new leather jacket. He had tried it on upon arrival, delighted to find it a perfect fit.

'Goodnight, *Nona*.' He pecked his godmother's cheek. 'Thank you.'

Calliope took her godson's head between her hands and kissed his forehead, her eyes misting over. 'No Panagoulis heroics, please!' She held on to his arms, willing him to listen. 'Promise me!'

He flung his scarf over his shoulder. 'Fine, *Nona*, I promise.' He gazed at her for a moment. '*What?* I promised, didn't I?'

'Don't forget,' Calliope said, pressing her cheek to his.

He pulled back and gave her a mock salute. '*Yassou, Nona!*'

He left with his new ID in his jacket pocket. The cousin he was impersonating had briefly studied medicine in Athens but had returned to Mytilene after failing his exams, to take over his father's pharmacy.

Calliope returned to the party. The room was warm, hazy with cigarette smoke. The guests huddled in small, animated clusters, eating, laughing, discussing Papadopoulos's educational reforms, the new language laws, the revised textbooks.

University students represented the most ardent opposition to the regime. There was, Aristides had told Calliope, a junta-appointed campus organisation whose members spied on students. His girlfriend had an uncle at the Security Police. He had tried to talk Dorothea into becoming a campus spy, but she had declined, claiming a heavy workload.

It was almost midnight. Calliope refilled her wine glass and sat down by the fire to chat with her publisher. A dapper, trilingual man, Titos had been educated at the Sorbonne, then returned to Greece to found a publishing house. He was the sort of man who could carry on an intense conversation with someone while still following everything going on around him. Getting a forged ID had been his idea.

'Are you all right?' he was asking now.

Calliope made a vague gesture. 'I'm worried about Aristides,' she said. Her toe was still aching, clad in the stylishly pointed shoe.

Titos regarded her for a moment. 'Is there anything I can do?'

'I doubt it.'

They talked about this and that: books Titos liked but couldn't publish under the new regime, an outspoken nephew's expulsion from the Bar. Calliope had yet to finish work on a novel Titos hoped to publish. She was vaguely thinking of translating a German memoir by an SS officer's son, she said.

At this, Titos leaned back and shifted his legs. The room was hot. He slid an index finger into his turtleneck and stretched it away from his throat. 'Have you heard from Lorenz lately?'

'Yes.' Calliope's eyelids flickered. She hadn't had a word from him for months but had finally received a letter just the other day.

Titos dragged on his cigarette. 'Did he tell you about Alicia?'

'Yes. It doesn't sound good, does it?'

'Tasia says ovarian's the worst.' Titos exhaled. Lorenz had been planning a trip to Athens, to research a non-fiction book about post-war Greece. He had cancelled the trip for the second time, after hearing his wife's prognosis.

Calliope sat smoking, staring into the fire. The flames crackled, spitting against the blackened screen. 'I have to write to him,' she said after a while. 'I don't know what to say... I have nothing to offer but platitudes.'

Titos sighed. 'Such a nice woman,' he muttered.

'Yes.'

Eager to change the subject, Calliope reminded Titos of his promise to visit Molyvos.

'One of these days,' he said. 'Maybe over Easter?'

Calliope was expecting a German interviewer then but thought they could manage. 'Do come,' she said, idly stroking the hosts' cocker spaniel. 'I'd like you to meet Rupert.'

Titos levered himself out of his chair. 'I'll speak to Tasia and let you know,' he said, returning to his social duties.

Several guests were preparing to leave. A baby, who had been sleeping in the guest room, was squalling in the hallway. Calliope thought of Aristides bawling in her arms after being baptised, of the first time he'd asked her why he had a *Nona* but no mother. She told herself she should be going as well. All evening, there had been the steady rumble of street traffic, but now she registered the honking of cars, the wailing of an ambulance. Not for the first time, she decided she really wouldn't want to live in the city. She much preferred crickets' songs and nightbirds' cries to the frantic sounds of the ever-expanding capital. All that awaited her this evening were the anonymous streets, the empty hotel room with its mothball smell.

She went to say goodnight.

VI

Calliope and Eva Reinhardt sat at Orpheus's Head, chatting over ouzo and appetisers. It was the German journalist's third day in the village. A portable recorder was whirring on the edge of the table; a camera in a brown leather case lay beside it, its strap coiled like a sleeping snake.

The feminist magazine's international feature profiled women who had distinguished themselves in various parts of the world. Calliope was pondering a question that Eva had put to her. Had there been a key event responsible for awakening her feminist consciousness?

'Not really. I believe it was a cumulative set of events. Events and occasional observations.'

The first thing she recalled had taken place when she was twenty. It was the year she began teaching, the year one of their neighbours – a young, battered wife – had come to cry on her mother's shoulder, only to go back to her husband because she had no other options.

'Sadly, that happens everywhere. Even in Germany,' said Eva.

Eva Reinhardt had come to Molyvos for a week, combining a spring break with an interview for *Sie* magazine. She was a sturdy-looking woman, taller than Calliope, with emerald-green eyes and straw-coloured hair that sat on her head like a helmet, gleaming in the sun. She was an unabashed lesbian.

The thought of making love to a woman intrigued Calliope. Was it really possible for a woman's body to thrill at the sight of another woman's breasts or buttocks? She thought of Lorenz, who was a friend of Eva's, and whose body – the mere thought of his body – could still tug at her heart. Eva had not asked about him. They talked about Greek customs, the inequities of the dowry system.

'The thing about tradition,' said Calliope, 'is no one thinks to question it. But once you do, once it occurs to you, it's as if the scales have fallen from your eyes!'

One day, she had attended the blessing of a former pupil's newborn daughter. 'It's an ancient religious ceremony,' Calliope explained. 'It takes place in church, when the child's forty days old.' She had been to such ceremonies countless times yet had never stopped to question the fact that a male child is borne by the priest to the Holy Portals, whereas a female is taken only as far as the narthex.

'Oh?' Eva blinked at Calliope greenly, like a curious cat. 'Why is that?'

'The Holy Portals lead to the altar. A newborn boy gets to be displayed before God, but a girl? Never!'

This statement, too, elicited a small chortle. Eva sat for a moment, staring out to sea, then picked up her camera and snapped a fisherman puttering about in his boat. Half a dozen rowboats were moored to the quay, bobbing in the water. From the kitchen wafted the smell of wine-braised octopus.

'Anyway,' Calliope continued, 'I think that was the day I began to see the connection between the child-blessing ceremony and the fact that there had never been a woman on the village council.' She waited for Eva to finish making a note. 'Ready for coffee?'

'Yes. No sugar, please.'

Calliope signalled to Nikki, wondering whether she had heard the rumours about her daughter's involvement with Ed Bell. Artemis was nowhere to be seen but, walking up from the harbour a little later, Calliope and Eva ran into Ed himself. He was on his way to the harbour but had stopped by the sea wall to scribble something in his notebook.

Everyone knew Ed had taken a year off from his advertising job to write a novel about his Russian grandparents, but eighteen months later he was still in Molyvos, still whipping out his notebook at every opportunity. He was tall and thin and had an odd habit of frequently licking his lips, like a man trying to solve a complex problem, contemplating an impossible set of options.

Calliope introduced her guest, then she and Eva meandered down to the beach. The sea was still too cold for the natives, but Eva insisted on swimming, until she spotted jellyfish floating on the cresting waves. She had once been stung so badly her arm had swollen like a balloon, she said.

The beach was deserted, except for Dora the weeper's sons, who liked to hang around their aunt's seaside kiosk. The feta had made Eva thirsty, so they bought lemonades, then went to sit on a bench, watching seagulls glide over the darkening water. Dora's sons were climbing up a tree, laughing when they reached the top. Calliope thought of little Aristides playing on the beach. She recalled a summer afternoon when he stood at the water's edge, trapping minnows in an empty jar. He trapped them cheerfully, calling out to her over his shoulder. He did this for a while, but suddenly stopped, opened the lid, then tossed the minnows back into the waves.

'Why did you do that?' Calliope recalled asking.

'I felt sorry for them,' Aristides had answered.

She had never known a more tender-hearted child.

VII

Excerpt from Calliope Adham's journal – 20 December 1969

They had hoped she would last at least until Christmas, but it was not to be. Lorenz's letter was brief. I don't know what to say. What can a former mistress say at a time like this? Am I even entitled to offer comfort for the death of a wife I myself have wronged? Once more, I seem to be swimming in very stormy waters, partly because of Lorenz's grief, but also because I can't help feeling culpable.

And then there is Aristides, who is neither writing nor calling. I can't sleep at night, brooding on Alicia and Lorenz, and worrying about Aristides. I have pressed him to accept Alexandra's invitation, but he refuses to go into exile. Meanwhile, Louizos, the police chief, has been demoted for 'non-fulfilment of official duties'. It seems he did not arrest enough villagers. I don't know him well, but he seems almost relieved not to be in a position of authority any more.

I've also had a letter from Alexandra, saying that her American nephew has fled to Canada, dodging the draft. I suppose that if

I were living in the USA, I would be taking part in anti-Vietnam demonstrations. Aristides hates the Americans, but at least they have not taken away the right to protest. The most difficult thing about being underground, he says, is not being sure who can be trusted. I don't know what I'd do without Rupert. I'm looking forward to finally visiting London. It will be good to get away for a while, though I continue to feel tense about tying the knot.

No one else seems to share my reservations about marriage. Eleni's daughter is getting engaged. Her future husband is a Cretan archaeologist, whom she met when he came to borrow a library book. Alexandra, too, has met someone she likes – a recent refugee she refers to as her Melancholy Hungarian.

Our village is quickly changing, attracting a growing number of foreign artists. One of them, a homosexual Australian painter who has been studying in Paris, has been here for two months but is hoping to come for a longer stay. Ed Bell says it's because of all the sex-starved soldiers, but who knows? Ed himself is in love with Artemis, but it seems they can't get married: he is half-Jewish and will not convert. I hope they have the sense to elope to Cyprus for a civil marriage.

Uncle Mandras, meanwhile, spends much of his time rooting for Papadopoulos, ranting about the decadent example foreigners are setting. Poor Papadopoulos: he wants to attract tourists but only if he can make foreign men cut their hair and women leave their miniskirts and bikinis at home before coming to enjoy our beaches.

Rupert and I are flying to London on Tuesday, but I can't stop thinking about Aristides or Alicia.

Someone is at the door.

VIII

Eleni said, 'I've brought your post.' She reached into her bag. 'Am I early?'

'No, no. I'd just lost track of time. Ouzo?'

Eleni nodded, peeling off her sweater. They were well into December, but the morning had swept in with a springlike sunshine. She smiled, watching a half-grown kitten chase a ball of yarn. 'Rupert not home?'

'He had to go to Mytilene. He should be back any minute.' They went into the kitchen, where a meatball casserole was simmering. 'So much to do before we leave,' Calliope said. It was Wednesday, a day on which the two friends routinely got together to share a meal and discuss *kentro* business. Eleni was scratching the edge of the day divan, trying to attract the kitten.

'Are you excited?'

'More anxious than excited, I think.'

The kitten leapt up from the floor and arranged itself in Eleni's lap. 'Why?'

Calliope picked up the post. She hated not being able to speak English properly, dreaded meeting Rupert's family and sounding like a child.

She was saying this to Eleni while sorting the post, but suddenly stopped with a surprised exclamation. She had not expected the January issue of *Sie* before Christmas, but there it was, including Eva's interview. Calliope studied her own colourful image, making an ambiguous sound that might have been interpreted as either disdain or satisfaction.

'Rupert calls this my Joan of Arc look,' she said, making Eleni smile.

Eva had captured Calliope with her chin in the air, a suntanned woman with shoulder-length hair, her unflinching eyes fixed somewhere beyond the camera. She had been carefully posed in front of the glittering sea. A second photograph showed her sitting in the *kentro* library. There was also a photo of the village, picturesquely perched on its fortress-crowned hill.

Eleni was trying to read the bold black caption. 'What does it say?'

'It says…' Calliope essayed a deep, theatrical voice. '"Calliope Adham: The Power to Decide."'

'Decide what?' asked Eleni.

'Oh, it's just something I said during the interview. I was quoting Napoleon: "Nothing is more difficult, and therefore more precious, than to be able to decide."' She shrugged, casting the magazine aside. 'Did you say ouzo?'

'Yes.'

Calliope got to her feet and went into the pantry to fetch a bottle of ouzo. 'Everything all right at the *kentro*?'

Everything was fine, Eleni said, though she was tired, having been awakened after midnight to deal with an obstetrical crisis. She rose and moved to the table, the kitten clinging to her skirt. She was about a decade younger than Calliope but growing heavy around the hips.

Calliope set down two glasses and a dish of olives. 'Who was it this time?'

'A Vafios shepherd's wife. You wouldn't know them,' said Eleni. 'By the way, are you still looking for someone to clean Elpida's house?'

'Yes. You know anyone?' Calliope had tried to oblige her cousin, but finding a cleaner wasn't easy now that everyone had enough to eat. She had asked her own housekeeper, but Evanthea had her hands full.

Eleni said the shepherd's mother might be interested.

'Ask her to come see me.' Calliope checked the time. 'I wonder what's keeping Rupert. He should have been here by now.'

She lit another cigarette. The serpentine road to the capital required vigilance at the wheel, but taxi owners often drove with their heads twisted backwards, carrying on political arguments. There had been a road accident the previous month. A three-wheeler had slammed into a Petra taxi, landing the driver in intensive care.

She began to beat egg whites, adding a slow stream of lemon juice. The meatballs were ready. She stirred the sauce into the pot and was slicing the bread when she finally heard the garden gate open. Turning, she saw Rupert plod among the trees, lugging two shopping bags. He looked unbearably tired. He pecked her cheek, then stepped into the kitchen, dragging his feet. Calliope had an odd feeling that he was avoiding her eyes, like a man coming home with a guilty secret.

He set the shopping bags down, greeted Eleni perfunctorily, then sank on to the divan and began to unlace his shoes.

'What is it, dear? Did something happen in Mytilene?'

Rupert began to speak, then bent over to shuck off his shoes. He sat for a moment, bleakly watching a cat chase a lizard. He tugged at his collar.

'I just ran into Mathaios,' he finally said. 'He was on his way to see you.'

'Mathaios the mayor?'

Rupert reached for Calliope's hand, holding it for a moment. 'They've arrested Aristides.'

'Aristides!' Calliope held on to Rupert like a drowning woman. 'How?'

'I don't know. His girlfriend phoned. She'll wait for your call around six.' Rupert kissed Calliope's forehead. 'Mathaios said you can phone from his office.'

'From his office,' Calliope echoed. She got to her feet, intending to do something of vital importance but unable to think what it was. She felt light-headed and unbearably warm. 'Yes, I'm going to...' she managed to bring out.

The rest of the statement slipped away from her. The floor was heaving under her feet. For a moment, she continued to stare at the dust motes dancing in a shaft of light, could hear Rupert's voice speaking across a widening distance. But then her knees gave way, and his words began to fade, caught in a web of thickening darkness.

IX

They had been on their way home from the fortress and there, lying under a pomegranate tree, was a dead baby owl. Aristides must have been three years old. He had gone down on his haunches and was studying the stunned-looking carcass.

'What's the matter with the baby owl?'

'It's dead,' Calliope said, glancing at the setting sun.

'Why?'

'I don't know. Maybe it fell out of its nest.'

'But why is it dead?'

'I don't know… everything dies sooner or later.'

'*Kyria* Maria's baby son died when she wasn't looking.'

'Did he? He must have been very sick.'

Aristides took Calliope's hand. 'I get sick sometimes.'

'Everybody gets sick from time to time.'

'But I don't want to die!' Aristides wailed. 'I—'

'Oh, you won't die,' Calliope said, bending to kiss the child's peach-soft cheek. 'Not until you are an old, old man with a cane and a long grey beard.'

'I don't want to grow a beard!'

'You won't have to. It'll be up to you.'

A moment went by. The sun went on sliding behind the mountains. 'Will I still have to die?' Aristides asked, his face tilted towards hers.

'Without a beard? Well, maybe not.'

The memory ensnared Calliope as she stood outside the grim edifice housing the General Security Headquarters in Athens. She had stationed herself across Bouboulinas Street, gazing at the barred windows. It was impossible to know which floor Aristides was being detained on, let alone whether he was being tortured. Dorothea had said that his being held at Bouboulinas, rather than at the notorious military police headquarters, was something to be grateful for.

No one knew why Aristides had been arrested, or even which underground organisation he belonged to. Someone who had been with him, who had managed to escape, had left a message for Dorothea, telling her about the arrest.

Dorothea had not been able to see Aristides either. Only legal counsel were admitted at this stage of the process. Calliope and Rupert had taken the night ferry to Piraeus. They arrived around eight a.m., going their separate ways. It was a crisp winter morning, with a sun so brilliant it seemed like a personal taunt. They had arranged to meet Calliope's cousin later, but Rupert headed straight for the British Embassy, hoping he could pull some strings there. Aristides was not a British subject, but Rupert knew someone who just might have the right contacts.

Calliope's heart was clogged with dread. Grigoris had promised to make enquiries; Dorothea was trying to get more information. She had arranged to meet Calliope at eleven, at a café across from the National Archaeological Museum. It would be their first meeting.

A face appeared at one of the prison's upper windows, peering through the bars. It was impossible to identify the man, but as she stood there, eyes riveted to the window, Calliope felt her private sorrow explode. It was unlikely to be Aristides, yet she couldn't shake the feeling that she had succeeded in summoning her godson with the sheer force of her sorrow, that he could see her now, peering up at him, and might draw some small consolation from her presence.

She raised her right hand in a wan gesture, then let it drop, swept by fresh desolation. Sobbing, she headed towards the café. If only she knew what her godson's crime had been! She had, at first, resisted contacting Grigoris – she disliked appealing to anyone indebted to her – but finally made the call. For Aristides, she would contact the devil himself if need be.

The café was spacious, with half the tables already occupied. Calliope threaded her way towards a corner table. She took off her coat and eased herself into a chair, facing the entrance. The room hummed with conversation. She was lighting a cigarette when Dorothea came in, with the breathless air of a woman trying to catch a departing bus. She paused at the entrance, squinting, eyes sweeping the room, then whipped out a pair of spectacles. Finally, she recognised Calliope. Aristides had kept a photograph of his godmother, next to one of his parents.

Calliope had her hair gathered into a clasp and was wearing a tweed suit, a barely ironed blouse; Dorothea wore a short red jacket. She was a long-legged young woman with striking eyes, large and earnest, the colour of an overcast sky. She would have been beautiful if not for her prim mouth which made Calliope think of a censorious headmistress. She apologised for being late. She had been detained outside the campus and questioned, not for the first time.

'Why?' Calliope released a puff of smoke. 'They don't know about your connection, do they?'

'No.' The Security Police often did random checks around the university. The classmate she had been with looked a little scruffy. 'Fortunately, we both had the right backgrounds.'

'Thank God.' Calliope wondered whether Dorothea's Security Police uncle would have the power to intervene if she were arrested. They sat leaning towards each other, pale and intent, speaking in hushed voices. Security Police agents often wore civvies, blending into crowds, eavesdropping on private conversations.

'I have the information you wanted,' said Dorothea, burrowing in her bag. Still squinting, still reluctant to wear spectacles, she retrieved a folded note, sliding it across the table. Scrawled across the lined sheet of paper was the name of an Athenian lawyer. Angelos Solomos. 'I just hope they don't know who Aris really is. I don't think they do.'

Calliope looked up from the note. 'What makes you say that?'

Dorothea hesitated. A stranger who had been reading a newspaper was rising to leave. She waited for him to go. 'If they did, he would be at the ESA,' she said.

The ESA – Elliniki Stratiotiki Astinomia – was the dreaded military police; its detention cells were said to be reserved for the staunchest dissidents.

Calliope set her cup down. 'So you do know what he's been up to?'

Dorothea dropped her gaze. 'Yes.'

'But you're not going to tell me?'

'Sorry.' Dorothea shifted her bottom. 'I gave my word.'

Calliope sighed, then sat silent for a long moment, her tongue probing a mouth ulcer on her inner cheek. She was fighting a small surge of resentment, knowing less about her own godson than this young, earnest stranger.

Dorothea, too, seemed to be striving for composure. 'My father would kill me if he knew I've been seeing him.' She sat staring bleakly at the window, the dead leaves drifting off tree branches. Calliope didn't know what to say.

'Do they know where you stand politically?'

'Not really. They like to think I'm ambivalent. Which is... well, it's not exactly a lie. There are positive things the junta has achieved.' Dorothea paused to blow her nose. 'You may despise their tactics,' she continued, 'I despise them myself, but you can't deny they've brought both economic growth and stability.'

'Oh, but think of the price!'

Calliope was nothing if not familiar with right-wing arguments: the junta had promoted international investment, unemployment was at an all-time low, inflation was down, farmers were prospering thanks to new grants. Some of it was true, but the last thing she had expected was to hear such talk from Aristides's girlfriend.

On the other hand, Dorothea was saying, she could not accept the regime's brutality, the disregard for civil rights. She spoke dispassionately, like someone reviewing the facts in her own mind, striving for objectivity.

'But you're not involved in student politics, I take it,' said Calliope.

'No. I'm too much of a coward,' Dorothea said. She seemed a little rigid but, disarmed by her candour, Calliope asked about her plans for the future.

Dorothea was studying law, hoping to become a judge some day. They talked about the Greek justice system, then Calliope glanced at her watch, signalling for the bill. She was meeting Rupert at Grigoris's office at one thirty. They had cancelled their flight to London.

'Are you going to contact the lawyer?' Dorothea asked.

'Probably. What do you know about him?'

'He's excellent. Unfortunately, his services don't come cheap,' Dorothea said.

'Don't worry about that.' Calliope sighed. All night, she had been haunted by images of crushed testicles and ripped fingernails and cigarette-burned soles. She had woken up, howling, just before dawn.

'Will you let me know what your cousin says?' Dorothea asked.

'Yes.' Calliope took down a telephone number. It was not Dorothea's parents' number but that of a close friend: someone Aristides trusted.

'You can leave a message for us.'

X

Grigoris Metrophanis had made lunch reservations near his Piraeus office. By the time Calliope arrived, though, Rupert had left a message, saying he was going to dine with his embassy contact and would see her back at the hotel.

Grigoris conveyed the message, then led Calliope into his office, trailing the scent of the cologne he had been wearing for decades. He had good news, he stated without preamble.

'Really?' Calliope lowered herself into a leather chair, her eyes fastened on her cousin's face.

'Very good news.' Grigoris settled himself behind his desk, stopped by a knock at the door. 'Come in!'

The office boy entered, bearing a tray suspended from brass chains. He offered Calliope a cup of coffee, discreetly placed a cup on his employer's desk, then turned and padded, bow-legged, out of the office. The room was sunny and elegant, in a ponderous sort of way. There were photos of ocean liners on the walls; a model of a new ferry rested on the massive desk.

'So, as I was saying, it looks good. It seems the police don't know who he is.'

'Oh! Why then… what's he supposed to have done?' Calliope asked. She had noticed that Grigoris's tie was askew and this small detail in this fastidious man unexpectedly touched her, suggesting as it did neglect of his own affairs. Somehow, within the folds of middle-aged flesh, a boyish face seemed eager to assert itself.

'I don't know about Aristides Dhaniel,' he was saying, 'but Konstantin Katranides will probably be found innocent.' Grigoris tugged at his shirt collar. 'It seems he just happened to be at the wrong place in the wrong company.'

The putative Katranides had stopped for a drink with the former editor of a student paper, a man suspected of distributing subversive pamphlets.

'And? Did Aristides have anything to do with the pamphlets?'

'Who knows?' In his statement, Konstantin Katranides claimed to have run into the erstwhile editor at Omonia Square, deciding on the spur of the moment to have a drink with him at a nearby *ouzeri*. The editor's name was Michalis Orphanos.

'Is Orphanos the one who managed to get away?'

'Yes.' Aristides had reportedly been sitting with his back to the entrance when the Security Police agents entered. Orphanos instantly recognised them and bolted towards the toilets, vanishing through a service entrance.

'So that's all there is to it?' Calliope was gingerly approaching the beckoning light of hope. 'They have nothing on him except a drink with a suspected activist?'

'So I'm told,' said Grigoris. 'They fingerprinted your godson and found no match to the pamphlets.' He took a sip of coffee, pondering his own words. 'Naturally, they're going to check out his story, but... well, I gather the editor had indeed been a classmate of Katranides.'

Calliope sat digesting all this. 'How reliable is your source?' she eventually asked. 'I was thinking we should—'

'Highly reliable,' Grigoris cut in. Angelos Solomos was a personal friend, he said, one of the top lawyers in town. He had already been in to see Aristides.

'Angelos Solomos! He has met Aristides?'

'What, you know him?'

Calliope explained about Dorothea, then reweighed the facts, absurdly buoyed by the coincidence. 'So, if his story checks out, they're going to let him go?'

'Probably. Solomos says his background's impeccable.'

He was, of course, referring to Aristides's assumed background. Any knowledge of his true parentage would have instantly doomed him.

Grigoris's private line began to ring. He spoke laconically, while

Calliope sat smoking, watching spokes of light play on the walnut desk. Grigoris said it was not a good time; he was busy now. 'I'll call you back.'

'How long do you suppose it'll take?' Calliope asked.

'Who knows? Our bureaucrats think they get paid just to kill flies.'

Calliope sighed. Grigoris decided it was time to eat.

'Shall we go?' He clapped his hands on his knees, hauled himself up, then came around the desk. 'Stop worrying; Solomos promised to call tonight.' He gave Calliope's shoulder an avuncular squeeze, then strode towards the coat stand. The restaurant was not far, he said, stepping out into the winter dazzle.

It was almost Christmas, but chrysanthemums were still in bloom around the flower beds; oranges peeked out of the green citrus foliage.

'Have you had any luck with the house?' Grigoris asked after a long silence.

'Yes – I'm sorry, I meant to tell you.'

An Australian artist wanted to rent the house, but not until March, Calliope said, stepping into the restaurant. It was said to be the best eatery in Piraeus. The smell of lamb and okra wafted out of the kitchen.

'March is fine, I suppose,' said Grigoris, scanning the crowded room. All he wanted was to prevent the house from going to wrack and ruin.

Calliope pointed to an empty table.

'I think I've also found a cleaner,' she said, pulling out a chair. Half her mind had retreated, the other half was relieved to have stumbled on a suitable topic. Now that Aristides's case had been hashed over, there wasn't much for them to talk about.

Grigoris asked who the cleaner was.

'Oh, a widow named Pelaghia. I don't think you'd know them. Her son's a shepherd... somewhere outside Vafios.'

'I see.' Grigoris's eyes kept roaming around the humming restaurant. Calliope, thinking he looked bored, latched on to a story Eleni had told her about the reclusive shepherd. Pelaghia's son had been at his wits' end because of a mysterious ailment afflicting his flock. Three sheep had died one after the other and the shepherd was convinced they had been hexed by the evil eye.

Grigoris shook his head, reaching for his spectacles. 'The Americans are sending men to the moon, and we're still ruled by the evil eye.'

'Yes, indeed.' Calliope sighed. 'The evil eye in the countryside and evil ears in the capital,' she quipped, opening her menu.

But, almost immediately, her eyes shot up, flying to scan the surrounding tables. Oh, there she was again: a fifty-five-year-old woman still blurting her thoughts like a reckless child!

'I'm sorry,' she muttered, stricken. 'Sorry... I wasn't thinking.'

Grigoris said nothing. He glanced at the other diners over his reading spectacles, then resumed studying his menu.

THREE

I

16 April 1970

Dear Alexandra,

Your letter reached me only yesterday. Please forgive me for not keeping my promise, but the three weeks Aristides spent in jail have taken their toll. Somehow, I managed to keep going until he was released, but then I contracted bronchitis and had a hard time shaking it. We were in Athens for Easter, but I am finally settling back into my routine. The bronchitis forced me to give up smoking, but I've become addicted to chocolate, which I enjoy but which does nothing to calm my nerves.

I can't believe three months have passed since Aristides's release. Why is it that the older we get, the faster time seems to fly? By now, Christmas is a blur, so I'm not sure how much I told you on the phone. Aristides was freed only because they never discovered his true identity. He had not been tortured, but they did rough him up ('You will talk here, or we'll make you spill your mother's milk!').

One day, they made him witness someone's transfer from the torture chamber. This shook up Aristides, but not for long. There was a point when I thought he might cave in and finish his doctoral dissertation in Paris. A few days later, though, he changed his mind again, maybe because of his girlfriend. I tried to find out how serious he is about her, but he seemed evasive. One thing I know: he was very lucky they thought him small fry and did not bother to dig too deeply.

For better or for worse, Aristides is an optimist, but Rupert says he's just about ready to start lighting candles to the saints – to keep Aristides out of harm's way, but also to ensure that we finally make it to London next Christmas.

We spent part of Easter with Aristides and Grigoris, then with my god-daughter and her fiancé. His parents and Eleni were also there, but I'm so glad to be back at work!

I was happy to hear that things seem to be working out between you and Tibor. For what it's worth, I think you should go ahead and let him move in, if that's what you want. Your children will just have to accept it. But here I am, meddling again! I'd better stop and go do something productive. Lorenz Umbreit will be in Athens this summer for his new book, but I am behind schedule with everything.

My best wishes to you and Tibor. And, once again, thank you from the bottom of my heart for offering to help.

Yours,

Calliope

P.S. A telephone network is being set up on the island. The kentro *has been promised a connection soon, but I'm not holding my breath.*

II

Calliope said, 'Umbreit is coming to Athens next month to research his book.'

'The political book?' asked Rupert, a soup ladle at his lips.

'Yes.' Calliope hesitated. 'The thing is, he'd like to come to Molyvos for a short visit. Would that be all right with you?'

'I suppose,' said Rupert after the briefest pause. He reached for a lid and covered the simmering pot. 'Are you thinking of having him stay here?'

'No. He wants to stay by the sea. At the Delphinia.'

'In that case, he doesn't need our permission, does he?'

Calliope hesitated. 'But he's asking anyway, Rupert.'

'I'm surprised he's not worried about the villagers. They're not going to welcome him with open arms, are they?'

'He doesn't think anyone will recognise him after all these years. He's much older; he's grown a beard.'

'Still.'

'It's been a quarter of a century, Rupert! German tourists are everywhere now.'

'If you say so. I shouldn't want to come back if I were in his place. Coffee?'

Calliope nodded, staring out the window. She thought she must go and collect the drying laundry before birds left their mark.

'Why does he want to come here anyway?' Rupert was asking. 'I should have thought he'd try to avoid any reminders of the Occupation.'

'I think he's just hoping to get over his writer's block,' Calliope said. 'It's been a year since his wife died... he hasn't written a word.'

'I see.'

'He's afraid he'll never write another novel. He started this new book because he's interested in our politics, but... well, he's a novelist. It's what he loves to do.'

'Right.' Rupert stood watching the coffee pot. 'It might actually work,' he said after a moment's reflection. 'Coming back is bound to shake him up, I suppose.'

The coffee rose, frothing. Rupert poured it into two demitasses.

'How long is he planning to stay?'

'A week, I believe.' Calliope paused for a moment. 'He won't come if he thinks it's going to cause any problems, Rupert.'

'Well, as I said, he might run into a problem or two if he's recognised.'

Calliope shrugged. 'I guess he's willing to risk it. He really is depressed,' she added, bringing the coffee cup to her lips. 'I just wanted to make sure it was all right with you.'

'It's fine with me,' said Rupert. 'Thank you for asking.'

They lingered over their coffee. It was the last Sunday in July. Not for the first time, Calliope found herself marvelling at Rupert's fair-mindedness. She recalled Pericles trying to stop her from meeting Lorenz in Athens and her heart stirred with love. She had told Rupert everything about Lorenz, had made it clear that their romance was over, but that Lorenz would always have a place in her life. For reasons she didn't quite understand, she found it easier to be perfectly open with Rupert than she had been with Lorenz.

They began to clear the table, but all at once, Calliope stopped.

'Rupert,' she said. 'You know I would never cheat on you, don't you?'

His eyes flickered. 'Yes, of course,' he said.

'But something is still bothering you. What?'

He paused. He dropped into a chair. 'I was just wondering how much Lorenz has to do with your reluctance to get married.'

'Rupert!' Calliope, too, sat down. 'I had doubts about getting married when I was nineteen! I've always had doubts.'

Rupert said nothing. He seemed to be thinking.

'Look,' she said, 'my doubts have nothing to do with how I feel about you. Nothing at all! I wish you'd believe me.'

'And… nothing to do with Umbreit?' Rupert spoke very gently, studying her face with a wistful sort of kindness.

'Absolutely not!' Calliope said. 'Anyway…' She fell silent.

'Anyway what?'

'Lorenz could never take your place. He could never live here. I could never live in Germany.'

Rupert sighed but remained silent.

'Look,' said Calliope. She, too, sighed. 'If you're going to be reading things into it, things that aren't there, I'll marry you, all right?'

Rupert raised his gaze. 'Oh, I wouldn't want to twist your arm.' He did not quite achieve a smile; his eyes were inscrutable.

'All right. Let me make myself clear,' Calliope said. 'I think marriage would be pointless. I honestly do. But, at this stage, it seems even more pointless to resist, since it means so much to you.'

Rupert shrugged. She went and sat on his lap.

'I don't want this coming between us,' she said, her arm around his neck. 'We'll get married, all right?'

'Wonderful,' said Rupert. 'See that you keep your word.' He reached out and gently tweaked the tip of her nose. 'Otherwise, I'll have to find me a young wench who'll wash my feet and bring me breakfast in bed,' he added.

But now, at last, he was smiling.

III

By the end of August, the countryside was a parched landscape of bleached rocks and desiccated gorse, of shrilling cicadas and tiny lizards darting in and out of dusty olive groves. It was late afternoon, but the sun was still high. Calliope was wearing a pale yellow head-kerchief, Lorenz a beige cotton hat and dark sunglasses. His hair was cut well below his ears; his beard was mottled with grey.

They had spent the afternoon in Eftalou but were heading back towards Molyvos. Lorenz stopped to take a snapshot of Calliope picking wild figs, then of a flock of sheep huddling around a leafy walnut tree. He lingered in the shade, greedily sniffing the air, clutching his new Exakta.

'If only this camera could capture the sounds and smells!'

The air smelled of sea salt and dry algae, of fig syrup and herbs and sun-ripened berries. There was the tinkle of sheep's bells, the incessant droning of insects. The waves came and went, splashing against hot rocks.

The road between Eftalou and Molyvos was still unpaved. Halfway to the village, two farmers looked up from a roadside orchard, one of them a young man whose left arm ended at the elbow. Calliope could not recall his name, but she knew he had been crippled shortly after the Civil War, playing with a hand grenade during a Clean Monday picnic.

The hand-grenade accident was the only mishap to take place

in recent years, but to wander about the village was to see Greek history grimly personified, she told Lorenz as they ambled on. There were still Anatolian refugees around, one of whom had had his eyes gouged by the Turks. There were men wounded during the Civil War, others born with birth defects during the Occupation. There was even an old man down in the harbour who had lost both feet in Macedonia.

All this, Calliope said, had happened in their lifetime. And now there was the junta. 'It goes on and on. A national nightmare with no end in sight.'

Lorenz was silent. They strolled on through the shimmering countryside. Calliope had stopped for wild blackberries when the late beekeeper's brother came toward them, riding his ancient mule cart. Nikiforos was short-sighted, but eventually recognised Calliope. He whistled at his mule, pulling on the reins. '*Yassas!*'

He was a peevish old man, with a look of perpetual bewilderment in his eyes, as though he were trying to work out the cause of the unsightly growths that had one day appeared on his face, like dark treacle hardening as it dribbled down his cheeks.

But this was not what he'd stopped to complain about. His stomach was bothering him, he said sourly. 'I woulda stayed home today, but it's time to extract the honey, eh?' Nikiforos and his wife lived in Calliope's own neighbourhood, so she was all too familiar with his ailments.

'I thought you were going to see the doctor last week,' she said, watching the old man squint in Lorenz's direction. The villagers were curious about the visiting foreigner but took him to be Rupert's relative. Lorenz had stepped aside to photograph a bird.

'The doctor, the doctor!' Nikiforos was saying. 'I did see him, but he wouldn't listen to me! He kept telling me to try a new medication, but you know how it is, *Kyria* Calliope, the doctor has his ideas, but we know what we know, eh?'

'What exactly is it we know in this case?'

'I have worms! I told you last time I had worms!'

'So, what happened? The doctor didn't agree with your diagnosis?'

'Of course he agreed! Could a man be wrong about his own stomach?'

'So what's the problem?'

'The problem, *Kyria mou*, is the medication. Didn't I just say so? He wants me to take medicine to get rid of the worms. I couldn't convince him: stomach worms are good for the digestion! Everybody knows that!' He gave her a disgruntled look, let out a vaguely resigned sound, then raised his whip as he said goodbye.

After he had gone, Calliope translated the exchange into German.

'And you thought I was making things up.' She chuckled.

The scent of fresh pine sap hung in the air. The pinewood was where Calliope had been kissed by Johnny the Australian, where Umbreit and Reis had almost caught her and her mother lugging live ammunition. The same thought must have flitted through his mind. They were silent entering the village.

'Oh, there's Zoe Samiou!' The deaf-mute artist was perched on a cement step, absorbed in sketching three black-clad crones huddled in a doorway. She had been sent to Mytilene to study icon painting but had quickly quit, turning her back on sacred art forever. Day in and day out, she drew village scenes, though no one showed the slightest interest in buying her work.

The three women were busy making *manestra*, cackling amiably at a French couple who had stopped to take photographs. The foreign wife was watching the three villagers roll dough between their fingers, the rice-like pellets spilling into their enamel bowls in a steady stream; her husband stood across the street, following Zoe's progress. He was a lawyer back home, but art was his passion, he was soon telling Calliope. When his wife joined them, they both fell to praising Zoe's *art naif*. The artist was deaf-mute, Calliope said, but had been drawing since the age of three.

'She has some fine paintings at home if you're interested,' she added on a sly impulse. 'I could take you there, if you'd like. It's not very far.'

The foreigners exchanged glances. They saw no reason not to. They left the three widows hunched over their pans and Zoe over her drawing pad. Lorenz wanted to have a shower. He headed back to his hotel, leaving Calliope alone with the foreigners, who went on to talk about their visit to the Theophilos Museum.

The museum was new, dedicated to the work of a local folk artist. Theophilos had died in his thirties, just as a celebrated Greco-French critic was beginning to establish his reputation abroad. There was a time when Molyviates would mock the peripatetic Theophilos, cursing as they whitewashed the murals he used to paint on unsuspecting hosts' walls. He died homeless, impoverished, friendless. Now the paintings were on exhibit in museums and fine art galleries all over Europe. The French couple compared Theophilos to the French Henri Rousseau. It was a pity, they said, that artists were so often unappreciated in their own lifetime.

'Unfortunately, posthumous recognition doesn't fill an empty belly, does it?' Calliope said. 'I think our Zoe will turn out to be the next Theophilos,' she added. 'I have two of her paintings on my own walls and I cherish them.'

'And how do you come to speak French so well?' asked the wife. She was a *lycée* teacher back home, an ample, red-haired woman named Manon; her husband was called Yves.

Calliope said she was a literary translator. 'My friend – the one you just met – is a German author. I'm his translator.'

'*Ah bon!*' Manon seemed about to add something, but they had just arrived at Olga's home. Calliope stood knocking at the door, a hot breeze blowing at her neck.

'Coming!' Olga Samiou appeared at the entrance, an old woman wiping her hands on her apron, peering at the strangers through a web of wrinkles.

Calliope introduced the couple. 'The foreigners are French,' she said. 'I think they might buy a painting. Show them the ones upstairs, Olga.'

'What, right now? The house—'

'They're not interested in your housekeeping, Olga *mou*! They want to see the paintings. I'm telling you; they are going to buy something! Go on, show them what you have. Tell them you won't accept less than six hundred drachmas.'

'Six hundred!'

'Well, bring them to me when you're done and maybe I'll let them bargain me down to five.' She turned back to the foreigners, looking apologetic. 'As you can see, she's not eager to sell. She has an idea that the work will be worth a fortune some day.'

The couple exchanged glances.

'Tell her we'd just like to have a look,' said Yves, beaming at Olga.

'Yes. Ask her if she has anything with fishermen or shepherds. Something rustic,' put in Manon.

'Go see for yourself,' Calliope said, motioning upstairs. 'Maybe we can talk her into letting you have something. I'll wait in the garden in case you need me.'

'*Merci!*' they said, speaking in unison.

And then they trudged upstairs, trailing the heavily perspiring Olga. Calliope stepped outdoors and sat under a pine tree, fanning herself.

It was an unexceptional August afternoon, but she would always remember that summer of 1970 as the year when Lorenz Umbreit returned to Lesbos, and when Zoe Samiou finally began to sell her paintings. Before he left, Lorenz himself bought three of them, though no one would ever discover the foreign art lover's real identity.

IV

One of Molyvos's new expats was a Belgian photographer named Hendrik Van Woert. Obsessed with doors, gates, portals, he had spent two months photographing entryways on the islands. He was showing Calliope a collection of his photographs, one of which she instantly wanted. The image showed a beautiful wrought-iron door to a Cretan house that was no longer standing. It had crumbled in a long-ago earthquake and was never rebuilt.

'Do you think I could buy this one?' she asked, turning to

Hendrik. He was a multilingual Belgian in his late twenties, as fair as a Viking, but with slanted brown eyes peering from under bristling eyebrows. Calliope was planning to frame the photograph and send it to Lorenz for his coming birthday. She was sure it would speak to him.

She was far less sure of what she would say in response to the letter she had just received. It was by now autumn; Lorenz had surprised himself by writing two short stories after returning home. He was a great admirer of Chekhov, his letter said, but somehow had never before considered writing short fiction. He was deeply grateful to Calliope and Rupert for making it possible. And to Nikiforos the beekeeper for inspiring his very first story.

Calliope was relieved to hear that Lorenz was writing again. For some time, he had been tortured by the idea that his divided love was what had caused Alicia's death. He had obviously let his guilt override his reason, he wrote in his letter. Sadly, exorcising his demons had seemed hopeless before his return to Lesbos. He'd found both peace and enchantment in the island's bucolic splendour and was contemplating buying a little cottage somewhere by the sea. Molyvos itself was probably too noisy, but Eftalou might be ideal for the summer, perhaps even an annual Easter visit.

Calliope had long believed that one could love more than one person at a time, though probably with different facets of one's psyche. She loved Rupert, but was nonetheless deeply attached to Lorenz and would, she felt sure, remain so to the end of her days. She had finally learned to accept the fact, but Alicia's death had made it impossible not to contemplate the irony of their current predicament: Lorenz was now in Heidelberg, widowed, and she was in Molyvos, attached to another man.

How the gods laugh at us, Calliope thought.

She had shared Lorenz's letter with Rupert, surprised to hear him confess that he had been more than a little jealous back in August. He considered jealousy a deplorable emotion and was ashamed to find himself capable of it.

'I feel I should be able to master it, but it seems I can't. I'm sorry!'

'Rupert!' Calliope stared, ignoring the cigarette stub in her hand. Both she and Rupert had gone back to smoking after Lorenz's visit. 'Why didn't you tell me?'

'What was the point?' Rupert stopped mid-stride to the fridge. 'He was here for a week; he was leaving soon. How was I supposed to know he would suddenly decide to buy a house here?'

Calliope closed her eyes. 'I'm so sorry.' She put out her cigarette and went to bestow a kiss. Rupert was not given to emotional outbursts, but who could blame him for being jealous, given her history? 'I don't know what to do,' she finally said, sinking on to the divan. They had just finished dinner, but the dishes had yet to be cleared. 'How can I stop him from buying a house if that's what he wants to do?'

'What can I say?' Rupert sat down too. 'I hate feeling possessive!' he said, as if sheer repetition might help him exorcise his unworthy feelings.

They were silent for a while. The fridge hummed, the drain in the sink gurgled. Calliope went on grappling with her inner storm.

That she was being offered an opportunity to see Lorenz for two months every summer, that she was being asked to turn down this unexpected gift! Had Rupert been more aggressive, she would have fought him over this, would have insisted on her rights, on Lorenz Umbreit's right to live wherever he pleased.

But Rupert was not Pericles.

'I'm not saying that you shouldn't see him,' he was soon saying. 'I would never presume—'

'I know, my dear.' She took his hand in hers, floundering.

One thing she was sure of. As she eventually wrote to Lorenz, destiny had not been on their side; it had merely enjoyed sporting with them. She explained the situation as tactfully as she could, taking care not to paint Rupert in a negative light. All the same, after much thought and with great reluctance, she decided she must respect Rupert's feelings. It was an extremely difficult decision, she wrote in her letter; she hoped with all her heart that Lorenz would understand and try to find a suitable cottage in some other village.

Maybe in a decade or two, she wrote, *when we resemble what*

Yeats called 'a tattered coat upon a stick', we will sit by the fire and chuckle at our youthful madness. But we are not there yet, are we, my dear? There is nothing I would like better than to see you more often, but as I told you once at the Grande Bretagne, I have all but stopped resisting the dictates of fate. I hope with all my heart that you will understand.

She promised to see Lorenz once or twice a year, in Rupert's company. She sealed the letter, then sat up half the night, groping for clarity. In the morning, she took the letter to Ed, hoping to catch him before he left for his morning stroll.

It was the most peaceful time of day, but peace proved elusive that day. It was only October, but already the incandescent summer was beginning to seem almost like a dream; the scent of approaching autumn tugged at her soul. As she arrived at Ed's house, a stray dog came from around the corner, tentatively wagging its bedraggled tail. Overcome by pity, Calliope stopped to pet the raw-boned mongrel, stroking its spotted, quivering haunches, swiping at her own mutinous eyes.

V

It was by sheer chance that Hendrik Van Woert was in Mytilene the following Easter when a local woman immolated herself in protest against her son's incarceration.

A history teacher, Theodoros Philippou had been arrested in Athens in February 1971 and, seven weeks later, was still in custody. The mother, a schoolmaster's widow, journeyed to the capital, only to be told that no visitors were allowed until after the preliminary interrogation. No one would tell her when this would take place, or indeed what her son's alleged crime had been. She went back twice, telling the gatekeepers that her husband had been shot by the Germans, her son had never been involved in politics, it was all a mistake.

It was all in vain. Returning to Mytilene, the fifty-four-year-old widow appealed to two local priests, but neither would intercede. She was referred to a lawyer, but his fees proved prohibitive. Two other lawyers were contacted but were too swamped to take on new cases.

On Good Friday, just before the traditional Easter procession, Katerina Philippou stationed herself outside Mytilene's cathedral and, possibly inspired by the recent immolation of a young Greek student, set herself ablaze, apparently hoping to draw attention to what many regarded as the church's collusion with the junta.

Katerina Philippou lived a stone's throw away from St Symeon's church but had chosen to stage her protest at the more imposing St Athanasios. The sixteenth-century cathedral's crypt held the relics of St Theodoros of Byzantium – her son's, as well as Mytilene's, patron saint. During holy days, the church was packed with worshippers from all over the region. Hendrik Van Woert, who had been invited to spend Easter with local friends, stood at the back, waiting to photograph the traditional candlelight procession.

The priest had just finished blessing the parishioners when a shriek was heard from outside. The priest went on chanting, but several men at the entrance dashed out, Van Woert following on their heels.

'Mother of God!'

'It's Philippou's mother! Go get blankets or something. Hurry!'

The crowd was quickly swelling. There were those who shouted and those who sped back into the church, colliding with others pushing their way through the open portals. Some of the witnesses crossed themselves; others had taken off their jackets and were trying to extinguish the tongues of flame. Two men came running out of the church, dragging an embroidered standard, while the sexton chased them, clutching a tablecloth.

'Use this, use the tablecloth, for God's sake!' he kept shouting.

Hendrik Van Woert had also rushed out to help, but quickly gave up and began photographing the live torch that was Katerina Philippou. She was swaying weakly, her hair burning around her face like some hellish crown. Her face was twitching, her arms rising and falling, as though she might soar towards the starry skies in a blaze of flames. He stayed just long enough to record the desperate attempts at rescue, then turned and took to his heels. It occurred to him, he would later tell Calliope, that there might be policemen in the crowd, and that one of them might decide to confiscate his film.

Katerina Philippou's husband had been among the ten civilians who, back in 1942, had been executed by the Germans in retaliation for the attack outside the Mytilene brothel. Had the poor woman finally gone mad, Calliope wondered. She praised Hendrik for keeping his wits about him. He had been right to suspect that his film would have been confiscated.

'We must find a way to publicise it,' she said, thinking.

Hendrik reached for his camera. 'Do you have any media contacts?'

'I do, but no one in Greece will touch this. I'm thinking of foreign media.' She was aware of Greek exiles' efforts to expose the junta's oppressive rule. It was hoped that, at the very least, foreign pressure might improve the treatment of political opponents.

'We must get the pictures out of the country,' she said, growing decisive. 'I'm going to phone Mytilene right away. I know someone who might be able to help.'

At the town hall, she placed a call to a man she had once been involved with, a prominent political journalist named Arghiris Economides. Their affair had ended on a sour note, but Calliope was sure her former lover would be glad to cooperate and was soon proven right. Arghiris knew an airline stewardess who might be persuaded to smuggle the package abroad. When could he expect the film?

The very next day, Calliope travelled to Mytilene and handed the film over, along with a typewritten commentary and three foreign contacts. At the top of the list was Rupert's son-in-law, who worked for the BBC and would do his best to get the photos shown on British television. Also included were phone numbers for Alexandra in Paris and Lorenz Umbreit in Heidelberg. One of the three was bound to succeed, she told Rupert on returning home.

'*Tu es formidable!*' Rupert exclaimed. 'The colonels are going to roar when the photos appear on foreign television.'

'They say a picture is worth a thousand words.'

Calliope managed a smile, though it quickly faded into a stifled yawn. She was feeling utterly exhausted, victim to recurring bouts of insomnia. When she wasn't brooding about the hapless mother, her thoughts would return to the cottage Lorenz was proposing to buy on the north-eastern side of the island. It was all in his latest letter. Skala Sykaminias was not as picturesque as Molyvos, but Lorenz said he and his sons were looking forward to spending their holidays by the sea.

He had been gracious about Calliope's domestic dilemma, and she felt grateful. And yet, there was no denying the obscure resentment she still felt on occasion. Resentment towards whom? She could not say. The spiteful gods, perhaps.

She had become both moody and irritable in recent days, as overwrought as she recalled being only during adolescence. The black mood generated by Lorenz's letter and the Mytilene tragedy persisted for days, fading only when news finally came that Hendrik's photographs were to be aired on the BBC.

The heart-wrenching images of Katerina Philippou's death would never be seen in Greece, but several foreign stations eventually showed the grieving mother going up in flames, causing the colonels to roar, exactly as predicted. The international outcries would be swift in coming, leading to the release of several innocent men, among them Theodoros Philippou, who promptly left for London, never to return.

VI

It was in order to reciprocate an invitation from Van Woert that Calliope decided to celebrate her name day by throwing a dinner party for the foreign Hellenophiles. It fell in early June, some nine months after Lorenz's visit. The Australian artist renting Elpida's house arrived with a new boyfriend from Marseilles. The artist was called Michael, his French lover was named Michel.

'M and M,' the Australian laughed, shaking Calliope's hand.

Hendrik brought a Canadian girl named Sylvie, who was interested in international dance. Unlike Molyviates, they all came casually dressed, bearing bottles of wine and ouzo. The atmosphere was less stodgy than at traditional name-day parties, dampened only by a mind-boggling piece of news: Ed Bell had just been arrested on suspicion of espionage. The authorities had received reports that he was in the habit of wandering in the countryside, scribbling in his notebook.

'You have to understand,' Rupert said, uncorking a wine bottle. 'Going out for an aimless walk in the hills is incomprehensible to Greek villagers; making notes is more suspicious than reading Trotsky.'

Everyone laughed.

'It's true,' Calliope said, though she suspected that, in this case, the arrest had more to do with Artemis's charms than with Ed's wanderings. Sylvie wanted to know who Artemis was and Hendrik explained, his arm around her beautiful suntanned shoulders. Sylvie was a lithe French-Canadian girl with avid eyes and an enigmatic smile hinting at tantalising thoughts.

Calliope said, 'I think they're just trying to get rid of him, now that her uncle's found out about them.' The secret affair had come to light after children had stumbled upon Ed and Artemis making love in an Eftalou cove.

'So now they've arrested him? Because he makes love to a Greek girl and walks in the hills?' Sylvie spoke with a strong French accent. She had come to Greece with an anglophone boyfriend, but they'd quarrelled and ended up going their separate ways.

Rupert said Artemis might have had something to do with Ed's arrest, but the authorities were genuinely paranoid about the disputed islands off the Turkish coast. A few months earlier, a pine forest had burned down, and everyone suspected Turkish arsonists. Could Ed have been spying for the Turks or Russians? He didn't really look like an American, Rupert had overheard someone say at the barber's.

All this was rehashed over a dish of stuffed courgette blossoms, while birds chattered in the trees and a dry-cleaning messenger from Mytilene did the rounds, hoarsely announcing pickup services. It was a radiant afternoon and they dined in the shade, surrounded by drowsy cats. Now and then, a breeze rose from the sea, dappling the tablecloth. The smell of grilled fish wafted from the outdoor firepit, swirling in with the scent of ripening fruit.

Rupert kept refilling the foreigners' glasses. Sylvie did a North African dance, making Calliope feel old. Old and jaded. The Canadian girl was twenty-six, exactly the age Calliope had been when she first met Lorenz Umbreit. She watched Sylvie dance among the fruit-laden trees, privately wondering whether the time would ever come when nothing at all could make her think of Lorenz.

VII

Friday was Eleni's day off, the only full day Calliope spent at the *kentro*. One Friday morning in August, she arrived at eight a.m. to find Varvara, the demoted police chief's wife, waiting at the entrance. She was accompanied by her six-year-old granddaughter, who was visiting from Salonika, and wanted to look at picture books. Or so Varvara said.

'Eh, *poulaki mou*, you love books, don't you?'

The child nodded vigorously, her wide smile complicated by missing teeth and pink bubble gum. She skipped across the threshold and into the library, where Calliope seated her at one of the low tables built for young children. The library assistant would come in the afternoon, after school hours.

Calliope placed a stack of picture books before the child, pulled up a chair for Varvara, and turned to go. 'I'll be at my desk if you need me.'

'Actually…' Varvara cleared her throat. 'I'd like to speak to you – in private.'

Calliope paused. 'Shall we go into the office then?' She supposed some domestic problem had arisen, possibly related to the visiting daughter. It soon became clear, however, that Varvara had come to warn Calliope of her own imminent arrest. She had been sent by Louizos, instructed to stress the urgency of the situation.

'They will probably come for you on Monday,' Varvara said, fidgeting with her fingers.

Calliope sat staring at Varvara, not a single muscle moving.

'What am I alleged to have done?' she asked impassively. *Could this be a trap*, she wondered, but quickly dismissed the notion.

Varvara was gazing at her with earnest intensity, tiny beads of sweat spreading above her lip. She was a woman in her middle years, with huge, haunted eyes. 'It's something to do with the American – the one they suspect of spying.'

'Ed Bell? What's it got to do with me? He's just an acquaintance.'

Calliope had spoken matter-of-factly, but maybe Ed had been forced to reveal her foreign correspondence? She sat for a moment, staring out, idly contemplating an old man who was ambling past, reading a newspaper. Her father used to look just like that, walking home from the *kapheneion.*

'*Kyria* Calliope,' Varvara was saying. 'I'm here to help you.'

'But I haven't done anything!' Calliope blurted. She could always say she had asked Ed to handle her mail because she did not want her private life exposed to the censor's scrutiny.

'They found his journal, *Kyria* Calliope. They've read it… they know everything.'

Calliope held herself very still, outwardly calm, inwardly aware of the slow chill seeping into her bones. 'But what can they possibly know?'

'They say you were responsible for smuggling out the Philippou photographs… you or your godson. They know you've been in touch.'

Calliope stiffened. She was silent for a moment, weighing Varvara's words. She knew that Ed was in the habit of scribbling notes for his novel, but not that he kept a journal. How stupid, how irresponsible of him to mention her, she thought, feeling hot all over. But then it came to her that if Ed was in fact innocent, he would have had no reason to expect the authorities to take an interest in anything he wrote.

'They don't really think he's a spy, do they?' she said, turning to Varvara.

'I don't know. Anyway, it's beside the point. The point is you should be thinking about leaving, *Kyria* Calliope. The new chief's in Mytilene, but when he gets back, they will come. Please believe me.' Varvara touched Calliope's wrist. 'There's no time to lose.'

'What are you saying, *Kyria* Varvara? You expect me to flee abroad? Just like that?'

Varvara's voice grew tighter, as if she were being forced to reason with a dim-witted child. 'Everybody knows how the authorities feel about the smuggled photographs,' she reminded Calliope. 'But… it seems they're also hoping you'll lead them to your godson. My husband says to go while you still can,' she repeated, fidgeting with her rings.

Calliope closed her eyes. She greatly appreciated *Kyrios* Louizos's concern, she said, but it was simply out of the question. She couldn't possibly leave everything from one day to the next!

'*Kyria* Calliope.' Varvara spoke severely. 'My husband respects you. He's risking his own neck because this is serious. You have a passport, don't you?'

Calliope nodded.

'There's a ferry leaving this evening. Take it – you and *Kyrios* Rupert. Take it! And don't tell anyone you're going,' she added. 'That's all I've come to tell you.' She pushed her chair back and rose, sighing, then reached again across the desk to squeeze Calliope's hand. 'The Virgin be with you.'

VIII

Calliope drifted through the house, darting from one mute object to another. She knew that her life as she'd known it was probably over. If only she could think. Think. Countless artists and intellectuals had fled abroad following the coup, yet she felt that she should have been given fair warning. It was Rupert who pointed out that a warning was precisely what she had been given.

'You're wasting time, Calliope!' He was pacing back and forth, rubbing his jaw. 'You trust Louizos, don't you?'

'Yes.' She trusted both him and Varvara.

'In that case, there's no time to lose,' Rupert said. 'For all we know, they're issuing an arrest warrant as we speak.'

'But—'

'There are no buts here, Calliope! We must leave this evening. We'll be in Athens in the morning, then—'

'But Rupert, be reasonable! You expect me to go into exile as if… as if I was going on a shopping trip!'

Rupert puffed out his cheeks and stood rubbing the back of his neck. When he finally spoke, his voice sounded brittle. 'Do you know what they'll do to you in Athens?'

Calliope continued to bite her knuckles, groping for clarity.

'How can I possibly leave?' she said, speaking to herself. 'The *kentro*—'

'Good God, Calliope! I don't seem to be getting through to you! There's no time to think about anything but saving your skin right now… you'll have to deal with everything else later.' He regarded her for a moment, his mouth a grim line. 'Start packing!' he said, abruptly decisive. 'Then go arrange for a taxi.'

He wheeled about and strode towards his own room. There was a spell of silence, during which a neighbour was heard beating a pillow over the balcony.

'I'm sorry,' Calliope said vaguely. She blundered towards the master bedroom – the room where she had been conceived and where her father died. A room in which she had changed nothing since Mirto's death, and where she now stood scanning the bed, wardrobe, curtains, her parents' wedding photo, her mother's iconostasis. It was a brilliant summer morning, and the windows were wide open, the room flooded with sunlight. A bumblebee buzzed in and out of a window. A farmer came lumbering up the street, hawking aubergines.

She had made it this far when a wave of anguish flooded her

heart. She felt like someone thrust into a dream landscape, where everything is familiar yet ruled by unknown imperatives. Rupert could be heard stirring below and, after a while, Calliope roused herself and crossed towards the wardrobe. She threw open its doors, then stopped and drew back, mutinous, collapsing onto the edge of the mattress.

'Rupert!' she wailed. 'Rupert!'

He came stumbling up the stairs.

'I can't do it, Rupert!'

'Darling! You don't understand, do you?' He seized her shoulders, his voice fraying. 'Listen to me! If you don't want to think of yourself, think of Aristides! They will torture you, just to find out where he is.'

'But I don't know where he is!' she cut in mulishly. 'How can they get it out of me if I don't know?'

'They'll get you to tell them about Dorothea. Believe me, they will! Then they'll work on her and get her to talk, tooth by tooth, fingernail by fingernail!'

'All right!' she suddenly yelled. 'All right!' She turned away from him, conscious of an intense need to shove her fist through the wall. 'I want a cigarette!' she said, sounding pathetic even to her own ear. 'Give me one, will you?'

'I don't have any.' He sighed: they had been trying to quit smoking.

'All right. Go. Go! I'll start packing,' she let out, defeated.

He hesitated, then turned and made for the stairs, leaving her to face decisions she felt incapable of making. How do you prepare for a journey when you don't know its duration? They might be gone for two months, or for the rest of their lives!

Calliope's first impulse was to pack everything she cherished. But after she hauled her suitcases out of storage, after she began going through her bedroom drawers, a peculiar but tenacious notion took hold of her brain. If she packed everything she valued, her departure would be final. If she *didn't* take anything of significance, her stay abroad would be temporary. Sooner or later, she would be back, as if her abandoned possessions had the power to effect her return.

That this line of reasoning was absurd Calliope knew perfectly well. She forced herself to do what had to be done, going through notes, books, accessories. She folded the clothes she expected to need in London. She packed a book she was reading, and a manuscript she was working on: a political satire written shortly after the coup d'état. She took her journal and her translation award, along with her dictionary. She took her favourite jewellery in case the house was broken into while they were away. Everything else she would leave behind. It would all be there, waiting, clamouring for her return.

Eventually, she went to see Kyriakos Himonas's brother, who now drove one of two village taxis. She returned home and sat down to write a note to Eleni, and another to Evanthea. The housekeeper would find the two notes when she arrived on Monday morning.

Her eyes blurring, Calliope sealed the two envelopes and left them on the kitchen counter. She set about making sandwiches.

Rupert came down and they picked at their food, desultorily discussing practical matters. There was a mobile bank that came once a week from Mytilene, but its arrival was somewhat erratic, so both Rupert and Calliope had cash stashed away; it would be enough for now.

Calliope was about to return upstairs when Rupert took her in his arms.

'This won't last,' he said, putting his lips to her neck. 'One day, Greeks will have had enough.'

He spoke with calm certitude, reminding Calliope of Lorenz whispering similar assurances about the end of the Occupation. That he had been right, that the war had in fact ended soon after, seemed to lend Rupert's words greater authority.

She was still trying to comfort herself hours later as she stood at the kitchen window, waiting for the taxi. Dusk was coming on when a lone kitten emerged out of the bushes, meowing plaintively. Calliope picked up the tiny creature and stood cuddling it, breathing in the familiar scents of her luxuriant summer garden.

The night promised to be calm. There would be no cancelled ferryboats, no reprieve. It was not yet dark, but the evening star was rising, and the moon emerged to stare down at her, complicated by smoke from a neighbour's chimney.

Suddenly, Calliope released the kitten and vaulted upstairs. She snatched two nightingale souvenirs Lorenz had brought from his travels, then several photographs: pictures of her parents and of Aristides, of Eli and his daughters, of Rupert and herself lounging in the garden, of Eleni and Athena, of Alexandra in Eftalou, and of a smiling Lorenz Umbreit, one arm resting around her shoulder, the other around his wife. She plucked all these photographs out of their frames, then stopped and surveyed the room one last time.

'I'm fifty-six years old,' she said to herself, 'and I'm about to become a fugitive.'

The words went jangling through her head, and she paused and waited for them to pass, the way one waits for a noisy cargo train to go by, spewing foul fumes into a blameless sky.

IX

It was easy to spot the soldiers and uniformed policemen but impossible to identify members of the Security Police. Calliope knew they could arrest anyone they deemed suspicious: without a warrant, without so much as an explanation. She had heard of people being jailed without formal charges ever being laid. Now and then, dissidents disappeared, their families unaware of their whereabouts. She thought of her godson, whom she was about to leave behind. She closed her eyes and drew a long breath, backing away from the jolt of pain.

She was in an airport queue with Rupert, waiting to check in. Unreasonably, she had drifted from a bullish reluctance to leave into a dread so intense it felt like foreknowledge: she was going to get caught, would, at the last moment, be prevented from making her escape and end up in a torture chamber. Whether or not the authorities had already been alerted, some bored Security Police agent might take it into his head to detain them. Rupert, with his shaggy beard, could easily be mistaken for a member of the Greek intelligentsia.

For years, Calliope had been praised for her inner strength, her ability to tackle other people's problems. Yet now, about to leave her homeland, she was vainly groping for solid ground. She had been lucky during the Occupation, if only because Lorenz had been swayed by his feelings. She did not think she was likely to be so lucky again.

Back on the ferry, Rupert had done his best to dispel her anxieties. It was Saturday, it was August, it was when public servants took their annual holidays. 'You know how efficient your Greek bureaucracy is. At the best of times.'

'What worries me is that Himonas's wife might have said something.'

'What if she did? She doesn't know why we're going to Athens, does she?'

'No.'

'There you are. Stop fretting.'

Calliope sighed. Rupert was right: even assuming that word eventually got around, that every village policeman knew about the imminent arrest, she would have to be extremely unlucky for news of their flight to reach Athenian authorities in time to stop her departure. It was possible but highly unlikely.

The queue went on inching its way to the check-in counter.

'They're doing spot checks,' Rupert whispered a few minutes later. The customs agents were there to prevent the smuggling of Greek currency and subversive pamphlets. And that was all, Calliope reminded herself. There was nothing to worry about, unless they decided to read through her manuscript. All she had to do was make sure she didn't overreact if they questioned her.

'They're running late,' she said quietly.

Olympic Airlines departures were notoriously unreliable, but BOAC had been all booked up. Fumbling for a cigarette – she had taken up smoking again on the ferry – Calliope watched as the agent singled out a lone passenger, asking him to step aside with his bulging suitcase. It came to her that the choice might not be random.

What if there was something they were trained to detect: some facial flicker, some telltale cue? What if they were under instructions to alert the Security Police?

Calliope put her hand to her brow. Neither she nor Rupert had slept much on the ferry. They both looked exhausted, but Calliope was hiding her fatigue behind dark sunglasses. Now that she was finally at the airport, her dread of an arrest was beginning to fuse with a more complicated emotion. She felt as if she were guilty of some appalling betrayal: a mother turning her back on her needy child, a cowardly captain deserting his sinking ship.

The airport was crowded and hot, the stale air reeking of sweat and floor-cleaning detergent. Sighing, Calliope drew her damp hair into a clip. She kept replaying Rupert's assurances, reflecting that equanimity came more naturally to an Englishman. The thought was faintly rancorous, as if the English had been blessed with some small but unfair advantage in coping with life's travails.

Although tourism was said to be on the downswing under the junta, the check-in queue included several foreigners. They seemed quiet and aloof, while all around them native families argued, laughed, scolded rowdy children. Rupert stood brooding next to Calliope, his legs apart, a finger stroking his beard. He glanced at his wristwatch.

At that moment, the customs agent looked up.

'Step this way, please, sir.'

Calliope froze. The agent was a scrawny man whose right eyebrow was slightly higher than the left, fixed in an expression of permanent scepticism. He appeared bored, stifling a yawn, waiting for them to heft their suitcases up for inspection. Calliope swallowed hard.

'How long are you planning to stay abroad?' the agent asked, unzipping a suitcase. He had a thick moustache and long, narrow eyes, like slivers of black liquorice.

'Until St Basil's,' Calliope said. She slipped her holdall off her shoulder and onto the inspection table. The agent looked rather sour, like a man with heartburn.

'What's the purpose of your trip?'

'My fiancé is English,' Calliope said, gesturing towards Rupert. 'We're going to be married in London.'

The agent glanced from Calliope to Rupert, his eyes unreadable. He asked whether they had any currency to declare and seemed satisfied with the answer.

'Are you taking printed material with you?'

'Yes.' She was a translator, Calliope explained, and needed to finish a book while she was abroad. She had a deadline to meet, she babbled.

The agent continued to look preoccupied, riffling through suits and dresses. He peered into the suitcase's inner pouches, into bags and boxes. He seemed interested in her folders.

'That's all for my work,' Calliope said, achieving the vaguely put-upon look any woman might wear watching a stranger paw through her carefully packed possessions. The agent was beginning to look like someone who just might decide to skim through her manuscript. When he came upon the translation award, he stopped and examined it, glanced at her briefly, then grew perfunctory.

Rupert watched all this impassively, fidgeting with something in his pocket. When Calliope's suitcase had been approved, he stepped forward to help her reorganise her belongings. A second agent had meanwhile emerged from the back, swaggering towards them. He paused, popped a Chiclet into his mouth, then briskly went about inspecting Rupert's luggage.

Calliope's mouth felt parched. She was saying she needed a drink when a public announcement came on, instructing passengers to proceed to passport control. There was a sudden flurry in the crowd, a spate of rising voices. A blond child, who had been playing with a balloon, gave it one final smack and spun to follow his parents, sending Calliope's muddled thoughts back to Aristides.

She stood gazing after the little boy, perspiration spreading between her breasts. She was wearing a light, short-sleeved summer dress, but the heat was like gauze clinging to her skin. The second customs agent was more cursory, as well as more cordial than his older colleague.

'Have a good trip!' he drawled.

And then it was over – or so it seemed for a moment or two. They turned away, barely breathing, and began to make their way through the restive crowd.

X

'It's a good thing they didn't discover my Trotsky,' Rupert said, winking at Calliope. They were approaching the passport control queue.

'Shhh!' Calliope hissed. 'They might take you seriously!'

Rupert waggled his shoulders. 'This must be the only European airport without air conditioning,' he said.

Calliope was silent, nervously peering about. If they were going to be stopped, it would be here, she said to herself. In the next few minutes, her fate would be revealed: imprisonment or exile. She pulled off her sunglasses, swiped the bridge of her nose, then replaced the shades. In front of her, a foreigner was gently rocking a fussing baby nestled in a corduroy carrier. A French flight crew went by, laughing.

'Won't be long now,' Rupert said, clutching their passports. The queue was creeping forward. The foreigner ahead of them tried to slide a dummy into her child's mouth, only to see the baby's agitated fist knock it down to the dirty floor.

'Next!' The passport inspector was poking in his ear, casting a languorous glance towards the fidgeting passengers.

He was a fat man with scant hair and prominent eyes that took in Calliope's voluptuous curves with an air both weary and speculative. His fleshy lips turned up slightly, promising a smile, if only it weren't so hot, if he weren't so worn out.

He glanced at her passport photo, then raised his gaze and studied Calliope more closely. She reminded herself: he was merely comparing her to the photograph, in which her hair was loose and her eyes exposed, carefully outlined with kohl. She raised her hand and theatrically whipped off her sunglasses, smiling straight into the glass booth.

The inspector paused for a moment, and finally smiled back, slapping the passport shut. He shifted his gaze towards Rupert.

Calliope stepped forward, conscious of her throbbing temples and her swollen feet. She was wearing flats, but by the time they entered the departure lounge, her legs refused to carry her any further. She slumped into the first vacant seat, a hazy feeling settling over her as she waited for their flight to be announced.

There were no soldiers or policemen about, but her fear had yet to release its clutches. It was only after boarding, after the jet had taken off, soaring in the radiant sky, that she felt the last vestiges of dread start to dissipate.

Calliope leaned back with a long exhalation. She sat flexing her feet and chewing on a mint for the next few minutes, dimly aware of the rumble of engines, the distant clatter of china. Somewhere in the back, a baby whimpered, then broke into a prolonged wail. Rupert squeezed Calliope's hand.

'Everything's going to be fine,' he said.

For a moment, Calliope was silent. She turned towards the window, taking in the bleached-looking houses, the blue sweep of glittering sea. She sat gazing out, struggling against a fresh flood of grief. All at once, her face puckered, and she twisted away from the vanishing view. She had made up her mind not to complain if they managed to escape. Yet there she was, burying her face in Rupert's shoulder, her chest heaving.

'I can't bear it!' The words had erupted against her will. 'I can't!'

Rupert had no comforting words to offer. Unbuckling his seat belt, he cradled her in his arms, mutely stroking her scalp. The jet had reached its flying altitude, but the infant went on shrilling. Calliope was weeping quietly, her thoughts slipping back to the night her father died, then the morning on which she found her mother dead, crumpled up on the kitchen floor. She thought of Aristides, unable to imagine where he might be, or what he was doing. All these thoughts twisted her heart again. She was being whisked away, through an endless realm of fleecy clouds, towards unfathomable exile. Abandoning them all.

FOUR

I

Dear Eleni,

How wonderful to hear from you! I can't tell you how much your letters mean to me, even if I must dispel some of your romantic notions about England. I was amused to hear you say that my descriptions of our London life made you feel as if you were here with us. I hope you will come for a visit soon but, believe me, it's not anything like the novels you've mentioned.

London remains a fascinating city, I suppose, and, as you say, it is interesting to explore a different culture, but there are many days when I feel I am languishing in this grey kingdom. In some ways, it is a truly dismal place, especially at this time of year.

Don't think I've forgotten how miserable winter can be in Molyvos, but back home, there were always brilliant days to break the gloom, whereas here, there are weeks when it seems as if the sun will never come out again! Sometimes, on rainy days, I find myself longing for the sound of the sea, the smell of burning wood, of salt-scented air. Last week I had an intense craving for hahles, *like a woman in the grip of a tormenting pregnancy. It's astonishing, the things one can get nostalgic about! That I should prefer roosters' calls and the bleating of sheep to the mayhem of urban traffic may* be understandable, but how can I explain the absurdity of going to the cinema and missing whistles and catcalls? Sometimes, I miss the very things I used to complain about! I can't help admiring British civility, but there are days when I find the English intolerably insipid. I sit opposite them on the underground and their faces are as blank as fresh sheets of paper. There is so little human warmth, or humour, or charm, and even less joie de vivre. I can now see why Rupert fell in love with Lesbos, and why Lorenz keeps wanting to return.

He is back in Germany now, reportedly hard at work. I, too, am busy, trying to finish the book I told you about. I am working at twice my usual speed because the French are eager to publish it, and because I know it's bound to open the world's eyes to Greek realities.

I am also working on my English. It seems to be improving, but I still feel handicapped, if only because it's hard to be clever in a language you haven't mastered. Rupert likes to say that he contrived to get me exiled so as to force me to perfect my English, but no linguistic triumph is worth the homesickness I feel. How, I wonder, was he able to abandon his home and people and settle in Molyvos? It seems that, no matter how well you know someone, there are things about them you will never understand.

Which brings me to a piece of news I have saved for the last: Rupert and I finally tied the knot, so I am now a respectable English lady! But, please, don't congratulate me. Congratulate Rupert, if you like, if only for having persuaded me to do something I consider pointless.

I try not to think about my Molyvos home, especially the chores I have saddled you and Evanthea with. I miss you and Athena but was happy to hear you are all doing well. Rupert is trying to arrange an exhibition for Zoe at a local gallery and says it looks promising. I have sent you something under separate cover and hope it reaches you in time for St Basil's. Please write again soon and let me have more Molyvos news.

Love and kisses,
Calliope

II

Every spring, there would be the penetrating smell of whitewash, of burning firewood and roasting lamb, and the scent of wisteria mingling with the smell of sea salt. By the time Easter arrived, every house and privy would be scrubbed and whitewashed, every courtyard decorated with fresh flowerpots. Beyond the walls and gates, children would screech and chickens cluck, and birds warble among blossoming fruit trees. On Easter Saturday, the women would queue up at the butcher's for fresh lamb, laughing and gossiping, while the men chaffed each other, collecting firewood.

Such were the things for which Calliope found herself yearning during her first spring in London. The Greek exiles exchanged the traditional *Christos anesti* greetings; they celebrated the Resurrection with the usual candles and incense and *maghiritsa*, but the scents of an Aegean spring permeated Calliope's dreams, making the English reality seem pitiful, like the efforts of a conscientious but hopelessly dull pupil.

She was as busy in London as she had been in Molyvos, still engaged in literary translation, and writing for the Greek branch of the BBC. There were political meetings aimed at toppling the junta, pamphlets to be edited, immigrants to be helped at the Hellenic Centre. Although her campaign for a battered-women's shelter had fallen on deaf ears, she had at least managed to establish a referral service. Rupert was teaching an advanced linguistics course at the University of London. They had English and Greek friends; they had a fine house in Hampstead; they had Rupert's children and grandchildren. And yet, everything about her life seemed provisional to Calliope, as if she were merely biding her time.

On 21 April 1972, the junta would be celebrating the fifth anniversary of the coup, but in London, a demonstration was being planned in front of the Greek Embassy, followed by a film and lecture at the Hellenic Centre. In late March, the evening following Orthodox Easter, a panel discussion took place on Greek radio. Calliope had been invited to chair it, only to find herself caught between the leftists and rightists, the monarchists and the Trotskyites, all trying to outshout each other.

Wearying of them all, she headed straight home after the broadcast. The following evening, she was to attend a meeting to discuss strategies for publicity and fundraising for a Greek library. She had made it her habit to watch the Greek news in the evening and the English broadcast during lunch with Rupert. The day of the meeting, they sat down in the kitchen, turned on the television, and heard about the murder of a nine-year-old girl.

Meredith Yealland had been on her way home from school, had stopped to buy a lollipop and was never seen or heard from again. Now her body had been found on Hampstead Heath, a stone's throw away from the Ealings' residence. This was shocking enough, but then the girl's parents were interviewed in their Knightsbridge home, a golden retriever slumped at their feet.

'I can't believe it!' Calliope exclaimed halfway through the interview. She said it in French, the language they still spoke at home.

Rupert glanced at her. 'Dreadful business,' he muttered. The child had been molested and strangled, then dumped behind a clump of trees.

Calliope shook her head. 'Look at the mother, though!'

'What?' said Rupert.

'She's made up like a movie star! Look at her: she's been to the hairdresser's, for heaven's sake!'

Rupert sank his teeth into a sandwich but did not reply. The Englishwoman was speaking of her daughter's accomplishments. She was impeccably dressed, powdered, dry-eyed.

'You'd think this was about some medal the child has won!'

Rupert was silent. A spring wind was flapping through the garden, rustling in the chimney. Calliope pushed her plate aside. She rose to get the kettle, her thoughts wandering back to a distant day when a fire had swept through olive orchards in Eftalou. She recalled the village women's grief at seeing their trees gone, income-generating trees that had been in the family for generations, but still only trees.

'You should have seen those women!' she said to Rupert. 'They flung their arms around the scorched trunks and wept. How can a mother sit and talk about her murdered child and not shed a tear? How can she be thinking of her hair, I ask you?' Calliope shook her head. If she spent the rest of her life in London, she still wouldn't understand the English!

This sentiment being all too familiar, Rupert kept his thoughts to himself. He had given up explaining that the English took pride in mastering their emotions. He finished his tea, wiped his mouth, and returned to his memoirs. Calliope decided to take a nap before going to the fundraising meeting.

She awoke to find it raining again – raining cats and dogs, as Rupert would say. She was often vexed by the English language, whose idiomatic expressions left her feeling defeated. At a university party, she had heard Rupert say 'I'm pulling your leg' to one of his students. Her English cleaner had spoken of 'spilling the beans', leaving her thoroughly mystified in her own kitchen.

The rain was coming down in torrents, lashing at fresh tulips and baby daffodils. Calliope washed her hair and made up her face. She dressed carefully, observing that only her skin seemed to be benefitting from her exile. At fifty-seven, she was more attentive to her looks than she had ever been back home. She weighed herself daily, and fussed over her appearance, as if its neglect might leave her inner self doubly vulnerable.

The Hellenic Centre meeting was scheduled for eight p.m. There were a few blocks to the underground, but Calliope had recently acquired a hooded waterproof raincoat and vinyl boots. Fully protected, she rather enjoyed walking in the rain: the play of neon lights in the puddles, the muted sounds of traffic. By evening, the rain had slackened, but the streets remained virtually deserted. There was a bookshop Rupert frequented, and a pastry shop Calliope had gradually learned to resist. There was a restaurant they occasionally ate at, and an art gallery with vapid paintings. Outside a brightly lit snack bar, two Africans stood in their paint-splattered clothes, waiting out the storm. Huddled deep into their skimpy jackets, they had been laughing, but stopped and stared at Calliope from under the green awning.

Calliope walked on, feeling a pinprick of obscure guilt. She had almost arrived at the underground, was about to turn the corner, when a lone man came up the street, clutching a black umbrella. Approaching her, he flicked his cigarette into the gutter and peered at her in the light of a street lamp.

'Excuse me,' he said. He was some sort of foreigner, a youngish man wearing a shabby coat and scarf. He was looking for Urquhart Street, he said. He pronounced it *Your-cart*.

'Is it around the heath?' Calliope asked. She had noticed how the English avoided contact with foreigners, reluctant to stop even in broad daylight.

He hesitated. 'Maybe I don't pronounce it right,' he suggested, with a small, crooked smile. 'I show you.'

Saying this, the stranger made as if to retrieve a note from an inner pocket. Instead, with a quick, dramatic motion, he tugged at his belt and flung his coat open, pinning Calliope with the intensity of his gaze.

Except for the scarf, the man was stark naked.

Calliope shrank back, her mind chaotically fighting to grasp what the man was after. On first exposing himself, the stranger had made an odd guttural sound, but was now staring at her with smouldering eyes. Calliope knew nothing about exhibitionists. Was this meant to be a seductive gesture, a lonely man's attempt to impress her with the goods on display?

The goods were impressive. The stranger was powerfully built and magnificently erect. Although some facet of her mind understood that she was meant to display shock, what she mostly felt was a muddled blend of pity and curiosity. Many hours would pass before she could make sense of her own feelings, but one thing she knew: the spasm of pity had something to do with the man's foreignness. This was a city that could drive anyone crazy, she would think much later.

The encounter with the stranger seemed interminable but could not have lasted more than a minute. They stood face to face in the light of the street lamp, the rain throbbing around them, the cars slithering by. The moment he had exposed himself, the man's eyes had grown bright with challenge. He stood clutching his umbrella, the rain drumming on the taut canopy, while Calliope's skin tingled. The odd mix of astonishment, fascination, and fear somehow felt familiar and, as a truck came trundling by, her wayward mind suddenly conjured up her own wedding night.

A little hiccup of nervous laughter accompanied the memory. Calliope stepped aside, shaking her head. She was starting to walk away, only to find herself vehemently spat at. The stranger was staring at her with unmistakable loathing.

'English bitch!' he flung at her retreating back. At least that's what he meant to say. The words came out sounding more like 'English beach'.

Calliope continued walking. The realisation that she could now be mistaken for a native, could pass judgement on a stranger's English, only compounded her inner distress. It was all a muddle and for some reason it seemed to bruise her soul as she approached the underground. Behind her, the rain went on falling, pelting the thwarted streets.

III

Nineteen and a half months later, in November 1973, Calliope was admitted to hospital with acute peritonitis, missing news of a momentous event taking place in Athens. The surgery lasted four hours, the hospital stay two and a half weeks. On being discharged, Calliope received a package from Lorenz, containing Deutsche Welle footage. It was an edited record of a Greek student strike that had unexpectedly turned into a massive protest against the regime.

'If you look carefully,' Lorenz wrote in the accompanying letter, 'you will spot me on the sidelines, but you won't have to look hard to recognise your godson.'

Lorenz had flown to Athens on the second day of the protest, when it became apparent that the event might warrant coverage in his new book. Calliope arranged to have the documentary shown at the Hellenic Centre. Seated beside Rupert, she watched intently as the black-and-white images began to flicker across the screen.

Athens's Polytechneion was the most prestigious engineering and architecture school in Greece (one that Papadopoulos himself had attended without ever graduating). The students had barricaded themselves behind the gates, their makeshift radio crackling all over the capital. It was Wednesday morning, 14 November 1973.

'This is the Polytechneion, the Polytechneion, the standard-bearer of the struggle against the dictatorship and for democracy!'

The Athenian student's voice made Calliope shiver in her auditorium seat. The room smelled of wet umbrellas and damp footwear, an odour she would forever associate with bitter exile. The Polytechneion student was appealing to Greeks from all walks of life to unite in the liberation of their homeland.

'Citizens of Greece: we are unarmed. Our only weapon is our faith in freedom!'

The school was situated on one of Athens's busiest thoroughfares, but all city buses had come to a stop, with waves of passengers impulsively joining the restive crowd. Soon, students, workers, and farmers were marching together to the sound of the national anthem, waving flags and banners, brandishing placards.

'Down with the junta!'

'Bread, education, freedom!'

'Fight against the bloodsuckers!'

By Friday, the crowd numbered in the thousands but, as Umbreit would eventually write in his letter, Aristides Dhaniel was easily recognisable. The camera had caught him by the school gates, clutching a megaphone in his left hand, the right raised in a victory salute. He flashed a joyful grin, then turned and mounted the platform to introduce one of the key speakers.

In London, Calliope and Rupert watched in silence, their knees grazing against one another's. The rest of the audience was silent as well. There was an occasional cough, a clearing of the throat. The rain went on drumming against the windowpanes.

The Athenian speeches continued. The demonstrators kept waving their fists and placards. Just outside the school gates, a policeman was photographed wrestling a demonstrator into a headlock. The rousing music played on and on.

When the riot police arrived, the camera shifted focus, and this was when Calliope spotted Lorenz, one of several men running down the street. A Norwegian tourist had been hit by a stray bullet and that was where Lorenz seemed to be heading. Meanwhile, two Greek girls were shown dragging an injured student into a hotel. The hotel owner, Lorenz had told Calliope, had been going around with platters of food, exhorting the students, 'Eat, eat, you can't fight for freedom on an empty stomach!'

The police went on thumping, harassing, arresting.

'Down with Papadopoulos!'

'Down with the CIA!'

All this was still going on when army trucks stormed the scene, spewing out troops in battle fatigues.

'Please don't shoot your own brothers!' the broadcasting student beseeched the soldiers. 'Please do not spill Greek blood!'

The khaki-clad men appeared to be listening; some could even be seen sheltering protesters from the club-wielding police. The bullets went on flying. In the background, there was the wail of sirens. The student pleaded with doctors and surgeons to come forward. The electrical lights flickered. The municipal power plant had been shut off, but the engineering department had its own generators. At midnight, a tank could be seen, steadily rolling towards the Polytechneion gates.

'Brothers in arms!' the student's choked voice continued. 'Do not obey the orders you've been given! Do not raise your weapons against your own brothers!'

He kept imploring the tank to stop, to heed the voice of the people, but the only response came from a military officer, who leapt out of the tank, shouting: 'The Greek army will never negotiate with anarchists!'

It was a moment Greeks would never forget. In London, Calliope grew limp, sagging against Rupert's shoulder. The army officer had disappeared from view, but the tank went on creeping towards the school gates. The Polytechneion student was singing the national anthem when the tank blasted its way through the gates, trapping the students but inexorably moving on.

Calliope slid down in her seat, a tiny squawk of protest escaping her mouth as she watched the historic event reach its tragic climax.

The documentary had come to an abrupt end, but Calliope remained in her seat, bitterness rising from her gut. Within days of the Polytechneion protest, over two thousand students had been arrested; hundreds had been wounded. The number of dead was unknown and would be debated for decades to come.

Aristides, it seemed, had managed to escape unscathed. While Calliope was still in intensive care, he had phoned Rupert to say he was safe. Discharged from hospital, Calliope called her godson's sisters. She kept calling his aunt, his cousins. No one knew anything about his whereabouts. By December, Papadopoulos had been overthrown, but there was still no word from Aristides. Calliope had made several attempts to contact the number Dorothea had given her. One evening, an unknown woman finally answered.

'Is Aristides there by any chance?'

'Aristides? No!'

'How about Dorothea? May I leave a message for her?'

'Sorry, it's not possible.'

'Why not?' Calliope persisted. 'Is Dorothea—'

'She's not here, she's not coming back.'

'But why? What happened to her?'

There was a brief pause, during which the line crackled a little. The Athenian let out an exasperated sound.

'Please don't call here again,' she snapped. And then the line went dead. Calliope hovered by the phone all night, waiting for it to ring.

IV

Dear Lorenz,

My beloved Aristides is behind bars again. Somehow, he had managed to evade both police and tanks, sheltered by an architecture professor whose daughter had been involved in organising the protest. It seems Aristides spent the second night of the demonstration with this girl, and that Dorothea had somehow got wind of it. He may have even told her himself; perhaps he had decided to break up with her – I don't know. But, as Rupert says, 'Hell hath no fury like a woman scorned.'

To make a long, tragic story short, Dorothea ended up betraying Aristides. I suspect she acted in a moment of terrible confusion and may well be repenting her vindictive impulse. Alas, neither my cousin nor Angelos Solomos can do anything this time, especially not with Brigadier Ioannides at the helm. Aristides's sister tells me that, in comparison with this thug, Papadopoulos could almost be considered a benevolent dictator. He, at least, liked to pretend that the suspension of civil rights was just a temporary measure; he might have even believed it. Ioannides makes no promises and does not bother pretending. His henchmen are everywhere, and Athenians are in a state of terror so deep that the atmosphere in the capital, people say, is like that of a graveyard.

Oh, my dear, I can't tell you how impotent I feel, trying to carry on with my safe English life, while everything inside me cries out for intervention! That I can do nothing to help – can't even speed up the process – fills me with indescribable rage.

This is one of the most harrowing periods I have ever known. I've always found it hellish to deal with uncertainty and don't know how I'll endure the next few weeks or months – however long it takes before we get any news. Yesterday, some local clairvoyant left a leaflet in our postbox, and I ended up dreaming about Zenovia Antoniou, the Molyvos fortune teller. I woke up thinking of a long-ago

day when she offered to read my coffee cup. Kimon was fighting in
Albania at the time, but I flatly refused. I did not believe in fortune
telling or destiny, I remember saying. Well, I think I believe in it now.
Certainly, I understand the need for hope that keeps crystal-gazers
in business.

Thank you for the American postcard. I was intrigued by your
impressions of New York and will look forward to hearing more
when we see you in the summer. I am also looking forward to finally
meeting your sons. To think that one of them is about to graduate
from university!

Rupert and I had planned to go to Paris for Easter but have
cancelled our plans. In any case, we expect to be here in July.
It's good to know that your book is virtually finished. I myself am
between projects. I spoke to Stamoulis just before Christmas and he
tried to interest me in a new Greek novel, but I am not up to it – not
while I sit here, biting my nails. Titos and Tasia send their regards,
as does Rupert. I hope your American visit continues to fascinate
and inspire.

Yours,
Calliope

V

They said he had jumped out of a detention-room window. It was
something they often said in those days, something that Calliope
could not imagine Aristides doing, but who could say for sure? How
could she possibly know what they had put him through once they
discovered his true identity?

In years to come, the date of the Polytechneion protest would be
ardently observed as a national holiday, but in the summer of 1974,
when Lorenz Umbreit and his sons stopped in London on their way
to Lesbos, the brutal Brigadier Ioannides was still wielding power.
In late June, there had been a sensational attempt to assassinate

Cypriot President Makarios, but the coup d'état had been foiled, leading to a Turkish invasion, with thousands of Greek Cypriots fleeing for their lives.

The political chaos was rehashed daily on Greek radio, but Calliope had lost interest in the news, as in so much else. The day she received word of Aristides's death, she crawled into bed, contemplating her memory's finest gems. Between late February and the end of May, she spent every day under a heap of blankets: weeping, trying to read, listening to requiems, eating few meals but huge quantities of chocolates. Asleep and awake, she dreamed of summer skies wanton with stars, of the hum of insects on hushed afternoons, of a child's bare feet running across cool marble floors, and bedroom curtains stirred by gentle sea breezes. Above all, she dreamed of the sea, mist-shrouded in the early morning, silvery in the moonlight. She was, she told Rupert, living for the day she would see democracy restored to Greece. She could finally go home then. She would die in peace.

And then Eleni arrived from Greece, grey-haired but bright-eyed as a girl, invited by a despairing Rupert to come and celebrate her fiftieth birthday in London.

In Eleni's company, Calliope felt free to unleash her grief without regard for English restraint. She wept copiously, uncontrollably, sharing her private conviction that Aristides would still be alive if she had been there to marshal help, if she had never got talked into leaving. The feeling might be irrational, yet it seemed imperative to hold on to both guilt and anguish, as if to let them go would be tantamount to turning her back on her godson's memory. What she did not voice was the searing thought that she was mostly being punished for other, unrelated sins.

Days went by. Roused by a nagging sense of duty, Calliope eventually rallied herself and took Eleni to Oxford, to Stratford-upon-Avon. Eleni was flushed with excitement, but Calliope showed little interest in the sights, or in sharing details of her English life. The only way to animate her, Eleni told Rupert, was to share some piece of Molyvos gossip, especially if it involved one of her former pupils.

It was on the way back from Oxford that Calliope first heard about Pavlos Rozakis, the post-war *kapheneion* owner, who had turned down a marriage proposal for his daughter because the suitor belonged to a right-wing family.

'When will it all end, I ask you?' Calliope said, seated next to Eleni on the homebound train. 'Are we ever going to be a normal, undivided nation?'

'My son-in-law says it will take two generations,' Eleni replied.

She stayed in London for a month. There was her own birthday, and then Calliope's name day, but also a great deal that had been neglected on the domestic front. Eleni had quickly taken charge and, a little ashamed, Calliope forced herself to participate in the belated spring clean-up. She might have, after Eleni's departure, crawled straight back into bed, but it was by then summer, and she was beginning to look forward to another visit.

Lorenz was coming to London. With his two sons.

VI

Lorenz had recently returned from America, had arranged to stop in London on his way to Greece. It was late July. Still given to unpredictable crying spells, Calliope marshalled all her inner resources for this long-anticipated visit. She planned a simple but elegant menu, took a dress to be altered, ironed a tablecloth. Rupert would be at the university all day, but everything was proceeding according to plan. The creamed almond soup had been prepared the day before. Fruit and vegetables had been washed, the Cornish hens marinated. She was going out to have her hair cut, pick up her dress, buy pastries or cake. And flowers; she could not recall the last time she had bought flowers.

Walking away from the hair salon, Calliope stopped at the cleaner's and the florist's, purchased an Italian cake, then hurried home to get ready. She had hoped to serve dinner in the garden, but one look at the surly sky and the plan was scrapped. Unlocking the door, she could hear the phone ring, but it stopped before she could reach it.

Calliope arranged the roses and snapdragons, then carefully flipped the halved hens in their herbed marinade. When Rupert called to remind her to refrigerate the wine, she assured him everything was under control. She was going to set the table, then have a leisurely bath. Rupert said he should be home before five.

'Take your time. They won't be here before eight o'clock.'

It was beginning to drizzle. She hastened to end the call, darting out to collect a bra from the laundry line. Then she made her way upstairs, vaguely disgruntled by the dismal weather. In Molyvos, rain in late July was a rare event.

It was time for a bath. She turned on the taps, added fragrant oil, then paused to study her new haircut in the bathroom mirror. It was the first time in months that she had given any thought to her appearance. Not having weighed herself all this time, she had been shocked to find that none of her good dresses fitted any more.

She reached down to test the bathwater. Not quite hot enough. She used the toilet, turned off the taps, and was about to step into the hot bath when she heard the telephone ring again.

'*Ach, sto diablo!*' Darting out of the steamy bathroom, she almost tripped over a bedroom slipper. She managed to right herself, then lunged for the telephone, surprised to hear Lorenz's voice. It seemed her heart could still stir at the sound of his voice, though she had spoken to him only yesterday, after he had landed at Heathrow. She supposed he was phoning to say they were running late.

'Calliope!' He sounded like a man calling across a bustling street, trying to catch a passing friend's attention.

'Lorenz! Is everything all right?'

'You haven't heard, have you?' He spoke breathlessly, the news rippling out of his mouth before she could utter a single word. 'They're gone, Calliope! They—'

'What?' Calliope could feel prickles of sweat spread under her arms. She had, in recent months, found herself feeling mentally sluggish but was now quick to feel alarmed. 'Who are you talking

402

about, Lorenz?' She sat staring at her yellowing toenails. His sons – was he talking about his sons?

'Oh my God! The junta, Calliope! I tried to phone earlier, but—'

'The junta is gone?' There was a small, barely audible, gasp. Calliope went still, clutching the receiver. 'How—'

'They've finally thrown in the towel. Karamanlis is being recalled from Paris. It's all over, my dear!'

'All over,' Calliope echoed. She was conscious of a blossom of happiness beginning to unfurl within her. She covered her eyes with her hand and sat on the edge of the bed, forsaken by words.

'Calliope? Are you there?'

'Yes.' She tried to steady her breath. 'I'm here.' Had he, had anyone, called her with this news before February, she would have danced with abandon in a public square, would have sung the Greek anthem from her Hampstead balcony. 'I can't believe it,' she muttered into the mouthpiece.

'You can go home now!' Lorenz was saying. He made a soft sound: something between a sigh and a chuckle. 'I'm so happy to be the one breaking the news!'

Calliope swiped at her eyes. 'Oh, Lorenz!' she said. 'Lorenz…'

'We're going to celebrate tonight!' His gaiety was like a sea breeze sweeping through musty rooms. 'I'm going to bring champagne.'

'Yes, that'll be nice,' she said – a polite, slightly distracted hostess.

There was a brief pause. He had, it seemed, just grasped the nature of her inner tumult, had no doubt failed to do so sooner because of his own excitement.

'Would you like me to come now?' he asked, abruptly solicitous.

'No… no, I'm not ready,' she said, her nostrils detecting the smell of her own stale sweat. 'I must phone Rupert and let him know,' she added. The rain was steadily gaining force, pelting the cowering garden.

'I'll see you later then,' Lorenz said after a brief hesitation. He was about to hang up when, all at once, the news shook Calliope's brain.

'Oh, Lorenz!' she cried, tears spilling out of her eyes. 'I still can't believe it!'

'Believe it, my dear!' He let out a deeply familiar laugh, at once tender and melancholy. A car was coming up the street, crawling to a halt under the bedroom window. In the garden, crows could be heard, bickering noisily above the rain. The English world went about its usual pursuits, damp and grey and impervious.

They said goodbye. Calliope replaced the receiver. She paused for a moment, picked up the phone once more and began to dial. But then she glanced at the clock. It was almost six. Rupert would be close to home. She told herself she should hurry and have her bath, but instead groped for the remote control and, perched on the edge of the bed, aimed it at the television.

Just in time for the six o'clock news.

The news would be all over the world by now, duly disseminated by scores of foreign correspondents. The BBC report was being transmitted from Athens by a young, hoarse-voiced reporter, who had stationed himself in front of the parliament grounds, surrounded by a crowd of jubilant, sun-bronzed Athenians.

'*Dimokratia*!' they chanted, delirious. '*Di-mo-kra-ti-a! Di-mo-kra-ti-a!*'

The camera swept the historic square, zooming in on a pack of frisky stray dogs. The dogs were scampering down the broad marble stairs, briefly catapulting Calliope's thoughts towards a distant but vividly remembered day: the April Fool's morning when she and Lorenz had been caught in a sudden downpour. On this very spot. In retrospect, the events that followed seemed rather predictable, but who could have guessed that one day, she – Calliope Adham – would find herself in a London bedroom, childishly hugging a velvet cushion, while, back home, her own people celebrated a historic triumph?

If the thought of Aristides was inevitable, so was the slashing pain. It took enormous skill – skill as well as steely resolve – to get through the most ordinary of days, feeling all the while as if some crucial organ kept ceaselessly bleeding within your body.

This was no ordinary day, but one that nonetheless made banal demands.

Calliope reached for a tissue. Turning the television off, she levered herself from the bed and padded across the room, her bare feet sinking into the plush carpet. Out on the street, a car door slammed, and voices were heard, muted by rain. A faint floral scent wafted out of the bathroom, but the rest of the house, the entire dreary city, seemed to smell of nothing but rain: punitive English rain that might go on falling for days now, its sole allegiance to verdant parks and pastures.

The bathwater was lukewarm. Leaning over the claw-footed tub, Calliope refilled it, listening to a Barbra Streisand song playing at a neighbour's. Then a motorcycle went by, its roar setting another neighbour's dog off. The vehicle quickly vanished, but the dog went on barking. Soon, a man's voice was heard, snapping at the dog; a child broke out in a sudden wail. Was the world always so intrusive, so egregiously noisy?

The thought was accompanied by a heavy sigh. Calliope was fully immersed in her hot bath before both crying and barking finally ceased, and it was only then that she became aware that Rupert had arrived. He was fumbling outside the front entrance, sliding a key into one lock, and then into the other. She heard the front door open, then close again: gently, quietly.

It was almost evening now. The rain was still whispering. In an hour or so, under the same alien sky, Lorenz Umbreit would be on his way over, possibly bringing a new nightingale sculpture from America. She supposed there would be more of them in the years to come; she could almost see them now, vividly displayed on the massive desk in her Molyvos study, overlooking the sea.

A rare collection of cherished souvenirs, fragile and eloquent.

HIGHLIGHTS OF MODERN GREEK HISTORY

1821–1829	War of Independence following four centuries of Ottoman rule.
1832	European powers officially recognise Greece's autonomy.
1843	Greece becomes a constitutional monarchy.
1897	Greco-Turkish War over Crete. The island would not be incorporated into Greece until 1913.
1910	Eleftherios Venizelos is elected Prime Minister, ushering in a controversial twenty-five-year political era, marked by the hope of recovering Ottoman territories long inhabited by ethnic Greeks. This would become known as Venizelos's Great Idea.
1912–1913	Balkan Wars bring about a partial realisation of the Great Idea. The island of Lesbos becomes independent.
1914–1918	Venizelos and King Constantine clash over the advisability of maintaining neutrality in the First World War. This conflict (known as the National Schism) marks the beginning of intense political upheaval, dividing the Greek nation into Venizelist and royalist camps. Allied pressure, however, forces the King into exile. With Constantine's younger son, Alexander, on the throne, Greece enters the war and gains several new territories after the Ottoman Empire is carved up by the Allied victors.

1920	Venizelos survives an assassination attempt but is defeated at the polls. King Alexander's unexpected death from a monkey bite leads to a national referendum. King Constantine returns to the throne.
1921–1922	Encouraged by Allied promises, Greek troops invade Asia Minor, only to be abysmally defeated by the Turks. This event is thereafter referred to as the Great Catastrophe.
1923	King Constantine abdicates and is succeeded by his elder son, George II. The League of Nations orders Greece and Turkey to undertake a formal exchange of their ethnic populations, uprooting ancient Greek and Turkish communities. Forced to absorb 1.5 million Anatolian refugees, Greece finds itself in economic ruin, beset by prolonged political upheaval.
1924	Proclamation of a Greek republic. Venizelos has returned from exile but is once again defeated at the polls.
1924–1935	This period is notable for its dire economic conditions and violent political strife, with coups and counter coups taking place, eventually resulting in the restoration of the monarchy. The nascent Communist Party gains in popularity.
1936	National elections result in a hung parliament, with the Communist Party holding the balance. Ioannis Metaxas, a former royalist general, becomes Premier and, with the King's support, establishes a dictatorship.
1940	Having occupied neighbouring Albania, Italy demands a right of passage through strategic Greek territories. Greece refuses and, despite the threat of a German invasion, goes into battle against the Italian aggressor.

1941	Germany invades Greece and, along with its Italian and Bulgarian allies, occupies the country, while the Greek government goes into exile. In the mountains, several resistance groups are formed, some communist, others anti-communist, but for now sharing the same patriotic goal.
1944	End of the German Occupation; the Greek government-in-exile returns to Athens.
1946	Civil War between communist and royalist supporters breaks out.
1948	The Soviet Union breaks off relations with Yugoslavia, forcing Greek communists to choose between Stalin and Tito. When the majority opt to side with Moscow, Tito closes the Yugoslav border and disbands guerrilla camps inside his country, causing internal conflict within the Communist Party. General Papagos launches a fierce anti-communist campaign, further weakening an already splintered Communist Party.
1949	A formal treaty brings an end to the Civil War.
1954	Greece becomes embroiled in Cyprus, the majority of whose population is ethnic Greek.
1955	Constantine Karamanlis, a royalist supporter, is elected Premier, dominating Greek politics for nearly a decade.
1964	George Papandreou Senior, an opponent of the monarchy, is elected Prime Minister.
1967	Right-wing army officers, led by George Papadopoulos, stage a coup, ostensibly to prevent an imminent communist takeover.
1973	The monarchy is abolished, and Greece becomes a presidential republic.
1974	A failed coup in Cyprus brings about the downfall of the military junta. Constantine Karamanlis is recalled from exile to form a new government.
1975	A presidential democracy is proclaimed.
1981	Andreas Papandreou is elected Prime Minister, heading the first socialist government in Greece.

GLOSSARY

Agora – Marketplace

Ameletita – Testicles (literally: unmentionables)

Anatolia – The Anatolian peninsula (sometimes referred to as Asia Minor) today constitutes the Asian portion of Turkey.

Baba – Father

Christos anesti – Christ is risen

Dimitris – Demotic version of Dimitrios

Dimokratia – Democracy

Eleftheria – Freedom

Evzones – An elite military unit and the official Presidential Guard of Greece

Fustanella – A traditional <u>pleated</u> <u>skirt</u>-like garment resembling a kilt

Gliko – Spoon sweet

Hahles – Biscuits made of *trahana*

Hamam – Turkish bath

Kale – A common, untranslatable vocative (literally: good one!)

Kalimera – Good morning

Kalispera – Good evening

Kapheneion – Coffee shop

Kentro – Centre

Koritsi mou – Term of endearment (literally: my girl)

Kritharaki – A type of home-made pasta

Kyrios – Mr/Sir; *Kyria* – Mrs/Madam/Lady

Maghiritsa – A traditional Easter soup made with leftover lamb parts

Manestra – Rice-like pasta

Mou – My

Nona – Godmother

Ohi Day – Holiday commemorating Metaxas's rejection of Italian demands (literally: No Day)

Ouzeri – A bar specialising in ouzo and appetisers

Paidomazoma – The mass abduction of Greek children during the Civil War

Panaghia mou – Holy Virgin

Pantopoleion – General store

Papadhia – Priest's wife

Papa – Papas – Priest

Pedhi mou – Term of endearment (literally: my child – though sometimes used in addressing adults)

Periodos – Menstrual period

Phile – Friend (vocative case)

Poulaki mou – Term of endearment (literally: my little bird)

Popo – Backside

Plateia – Town square

Rizogalo – Rice pudding

St Basil's Day – First day of the New Year

Stifadho – Meat and onion stew

Sto diablo! – To the devil!

Thee mou! – My God!

Turkospori – Seeds of the Turks

Trahana – A blend of cracked wheat and yoghurt, fermented and dried, served as soup or porridge

Yassou – Hello/Goodbye (singular); *Yassas* – Hello/Goodbye (plural or formal)

Yaya – Grandmother

ACKNOWLEDGEMENTS

This novel was years in the writing and could not have been completed without help from friends, strangers, and several other authors. I am indebted to the following:

Kevin Andrews	*The Flight of Ikaros*	Weidenfeld and Nicolson, 1959
Philip P. Argenti	*The Occupation of Chios by the Germans and their Administration of the Island*	Cambridge University Press, 1966
Richard and Eva Blum.	*Health and Healing in Rural Greece*	Stanford University Press, 1965
Susan Borg and Judith Laskor	*When Pregnancy Fails.*	Bantam Books, 1989
Louis de Bernières	*Captain Corelli's Mandolin*	Martin Secker and Warburg, 1994
Kazantzakis, Nikos	*Freedom and Death*	Faber and Faber, 1956

Nicholas Gage	*Eleni*	Ballantine Books, 1983.
Pavlos Matesis	*The Daughter*	(Translated by Fred A. Reed) Arcade, 2002
Mark Mazower	*Inside Hitler's Greece.*	Yale University Press, 1993
Yorgos Tsalikis	*Katohi*	Athens, 1977
Vardaros, Leonidas	*All of Us, Effendi (telefilm)*	
Zinovieff, Sofka	*Euridyce Street*	Granta Books, 2004

I am deeply grateful to Eleni Eliadis and Toula Karahaliou for their countless contributions, and to Louis de Bernières, Maureen Freely, Nicholas Gage, Sofka Zinovieff and Jeannie Marshall for their early support. For information pertaining to the Civil War and junta years, many thanks to Yannis Karafyllis, Rallou Kralli and Yannis Konstantellis, Alkman Granitsas, Leonidas Kallivretakis, Theodoros Adamopoulos of the Greek Film Archives, and Despina Zervon of ERT Television Archives; thanks, too, to the Athens News and to all the Molyviates who answered my endless questions; to Eva Stachniak, Judy Yelon, and Sofka Zinovieff for early feedback; to Yorgos Kaklamanos, Roger Taylor, Christos Velentzas, Laurie Kezas, and Montreal's Goethe Institute for contributing to my research; to Margot Granitsas, Margaret Rumscheidt, and Michael Osmann for help with translations. I am grateful to my eagle-eyed editors Ross Dickinson and Cari Rosen at Legend Press, with heartfelt thanks to the latter for championing this novel and being an exceptional pleasure to work with. Last but not least, my endless thanks to my daughter, Ranya, who was always there when my light was low.